Her rescuer held up a horse...

...and she caught a brief glimpse of his face through a short break in the rain, but as she leaned toward him, her foot caught in one of the straps and she fell hard against his chest, nearly knocking the breath out of her. She thrust her hands forward and caught herself on the area just below his shoulders, and she forced her eyes upward to look into his face.

"Are you all right there, little lady?" he asked, his mouth widening into a broad grin. "If you wanted to snuggle a little longer, all you needed to do was ask."

Heat flooded her face as she met his eyes.

There was no mistaking it this time. Will Redbourne stared down at her, carved dimples adding interest to his firm jaw and beautiful face. His deep brown eyes, framed by long, thick lashes, held hers captive. Her voice betrayed her as she opened her mouth to speak. Nothing came out. The dimple in his cheek deepened and his hands wrapped around her waist as he twisted her around and set her down safely on the boardwalk.

He walked to the opposite side of his horse and unlatched her satchel, handing it over to her, sopping wet on the outside. He tipped his hat and winked.

"Ma'am," he said before collecting the reins of his horse and walking into the livery.

She watched him until he disappeared behind the oversized doors.

Just breathe.

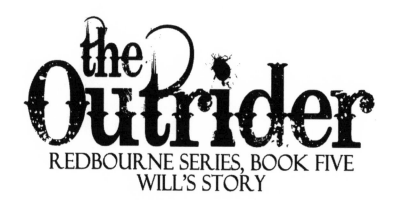

the Outrider

REDBOURNE SERIES, BOOK FIVE
WILL'S STORY

KELLI ANN MORGAN

inspire books

Inspire Books
A Division of Inspire Creative Services
937 West 1350 North, Clinton, Utah 84015, USA

THE OUTRIDER

An Inspire Book published by arrangement with the author

First Inspire Books paperback edition August, 2016

ISBN-13: 978-1-939049-29-2
ISBN-10: 1939049296

Printed in the United States of America

PRAISE FOR THE NOVELS OF AMAZON BESTSELLING AUTHOR

KELLI ANN MORGAN

"...a roller coaster. Action, suspense, excitement, all rolled together. What a fun experience."

—*Rocky Palmer* on THE OUTRIDER

"The Redbourne men are the most amazing characters in the American west!"

—*Lesia Chambliss* on THE IRON HORSEMAN

"...beautiful settings, sweet romance, and an adventure so intricately woven that it will keep you guessing till the end."

—*Tennille Rasmussen* on THE BLACKSMITH

"Twists and turns of the story line keep you on your toes as you, in a page turning search, look for what comes next...."

—*B.D. Mann* on THE BOUNTY HUNTER

"It was very hard for me to go to sleep without finishing this book, it was so romantic entertaining and mystifying."

—*Patricia Collins* on THE RANCHER

"...an incredibly compassionate and passionate story."

—*Donna Feibusch* on JONAH

"Kids hungry? That's too bad! Mama can't put the book down- better find the crackers in the pantry!!"

—*Jennifer Sisneros* on LUCAS

"Well developed characters, romance and action. I was emotionally connected... Sit back, relax and enjoy another Deardon heart throb."

—*Forever Fan* on NOAH

"Highly enjoyable and very entertaining..."

—*R. Miller* on HOLDEN'S HEART

ACKNOWLEDGEMENTS

To all of you who read my stories and share with me how much they've meant, how they've touched you, or how much you enjoy them and are anxiously waiting for more. You make the blood, sweat, and tears that sometimes come with the writing of a book more rewarding than you'll ever know.

To my amazing beta readers who are so willing to provide me with critical feedback that helps my stories come to life. Thank you, Jennifer, Kim, and Janene! I appreciate all you do and couldn't have done this without you!

To my copyeditor, Rocky, who is incredible at his job. Thank you!

To my fellow writers, retreat buddies, and colleagues—thank you for the wonderful support system and lasting friendships.

And, as always, to my own charming husband who believes in me and provides the emotional support and encouragement to finish what I start. And for sitting up with me until all hours of the night blocking action scenes with Lego®. You are my hero, babe. I'd be lost without you!

To my closest friends in each aspect of my life—
Jody Allsop, Susie Dawson, Lesli Lytle,
and my wonderful mother, Carolyn Palmer.

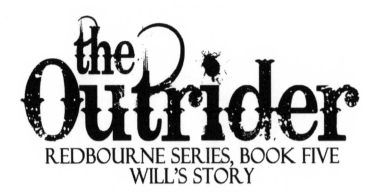

REDBOURNE SERIES, BOOK FIVE
WILL'S STORY

CHAPTER ONE

Kansas, Early April 1870

Elizabeth Archer looked around at the ranch she'd purchased in a fake name and breathed out a heavy sigh. Since she didn't know the legalities of unmarried women being allowed to own land in this state—let alone a British immigrant, she had pretended to have a husband, which had seemed like a good idea at the time.

Elizabeth stood in front of her dilapidated house, hands on hips, and blew at a stray lock of hair dangling in front of her eyes. Shutters had fallen away from the windows in disarray and the paint on the house peeled from the wood. There was no shortage of work to be done and she almost wished the husband she'd invented really existed—if only to help get the place in order.

Woof. Woof.

She giggled as the large, loveable red coonhound who'd become her travelling companion somewhere near the Missouri-Kansas border, chased a squirrel up the enormous tree looming heavily over the big wrap-around porch at the side of the house.

"Come on, Caspar. Let the poor thing alone." She heaved up the bucket she'd filled with water from the well and marched up the front steps, the dog on her heels, and strode through the house into the disheveled kitchen. Maybe a good day's work would tire her out enough to banish the unwelcome memories that invaded her thoughts more often than she cared to admit.

Caspar happily settled into the corner where minute whimpers and squeals came from the pups she'd delivered just a few days ago. It had been quite the surprise for Elizabeth to discover that her travelling companion had been expecting.

Elizabeth had already cleared away most of the clutter around the house over the past few days, but the surfaces of the counters, tables, and floor were still caked in a layer of dirt and grime. It was no surprise that the man from whom she had purchased her new home had lived alone, as she didn't imagine there was a woman alive whose house would be in such disarray. She knelt down beside the bucket, plunged the thick brown sponge into the soapy water, and started scrubbing the dirty wood floor.

Now that she'd had time to think it through properly, starting out in a new place with such a blatant lie probably had not been her brightest idea, but as an unmarried woman in a new land, she hadn't wanted to deal with the questions that would accompany her purchase. She just wanted to start over in a place she could call home. A place where she could feel safe. Away from the family—the father—who had betrayed her trust.

Luckily for her, the previous tenant had sold her, or rather her imaginary husband, the house with a good majority of his belongings still inside. It had been an odd exchange, but she hadn't been in much of a position to ask questions.

The kitchen was on the small side, but cozy. A nice pot-bellied stove sat at one edge and a tall counter-sized table had been bolted to the wall. She'd only been settled in a few days and supplies were already running thin. She'd need to make the trip into the small town of Stone Creek for foodstuffs and other supplies soon, but dreaded the questions that undoubtedly would be cast in her direction.

"Ferguson, you backstabbing coward, get out here!" someone shouted from the yard.

Caspar barked.

Elizabeth shot up to her feet, wiped her hands on her apron, and tiptoed toward the front of the house. She pulled the shotgun from the corner and held it firmly as she pulled open the large, raggedy wooden door, keeping the second, thinner door, shut.

"Mr. Ferguson no longer lives at this residence," she called out through the screen at the top of the outside door.

Three mounted men, who looked like they'd never heard of a razor, fanned out in front of the porch steps. The hair on the back of her neck stood on end and a feeling of unease settled in her stomach.

"And who might you be?" one of them asked as he dismounted, handing the reins to his companion, then started cautiously up the stairs.

Elizabeth took a step back and aimed her gun at the man's chest.

"Whoa now, little lady. No one here's gonna hurt ya. We just wants to know how we can find old Ferguson."

"I assure you I am unaware of your Mr. Ferguson's whereabouts. He sold me…and my husband the place. He said he was moving back home. Somewhere back east. That is all I know."

The man took the last step between them, right up next to the door, his face nearly touching the screen. "Where are you from, li'l lady?" he asked, his chin lifted as he stared down at her through the screen, his eyes squinted in scrutiny.

She could lie, but her voice had already given her away, and she made a mental note to use an American accent from here on.

"Wales," she stated matter-of-factly. It wasn't exactly a lie.

Her mother was from Wales.

The man scoffed. "What kind of a place is....Whales?" His face contorted in a sneer and the others joined in his mockery.

She needed to get rid of them.

"If there is nothing else, gentlemen," the word sat loosely on her tongue, "I am quite busy."

"Well, see now, Old Ferguson took somethin' of ours and we intend to get it back. You don't need to worry your pretty little head over that. If you'll just let us in, we can take a look and then we'll be gone quick as a jack-rabbit."

"I told you, I do not know anything about Mr. Ferguson or to what you are referring. Now, it is time for you to move along."

He laughed—an ugly, leering sort of sound.

"Did you hear that fellas? It's time for us to move along."

The others joined his raucous display.

All of a sudden, the mock amusement left his face and he pouted his lips and raised a brow as he leaned up against the door.

"It's been a while since I been with any kind a lady." He picked something out of his teeth with his tongue and reached for the door.

She cocked the gun, her jaw set firm and her eyes narrowed. *Ewwww.*

Caspar came bounding up to the door, barking loudly. The man jumped backward, nearly tripping over his own feet as he grasped for the rail to steady himself. The last thing she needed was to blow a hole in the side of the house that she aimed to repair, but she was not about to allow the brute anywhere near her either. Caspar's presence emboldened her and she narrowed her eyes at the man.

"I would not do that if I were you," she said, cold and smooth, with more confidence than she felt.

The man met her eyes, assessing her intentions as he took an emboldened step toward her, raised an arm, and leaned against the door.

"You say Ferg sold the place to you and your husband?"

She nodded.

"Where is he? Your husband, I mean?"

"He…is on his way back from town. He will be here at any moment. And I can assure you that he is not the kind you would want to trifle with."

"Well," the lumbering oaf said, pushing away from the door, "you tell your man that we want to speak to Ferguson or we'll take what he owes us out of this place." He kicked at the railing pillar before descending the stairs in a rush. "We'll be back by the end of the week."

Elizabeth had heard these types of threats all too often, but never had they been directed at her. Were all American men out west this ill-behaved? She'd dealt with hooligans like these before.

Worse even.

Her father employed many lowlifes to help him in his shady business dealings back in England and she had fled to America in the hopes that she would never have to see them again. She'd wanted, no, needed to start over somewhere far away from her father and the pugilistic world she'd grown up in. Had she traded one sort of brute for another?

Elizabeth had been alone for several months in her travels—joining other groups as they'd made their way west, but this was the first time in a long stretch she felt it. Loneliness encroached upon her like night on a fading day. Inevitable. Inescapable. She stood, staring through the screen door, long enough to watch the last man's hat disappear beneath the hillside before she wobbled backward and fell into the chair behind her, breathing out her last ounce of courage.

Her man? At least the lie had saved her. For now.

Elizabeth fanned herself and frowned at the thought of the ruffians returning and destroying her new home. She'd spent a good portion of her money buying this place. It wasn't anything like the estate in England, but it was hers—well, sort of. Legally, it belonged to a man who didn't exist, but no one had to know that information. She'd figure out a way around it sooner or later, but for the moment, it would buy her some time. After all, a woman couldn't be Sterling Archer's daughter and not learn a few things about how to defend herself.

"Stop feeling sorry for yourself, Elizabeth Archer. There is too much to do." And with that, she pushed herself out of the chair, set the shotgun in the corner, and went back to work.

Jab.

Jab.

Feint.

Jab.

William Redbourne ducked away from the ferocious Norwegian brawler, whose width nearly doubled his own. A whirl of crisp air curled around Will's perspiring shoulders, hardening his skin to gooseflesh.

Cross.

Jab.

It had been a long time since he'd been in a ring and he missed it. He missed the control, the heart-thumping surge of energy, the taste of victory.

Will had worked alongside Sven on multiple occasions on various jobs protecting high-profile passengers traveling west on the stage. They'd started out as rivals, but had quickly become friends. But even a friend needed to understand the lengths Will would go to in order to protect his family—especially his little sister.

Jab.

Duck.

Uppercut.

"William Trey Redbourne!"

To his defeat, he allowed the sound of his mother's voice to work its way into his thoughts, taking his focus momentarily from his opponent.

Too long.

BAM!

Pain sliced through his jaw, ricocheting through his ears and spinning around in his head.

An elongated, loud whistle sounded.

The cheers and groans of the men in the room fell silent as quickly as they had erupted. Will worked to recapture his focus, raising his forearm for some semblance of protection and waited, but there was no follow up blow. He reached out, barely able to keep his footing. It had been a long time since he'd been clocked so hard, but why wasn't the Norwegian finishing the bout? He shook his head, clarity finally beginning to return.

"Mama?" he asked as the blur around his vision cleared. He dropped his arm to his side and blinked, shaking his head once more.

Leah Redbourne stood in the center of the makeshift arena like a wall between the two fighters. "The territory Marshal has been in town inquiring about you and any fights that may have been organized for local entertainment," his mother said loud enough for the men in the crowd to hear. "I wouldn't be a bit surprised if he's already on his way out here to the ranch. After all, my son has earned quite a reputation." Though her brow was raised in a challenge, there was a proud gleam in her eyes and Will couldn't help but grin. She wasn't as angry as he'd expected her to be.

Several of the would-be spectators pushed their way through the crowd and headed toward the now open barn door.

"Sorry, Will," Mr. Jenkins, the shopkeep called back over his shoulder. "My wife'll have my hide if I don't get back soon," he said apologetically as he rushed out of the building.

"I can't be sure," his mama continued, "but last I heard, organized bare-knuckled brawls are illegal in Kansas."

Will hoped his mother wouldn't notice the quick exchange of monies between the rest of the men in attendance as they hurriedly made their way out of the barn, but he knew better. His mother didn't miss a thing.

He caught sight of the Norwegian just as he reached the edge of the barn. Sven stopped near the entrance, his mouth opening and closing in conversation with someone obscured by a tall stack of hay bales. Will shifted his balance and twisted his head to see to whom the man was speaking. After a moment, his little sister, Hannah, stepped into sight, a smile touching her face.

Women. He shook his head. *Fickle. The lot of them.*

He'd seen it hundreds of times—women who changed their minds like a leaf on the wind. How could he defend her honor when she smiled at Sven like that? Encouraged him? She was too pretty for her own good.

At least, it seemed, his outriding partner had apologized for his actions. As he disappeared from sight, Hannah caught her brother's eye and nodded at him with a grateful smile. He shook his head, realizing that it didn't matter what trouble she got herself into, he'd do most anything for his little sister.

After Hannah retreated toward the house, Will's focus returned to his mother. "Which marshal?" he asked, walking over to his bench and reaching for his towel.

"Does it matter?" His mother followed.

"Yes, it matters."

The last time Will had encountered a marshal, it had been a few counties over and he'd embarrassed the man in front of a roomful of young, eligible women—on one of whom the lawman had been sweet.

If a marshal really was on his way, and it was the same man, Will might be in for a whole lot more trouble than anyone suspected. Not all lawmen were as respectable as his brother, Raine. Or even Rafe, who'd turned to bounty hunting after a woman broke his heart just a couple of years back. And Will didn't know enough about Marshal Fenton to know what kind of man he was or if he could be trusted. He only knew he wouldn't blame the man for holding a grudge.

Will raised a brow, pain stabbing against the back of his eye.

"All right, well, let me look at you," Leah said as she reached up and placed her hands on his shoulders, pushing him into a seated position on the bench where he'd lain his clothes.

Will sat down, knowing what he must look like, especially after taking that last hit. She would worry too much. He was sure he'd looked worse.

"Oh, William," she exclaimed, "your beautiful face." His mother tsked as she reached out and cradled the air beneath his chin before gingerly placing two fingers against his jaw and lifted it upward. "Cole," she called to her youngest son, "go into the house and retrieve my poultice."

"Yes, ma'am." Cole and his friend, Alaric, both jumped down off the bales of hay that had acted as seating for the unauthorized event and headed for the house.

Will hadn't intended to have a prize fight in the barn, but somebody had needed to teach the scoundrel a lesson after he'd been clumsy enough to knock Hannah into the pond, and then laugh at her. He figured fighting in the barn would be better than a brawl in a saloon, but the disappointed look on his mother's face told him otherwise.

"Mama, I…"

"Shhhh…" she said quietly, sitting down next to him on the bench, patting his leg. "I'm just glad you're all right."

It wasn't the first time Leah Redbourne had said those words to him after a scuffle and he sighed as his mother fussed over his injury. Will knew how hard it must be for her to try and understand his desire to fight. Hell, *he* barely understood what drove him to fight—other than he was good at it. And Redbournes loved doing what they were good at.

Will had been home just a few months shy of a year from his studies at Oxford University in England, and had done nothing to utilize his education. He'd had a taste of life outside the ranch and he wanted more. Needed more. And that was precisely why he was leaving again. He'd been taught from a very young age to take advantage of every worthwhile opportunity and his next adventure was more than worthwhile.

He wanted to see the world. To explore. He'd finally found the right ship for the right price. Soon, he'd make a name for himself outside of the ranching community and he would make his parents proud instead of constantly worried.

"Darius Fenton," his mother finally told him, pulling a cloth from her pocket and dabbing at his wounds.

Will's brows scrunched together.

"That was his name. The marshal. Darius Fenton."

Will winced.

"Sorry. Mrs. Jenkins sent her young Phillip with a message as soon as the lawman stepped foot inside her store. We're lucky the man didn't stop at the telegraph office first. Mrs. Hendersen would have marched him out to the ranch herself."

They both laughed. Will's chuckle mixed with a pained groan.

If Fenton was sniffing around, it didn't bode well. Of course, there weren't many men who could go up against the Redbourne clan unscathed. And other than Levi, all of his siblings were living in one place or another on Redbourne Ranch.

Technically, he hadn't broken the law. He was settling a score with a man who'd disrespected his family. It wasn't his fault the fight had drawn the attention of many of the men from town and the surrounding ranches who'd wanted to watch.

Will scoffed at his ability to rationalize. If the marshal needed something from him, he would stand up and take responsibility for any of his own actions.

Cole stepped back into the barn, breathing heavily from running from the house. He twisted the lid from the small clear jar filled with their mother's special healing concoction and held it out for her, along with a freshly filled bucket of water and a rag.

"Thank you, dear," Leah said with a warm smile, dipping her fingertips into the creamy substance. She stood and turned to face Will, shaking her head and gently placing her hands over the wounds on his face.

He clenched his teeth as she grazed over the cuts and bruises on his jaw, cheek, and the sensitive area just below his eye, but he refused to show discomfort—suddenly grateful his mother had not been in England to witness the aftermath of some of his most brutal fights there. Some of which even *he* wanted to forget.

Especially his last one.

CHAPTER TWO

Three weeks later, Saturday

Glass broke.

The faint echo of Caspar's bark penetrated the barrier of Elizabeth's restless dreams.

"What is it, girl?" she managed groggily, still unsure if the sound had been real or imagined.

The barks grew louder and more frequent. She slowly opened one eyelid, but quickly closed it again. The sun hadn't risen yet, so why should she?

The weight of Caspar's body as the pup pounced on top of her jolted her awake. Elizabeth's eyes drew wide and the sweet stench of wood-smoke filled her nostrils. She sat bolt-upright in bed. Thick grey swirls of haze filled the room, lit only by the faint light of the moon. She coughed, the smoky air burning her lungs as she drew breath. She threw back the covers and jumped out of the bed and onto the chilly floor, pushing her way through the haze toward the door.

Flames licked at the frame of the house, but the stairs had yet to be touched. Elizabeth slipped down to the main floor, ran into the kitchen, and grabbed her bucket of soapy water and a woven rug. After several attempts to beat the flames down,

Caspar barked a warning, grabbing onto the bottom of her nightshift with her teeth, coaxing her from the burning house.

"Oh, no," she exclaimed, waving a hand in front of her face. "My books." An entire bookcase, full of her most prized works of literature and study, was ablaze, scorched pages turned to ash and floated menacingly through the air.

After a few more unsuccessful slashes at the fire, Elizabeth dropped the singed rug and relented, coughing heavily as she fought her way through the smoke into the kitchen. Caspar's pups whimpered, their high-pitched barks calling out to her. She swooped their basket into her arms, grabbed a few of her favorite books off the shelf, an old pair of shoes, and a shawl, then headed out to the edge of the front lawn with Caspar at her side.

The coonhound barked again and ran back into the house.

"Caspar!" Elizabeth yelled, the gesture like a burning match against the back of her throat. Why would she go back into the house?

A loud crack focused her attention to the spot where her dog had disappeared inside the building.

Crash!

The greater portion of the roof over the living area caved.

"Yelp!" the dog cried out in pain.

Then…nothing.

Elizabeth set the basket on the ground and leapt toward the house, but the heat from the fire was too great. She waited, her hands twisting in front of her as she listened for any sign that her only friend may have survived the collapsed roof.

Still nothing.

Elizabeth dropped to her knees, unable to hold herself up any longer as the building she'd worked day and night to turn into a beautiful place she could call home was now consumed in flames. The heat from the fire stretched the skin of her face. Her arms, covered in soot and grime, her hands red and blistered, folded in her lap. She sat back onto the heels of her feet and dropped her head, squeezing her eyes shut, pushing the tears that had welled there to slip down her cheeks.

Caspar! she grieved silently.

Her shoulders shook as sadness racked through her at the tremendous loss before her. Her home. Her loyal companion and friend. She opened her eyes and lifted her chin, staring helplessly into the rage of devastation as it rose into the darkness of the night sky, etching her pain on the black canvas with a pulsing orange haze.

Lord, help me. What am I going to do now?

She'd spent most of the money she'd brought with her from England in buying supplies and materials to fix up the house and make it her own, and the rest was now going up in flames, hidden inside a small box of her mother's with all evidence of her life in England. Everything she had in the world would soon be nothing but embers on a plot of land in the middle of nowhere.

A horse neighed nervously in the fire-lit night air.

Luckily, the barn was far enough away from the house that the animals would be safe. At least she'd have the buckboard that she could sell in town. But, other than the few books she'd been able to salvage, everything else she owned was in that house. She lay down against the earth on her side, watching the flames from the fire burn her home until the weight of her lids could no longer bear to remain open.

Voices soon filled her head and Elizabeth fought to distinguish whether they were part of a dream or reality and strained to listen to what was being said. Someone lifted her from the ground and she willed her eyes open. A light fog blurred her vision, but in her exhaustion she saw the impossible. The face of William Redbourne.

"Wi—" she tried, but she could not get his name to sound through her scratchy, dry throat.

"She needs water," a woman's voice finally broke the haze of Elizabeth's exhaustion. "Lie her down here."

Elizabeth didn't want to leave the comfort of Will's embrace. His strength. And she clung to him as best she could, but to no avail.

"It'll be all right," he assured with a voice a little deeper than she remembered. He gently laid her down against a wagon's hard wood back, his sudden absence causing a chill to pass over her.

Elizabeth's lashes fluttered open again and she looked up into the kindest green eyes she'd seen in a long time. She tried to sit up.

"Welcome back," a young woman said as she placed a hand behind Elizabeth's back to help. "I'm Grace." She appeared to be about Elizabeth's age, her nightshift peering out from beneath her thick woolen coat. She wrapped a large, heavy blanket around Elizabeth's shoulders and sat down next to her in the back of the buckboard.

Elizabeth glanced around, but it seemed that Will's face had been nothing but a mirage, a vision of her past catching up with her. Haunting her. She tried to smile at the woman, but fearing she'd fail completely, she simply nodded. "Thank you," she finally managed with the best American accent she could muster. She shivered against the cold of the unusually crisp April night and snuggled deeper into the warmth of the blanket, breathing deeply to help keep her calm.

"What's your name, honey?" Grace asked quietly.

"El…" the rest of her name danced on the tip of her tongue, but she wanted to rid herself of her father's reputation and everything he stood for. When she'd come to America, she hadn't wanted to be Elizabeth Archer, daughter of Sterling Archer, wealthy and distinguished fraud and master crook. "Eliza Beth," she offered instead. "Eliza Beth Jessup." Jessup had been the name she had used to purchase the home and it fell off her tongue more easily than she would have expected.

"Did Ferg get out all right?" Grace asked, a worry line appearing on her young forehead.

"Mr. Ferguson?" She needed to explain, but her head still seemed a bit groggy. "Um, well, Mr. Ferguson sold me...us...me—Mr. Ferguson sold *me* the house just a week or so ago. I haven't seen him since."

"Were you alone?"

Elizabeth had a choice to make. She'd lied about being married to buy the property and then again in an attempt to scare off some ruffians, but somehow it didn't seem right to keep pretending with this woman who had been so kind. Lying about her name was one thing, but to pretend she had or lost a husband was another entirely and she breathed out deeply with a nod.

"It was just me and the dogs." Relief washed over her as she spoke the truth. It was as if the husband lie had been consumed in the blaze.

"Do you have any family close by?"

What could she say?

"I...I don't have a family...anymore. It...it's just me." It wasn't a lie, was it? She'd left. Hadn't looked back. She hated the stutter that accompanied her words. *You are stronger than this, Elizabeth Archer!*

She reached up to the small gold pendant that dangled from a chain around her neck. It had once belonged to her grandmother and now served as a reminder of how strong she could be in the face of adversity. She rubbed it between her fingers for strength.

"I'm so sorry, Eliza Beth," Grace said, picking up the corner of the blanket that had fallen from her shoulders and tucked it tight up around her neck.

"How did you know that I was out here? That I was in trouble?"

"My husband," Grace answered with a smile. "He said he had a feeling that something was wrong and I learned a long time ago to never ignore a Redbourne gut."

Redbourne? Elizabeth gulped. *Husband?*

"As soon as we stepped outside, we could smell the fire. The blaze was big enough that it wasn't hard to see it in the dark." She twisted enough to look Elizabeth in the eyes. "I'm so sorry for your loss."

Elizabeth barely heard what Grace was saying as she marveled over the revelation that it had been real. He *was* here. Will Redbourne had indeed carried her to the wagon and he was…

Married.

Her heart dropped into her stomach and a fresh wave of tears welled up inside of her—though she refused to let them spill in front of a stranger, no matter how sweet she had been to her. Elizabeth could not explain why the thought had affected her so. It wasn't like she had a claim on the man. She had never even met him in person. But, still, he'd inspired her to be a better person and to stand up for what was right.

She stole a quick glance at Grace. Will had done well for himself. Grace was beautiful. And kind.

"He's just gone around back to get you some water," Grace said, pointing toward the back of the house. "My husband," she clarified. "He knows his way around this place. Helped Ferg out quite a bit."

"Look who I found whimpering around back by the pump." The tall, blond man made his way to the back of the wagon.

Elizabeth's focus fell to the animal clasped in the man's arms and not on the man himself. She didn't know if she could bear to look at William Redbourne, knowing he was now a married man. Regret clenched at her chest. She'd had her chance to meet him and had walked away from it out of fear.

"Caspar!" she gasped when she realized the soot-stained leathery flaps hanging over Will's arms were the coonhound's ears. She was alive!

Elizabeth jumped down from the back of the wagon, her legs barely able to support her weight. As she stumbled, the man caught ahold of her elbow and lifted until she was able to stand sturdy.

A welcoming bark tugged at her heart strings and she rushed forward, wrapping her arms around the injured dog, ignoring the pain in her hands as they rubbed against the man's thick jacket. Caspar happily licked her face in greeting. Despite her best intentions, Elizabeth fell on the animal's neck and began to sob, hiding her face from immediate view.

"Careful now," his deep voice cautioned. "She's hurt. We'll need to get these burns tended to quickly or they could become infected. We'll take her into Stone Creek tomorrow. The doc is not only good with people."

Reluctantly, Elizabeth pulled away and forced herself to look up into Will's face. An unsettling anxiousness filling the pit of her stomach like a quarry of rocks.

"Thank you for finding her," she said quietly. "And for finding me."

When the man looked down at her and smiled warmly, Elizabeth was taken aback. This man was not William Redbourne. While they had similar features and stature, Will's eyes were a rich, dark brown with amber hues and his jawline square. This man's eyes were light—though hard to tell the exact color in the dim light, and his face much narrower.

She breathed out a sigh of relief, though she wasn't sure why. She hadn't seen Will since he'd returned home from England and was not sure how he would react if he discovered who she was. After all, he was not exactly on the best terms with her father after everything that had happened. Not after the way he'd left things.

"Are you all right?" the stranger asked.

She'd been staring at him way too long to be appropriate. She cleared her throat.

"Yes, I am fine. Sorry. You just reminded me of someone I had not thought about in a long time is all. I will be fine." She pulled her shoulders back and stood up as tall as she could, still a good foot shorter than the man. She scratched Caspar's ears.

"I get that a lot." He flashed a smile that made Elizabeth begin to understand what had attracted Grace to him. "Name's Ethan, ma'am. We live just over the ridge there on Redbourne Ranch."

There it was again.

Redbourne.

It had to be a coincidence. The likelihood of running into Will or his family a continent away from home was slim, if not impossible.

Ethan glanced over at the burnt rubble. "I'm afraid there's nothing more we can do here tonight. The fire's just about run its course"

"You've done so much already. Thank you."

"Oh, I almost forgot. This dog of yours must have dragged this potato sack out of the house. It was lying in the dirt under one paw when I found her, and she nearly took my hand off when I first tried to pick it up. She must have thought it was important. I'm sure it's of little consolation, but it's pretty heavy. There might be something worth salvaging inside." His voice sounded hopeful.

Elizabeth looked down at the charred material of the sack and graciously took it from Ethan's hands. It *was* heavier than she'd remembered. She opened the top of the bag and pulled out a beautifully carved chest.

"It was my mother's." Relief washed over her. At least she hadn't been left completely destitute. The box had everything that was left of her money, a few photographs of her family, and a large ruby pendant that had been passed down from mother to daughter for generations.

"Thank you for bringing it to me." She wiped a layer of black soot from the edge and noticed the latch was bent. Maybe she could have someone in town fix it later.

"Don't thank me. Thank this pup of yours. I can't say I've ever seen an animal with that kind of instinct before, but I guess there's a first time for everything."

Elizabeth leaned close to Caspar's face. "Thanks, Cas," she said with heartfelt gratitude as she squeezed the dog as much as she dared without hurting her. She turned to Mr. Redbourne. "I thought I had lost her. I still cannot believe she went back into the house while it was burning."

"You've either got a right brave hound there, ma'am, or one with a few logs short of a pile."

They all laughed.

The weight of the box shifted and a tiny whimper came from inside the unlocked chest. Elizabeth opened it to discover the runt of Caspar's litter noisily rooting and pawing at the sides.

"Ah," Ethan said with a laugh. "Now, that makes a lot more sense. She went back in for her babies."

"How did you get in there?" Elizabeth asked, confused at how something so small could have gotten into the closed container. She glanced over at the hamper where the other four puppies played. "Just one," she nodded at the basket. "I must have missed him. I grabbed all of the others on my way out."

The little one in the box started to whimper. She looked down at the runt, reached in, and pulled him out, cradling him against her chest.

"I am not sure how he got out of there. He would have had to climb over all the other pups."

"A real fighter," he said with a nod of approval.

Elizabeth pulled the puppy away from her to look into his face. "You're going to be trouble, now aren't you, little one?" She asked as she scratched behind his ears. "I've always had a soft place in my heart for a fighter."

Grace squealed when she picked up the basket with Caspar's four little puppies. "They are adorable," she said as she carried them over to the wagon. "Ethan, maybe we can—"

"Nope."

"But—"

"Nope."

Elizabeth stood up straight and looked back at the house. Several persistent flames still licked at the frame, but most of the building had collapsed onto itself into a few large heaps.

"Did Ferg go for help?" Ethan asked as he laid Caspar in the back of the wagon next to the basket of pups. She seemed quite content to stay put atop the thick wool blanket. "I didn't see his horse in the stable."

"I guess he didn't tell you either," Grace said, placing her free hand on her husband's arm, still snuggling with one of the pups. "Ferg moved back east, I'm guessing to be closer to his son, and sold the house suddenly to Mrs. Jessup last week."

A silent glance passed between Ethan and Grace.

"What is it?" the exchange did not go unnoticed by Elizabeth.

"It's nothing." Grace said with a giggle as the pup she was holding licked her face.

"Ferg was an eccentric old man and sometimes he didn't always associate with the most respectable crowd."

"I am afraid I am already quite aware of that fact."

Ethan and Grace both looked at her, their heads tilted in the same direction.

"There were some men who stopped by last week who seemed a little...rougher than most of the men I have encountered in Stone Creek. They were less than hospitable and made a few threats."

Grace tucked the puppy in her arms close to her body and reached out to touch Elizabeth's shoulder. "Are you all right? Did they hurt you?"

"I think the shotgun I had aimed at the door deterred any tomfoolery." She laughed half-heartedly, but neither of the Redbournes had even a hint of a smile on their faces.

"Ethan," Grace said, shaking her head and turning to her husband, "you don't think that..."

"I think we need to talk to Raine."

"What's wrong?" Elizabeth asked, an unsettling sensation

welling up in the pit of her stomach. Now that the flames had diminished and the house had all but collapsed completely, the night was returning to solemn darkness and Elizabeth found it hard to read the expressions on Ethan's face.

"At least it won't turn into something like what happened in Florence City."

Both Ethan's and Grace's brows scrunched together.

Elizabeth shook her head. She always spouted useless facts when she was nervous. "Surely you heard about it. Hoodlums started several homes on fire and within the week, the whole town went up in flames."

"I've never heard of Florence City," Grace said quietly.

"Exactly." Elizabeth had read all about the small Kansas town in one of her history lessons with her American tutor.

Ding. Ding. Ding.

Bells sounded in the distance.

"That is the watchmen's bell. They must have seen the smoke," Ethan said with a nod of his head. "The others will be here soon enough."

"Others?"

"My brother, Raine, is the deputy in town. He leads a nightwatch of men who respond to incidents like this." He looked back at the burning house. "You are one lucky young lady, ma'am. This fire burned more quickly than most I've seen. Do you know how it started?"

Elizabeth thought for a moment, her brows scrunching together as she tried to remember. It had all happened so fast. *The window.*

"I was in bed. Caspar woke me up and I heard glass breaking downstairs. I thought maybe a window pane had fallen and shattered against the wooden floorboards, but then my room started swirling with smoke. When I reached the stairs, the living room was already on fire." She shuddered at the recollection.

Grace reached up and rubbed Elizabeth's shoulder, as if to

offer strength.

"I ran to the kitchen and doused some towels and the rug with water from the buckets I had been using earlier to clean up the place, then I tried to beat out the flames." She wiped the back of her wrist across her forehead as if reliving the heat from the fire. "Caspar started barking, but I have worked so hard making the place my own, I did not want to just leave it to burn. I put everything I have…" she turned to look at the smoking remains of the place that was to be her home, "…into this house." Her shoulders dropped.

"I'm glad you changed your mind before it was too late," Grace said, understanding lining her voice.

Elizabeth turned to the woman with a half-smile. "It's because of Cas. I don't know how long I would have stayed. The obstinate dog bit onto my skirt, growling and tugging until I finally dropped my rags and followed her out into the yard."

"You're a good girl, Caspar." Ethan scratched the top of the hound's head.

The melodic sound of horse's hooves beating in rhythm filled the distant silence as several men rode up with shovels, buckets, and blankets.

"Ethan," one of the men called out as he dismounted and joined them, "did everyone get out all right?" He glanced from Ethan to her to Grace and back to her again.

"Looks like we're a little too late. What happened here?"

"My house burned down," Elizabeth said matter-of-factly.

The handsome man focused on her a moment. "Forgive me, ma'am. I didn't mean to sound insensitive. I don't believe I've had the pleasure." He removed his hat and cradled it in his arm. "I'm Deputy Raine Redbourne, ma'am. You must be Mrs. Jessup."

She looked up at him with surprise, as did Grace and Ethan.

"A couple of the boys in town were grumbling about something Mr. Ferguson had taken from them. They mentioned that there was a new couple who bought his place, so I stopped off at the telegraph office to check the record. Where is your husband, ma'am?"

The question was simple enough.

Heat flooded Elizabeth's face. She couldn't quite meet the deputy's eyes. She'd heard that confession was good for the soul and if at any time her soul needed something good, it was now.

"I have no husband, Deputy."

Grace nodded her encouragement.

He scrunched his brows together. "I'm not sure I understand, ma'am."

"Raine," Ethan spoke up, "it's been a long day and I am sure Mrs. Jessup is very tired. Do you think we could do this in the morning instead?"

"Yes, of course," he said with a nod toward Ethan, then he turned back to face her. "But I'm afraid I have to ask you a few more questions first. I know it's hard, and I know you're tired, ma'am, but it isn't everyday someone's home burns to the ground." He dropped his head a little to meet her eyes. "Are you up for it?"

Elizabeth waited a moment, then nodded.

"I'm so sorry for your loss, ma'am. Do you have any idea what may have started the fire?"

"Winston Driscoll and his boys paid her a visit a few days ago. Threatened her," Ethan said, stepping midway between her and his brother.

"How do you know Mr. Driscoll, Mrs. Jessup?" the deputy asked, ignoring Ethan and stepping sideways so he once again faced her.

"I am afraid I do not know the man." She shrugged. "He said that Mr. Ferguson had something of his and that if he did not get it back, he would take what was owed out of the house."

What could have possibly have been gained from the man actually burning down the house?

"Did he threaten to hurt you in any way?"

Elizabeth felt the heat rise again in her face, but didn't

respond immediately.

"I see," Raine said.

"Apparently, she's pretty handy with a shotgun," Ethan said with an encouraging smile and a wink.

"Understood." Raine placed his hat back on his head. "I apologize that we didn't get here in time to save the place, ma'am. I'm sure that we'll be able to round up enough men to help you rebuild whenever you're ready." He tapped the front of his hat and then turned to Ethan. "I'll head out to Driscoll's place tomorrow and see what Winston has to say." He nodded at Elizabeth. "Ma'am."

"Thank you, Deputy," she said.

He nodded briefly, then walked over to where a group of men stood, holding up their lanterns to look at the scorched remains of her home.

Ethan cleared his throat.

"If it's all right with you, Mrs. Jessup, Grace and I would like you to come home with us. Tomorrow we'll worry about what needs to be done here, but for now, I think it'll do you good to get some sleep." Ethan extended his hand.

My books.

Elizabeth held up one finger and dashed over to where she'd dropped the few books she'd been able to salvage. She scrunched down, careful to keep the puppy securely tucked in one arm, and picked up her books one at a time until all had been collected. Out of all the volumes she'd brought with her, only five were left for her library. And she longed for her expansive collection back home.

At least you have these, she told herself with a grateful nod.

Ethan relieved her of the books, setting them on the floorboards beneath the driver's seat.

Unsure of what tomorrow would hold, Elizabeth climbed into the back of the wagon alongside Grace and a restless Caspar and the pups. She kept the runt snuggled tightly into her chest and pulled the blanket up tighter around her shoulders.

"Grace?" Elizabeth asked.

"Um-hmmmm," the woman said softly as she turned to face her.

She needed to ask, but was unsure how to do it.

"If I ask you something, do I have your word you will not say anything?"

"Of course."

"William Redbourne. Do you know him?"

Grace turned a surprise look on her. "Handsome? Tall? Blond? Dimples that won't quit, but stubborn as all get out?"

"That's him." Elizabeth wasn't sure whether to be excited or fearful at the realization they were so close.

"Will is Ethan's brother. How do you know him?" Grace asked with a devious smile.

Elizabeth held her mother's charred box close to her scorched bosom.

"We've never actually met, but I saw him fight many times while he was at school."

"England?"

Elizabeth nodded.

"Will speaks fondly of his time overseas. I'm sure he will be thrilled to meet you."

"I'm not so sure of that. Maybe you can drive me into town in the morning. I'd just assume that Mr. Redbourne not know about me."

"Nonsense," Grace said with a shake of her head. "Will might be a fighter on the outside, but he's got a heart of gold."

Elizabeth didn't respond, skeptical of the woman's optimism. Grace didn't understand the history Will had with the Archer family. It would be best if she just kept to herself and never looked back.

"Did you know that one cubic foot of gold weighs a half of a ton." Elizabeth's hand flew to her mouth. She would have to work harder to keep her words in check. "I'm sorry. I cannot seem to help myself."

Grace narrowed her eyes with a pursed-lip smile. "I guess he has a very heavy heart."

They looked at each other. Elizabeth held her breath, her eyes wide, then suddenly the humor of Grace's statement bubbled over and they both laughed.

"Don't you worry. He's out of town right now," Grace continued, "but I am sure he will be back by the end of the coming week." She nodded, then reached out, taking hold of Elizabeth's hand, and squeezed. "It'll all work out. You'll see."

From your lips to God's ears.

As long as Will Redbourne didn't find out she was Sterling Archer's daughter, there might just be a chance that everything would work out fine. But, if she stayed in Stone Creek, it would only be a matter of time before he discovered the truth of her heritage. No, she couldn't risk it. Not if she wanted any chance of living a life outside of her father's devious shadow. It seemed the time had come, more quickly than she'd expected, to move on. To find another place to call home.

The question was, where would she go?

CHAPTER THREE

Colorado City, Colorado

"I'm done," Will told Sven as they rode into town and stopped in front of the General Store. He only had a few weeks left before he would be returning to England and he wanted to spend as much time with his family as he could before he left. Taking on another job, no matter how small, would be a distraction he could ill afford.

He'd already been working as an outrider for the stagecoach company for longer than he'd planned and he was anxious to get home. There were a lot of preparations to be made, and with the money from this ride, he'd have enough to finally purchase the ship waiting for him in Boston.

His friend's brows knit together.

"I have been offered a position at the University of London to teach for the next few years and I have a lot to get done before I leave," he explained as they both climbed down off their horses.

"London?" Sven asked with a raised brow. "Does your mother know?"

Will hadn't been able to muster enough courage to tell his family about his new position in England. His mother loved having her children close to home, but with Rafe and Levi travelling all the time, he figured it wouldn't be much different, he'd just be riding the ocean waves instead of a horse. The job included the opportunity to assemble a crew for his ship and to explore.

"I didn't think so," Sven mocked. "Come on, Will. It's just one more run to Kansas City. You wouldn't even have to take the train with them to Denver. Good money," the Norwegian man coaxed as he strapped his horse to the short wooden railing. "Twice as much as this one and less than a quarter of the distance."

"You know I don't care about that." Truth was, ever since his brothers, Levi and Ethan, had both found that finding love agreed with them, Will had started thinking more about settling down himself, getting married and having a gaggle of children of his own, but there were a few things he wanted to do first. *Needed* to do first.

"And on top of the bankroll, we'll be escorting three beautiful women across God's lovely countryside," Sven continued. "Not like these two," he said, pointing to the wealthy man and his attendant standing just outside of the bank.

Will narrowed his eyes at his friend. "How in the world you think you are going to find a wife escorting mail-order brides to their intended grooms is beyond me. They're spoken for," he said with a shake of his head. "That *is* the whole idea."

"I know," Sven said as he climbed the stairs and walked into the mercantile. "But a lady can change her mind, right?"

Will shook his head at the absurdity of his friend's scheme. "I think he's gone mad, don't you think, boy?" he whispered in Indy's ear.

Independence, Will's black gelding that sported a white star on his forehead, dipped his head into the waiting trough for a long drink and Will patted his side before following the broad shouldered man into the store.

He'd never intended to be an outrider for the stagecoach

company, but when the opportunity had presented itself, he hadn't been able to pass up the chance to see the vast open spaces of the west for himself. Going abroad had whetted his appetite for exploring and he found himself growing restless sticking around the ranch day after day. Besides, the money was good. He came from a wealthy family himself, but he'd been taught early on that a man needed to make his own way in life. He couldn't expect that everything would be handed to him without effort.

Ranch life was as much in his blood as any Redbourne's, and he enjoyed the work—it gave him perspective—but something was missing in that life for him. Fortunately, studying abroad had given him a chance to see what else life could offer him and he'd finally begun to figure out exactly what it was that drew him away and where his purpose lay.

"When are you leaving?" Sven asked as he bit into one of the apples he'd just purchased from the clerk, tossing Will the other delicious, red fruit.

"A couple of weeks."

"That's plenty of time. If you cut out the train and just accompany the stage, this next run will only take a day or two. Tops."

Will smiled and bit into his apple as the Norwegian tried to convince him. He and Sven had put their differences behind them. Their bout in the barn last month had been foolish and he knew it. Sven had not intended to show any disrespect for Hannah, but in Will's way of thinking, ignorance was no excuse. At least now, the man would be more aware of his surroundings and had gained a better understanding of how protective Will was of his little sister or any of the women in his life. The men had gotten along just fine since that day.

"I'll think about it," Will offered. He knew that if he gave the man a little hope, it would earn him a few moments of peace, then Will could let him down a little later. He needed to keep his eye on his future. And being an outrider was not it.

"I knew you'd come around," Sven said with a satisfied smirk.

"Come on." Will walked past him and out the door.

It was time to go home.

Kansas

Sunday services, followed by supper at Redbourne Ranch, had Elizabeth on edge. She still hadn't come clean about who she was, and coming face to face with Will Redbourne would bring everything out into the open, showing her off in a less than perfect light.

She wished she'd just told Mr. Redbourne and his wife everything last night. While she'd never actually met Will, his history with her family was not pleasant. She'd seen him fight on many occasions from her father's box at the ring, but things had gotten ugly when he'd stood up to her father. Everyone did what Sterling Archer wanted or they paid a hefty price.

Well, not everyone.

Sadness descended upon her like a candied apple melting in the sun. She'd lost her home and most everything in it. And the things she'd been able to salvage would not be worth much to the average person. She knew the time had come for her to move on from this place, but with little money, opportunities for a woman to strike out on her own were few.

If she stayed in Stone Creek, the truth would be inevitable. Will had history with the Archers and that was exactly what she'd wanted to avoid. She needed to go where no one knew her or her family. There was no longer a choice. She had to leave.

Knock. Knock.

"Eliza Beth," Grace called from outside the door, "are you ready to head up to the homestead?"

She took a deep breath as she looked into the mirror above

the vanity in the corner of the room where she'd slept and swept down her rosy top with her hands. Grace had lent her a dress to wear. It was a little too short and a little too tight in the waist, but it was leaps and bounds better than wearing her now ragged and singed nightshift to dinner with one of the most prominent families in the territory.

She pinched her cheeks. "Coming."

When she opened the door, Grace greeted her with a genuinely pleased smile. The young woman's green dress accentuated the emerald flecks in her eyes. She fit her name. She was the epitome of what Elizabeth would consider refined and she mused at how well the woman would fit in with the ladies of high social breeding back home.

The woman wove her arm into Elizabeth's and guided her down the short staircase and out the door to where her husband had already hitched the wagon and, to her surprise, the deputy had decided to join them for what she believed was supposed to be a short trip out to the main homestead on Redbourne Ranch.

"Gracie!" a tall young man called from the porch.

"I'll be right back," Grace said as she turned back for the stairs.

"I don't know why you're making me wear this get up anyway. It's just dinner," he said, pulling at the collar of his shirt where a tie dangled haphazardly at his throat.

Elizabeth smiled at the exchange. The youth reminded her of the brother just older than her at that age—full of attitude and sass. Then, her smiled faded. Jeremy was the one she missed most of all.

"Jack, we need to look nice," Grace said as she slapped away his hand and proceeded to fix the young man's tie.

"Why doesn't Ethan have to wear a tie?"

"'Cause my sister is younger than me and can't tell me what to do," Ethan said, stepping out of the house in a freshly pressed, button-down shirt—his hair combed neatly and his face clean-shaven.

"Ma'am," the deep sound of Deputy Redbourne's voice geared her attention away from the conversation on the porch. Raine tipped his hat as he brought his horse up alongside the buckboard seat. "We've been back out to your place and walked the premises. I'm afraid there isn't much left, but going over the debris from the house, I did come across something that makes me believe the fire may not have been an accident."

"What do you mean, Deputy?"

Raine reached down into his saddlebags and pulled out a small cloth-wrapped bundle. He rolled the contents out into his hand where he held up the neck of a blackened whiskey bottle for her to see. "I found this just below the section I believe was the windowsill."

Elizabeth opened her mouth to say something, but words would not come. That bottle had not been there yesterday after she'd scrubbed the floors and she certainly did not keep spirits in her house, so how did it get there?

"Funny thing," he said, "that smell is not alcohol, it's kerosene." He paused long enough for the words to sink in.

Someone had set fire to her house. On purpose.

"I'm afraid it looks like arson, ma'am."

Arson? Why would anyone want to burn down her house?

"I think maybe it's time for us to have that little chat now."

"Come on, Raine. We'll be late for church and you know what Mama says about people who are late to church."

"I know. We'll all be heathens," he laughed. "Just tell me one thing, Mrs. Jessup," he said as he turned to her. "Is there anyone who may want to hurt you?"

Several of her father's business associates came to mind, but they were all back in England. And she couldn't imagine her father trying to actually have her killed—not even after the way she left. Besides, no one from her old life had any idea where she was, so she looked the man straight in the eyes as she replied confidently.

"No, sir. I am new to Stone Creek and have not had many

opportunities to meet the people here. The only acquaintances I have are Mr. and Mrs. Redbourne." She jutted her chin toward Ethan and Grace who now joined them at the wagon.

Grace climbed up onto the seat next to her and took a hold of the reins. Ethan and Jack both mounted horses to ride along beside them.

"We just want to keep you safe," Deputy Redbourne said with a wink. "Normally, Stone Creek is a real nice place. I'm sorry you've had a rough go of it in the first few weeks." He tipped his hat again. "Rest assured, we'll get to the bottom of it." He wrapped the bottle back up and placed it carefully in his saddle bag. "Let's go."

Grace leaned close. "Don't worry," she whispered, "these Redbourne men won't let anything happen to you." She wrapped an arm around Elizabeth's shoulders and squeezed. "And, I thought you might want to know that Will is still out of town, so you don't have to worry about running into him. It's just supper at the ranch. With his family," she added with a grin.

"*Just* supper. At Redbourne Ranch." Elizabeth snorted. Her eyes shot open and her hand flew to cover her mouth and nose. Heat filled her cheeks as she lowered her hand. "With the Redbournes." She inhaled, then exhaled slowly. "Did you know…"

Bite your tongue, Elizabeth Archer.

Grace giggled. "I'm excited for you to meet Leah, their mother. You'll love her. Everyone does. And she loves smart, educated women. You'll fit in just fine."

Elizabeth tried to smile, but the flutters in her stomach would not be calmed, and a twinge of disappointment crept in that the prize fighter would not be joining them. Entertaining thoughts of Will Redbourne was dangerous. She couldn't blame him for what had happened, but he might blame her. She'd wanted to leave her life behind, to start over in a place where no one had ever heard of Sterling Archer or his family, but she'd obviously not gone far enough.

"When will he be back?" she asked Grace, trying to mask the interest in her voice. She needed to leave before he returned. To get as far away from him as she could.

"Ethan said he would be back by the end of the week."

"Friday or Saturday?"

Grace shrugged and raised her hands lightly, palms up. "Friday?"

"Friday," Elizabeth confirmed with a nod.

That gives me about five days.

Surely she would be able to find a way out of town by then. A little voice crept inside of her head as she looked over at her new friend and suddenly she wasn't at all sure she wanted to leave…Will Redbourne or not.

Grace was the first person she'd met since coming to this little town to whom she felt a kinship and she dreaded the sense of loss that would come when she left. At least for the short while she would be staying in Stone Creek she hoped they could be friends.

Leaving home had come at a cost. Friends, family, everything familiar and comfortable were all a continent away. But the price of staying would have been greater. It had been a long time since Elizabeth had been able to talk to anyone and it felt good to have someone in her life she felt she could trust. Almost.

As they crested a large hill, Elizabeth looked down at what could only be the heart of Redbourne Ranch. Several outbuildings surrounded by trees, corrals, and open fields dotted the landscape around the largest home she had seen since coming to America.

"Suddenly, I am not feeling so well. Maybe we should go back and I will lie down for a bit."

Grace laughed. "You are going to love them," she said with a smile. "And they are going to love you. All of the Redbournes appreciate a woman with smarts."

That is exactly what I am afraid of.

CHAPTER FOUR

Just Outside Colorado City

"I think there are three of them," Sven whispered from his place behind the large tree trunk.

Will closed his eyes and took a deep breath, his gun drawn, and his wealthy charge huddled up behind him. They had been ambushed just outside of Colorado City. Several masked gunmen had fired on the stage and they'd had to pull up behind a crag jutting out from the side of the road for protection.

The driver now lay on the ground just a few yards in front of them, blood oozing from a shot to the shoulder. Will quickly assessed his surroundings. There were not a lot of places to take cover and bile burned his throat at the idea of taking a man's life. He'd come all too close to that once already and he hadn't needed a gun to do it.

"Stay put!" he warned his friend.

Otis, the stagecoach driver, groaned, tossing his head from side to side.

Will could not leave him exposed. As one of the riders came into view, Will stuck his head out from behind the stage long enough to get off a warning shot.

"We're going to die out here in the middle of nowhere,

aren't we?" whined the sniveling man he'd been charged to protect.

Will glanced over at Mr. Warding as his tall, gangly assistant pulled a perfectly folded white handkerchief from his pocket and handed it to his employer, who dabbed at the little beads of sweat forming on his brow.

"Thank you, Kells," Mr. Warding spoke under his breath.

Will shook his head. "Not if I have anything to say about it," he returned gruffly, marveling at how differently this man handled his wealth than his father. Jameson Redbourne would no more allow a man to follow him around to attend to his every need than he would wear a woman's dress to church on Sunday.

Another shot sped by and Will backed up tighter against the wheel of the stage. His mind raced. He knew what needed to be done, but he prayed there would be another way to keep those under his protection alive and unharmed. He looked over at Sven who nodded his willingness to do what was necessary.

"Stay!" he commanded his charges.

"And just where do you think I'm going to go with ruffians like that out there?"

Will narrowed his eyes at the annoying man, his lip curling slightly into a snarl.

"I'm staying," the man affirmed, his hands up and patting the air in front of him.

"You?" Will asked the man behind Mr. Warding.

He dipped his head affirmatively.

He stared at them both another moment. Satisfied, Will turned to look at Sven with a nod. He waited only long enough for his friend to return the gesture before darting out from behind the stagecoach. He fired off a couple of shots amidst those Sven sent to the other side of the ravine, as he traversed out into the open, wrapped his hands beneath the driver's shoulders, and dragged him back behind the protected ridge.

A shot whizzed just above his left ear, grazing the tender flesh there, but he did not stop moving. To his amazement and relief, the team of horses strapped to the stage, while anxiously prancing about and pawing at the dirt, had not bolted. Luckily, the back half of the oversized wagon was tucked up behind a rocky ledge, providing extra protection against the attack.

"We've got to stop the bleeding," he told Mr. Warding as he laid Otis down at his feet. "Where is your man?" he asked as he glanced around, but the attendant, Mr. Kells was nowhere to be seen.

Mr. Warding looked behind him as if he hadn't noticed the man was gone.

Idiot!

How was he supposed to protect a man who was senseless enough to run off in the middle of a robbery? Or a gunfight?

"He's…um," he shook his head in frustration. "I don't know. Maybe he's gone for help. Yes, that's it. He went to get help." He wiped his head again with the little white hankie as he leaned against the spokes of the wheel and heaved out a sigh.

"Listen to me, Warding. This man is going to die if we don't help him. Do you really want that on your conscience?"

The man's eyes grew wide. "What am *I* supposed to do? I'm not a doctor."

Will's patience with the wealthy land baron had all but run its course. "Your jacket."

Mr. Warding opened his mouth as if to protest, but quickly shut it again, pulling off his sleek overcoat and handing it to Will who had already pulled a knife from the side of his boot.

As he stabbed into the thick material, Mr. Warding whimpered and bit his lip.

"Do you have any idea how expensive that coat was?"

Will shot a look at the man that shut him up. He tore a few strips of material away from the jacket and pressed one of them up against Otis's shoulder. The driver groaned softly, color quickly draining from his face.

"Press here," he directed Mr. Warding, who scrambled to do as he'd been directed. He knelt down next to the injured man and held the cloth in place.

CRACK!

Several shots rang through the air. Will glanced over at Sven, who lifted his shoulders in a shrug and glanced out from behind the tree he was using as cover. He shook his head.

Silence passed for an uncomfortable amount of time.

"Anybody hurt over there?" a familiar voice called out.

It can't be.

Will's brows scrunched together.

Rafe?

Will pulled himself up off the ground and moved cautiously to the edge of the stagecoach to peer out from behind the splintering red-painted wood. There, walking toward him was his older brother, Rafe, pushing along two men whose hands had been tied behind their backs.

Will stood up straight and stepped out into the open, a grin spreading wildly across his face. Rafe had always had good timing.

"Rafe?" Will called out to him.

"Hey, Oxford, is that you?"

The brothers exchanged a quick hug, and Rafe slapped Will on his shoulder, a wide smile on his face. It had been ages since the siblings had seen each other.

"I'm sure glad to see you," Will said, his smile fading. "Otis has been shot."

The stagecoach driver was a personal family friend of the Redbournes. He'd taken many meals at their family table, often recounting his many adventurous tales of life on the road. Will couldn't bear the thought of losing him this way.

"How bad is it?"

"It's bad," Will responded.

"Where is he?" Rafe asked, a sudden urgency lacing his voice.

The two men in his custody stumbled as he roughly urged them forward. Suddenly, his arm shot into the air, his revolver cocked and aimed perfectly at Sven's head.

"Ought not try to sneak up on a man," Rafe said without even looking to see who was there. "A man could get himself shot like that."

A branch cracked beneath Sven's feet as he stepped out from behind his tree. "Don't shoot. I'm a friend. A friend," he said, his hands raised.

"He's my riding partner," Will assured when Rafe glanced at him for confirmation as he stepped between his brother and his prisoners.

"That was incredible," Sven cooed as he approached. "How did you know I was even here?"

"I could smell that cologne you wear from across the ravine," Rafe said with a chuckle as he returned his gun to his hip.

Will laughed too, then, his eyes narrowed as he thought about the attack. Rafe had two men in custody, but there had been at least three. "Where's the third man?"

As if on cue, a rider on horseback came around the angled rocks and charged directly at them, gun drawn, and bullets flying. Will sidestepped the assault, retrieving his pistol, and bracing himself on one knee, his gun aimed at the bandit.

Rafe slid one of his pearl handled, red colt revolvers from its holster and just as the man dared take aim, he fired. The would-be thief tumbled backward off his horse, landing with a thud in the rocky dirt road.

"I'm going to kill you, Redbourne," one of the captured men spat, lunging forward at Rafe, his hands still behind his back.

Will stuck out his foot and the man fell forward onto his face in front of them.

Rafe knelt down with one knee in the center of the man's back. "Wasn't such a smart move, now was it, Gruber?"

The man squirmed beneath Rafe's significant weight, his feet flailing behind him.

"Where's McElvoy?"

"Get off me, Redbourne, or you won't live long enough to regret it."

Rafe laughed derisively. "You say that like it's the first time I've heard a threat." He looked over at Will. "Hey, little brother, will you get me that rope?" He pointed to the fallen man's horse that had rounded back.

"How many more do you think there are?" Will asked as he slipped the braided cord from the strap at the side of the mount's saddle.

"The bounty note had four listed," Rafe said, returning his gun to its holster and taking the binding from Will. He tied up the man's feet. "I imagine that McElvoy isn't too far away." He looked over at Sven, then nodded at the bearded prisoner still standing across from them. "Make sure he doesn't move. I've got to check on Otis." He stood up and strode to where Will had tucked the stagecoach driver behind the ridge.

Mr. Warding was gone.

Coward. Nothing surprised him anymore.

Movement at the top of the cliff caught Will's eye.

"Rafe, look out!" he shouted.

It was too late. Mr. Kells had already jumped at Rafe from the top of the ridge, a knife in one hand. He toppled on top of his brother, lashing out with a cheap punch to his jaw. Luckily, Rafe had been able to deflect the man's stabbing arm and rid him of the weapon.

How had Will not seen it? He'd been travelling with the man for days, but had been too annoyed with the man under his protection to suspect anything sinister about the attendant. The more he thought about it, the more he realized that there had been way too many coincidences and mishaps on this run to ignore. Something was off and just didn't sit well with him, but there wasn't time to figure it out right now.

Will considered jumping into the fight, but he knew all too well that Rafe could handle himself—especially hand to hand.

He shook his head. Either this Mr. Kells had no idea who he'd just attacked, or he had a death wish. Will considered himself a pretty good fighter, but admittedly, Rafe was better—at least outside of the ring.

"Will!" Sven yelled.

Will looked back to see his friend lying on the ground, holding his head, and the prisoner who'd been restrained just moments ago coming at him with a large branch in his hand. He waited until the bearded brute was within a few feet before he shifted his weight, leaning to one side, allowing the man's momentum to take him beyond his intended mark.

"You all right, Sven?" Will asked without looking behind him.

"Yeah."

"How did he get loose?" As far as Will knew, Rafe had never tied a knot that a man could shake without help.

Kells.

"Don't…know."

By the time the charging man had turned back for him, he was prepared.

One, jab. Two, hook. Three, cross. Down for the count.

That was easy.

Rafe still tussled on the ground with his attacker.

Otis lay in a lifeless heap, no longer tossing his head about. Will rushed to his side. The man's breathing was shallow, almost non-existent. He pressed down against the wound with the torn cloth, trying to slow the bleeding.

Damn that Mr. Warding. Where is he?

"Rafe, what's taking you so long? Otis needs you. Now!"

It wasn't like his brother to prolong a fight.

"Just…give me…one…more…minute," Rafe grunted the words as his fists connected with their target. The two fighting men had worked their way down a little slope to the bottom of a small gulley.

Will held his gun on the man who had attacked him.

It was only a matter of minutes before his brother climbed back up the hill, his bounty incapacitated and strung over his shoulder. When he reached the top, he placed two fingers in his mouth and whistled.

Will turned to see Lexa, Rafe's large, strawberry roan mare, running along the ridge of the ravine until she reached the small clearing just a few feet from their position, kicking up dirt in front of him and shaking her head with a neigh.

"Where did you come fro…?" His question trailed as Rafe shouted directions at him.

"Will, get my bag," his brother urged. He quickly lashed the subdued attendant to the axle of the stagecoach, along with his cohort, and rushed to the side of the dying man.

"Lexa, girl!" Will said, reaching up to rub the mare's face. "It's good to see you, my old friend," he said, sliding his hands over her back and to the saddle bag where he thought Rafe would keep his curative bag. His brother had attended medical school for years before an unfortunate incident caused him to deviate from his course to become one of the most feared and revered bounty hunters in the territory.

Will retrieved the sleek black leather bag by its handles and hurried back to where Otis lay lifeless on the ground. "Is he…" he couldn't formulate the rest of the words.

"No," Rafe said, reaching up for his bag. "He's just passed out. For now. But if we don't remove the bullet straightway and stop the blood, there will be no waking up."

"What can I do?" Will asked, feeling more helpless than he had in a long time.

Rafe looked up at him. "Hold him down."

Will had learned a long time ago not to second guess Rafe. Otis certainly didn't look like he was going anywhere, but he knelt down next to the man and braced himself against his body.

His brother pulled some long metal tweezers from his bag, along with a bottle of liquid. He poured the disinfectant over the wound, then gingerly slipped the prongs of the medical tool into the hole in Otis's shoulder. The man convulsed in pain, straining against Will, who used every ounce of his strength to keep him as still as possible.

"Got it," Rafe said as he blew out a long breath, holding up the blood-covered slug.

Otis's body went limp.

"He'll rest easier now," Rafe assured him as he pulled a familiar white poultice from his bag and applied it to the stage driver's wound.

Their mother's salve worked wonders on all sorts of injuries and Will had no doubt that it would help stave off infection and aid in Otis's recovery. Rafe pulled a roll of white gauze bandage from his bag, binding the wound tightly. Finally satisfied that his patient was cared for, he pulled himself into a standing position.

"You did good, little brother," he said as he hauled Will into a tight hug.

"It's good to see you, Rafe." Will clapped his brother on the back before pulling away. "How did you know I was out here?"

"Didn't." He dusted his hands on the legs of his trousers, trying to wipe the blood off of them. "I've been after this Kelton McElvoy and his cohorts for weeks, and their trail led me here. Seems the good Lord just knew you needed looking after today," he said with a playful grin.

"I'm glad you're here."

"Me too."

"I've seen a lot of things in my days on the trail, but never anything like that," Sven said with admiration as he stepped in between the two men. "So, you're Rafe, the bounty hunter brother? I've heard a lot about you."

Rafe extended his hand, one brow raised as he looked at Will.

"Sven," the Norwegian offered awkwardly. The two men were of similar heights, but somehow his brother still seemed bigger than life.

"You coming home?" Will asked, knowing his mother would appreciate seeing her son.

"'Fraid not for a while. There's another job waiting for me after I turn in these brutes and collect my bounty."

Will understood.

Rafe was still hurting after being left standing alone on his wedding day, jilted, brideless. It would take time, but he knew that eventually his brother's heart would heal.

"Hmhmmm."

Will had nearly forgotten about Mr. Warding and he turned to see the cowardly man peek out between the spokes of a wagon wheel.

"How long might it be before we can get back on the road?" the little annoying man asked as he pulled himself out from beneath the stagecoach. The back of his trousers caught on the metal step rung. The loud rip of the thick material filled the momentary silence.

Mr. Warding's face turned a bright shade of red and his eyes grew wide, unblinking. He threw his hands to his behind and melted into the side of the coach.

They all laughed as the man opened the door and climbed backward into the passenger compartment, quickly pulling the door shut behind him. He poked his head out the window and looked up toward the axle to where his attendant now sat, slumped over and unconscious, but restrained.

"Why is my man, Kells, tied to the wagon?" He looked at Will. "I demand you release him immediately," he said as if trying to regain some of his dignity.

It wasn't working.

"I'm afraid that's not going to happen, Mr. Warding."

"Why in heaven's name not?"

"Because Kelton McElvoy is a wanted man," Rafe said, standing to his full height as he approached the stagecoach, "and I aim to take him in." He folded his arms and narrowed his eyes at Mr. Warding. "Do you see any problem with that?"

Mr. Warding opened his mouth nearly as wide as his eyes. He didn't say anything, but shook his head slowly.

"Good," Rafe said with a curt nod, then strode toward his prisoners.

Mr. Warding looked over at Will. "Your superiors will hear about this," he said, flipping his nose into the air and slowly backing into the shadows.

Will snorted a laugh.

McElvoy roused, jerking on his hands to try to get them loose from their bindings.

"I best be getting on the road," Rafe said as he checked on the man he'd shot. He dropped his head and closed his eyes before untying the men now in his custody from the axle and with little need for persuasion placed them on horses that had all been strung together and secured to Lexa's saddle. He picked up the body of the now lifeless man, threw him over his shoulder, and turned back to Will. "You fellas need anything else before I go?" he asked as he tossed the corpse over Lexa's rump.

Will didn't know how Rafe did it, but he always managed to take down the bad guys—even when the odds were against him. A big part of him wished he could be more like his brother.

"You going to be all right with all of them?"

"Awww, they won't be any more trouble, now will you, fellas?" he called out to the men now restlessly sitting bound astride their mounts.

"You won't make it to Edmonton alive, Redbourne," McElvoy spat as he attempted to loosen his hands again.

With all of three men secured together, as well as their horses, McElvoy had no chance of going anywhere or doing anything that Rafe didn't want him to.

"Are you doing okay?" Will asked, meeting his brother's eyes.

A flash of pain glanced off his brother's face, then was gone.

"My shoulder's a little stiff from the fight, but I've had worse." Rafe shrugged.

"That's not what I meant."

"I know."

Will nodded. His brother wasn't ready to talk about it. "Well, your timing was excellent—as always." Will shook Rafe's hand, then pulled him in for another hug.

"Glad I was here," Rafe whispered with a firm clap to Will's back, smiling as he pulled away. "Tell Mama…"

"I will."

Rafe nodded and headed back toward the horses.

"Be safe," Will called after him. He wanted to say more, but it wasn't the time. He just hoped his brother would come around sooner rather than later, but the realization hit that this could be the last time he would see Rafe before he left for England. He waved and watched as the bounty hunter led his charges across the ravine and out of sight.

Sven came up to stand behind him. "You Redbournes sure are a breed of your own," he commented as he placed a hand atop Will's shoulder.

Some of us, maybe…

He glanced over at Otis, who looked to be resting peacefully. Color had returned to his face and it no longer glistened with sweat. They would have to double back to Colorado City where Will knew of a skilled doctor who could take care of Otis while they finished the job.

It didn't take long for Will and Sven to fashion a makeshift travois for Otis out of the canvas covering the luggage on the back of the wagon and two felled lodge poles they'd been able to strip and secure with rope. Will and the Norwegian strode over to where the stagecoach driver lay and set the man carefully on the canvas structure that had been strapped to Indy's tack.

As Will placed a blanket over Otis, the man stirred and reached out to grab a hold of his arm.

"You've grown into a fine man, Will Redbourne. Thank you

for what you done here."

"I'm glad you're still with us," Will said with a smile. He patted the man's hand, then pushed himself into a standing position. "We'll see you soon," he said as he walked over to Indy and mounted.

Sven climbed up onto the stage, his horse secured to the rear of the wagon, and they headed back for Colorado City.

Will finally let himself relax a little as they made their way back the direction they'd come earlier that day. After they dropped Otis off with the doc, he hoped they could get back on the road without any more delays on their way to Denver. At least they could catch the train to Kansas City from there. It would be good to get home and spend some time with his family before his oceanic journey.

Visions of his ship, bobbing in the harbor, waiting to carry him and his crew across the sea filled him with anticipation and he smiled as he imagined the cool breeze of the salty sea on his face. He opened his eyes, surveying the ocean of surrounding grassland swaying in the warm spring wind and sighed. He'd waited a long time to earn enough money to purchase that ship, he supposed a few more days wouldn't hurt anything. As long as the man didn't sell it to someone else in the meantime.

CHAPTER FIVE

Kansas, Four Days Later, Thursday

Elizabeth's flesh puckered and the hairs stood up on the back of her neck. She glanced over her shoulder around the mercantile, but didn't see anyone out of the ordinary.

"Did you find a color you like?" Grace asked, eying the bolts of material in front of her.

"I'm sorry. What?" Elizabeth asked, pulling herself away from her suspicions. "Oh, um…" She forced a smile onto her face and held up the vibrant blue cloth. "What do you think about this one?"

"I think you'll put all of us to shame in that color."

Pleased by the compliment, heat touched the edge of Elizabeth's face and she smiled softly. However, she still couldn't shake the feeling that she was being watched and she glanced over her shoulder once more.

Grace and Ethan had been kind enough to put her up for the last few days, but it was time for Elizabeth to move on. Will was expected home soon and she wanted to be gone before he arrived.

"I just don't think I can go through with it, Opal," a young woman in a yellow dress with dark ringlets framing her face said to her friend. "I thought I could, but with my father still ill, I'm afraid my mother won't be able to do it alone. Besides, what if I get to Silver Falls only to find out that Adam MacKenzie is not who he says he is? What if he's actually a drunk? What if he can't read? Or worse yet—poor? I just don't think I have it in me."

"Oh, Winnie. He's already expecting you. Paid for your passage to Colorado and everything," Opal said. "Besides, what would you tell him?"

Guilt settled into Elizabeth's gut as she listened in on the women's conversation, but her interest was piqued. Paid passage to Colorado.

"I thought we were going to do this together," Opal persisted with a pout. "There aren't many men in this town, and I don't know about you, but I don't want to wait around any longer. We aren't getting any younger."

"We are hardly old maids, Opal Gailey!"

"If we stay in this town much longer, we might as well be." The young woman in the lavender dress picked up a travelling bag. "I think this one will be just perfect for our trip to Silver Falls, don't you?"

"Eliza?" Grace called from the front counter by the window.

Elizabeth stood up straight and picked up a large leather satchel, pretending to be checking the quality of the bag. She smiled at the young women who now looked in her direction, set down the bag, and started toward the front of the store.

"Coming," she called, hesitant to pull away from the conversation between the two young women. She wanted to know more.

Elizabeth had seen playbills with ads for those interested in becoming a mail-order-bride, but had never imagined that a woman would actually do it—travel across the country to the wilds of the west and marry a man she'd never met. It was so brazen, so improper, but right now, the opportunity looked more appealing than she would have ever expected.

When she reached Grace, her friend peeked out the window and subtly pointed across the street.

"I think you've caught the eye of that gentleman over there."

Elizabeth followed her friend's glance to where a tall, lanky man in a brown leather fedora stood watching them. The hairs on her arms rose and suddenly she felt the chill of the cool afternoon, even from inside the mercantile.

"Do you know him?" she asked Grace.

"I've never seen him before—though I've only been in Stone Creek myself for just a little more than half a year. Some of the ranchers and farmers here keep to themselves and there are plenty of faces still unfamiliar to me."

Elizabeth did not recognize the man, but there was something about him that seemed familiar.

"I think we should be heading back," she said, trying to ignore the pit that rested at the bottom of her stomach.

After Grace had paid for her goods, they stepped out onto the boardwalk. Elizabeth could not take her eyes off the gentleman, though she tried to hide her interest beneath the large hat Grace had insisted she wear.

When the man caught her eye, he took a step out into the street and headed toward them. He jumped up onto the wooden walkway and removed his hat with a slight bow.

"Excuse me for staring," he said, his soft British accent a reminder of home, "but aren't you Miss Elizabeth Archer? Sterling's daughter."

Heat drained from Elizabeth's face and her heart thumped heavily inside of her chest. Her mind raced, but she was unsure what to say. She'd thought of a thousand different questions people might ask her and had prepared her answers carefully, but that was not one she had anticipated.

Grace stepped forward and offered her hand to the man. "I am Grace Redbourne, and this," she said, turning her shoulders and raising a hand toward Elizabeth, "is Eliza Beth Jessup. May

I ask *your* name, sir?"

"Of course. Where are my manners?" he asked, wrestling with the hat in his hand. "My name is Gregory Cromwell. I am a professor at the University of London. Forgive my error." He bent at the torso enough to look around Grace at her. "Though the resemblance is uncanny."

Elizabeth fought the urge to pull her own hat lower on her head to further obscure her face.

"I apologize if I've made you uncomfortable, ma'am," he said, clearing his throat and looking back at Grace. "The daughter of an acquaintance of mine recently went missing and when I saw your friend here," he gestured toward Elizabeth, "it was like seeing a ghost." He took a step sideways and addressed her directly. "You look just like Miss Archer, my dear."

American accent, she reminded herself before speaking.

"Sounds like something out of one of my adventure novels," she said, trying to sound excited.

"I couldn't help but notice that pendant you are wearing. It is very becoming. I'm sure a piece like that comes with quite a history."

Elizabeth reached up and caressed the ruby dangling from her neck. Why had she worn her mother's necklace?

"I'm sure I wouldn't know. I bought it off a peddler somewhere outside of Boston," she lied, refraining from adding any history about the jewel. She bit her lip.

"Shame. Yes, well, I hope I haven't taken too much of your time." He turned to leave, but stopped and looked at Grace. "Ms. Redbourne, was it?"

"Yes," Grace said with a smile.

"Are you, by chance, a relative of Will Redbourne?"

Elizabeth swallowed hard.

"Why, yes, Professor." Grace glanced over at her. "Will is my brother-in-law. How do you know him?"

Elizabeth wanted to shrink away. If this man was an acquaintance of her father and he was looking for Will, it could only mean trouble.

Grace looked at her, a conspiratorial glint in her eyes.

"He was a student of mine at university a while back."

"What brings you so far away from home, Professor?" Grace asked.

"Will has not told you, has he?"

"Told us what?"

"Ahhh, it is to be a surprise then," he said, switching his hat between his hands. "I will not ruin it for him." He tipped his hat. "Ladies, it has been a pleasure to make your acquaintance." He placed the fedora back on top of his head and winked. "I'm sure I will see you tonight at Redbourne Ranch. Will and I have some business to discuss."

"Will has not returned yet from his last trip."

"If there is one thing I have learned about Will Redbourne, my dear, it is that he always follows through on his commitments." He smiled, then turned away from them and walked into the livery.

Elizabeth relaxed her shoulders and let out the breath she had been holding. She searched her memory, unable to recall ever meeting a Professor Cromwell, but he certainly seemed to know her.

Grace hooked her arm through Elizabeth's and leaned in close to her ear. "Elizabeth Archer, it's very nice to meet you."

Elizabeth pulled back for a moment trying to act as if she had no idea to what the woman was referring, but she'd been discovered. She could see it in Grace's eyes. Her secret was out.

"Don't worry," she said matter-of-factly, "my lips are sealed."

"Grace, I…"

"No judgements from me, Ms. Arch—I mean, Eliza Beth. We all have stories. I'll tell you mine if you tell me yours," she said, a thread of excitement weaving its way into her words.

Relief washed over her like water from a warm bath. The drama in her life could rival any of the penny dreadfuls she'd read, but she was glad she finally had someone she could confide in. Someone she could trust.

"What kind of a story could you possibly have?" Elizabeth asked.

"The kind that involves betrayal, treasure, and love," Grace responded without missing a beat.

Elizabeth stopped in front of the livery where their carriage had been boarded and looked at her friend with a full dosing of skepticism, shaking her head and hands on her hips.

"Honest," Grace said, crossing her heart.

Elizabeth's eyes narrowed, but she could see the sincerity written on Grace's beautiful features.

"What do you say we talk over a slice of warm peach cobbler?" Grace tugged on her arm, pulling her into the quaint little restaurant nearby that served the townspeople of Stone Creek. They took a seat at a table in the corner of the room, lit by two large curtain-bordered windows.

Grace pulled the scarf from around her neck and set it on the empty chair next to her, then looked up at Elizabeth, waiting.

Elizabeth shook her head. "It's a long story."

"My favorite kind."

Will's heart swelled as they crested the summit down into the valley of Stone Creek.

Home.

Redbourne Ranch could be seen in the distance and the thought of Lottie's home cooking made his mouth water. Sven could do many things, but preparing a tasty meal wasn't one of them.

They'd made sure that Otis would be well taken care of in Colorado City before seeing Mr. Warding into Denver. Will stretched in the saddle and took a deep breath of afternoon air, enjoying the familiar smells of the surrounding land. This last ride had taken something out of him.

"Why don't you join us for supper?" he asked Sven. "Lottie always makes more than enough, and if you are as tired as I am, it will do you some good to have a place to hang your hat for the night."

"I'd be much obliged. Thank you, Will."

As they pulled up in front of the ranch, Leah Redbourne descended from the homestead, wiping her hands on her apron, to greet them.

Will's body ached and he struggled to keep himself upright in the saddle. He hadn't felt so bone tired in a long time. A hot bath and a shave sounded like heaven. If his mother had anything to say about it, he would have both before he would be allowed into the kitchen.

The heavenly aroma of freshly baking biscuits clenched his gut, the scent itself melting in his mouth as it wafted through the front door of the house and reached his nose. He dismounted with some effort, but with a grin on his face that extended from ear to ear, he greeted his mother with a bear-like embrace.

"I invited Sven to eat with us," he said, looking down at her. "I hope that's all right."

"Well, of course it is," she said, squeezing his arm. She turned to Sven. "You are always welcome, Mr. Anderson. I'll start heating some water for you both to clean up before supper."

Will smiled to himself. It was good to be home.

"Your father and Tag just returned from Texas this morning. It'll be nice to have so many of us together tonight." Leah gathered her apron and turned back for the house.

Will's gut dropped. He had tried to tell his parents multiple times over the last few months that he would be leaving Redbourne Ranch for a short while, but hadn't been able to voice the words. He didn't think his mother would view five years as such a short while, especially so soon after returning home from university.

Will loved his family. He loved ranching and the clarity it provided him, but he still yearned for something more. The University of London wasn't expecting him for a while, though he'd be leaving for Boston in the next few weeks to purchase his ship and hire a crew.

His new position at the university would allow him time and means to explore—an adventure he couldn't wait to begin. With only a few weeks remaining, he aimed to make the most of his time here at the ranch and would tell everyone when the time was right.

Soon.

It took a while for them to brush down, water, and feed the horses, but when they made their way into the back stall of the barn, they were greeted by two over-sized, elongated basins that had been filled with hot water. Steam rose from the top like a hazy fog over the mountainside. Towels draped over the gate. Fresh cakes of soap, two straight-blade razors, and a hairbrush had been laid out in front of a mirrored base.

Will closed his eyes in gratitude as he inhaled deeply.

"You weren't kidding. It's like your own personal bath house right at home." Sven didn't waste any time removing his clothes and sinking down into the warm water. "This kind of living could do a man good."

Will laughed. "Just wait."

"Will," Hannah called from somewhere toward the front of the stable.

"We're a little busy," he called back.

"Mama said that Mr. Anders...on..." Hannah stepped into the back stall and froze. "Um...I'm sorry," she threw a hand to cover her unusually wide eyes. "I didn't see anything. I swear." She took a step backward, her arm knocking into the shelf that held dozens of cans and a few empty milk jugs. She squealed as they all came tumbling down on top of her.

Will hopped out of the tub, grabbed the towel from the gate's top rung, and draped it around his midsection as he rushed to help his kid sister.

She sat up, pushing a large milk can away from her. A deep-seated red burned into her cheeks as she looked up at him. "I'm sorry, Will." She shook her head. "I didn't—"

"Think," he finished for her. "Didn't listen. I told you we were busy."

She dared a glance at Sven, whose upper body was still visible above the basin, and the red in her face darkened another shade. "I'm sorry."

"Any broken bones?" Will asked as he helped her to her feet.

"I don't think so."

"Are you hurt?"

"Just my pride. Or what was left of it," she admitted with a sheepish smile.

He reached out to steady her by the shoulder and she winced.

"Maybe a bruise or two, but I'm fine. I've got seven brothers who've taught me how to be tough," she countered with a grin.

Will laughed.

Hannah leaned in close to him. "Is Mr. Anderson staying for supper?"

"What is it with you?" he asked, a little laugh in his voice. "Get on up to the house. We'll be there shortly."

A smile spread across Hannah's face and she clapped her hands together before turning on her heel and disappearing from the stable.

"A breed of your own, I tell ya," Sven said with a chuckle, dropping down lower in his tub.

"Maybe so, my friend. Maybe so." He glanced back at the stable door and thought for a moment before climbing back into the welcoming warmth of the water.

He reached over the side of the tub and pulled the folded image from his vest pocket. His ship. Well, it would be his once he made the trip to Boston, but he'd already made a gentleman's agreement.

Maybe it was time for a new breed of Redbourne. The seafaring kind.

CHAPTER SIX

Elizabeth watched out the window by their table for any sign of Opal Gailey. She needed to speak to the young woman before they headed back to Redbourne Ranch.

"Becoming a mail-order-bride is a huge step. And a little scary. Are you sure that is what you want to do? Just to avoid running into Will?"

"That's not the only reason, Grace. When I arrived in Stone Creek, I truly believed this was the right place for me."

"Then stay."

"I wish it was that easy. I bought a house—well, my pretend husband did anyway." She chuckled lightly under her breath and shook her head. She waited a moment before continuing. "After it burned to the ground, I realized that most everything I had brought with me—my books, my money, my clothes—were all gone and I had nowhere to turn."

"If money is what you need—"

"I need a purpose, Grace. I need a place I can call my own. I need..." What did she need?

"A man?" Grace supplied.

Elizabeth looked at her friend with a smile.

"Maybe. I don't know, but I cannot believe that my adventure is over. There is more for me to do. If it works out that I can find a home…" She leaned toward Grace with a smile, "…and a good man along the way, then all the better."

They both laughed.

"Seriously, when I left England, I knew I could never go back. I started a life here, and now, it seems, I will have to start again, somewhere else."

"Maybe if you just talk to Will, I'm sure he will understand."

"Will is a good man, but sometimes things just aren't meant to be. I thought Stone Creek would be my home, but life has other plans for me. *This* is my chance to move on and find that place. And after encountering the professor…"

"You don't want to risk your father finding out where you are."

Elizabeth nodded slowly.

Grace's eyes moved back and forth between Elizabeth's, searching, then she nodded her understanding. "I know what it's like to start over and how hard it can be. But, I want you to know that there will always be a place for you here." She placed a hand over Elizabeth's. "I feel like I'm losing the sister I never had."

"Me too. Thank you. You and your family have already been so generous. I'm afraid I don't know how I'll ever repay your kindness."

"Be happy," Grace replied. "That's all I ask. Be happy with whatever choices you make in your life." Her eyes diverted to something outside the window. "Oooo, look. It's Opal Gailey," she said, pointing at the young woman walking out of the milliner's shop.

Elizabeth pushed herself away from the table, but Grace caught her arm.

"You're sure this is what you want?"

"I'm sure. That stage is leaving tomorrow and I am going to be on it," Elizabeth said with more conviction than she felt. She hoped she was doing the right thing, but there was only one way she was going to find out.

Grace nodded with a sad smile and let go of her arm.

"You'd better hurry. I'll take care of this and then head over to the livery for the carriage. Meet me back here in an hour?"

"One hour," Elizabeth confirmed with a bob of her head, then hurried out the door and across the street. "Opal," Elizabeth called out to the young woman from the mercantile.

She turned around, swinging her head in such a fashion as if to show off her new purchase. The hat was quite extraordinary and exquisite—far from the type of hat Elizabeth would have thought to buy for a long trek west.

"Hello," she said, a blank expression crossing her features. Then, she smiled. "You're Grace's friend. Eliza Beth, right?"

"Right." It was funny. Elizabeth had been living at the old Ferguson place for a couple of months now, but a few days of being friends with a Redbourne made her someone worth knowing.

"I'm afraid I haven't taken much time lately to get to know the new people in town. You see, I'm getting married and I'm leaving tomorrow."

"I had heard that," Elizabeth said, unsure how to broach the subject without appearing the nosy neighbor. "Um…Opal…" She cleared her throat. "I was in the mercantile just a little while ago. I hadn't meant to eavesdrop, but I understand that you are taking tomorrow's stage to Colorado to be…a mail-order-bride."

"That's right," Opal squealed. "Can you believe it? Me. A bride."

"I hope you don't mind me asking, but how did you meet, eh…find your groom-to-be?"

Opal smiled widely and leaned over as if sharing a secret.

"I haven't actually met him. In person, I mean. There is a shortage of women farther west, where there are plenty of men searching for brides. I responded to one of the ads that I saw in the Stone Creek Chronicle from the Matchmaker Agency in a place called Thistleberry, Montana. They really are quite reputable and there are simply dozens of men to choose from in a variety of different locations." Opal looked as if she might burst with pride. "My Robert is a young tanner who just opened his first shop in a small town called Silver Falls in Colorado."

"The Matchmaker Agency, you said?"

"Yes."

"And, what about your friend? I heard her say that she has decided not to go. Is that still the case?"

Opal eyed her for a few moments before responding, as if trying to decide if she was shocked or honored that Elizabeth had 'overheard' so many details of their conversation. Then, she tsked.

"Poor thing. The reverend, I mean. He will be expecting a bride on the stage and all he'll get is Winnie's refusal letter."

"What if that wasn't all he would get?" Elizabeth dipped her head lightly to look Opal in the face.

The young woman placed a hand on Elizabeth's arm and smiled knowingly.

"Are you interested in becoming a mail-order-bride, Eliza Beth?"

Truth was, Elizabeth was ready to take on most any challenge at this point, she just needed to get out of Stone Creek before her father could find her.

"I might have some interest. Do you think the agency would be okay if someone took her place?"

"That, Eliza Beth, sounds like more than a little interest," Opal replied happily. "Winnie has made up her mind. She is definitely not going to Silver Falls. Oh," she said, weaving her arm through Elizabeth's, "I thought I would have to travel all that way alone with Gertrude. Thank heavens that will not be the case."

Elizabeth had no idea who Gertrude was or what she might be getting herself into.

"I'm sure Winnie has not notified the agency yet. I know she has the stagecoach and train tickets that she was prepared to return to her unfortunate beau with a letter of apology. So, I don't see why you couldn't take her place on the stage." She paused. "If you don't mind marrying a preacher."

"A preacher?" Elizabeth swallowed. She wasn't exactly the type to hold bible study classes or host sewing bee's or afternoon tea, but she guessed that if it was meant to be, she could be a preacher's wife.

"How old is this preacher, exactly?"

"Winnie would be the best one to talk to about that. She has exchanged several letters with the man. I was just on my way to meet her for lunch at Millie's Café. Would you like to join us?"

Elizabeth looked down the road to where Grace was speaking with Mr. Phillips at the livery. She looked at the large clock that towered over the town. She still had forty-five minutes before she had to meet Grace at the restaurant.

"It would be my pleasure," she said with a dip of her head.

Opal linked her arm in Elizabeth's and guided her across the street to Millie's place. It was a quaint little café with flowers in the windowsills and embroidered cloths on the tables. When the door opened, Elizabeth closed her eyes to soak in the atmosphere. It smelled like a little slice of heaven.

"We've got fresh, warm Strawberry Rhubarb pie on the menu today. Would you ladies like to try a slice?" Millie held a pot of coffee in one hand and dusted her apron with the other.

"That sounds divine, Millie," Opal told the establishment's proprietress.

"May I just have a glass of lemonade?" she asked. She'd already shared some pie at the restaurant across the way with Grace and didn't think her stomach would appreciate two in one day.

"Of course," Millie said with a smile.

Within moments they found the table where Winnie had been seated. Opal sat down next to her, and motioned for Elizabeth to sit on the other side of her. Winnie smiled half-heartedly as Elizabeth did as she'd been told.

"I am not sure I have had the pleasure," the second woman from the mercantile spoke while raising her glass to her small mouth.

"Winnie," Opal began, "Eliza Beth is a friend of Grace Redbourne. Since you have decided that you will be staying here in Stone Creek, wouldn't it be lovely if she went in your place?"

"Why would you do that?" the woman scrunched her eyes into slits as she evaluated Elizabeth.

She hadn't expected the question and it took her a moment to collect her thoughts.

"Well, Miss Winnie, hmhmm…" she cleared her throat, "I'm afraid there is nothing left for me in Stone Creek. I have no family to speak of, my home burned to the ground, and I want to start over, but that is hard to do without means."

Winnie leaned back in her chair. "Your house burned down? That is horrible. I am so sorry to hear of your predicament, but I am still deciding whether or not I should go."

"But, Winnie," Opal said, in protest, "I thought you—"

"Now, Opal, you know that I detest the idea of causing that man any more pain than necessary. My father seems to be getting better every day." Winnie said before taking another sip from the large glass of lemonade sitting in front of her.

It took everything Elizabeth had not to roll her eyes into the back of her head. She had encountered countless women with the same wishy-washy attitude as Winnie back home. How was a girl supposed to make any plans when dealing with someone so fickle? She would probably decide to make the trek only to get off the stage in the next town and coax some unsuspecting farmer into bringing her home.

"I am so sorry," Elizabeth said, deciding to play the girl's game. "I did not realize that you had changed your mind. I apologize for having wasted your time." She stood up and looked down at Opal. "Thank you for your kind offer. It would have been quite an adventure," she said as she turned to leave, placing a hand on the woman's shoulder. "Good luck, Miss Winnie. It is a shame really."

"What's a shame, Eliza Beth?" Opal asked with interest.

"Well, I was willing to pay what I could for your place on the journey," Elizabeth said as she shrugged her shoulders, "but—"

"How much?" Winnie said with a squeaky little voice, her finger twirling one of her ringlets.

"I'm sorry?" Elizabeth said, forcing the woman to speak a little louder.

Winnie looked at Opal, then back to Elizabeth. "I mean, it did take a lot of time and effort to coordinate the trip, to apply to the Matchmaker Agency and to write to my Adam. Your Adam," she corrected.

Elizabeth reached into her satchel and pulled out a few of her remaining bills, set them down beneath her hand, and slid them across the table to Winnie.

"Take it or leave it," she said with a fabricated smile.

Winnie glanced down at the money and looked up with wide eyes. "I would say you have been more than generous. Thank you." She picked up the money and tucked it away in her own little handbag.

Elizabeth had done a fair share of research into mail-order-bride services since learning of the potential opportunity, and she knew that Winnie had not paid a penny for her travel plans. The men requesting a wife were responsible for that purchase, as well as any other expenses a prospective bride might encounter along the way.

Opal had said that Winnie intended to return the tickets with a letter of apology. The young woman had proven herself shrewd, but Elizabeth didn't care about any of that. The woman's fears about leaving her family and comfortable life behind to venture out on the journey had worked out in Elizabeth's favor and now, a new adventure awaited her, just like those that she'd come across so often in her books.

"You have your money. Now, may I please have the tickets and other travel arrangements the preacher made for you?"

"Oh, of course," Winnie waved at the air.

Elizabeth extended her hand.

"You mean now? I don't have them with me," she placed a hand over her chest, "but I will see that you have everything you need by the time the stage leaves tomorrow. I'm sure you wouldn't mind delivering my letter to Mr. MacKenzie?"

"Not at all," Elizabeth responded with a slight bow of her head. "Tomorrow then. Opal." She nodded at her new travelling companion, then turned for the door, smiling to herself. Now, she just had to tell Grace and she'd be on her way.

When she reached the livery, Grace was in a pleasant conversation with a stout woman in a thick bustled dress with cherry-colored fringes.

"Here she is now," Grace said, holding out her arm toward Elizabeth. "Eliza Beth, this is Mrs. Blanding, the good preacher's wife. She tells me that the teacher at the school on the edge of town is leaving tomorrow on the stage and the position needs to be filled as soon as possible."

"It's very nice to meet you, Mrs. Blanding," she said with a slight bow of her head. She studied the woman for a moment, the trio standing in silence before the question plaguing her mind slipped from her mouth. "Do you like being a preacher's wife?" she blurted.

Grace stared at her open-mouthed, but quickly recovered.

"Do I like..." the woman cleared her throat. "Well, I've never really thought about that. Mr. Blanding is a good man and I enjoy the occasions I have to call on the women of this town." She stood up a little taller. "Yes, I suppose I do like being a preacher's wife."

Elizabeth breathed deeply, satisfied with the woman's answer.

"Though," Mrs. Blanding continued, "I never saw myself as the type." She turned to Elizabeth. "You know, the kind to host afternoon tea or organize a bazaar. But, here I am." She looked past them and concern found a place on her brows. "Excuse me a moment, ladies," she said as she slipped between them and over to where two young boys were in a tussle near the livery's front gate.

"Grace—"

"I know you have a plan, but the selfish part of me thought that with your love of books and your abundant knowledge, you would be just the person for…the…job. What's wrong?"

"I'm leaving on the stage tomorrow with Opal. And apparently, the town's teacher," she added, trying to find some humor in the situation.

Grace's shoulders dropped a little, but her smile didn't falter. "Are you sure this is what you want? A teaching position would give you a place. A purpose."

"I know. Thank you, but my mind is made up. I am going to be Mrs. MacKenzie—a preacher's wife."

Grace giggled. "That explains it."

"What?"

"I thought Mrs. Blanding was going to faint when you asked her if she liked being married to a preacher. The look on her face…"

"Was shocked, to say the least," Elizabeth finished.

They both laughed.

"I guess it was rather outspoken of me."

"Elizabeth, you are definitely one of a kind." Grace linked her arm in hers. "I don't care how far away you go, I know we will always be friends."

"I would not have it any other way."

Ethan pulled up in the buckboard. "You ladies ready?" he asked, jumping down and offering a hand to his wife, then to Elizabeth.

Normally, there would have been a lot to do to prepare for a trip like this one, but with no belongings to speak of, there was nothing to prepare—just a few goodbyes to say. The feeling was bittersweet.

By the time they pulled into Redbourne Ranch it was already near six o'clock. Supper would already be on the table. Ethan went to take care of the horses and the wagon, while she and Grace headed for the back door that led directly into the kitchen.

When they passed by the window, she caught a glimpse of the honest-to-goodness Will Redbourne already seated at the table. She laughed at herself for having thought Ethan was his brother. It was true they were similar in appearance, but the sight of Will took her breath away. He was even more handsome than she had remembered.

Elizabeth froze in place, her mind racing as to what to do.

"I think I'm just going to walk back up to your place to pack my things," she reasoned, though she knew her new friend would see right through her.

Grace glanced through the window. "Will's home."

Elizabeth nodded.

"Why don't you just face him? Tell him everything?"

Images of her brother's swollen face, his bandaged head and body streamed through her mind. While he'd certainly been deserving of the beating he'd gotten, she couldn't imagine that Will would be able to forgive or forget everything that had happened.

She shook her head. Breath escaped her and her heart sped within her chest.

"What are you two doing waiting out here?" Ethan asked as he joined them on the back porch. "Lottie made pot-pie tonight. With Tag and Cole home, we'd better hurry or there won't be any left."

"I'll catch up," she said, feigning a smile.

"Are you all right?" Grace asked, placing a hand on her arm.

"I'll be fine," Elizabeth whispered back. "I just need to catch my breath for a moment."

"It'll be okay. Talk to him and then, if you still want to leave,

I won't protest."

"Thanks, Grace."

The couple disappeared inside of the house. Elizabeth plastered herself up against the wall. She would not be joining them for supper tonight.

CHAPTER SEVEN

Lottie's chicken pot-pie had lived up to everything Will had expected and described to his friend. The succulent meat seemed to melt in his mouth along with the heavenly flaked crust on top. When he glanced over at Sven, he couldn't help the chuckle that sounded low in his throat. His broad-shouldered friend had closed his eyes as he chewed and his tongue swiped across his lips.

"This is a mighty fine meal, ma'am," Sven told Leah.

She smiled softly. "We are very blessed to have Lottie with us. She has a real talent in the kitchen."

"I'll say," the Norwegian said, eying the platter of little creamed custards topped with fresh-picked raspberries across the table.

Everyone at the table laughed and Jameson picked up the dish and held it out for Sven.

"Thank you," he said. "Don't mind if I do." He picked up one of the custards and set it down in front of him, scooping one of the raspberries up into his mouth.

The back door opened and Grace walked in followed closely by his little brother, Ethan.

"I'm sorry we're late," Ethan said as he hung his hat on the rack by the stairs. "We had some business in town that needed attending to."

"So," Jameson said, looking at the Norwegian as he picked up his napkin and wiped the corners of his mouth, "Will tells me that you are headed out on the stage tomorrow, taking a group of young ladies to Colorado."

Sven nodded, his mouth still full.

"We have property in Silver Falls," Tag said as he scooped up another bite of his savory pie.

"Mama spent a few summers there while granddad conducted business," Hannah chimed in.

Sven started to speak, but a coughing fit ensued.

Leah stood up and poured more water into his glass. "Are you all right, dear?" she asked.

"Wrong pipe," Sven choked out as he hit his chest with his fist. With a large gulp of water from his glass, he finally was able to swallow, then inhaled deeply.

"I heard it's not just a run-of-the-mill job." Ethan joined in the conversation. "I understand that it will be carrying the bankroll from Stone Creek to Kansas City."

"Nobody is supposed to know that," Sven said, swallowing hard, then coughed again.

"Mr. Collins at the bank has a big mouth," Cole said heartily.

Leah shot him a quelling look.

"Sorry," he said with his head bowed.

"I tried to get Will to come along, but he's too busy getting ready for his overseas adventure."

The table went silent.

Damn.

This is not the way he'd wanted his family to find out that he was headed back to England.

Knock. Knock.

Will laughed weakly, wiped his mouth, and pushed himself away from the table. "I'll get it." He scampered into the front room and swung open the door. "Professor!" he exclaimed, extending a hand to the man who had offered him the teaching position at the University of London. He'd nearly forgotten the man would be stopping by tonight. He glanced back at the kitchen.

Well, I guess now is as good a time as any.

"Come on in, Professor. We're just finishing up our supper. Would you like to join us?"

"Why, I would be delighted. Thank you," Professor Cromwell said as he stepped over the threshold.

Will took the man's coat and hung it on a nearby rack. If anyone could get his family to see the benefit of what he was planning, Professor Cromwell could. As he took a step toward the kitchen, the professor put a hand on his arm to stay him.

"May I have a word with you first?" he asked with a raised brow.

"What's on your mind, Professor?"

"In town earlier today, I can't be sure, but I swear I saw Sterling Archer's daughter on the street. She pretended to be somebody else, but it's her. I'm sure of it."

Will swallowed hard.

"Do you think Archer is in town?" he asked without hesitation.

"No."

"Then, what would his daughter be doing in Stone Creek?" Will asked.

"The girl has been missing for months. Sterling has scoured the countryside looking for her, sparing no expense. He's even put out a reward for her safe return. If she's here..."

The professor didn't need to finish that sentence. Will had had enough experience with Sterling Archer to know that he would do anything to protect what was his. And that included killing anyone who stood in his way.

"Do you think she's here against her will?"

"To that I cannot speak, unless your sister-in-law is holding her captive."

"What does Grace have to do with this?"

"They were together on the boardwalk today when I ran into them."

Will nodded in understanding. He'd never actually met Archer's daughter, but was all too well acquainted with the rest of her family. A pit formed in Will's stomach, but he tried to shake it off. He guided the man into the kitchen where the family was deep in conversation

"I think it's romantic," Hannah said, leaning on the table with her elbows. "Crossing the country in search of love."

Will rolled his eyes at the machinations of a young girl.

"Are you speaking of the mail-order-brides leaving tomorrow?" Will asked, interjecting himself into the conversation.

Everyone turned to look at him.

"Yes," Ethan said. "I think Grace is a little envious of the adventure that awaits her new friend."

"As if I didn't have enough adventures with you, my darling husband." Grace raised a brow at Ethan, her mouth widening into a grin.

Ethan pulled his wife in close to him and kissed her smack on the mouth.

There had never been a lack of affection in his family. Most everyone looked away, scooping food into their mouths—except for Hannah, who sighed as she leaned on her hands and watched the display.

Jameson cleared his throat and his brother tore himself away from his beautiful wife. Her cheeks were flushed, a smile touching the corners of her mouth.

"I just hope 'my friend' is not doing it for the wrong reasons," Grace said as if the conversation had never halted. Her voice grew a little louder and she leaned toward the back door so far, Will thought she might fall over. "I would feel much better if she wasn't travelling alone," she called out loudly. "There's a teacher's position opening in town and I thought it might be nice to have her stick around. No matter how hard it might be."

Will glanced at the door, but there was no one there. He shook his head.

Women.

"We're all right here, Gracie," Jack, her little brother, said as he stuck a finger in his ear and wiggled it around.

"Sorry." Grace wiped her mouth with her napkin.

Sven cleared his throat and coughed, holding a glass of water near his lips as he spoke. "There are two other ladies who'll be on that stage travelling with us to Silver Falls, and I'll be right there beside it, Miss Grace," he said. "I'll make sure to keep her safe." He took a drink.

"Thank you, Mr. Anderson. That is of some comfort."

"Everyone," Will announced, stepping aside, "this is Professor Cromwell from—"

"The University of London," Grace cut in. "It's nice to see you again, Professor."

"Mrs. Redbourne," he replied with a nod, stepping forward toward the table. "Please forgive my manners for intruding into your discussion, but were you speaking of the young woman whom you introduced me to earlier this afternoon on the boardwalk?"

"Yyyyes," Grace replied hesitantly. "Eliza Beth Jessup. From Oklahoma," she added unnecessarily.

"Who is Eliza Beth Jessup?" Will asked nonchalantly. He'd been away quite a bit, but for the life of him, he didn't recall anyone by the name of Jessup in town. Will sat down in his chair and offered Raine's empty seat to the professor. If this woman was the one who Professor Cromwell believed to be Sterling Archer's daughter, he wanted a look for himself.

"She's the gal who bought Old Ferg's place," Ethan said as he scooped some of the pot-pie onto a plate for his wife.

"The one that burned down?" Will asked incredulously.

"That's the one."

"Has Raine found out any more about how the blaze started?" their father asked.

"Where *is* Raine tonight?" Will wondered aloud.

"He said he'd be late for supper because he found a lead on the fire and had a few miscreants to round up for questioning." His mother took her own custard from the tray and dipped her spoon inside.

"I would have just thought the sheriff had him out doing rounds again. Doesn't seem he can stay out of the saloon long enough to do his job himself. He has to send Raine around to do it for him."

"Taggert Redbourne, bite your tongue," Leah scolded her son. "Sheriff Butts...

Smothered giggles surrounded the table.

Leah cleared her throat. "Sheriff Butts," she tried again, staring down anyone who dared the slightest smile, "has been very good to our family. He has had it tougher than most. Especially, after losing his wife and daughter in that disaster."

"I only meant that he..." Tag said, trying quite unsuccessfully to keep the smile from his face.

"I know what you meant, son, but we will not speak ill of others in this house. Am I understood?"

"Yes, ma'am," Tag said. "I meant no disrespect."

"That goes for the rest of you too," she said, eying each person sitting at the table, her gaze finally resting on their father, who cleared his throat and scratched at his face with the back of his hand.

"Yes, ma'am," they all said in unison.

"So, this Eliza Beth Jessup," Will started again, unable to quash the curiosity in him. "Has she lived in town long?"

"Why the sudden interest, Will?" Cole asked, eying him warily.

"No real interest. It's just that usually when someone new moves to town, we're all put on welcome duty and I wondered why I've never heard of the woman before now. That's all."

"We didn't discover she'd moved in until Ferg's place burned to the ground," his mother was quick to say. "Luckily, Ethan and Grace saw the smoke and were able to go and help."

Will bobbed his head, contemplative.

"You could ask her yourself," Ethan said between bites of his dessert. "She said she just needed a moment and she would be in. Come to think of it, I wonder why she hasn't joined us yet," he said, glancing toward the back door.

"You mean, she's here?"

"We left her out on the front porch just a bit ago."

Will pushed himself away from the table and dashed to the door. When it swung open, the porch was empty. He scanned the yard, but she was nowhere to be seen. A feeling of disappointment settled in his gut. He closed the door and returned to his seat, shaking his head at an expectant Grace. She arose from her seat to verify for herself.

"So, Mr. Cromwell," Jameson said, addressing the professor, "what brings you to the states?"

Will exchanged glances with the professor.

"Actually, Dad, I've been meaning to talk to you."

Everyone sitting at the table seemed to stop eating at that moment and look up at him. Waiting.

He cleared his throat.

"The University of London has offered me a temporary teaching position in the archaeological department, and…I have chosen to accept." He breathed out a sigh of relief at not having to carry that weight around with him any longer.

"Temporary?"

He could hear the hope in his mother's voice.

"We are in the middle of a large project that will guarantee your son's services for five years. Isn't that wonderful?"

From the look on his mother's face, wonderful was not the word he would use to describe it.

"Mama," he started.

Leah picked up her plate and with a half-hearted smile

headed over to the sink.

Will followed.

"Mama," he tried again.

Leah turned to him, her head held high, and placed a hand on his cheek. "I always knew you were meant for great things. You are smart, and kind, and maybe a little more adventurous than a mother would hope, but you have so much to give." She dropped her hand and turned away from him.

"It won't be forever."

"We've raised you to be your own man, William," she said as she placed both hands down on the counter as if to prop herself up. "You'll be a wonderful teacher."

Will opted not to tell his mother about the other opportunities that came with the job. She seemed to be taking this news better than he'd expected and didn't want to spoil it.

"How long do we have before you must leave?"

"It's still a bit off."

She looked up at him with a raised brow.

"Three weeks."

"Very well, then. Let's make the best of it, shall we?" Leah reached down, captured Will's hand in hers, and squeezed.

He bent down and kissed the top of her head. "I love you, Mama."

She closed her eyes and slipped an arm around his waist. "I love you, my not-so-little William."

CHAPTER EIGHT

Friday

"Come on, lazy bones. Don't you have a stage to catch today?" Will threw a folded pair of socks at his friend's head with a laugh. He sat on the edge of his bed and pulled on his own boots. The man in the other bed did not stir. "Sven!" he called loudly.

Still nothing.

Will stood up and crossed the room. He placed a hand on Sven's shoulder and turned him over. The man's skin was pallid and damp, his mouth was surrounded in a gum-like film, and his head was hot to the touch.

Cough. Cough. "Is it time to get up?" he asked wearily, attempting to sit.

"Not yet, my friend," Will said, concern working its way through his mind as he casually brushed the back of his hand against his friend's face. "Go back to sleep for a few more minutes."

Sven closed his eyes and sleepily nodded his consent.

"Mama!" Will called as he ran from the room and down the stairs. He found her in the kitchen peeling the shells off some hard-boiled eggs. "Mama, something is wrong with Sven. He's pale and weak, and his skin is really hot to the touch."

Leah dried her hands in her skirt as she ran into the washroom.

"Sounds like a fever," she told Will as she threw open cupboards and closed them, searching for something. "Tag and Cole should both be pretty close to home. Find them. Have them chip up a block of ice as quickly as they can. Then, fill the tub in the washroom and make it as cold as you can get it."

Will waited for further instructions, but they didn't come.

"Go!" she urged as she made her way up the stairs toward the twins' room where he and Sven had slept last night.

He didn't waste any more time. He hadn't seen many people who'd gotten sick so quickly, but it didn't bode well. Tag was in the corral with one of the new horses they had picked up on the drive. His ability to tame a horse was parallel to none.

Cole, his youngest brother, rode into the yard as if he suspected his help was needed. Will quickly explained the situation to both of them and without hesitation they dropped what they were doing and headed out to the shed where the ice box was kept.

When Will returned to the twins' room, Leah sat on the edge of the bed where Sven had been sleeping. Cool wet cloths had been strewn across his forehead.

"Will, we need to get him down to the washroom." Leah stood up and moved to the side.

Will strode over to the bed and leaned down to pick up his friend. Sven was not a small man, but with more than a little effort, Will was able to heave him up and into his arms.

Leah held open the door as wide as it would go, to allow him more space to maneuver. Once down the stairs, he laid his friend, clothes and all, into the freezing cold water of the washbasin. Sven only stirred a little with several low-seated groans at the brisk change in temperature.

"Here is the ice," Cole said as he opened the door to the washroom and stepped inside with a large bucket full of the frozen chips.

"Dump it over the top of him," Leah directed.

Cole did as he was told, then headed back out for another load. After several trips, the tub overflowed with ice chunks.

Will shivered as he watched the skin on Sven's arm pucker into gooseflesh.

"Tag's gone to fetch the doc," Cole called back as he headed out the door.

Will sat in the chair next to the tub, his elbows on his knees, and his hands cradling his face.

"There's nothing more you can do for your friend right now, son." Leah placed a hand on his back.

"He's supposed to be one of the outriders guarding the stage today. Someone should tell the new stagecoach driver that they will be down one outrider."

"It is a shame that there isn't anyone experienced enough and available to take his place."

Will looked at his mother, his brows meeting together above his nose.

"I mean," she said as she picked up a towel and started to fold it, "there *are* three innocent women who are travelling across the country, unaware of the bankroll that will be loaded in the back of their stage. It could be quite dangerous without anyone to protect them."

"You think I should go in his stead," Will surmised. He stood up, shoving his hands through his hair as he contemplated his options. He hated the thought of those women being left vulnerable on a stage carrying such a prized cargo.

Outlaws like Kelton McElvoy and his gang would be lying in wait around every corner if the word got out about the monies being transported and Will wondered why on earth the company would endanger the lives of these young mail-order-brides. It wasn't like there was only one stage that came through town.

"I think you are a protector. It comes naturally for you," his mother told him as she set the towels down and turned to him, raising her hands to his face. "You've always had the heart of a lion and skills to match. I know you well enough to understand that you need to feel useful. Needed. I have a feeling that it wouldn't matter what I said, you would do what you felt was right…whatever needed to be done." She dropped her arms down and captured his hands in her own.

"It's nice to know you have faith in me," he said, appreciating every word she'd spoken.

"I do and I always will. You are a smart man, William. No matter what you decide, I know you will find the best solution to this unfortunate dilemma." She squeezed his hands, stood up on her tip-toes, kissed his face, then turned and left the room.

"Just like her to leave me with my thoughts," he said loud enough she'd probably heard him. He waited, but there was no response. "What am I supposed to do now?" His voice softened, but he still spoke aloud. "Three weeks," he said as he paced the washroom, kicking at some stray towels that had fallen to the floor. "Three weeks, and then I'll be gone."

Will knew himself all too well to believe that this would be a one-time deal.

"I can't leave. How can I leave? I'm sure they can find someone else," he said with a satisfied nod. "I'm not going. Besides, Jem will be passing through town sometime today, or tomorrow, on his way down to New Orleans to fight for the heavyweight title," his short monologue continued. "That man taught me everything I know about boxing and was there for me at a time when I was far away from home and needed someone for support. I can't miss him."

"Well then…"

Will jerked around to see his friend slipping the rag from his forehead.

"…you'd better help me up." Sven's voice was weak. "Or, I'm going to miss the stage. I can't imagine that would be too good for those brides-to-be, or for my chances with any of them, for the stage to be down one trained guard." He tried to laugh, but coughed instead.

"Welcome back." Will rushed to the side of the tub as Sven attempted to sit himself up straight.

"I guess you really thought I needed another bath," he said with some semblance of a strained smile. "My clothes and all. It might just be me, but this one is quite colder than the last." He shivered.

Will's laugh accompanied a relived sigh. "I'd thought I'd lost you there for a bit, mate."

"You're not going to get rid of me that easily." Sven placed his hands on the side of the tub and tried to push himself up. "Just get me something dry to wear and my pack." The effort was too much for him and he plopped back down into the icy water.

Will jerked forward to try to catch him.

Sweat beaded thickly on Sven's forehead and Will recalled something Rafe had told him years ago, while he was on break from Harvard Medical School, about sweat being a good indicator that a fever had broken.

"Mama!" he called loudly, but rather than wait for her to return, he reached down and helped the large man to his feet. His clothes were drenched and dripping all over the floor as he stepped from the tub. Luckily, the washroom was full of towels. He carefully lowered Sven down onto one of the chairs. The Norwegian slumped against the back rest, his hands dangling at his side. He was weak and Will was worried.

"Where is he?" a man called from somewhere near the front of the house.

The doctor had arrived.

His mother opened the door, followed by the tall, robust man who'd been called out to the ranch more often than he'd probably liked.

"Mr. Anderson," the doc said, "I understand you've been feeling a little under the weather."

"You could say that, Doc, but I just need a few minutes and

I'll be fine."

"I'm sure you will, but why don't you let me have a look at you anyway."

"Will," his mother said, "run up and get him something dry to wear."

He glanced over at Sven, and with a nod, darted from the room and up the stairs. All of the Redbourne boys were tall and slender, but Sven's shoulders nearly doubled the width of his own. Rafe was the closest in size and so he headed into his older brother's room. It had not changed a bit since the day he'd left. His mother hadn't touched a thing. Will reckoned that she'd left it alone out of hope that Rafe would come back home sooner rather than later.

Sven's predicament weighed on Will's mind.

His friend was in no condition to accompany the stage to the train depot in Kansas City, let alone all the way to Colorado. Guilt tugged at Will's gut. He certainly had the capability to step in and take over, and under normal circumstances he would welcome the adventure, but between Jem coming and Will wanting to spend time with his family before he left, taking Sven's place on this job would be a sacrifice he wasn't sure he was willing to make. He owed a lot to the Englishman. If it hadn't been for Jem and his countless fighting lessons, Will didn't know if he would have made it back to his family in one piece.

With an exasperated sigh, Will grabbed the necessary clothing from Rafe's wardrobe and headed back downstairs.

"He's going to need rest. And lots of it," the doc said as Will pushed his way back into the room. A red-faced Sven was covered in towels, his wet clothes hanging from the rafters over the tub.

Will handed the dry clothes to his mother.

"Go ask Lottie to warm some of the chicken broth she used for the pot-pies, will you?" Leah smiled reassuringly. "And bring some of my willow-bark tea," she called after him.

When he walked into the kitchen, Raine sat at the table eating his late breakfast. A waft of savory aroma wove around Will and he glanced at the stove where a pot of broth had already been set to warm. He walked over to the cupboard above the sink and grabbed a tin full of his mother's special herbal tea.

"Querida," the little Spanish cook said as she walked into the kitchen. "This sopa will do your friend some good." Lottie picked up a ladle, spooned some into a bowl, and passed him on her way out the door. "I will take to him."

"Gracias, Lottie," he called after her. He pumped the kettle full of water and set it on the stove to warm, then pulled out a chair and sat down at the table next to his brother.

"Where have you been?" Will asked playfully, now able to relax for the first time this morning.

"The Hamilton's well caved in last night. Mrs. Hamilton has had to cart in all of her water from the river while her husband and a few of the neighbors have been working to clear the well. And with their four little ones, they needed someone to help out."

"So, Raine Redbourne came to the rescue and cleared out the well in no time at all, right?"

"Actually, I helped the oldest two children with their schoolwork and played with the others until their ma had finished making dinner and had gotten the youngest to bed." He took another bite of his eggs.

Will laughed loudly.

"And then, of course, I helped them clear the well." A grin spread across his face, but he didn't look up from his food.

Will watched his oldest brother for a moment. How could he ever live up to the standard that Raine had set for all of his younger siblings? He was proud of everything he'd been able to accomplish with his life—especially amidst the hardships that he'd seen. Losing his wife, Sarah, had been a real black moment in his life. In all of their lives.

"Mama said that you had a lead on the Ferguson fire."

"Three of the four suspected culprits are sitting in the jailhouse sleeping off their drunken stupor."

"You caught three already?"

Raine nodded, then slipped some shredded potatoes into his mouth and chewed heartily.

"And the fourth?" Will asked.

"He got himself caught in one of Old Ferguson's tree nets. It seemed only fitting that I leave him there to think on it for a bit while I got myself something to eat. He's not going anywhere."

They both chuckled.

"So, it seems Sven's fever has broken," Raine said, finally breaking away from his food long enough that he met Will's eyes.

"He's still weak, but it looks good. I guess." Will had no idea how good or bad the prognosis would be, but he figured if Sven was up and joking around, he was on the mend. The fever had come on so quickly. It was hard to imagine something unseen could have drained the robust man's strength in such a short period of time.

"I'm sure he'll be back to his old self in no time," Raine assured him.

"Not soon enough." Will blew out a heavy breath and hung his head.

"What's on your mind?" Raine asked as he leaned back against the chair, leaving the remainder of his meal in front of him.

"Sven is supposed to be the escort for the stage that leaves this afternoon."

"I'm sure Otis's replacement will get along fine with just one guard."

They had received word that the previous stagecoach driver was on the mend, but would not be returning to work for some time.

"That's just it, it's not only accompanying the three mail-order-brides that has me concerned, but the sizeable bankroll being transported to Kansas City on the same stage. There should be at least four guards, let alone the two they already have slated, but there is no way they will be able to make it safely with just one outrider."

Raine nodded his head, but didn't say anything.

A few moments passed in silence.

Raine sipped off his mug.

"I enjoy riding out with the stage," Will continued, "but," he looked up at his brother, "do you remember Jem Mace?" he asked.

"The boxer who took you under his wing?"

"That's the one. He's fighting for the heavyweight championship next week down in Louisiana and he'd be stopping through Stone Creek on his way to Kennerville, just outside of New Orleans. I've been waiting for an opportunity like this, since I never really got the chance to...to..."

"Say thank you," Raine filled in for him.

Will nodded.

"So, you have a dilemma."

Will nodded again, more slowly this time, his hands folded together on top of the table, his head hung low.

"Is that the only thing that's on your mind? Your only reason for denying the job?"

"What do you mean?"

"I mean, from what I heard from Mama, you are heading back to England soon and should have many chances to see Mr. Mace. Is missing the chance to talk to Mr. Mace really the only reason you don't want to take the job?"

Will thought about it for a good long while. Out of everyone in his family, Raine would be the one to understand.

"There's...a ship."

"Ahhh," Raine said, leaning back down onto the table with his forearms. "I thought it might be something like that."

"You know how much I've always wanted to have a ship of

my own to sail across the seas. To explore the world. My teaching position in England comes with a few more incentives than what I let on. I couldn't bring myself to tell Mother that exploring on a ship across the ocean is a part of my position with the university."

Raine rested his elbows on the table, his hands clasped together, and leaned his mouth against his hands as he continued to listen, but still offered no advice or suggestions.

"I am supposed to be in Boston in less than three weeks to finish the transaction. Three weeks, Raine. And then I'll be gone five years. Years! I want to spend every moment with the people who mean the most to me. It's not like there aren't any other men qualified to do the job. What should I do?" Will shifted his head enough that he could meet Raine's eyes.

"Well, I can't answer that, little brother. That needs to come from you. But trust your gut. You are a Redbourne after all." Raine smiled as he leaned forward to take another bite of his meal.

"My gut doesn't work the same as yours. Or Rafe's. Or even Cole's for that matter."

Raine paused for a moment before speaking.

"How many fights have you won in the ring?"

Will shrugged. He'd lost count. "Enough."

"How do you think you've been able to do that? I would imagine that any successful pugilist would need to depend on more than mere strength or technique. You win because of your ability to listen to your gut. I would venture to say, Oxford, that you are better at it than the rest of us. We just use it differently."

Will considered this information carefully. He had found a lot of success in the ring, but he'd always attributed it to the moves he'd learned and the hours of practice he'd put into it. What was his gut telling him?

His lungs filled with air, his mind cleared, and he knew exactly what he needed to do.

"Thanks, Raine," he said, pushing himself away from the

table.

His brother picked up his fork and stuck it into the remaining food on his plate. "Three ladies and a bankroll, sounds like there is a joke in there somewhere," he mused. "Hey, I've got some beef jerky drying in the smokehouse and I think Mama just finished a batch of her fruit jerky. You should load up. It's going to be a long ride," he said with a grin.

Will shook his head.

How does he do that?

Raine always knew what Will was going to do before he did it. He had a keen sense and a unique perspective on life. That was one of the many things Will loved and admired most about his oldest brother.

"What makes you think I'm taking the job?"

"You're Will Redbourne. A born fighter and protector. An adventure like this—was there really ever any question?"

Will picked up one of the biscuits from the basket and threw it at Raine. Then, he scrambled out the door with a loud laugh. He was right.

The stage would be here within the hour.

"Better get a move on, Will Redbourne," he told himself. "You are the replacement outrider."

CHAPTER NINE

Lightning cracked the sky, followed by a rolling roar of thunder. Elizabeth looked up just as the heavens broke above her. Why hadn't she accepted Ethan Redbourne's offer to give her a ride into town? She'd thought that with her simple satchel—containing nothing but a spare blouse and skirt Grace had been kind enough to give her, her mother's salvaged box, and a couple of books—she'd enjoy one last opportunity to really stretch her legs before the long journey to Colorado.

She'd been wrong. The ground grew muddier by the second and it was becoming more difficult to lift the skirt of her dress while holding onto her travelling bag.

"What do you have there, Caspar?" she asked as the red coonhound ran up in front of her, carrying something in her mouth. Elizabeth wasn't sure she even wanted to know. The dog seemed to have more energy than she'd had over the last couple of weeks as they'd weaned the puppies. They had just placed the last of her five little darlings this morning. Grace and Ethan had elected to take one and there had been several townsfolks who had been more than happy to provide homes for the others.

The methodic beat of horse's hooves sounded behind her and she turned to see the form of a rider approaching in the short distance. She raised her hand to shield her eyes from the rain, but it was difficult to make out any detail.

Another crack of thunder startled a short squeal out of her. Her chest reverberated from the low boom that spread across the sky. She breathed out in one quick heavy exhale, collected her skirt in her hands again, and trudged forward.

"Can I give you a lift into town?" the rider said as he pulled up alongside her, his hat riding low on his head, his face obscured by the rain.

She looked out at the road before her, the town a blurred mirage against a grey backdrop. It would be highly inappropriate for her to be so close to a man, but she was leaving this town and no one in Silver Falls, Colorado would ever know the difference.

"That would be most kind of you. Thank you." Her accent slipped a little, but she didn't care. It was not as if she would ever see this stranger again after today.

The rider dismounted his black and white horse and collected her bag from her shoulder, then secured it to the side of his saddle. She was grateful when he lowered a flap to cover the satchel for added protection against the elements. It would be such a shame to lose the only books she'd brought with her for this trip—especially her personally signed copy of *Alice's Adventures in Wonderland*.

The stranger turned back to her. "Do you ride?" he yelled through the curtain-like downpour. There was something definitely familiar about him.

"Of course," she called back, "when the need arises."

"It has." He held out a hand and helped her up onto the saddle, then climbed up behind her, scooping her up onto his lap.

She sucked in a breath, along with a dozen or so raindrops. It was highly inappropriate for her to be this close to a man, but she didn't protest.

"Where are you headed?" His hot breath grazed the tip of

her ear, sending gooseflesh down the length of her arms. A light thrill washed through her at the warmth of his body pushed up against her, his arms wrapping her protectively in their strength. Elizabeth swallowed.

"Come on, Caspar," she managed to call her dog instead of answering his question.

The sudden intensity of the storm made it nearly impossible to carry on any sort of conversation. Try as she might, it was near impossible to stay upright and away from him. After a few minutes, she gave in and relaxed against the man's firm chest, welcoming the surprising comfort she found in his arms.

It didn't take long before they reached town. The streets were understandably empty, other than a few patrons coming in and out of the more frequented establishments. To her delight, the stage had not yet arrived. She suspected that the sudden onslaught of rain had delayed its appearance. Opal Gailey and another young woman Elizabeth had never seen before, sat on a bench in front of the telegraph office, protected by the covered boardwalk.

Her rescuer pulled up to the beginning of the covered boardwalk next to the livery and lifted her off of his lap and slid down from the horse behind her. A swift gust of cool air swept across her back and she felt a momentary twinge of disappointment. She chastised herself at the terribly forward manner in which she had conducted herself with this stranger.

He held up a hand to help her down from the horse and she caught a brief glimpse of his face through a short break in the rain, but as she leaned toward him, her foot caught in one of the straps and she fell hard against his chest, nearly knocking the breath out of her. She thrust her hands forward and caught herself on the area just below his shoulders, and she forced her eyes upward to look into his face.

"Are you all right there, little lady?" he asked, his mouth widening into a broad grin. "If you wanted to snuggle a little longer, all you needed to do was ask."

Heat flooded her face as she met his eyes.

There was no mistaking it this time. Will Redbourne stared down at her, carved dimples adding interest to his firm jaw and beautiful face. His deep brown eyes, framed by long, thick lashes, held hers captive. Her voice betrayed her as she opened her mouth to speak. Nothing came out. The dimple in his cheek deepened and his hands wrapped around her waist as he twisted her around and set her down safely on the boardwalk.

He walked to the opposite side of his horse and unlatched her satchel, handing it over to her, sopping wet on the outside. He tipped his hat and winked.

"Ma'am," he said before collecting the reins of his horse and walking into the livery.

She watched him until he disappeared behind the oversized doors.

Breathe, she reminded herself.

"Was that Will Redbourne you just rode into town with?" Opal's voice sounded in her ear and she glanced back to see the young woman staring after him, a dreamy expression crossing her pointed features.

"I believe so," Elizabeth replied, still reeling from their brief encounter.

"Too bad *he's* not the outrider for our trip. It would make the journey much more interesting," the woman with Opal said with a giggle as both ladies turned back for the bench.

A little too interesting.

"I told you I would be here." Winnie emerged from beneath a wide-brimmed blue parasol, holding out a yellow stagecoach ticket-sized envelope. "Please tell Mr. MacKenzie that I am truly sorry about the change in plans and that I wish him the best."

Elizabeth reached for the small parcel, but Winnie held it tightly, unwilling to relinquish it.

"You are a braver woman than I, Eliza Beth. Good luck." She let go and disappeared almost as quickly as she had appeared.

Elizabeth glanced down at the envelope and reached inside to find well-laid travel plans. An itinerary outlining each phase of the journey had been carefully planned out and the appropriate tickets and vouchers had been included. The pastor had thought of everything. He seemed to be a man after her own heart. A schedule she could follow was exactly what she needed.

The clock in the tower at the center of town rang loudly. Elizabeth glanced up. One o'clock. Hopefully, the stage would arrive any moment now or they would be off schedule for the rest of the trip—especially, if the driver needed any sort of break. Elizabeth opened up the small coin purse she had inside of her satchel. There wasn't much left and she guessed she would need to scrimp if she wanted any food besides bread on the journey. She snapped it closed and tucked it down into the bottom of the large pocket on the inside of her bag. If they didn't leave within a couple of hours, they would miss the train in Kansas City and she certainly did not have the funds to try to rearrange the trip.

She figured it would take no more than a couple of hours to get to Kansas City and the train depot, and as long as everything went as planned, they would be in Silver Falls by Tuesday evening. Her heart hurt a little at the thought of having to start over…again. She just hoped that Colorado would have people as good, kind, and accepting as the Redbournes. At least she still had…

Caspar. Where's Caspar?

She put the tips of her fingers in her mouth and whistled for the hound, but she didn't come.

Where could that dog have gotten herself?

Hopefully, the stagecoach driver would not have a problem with her bringing the dog along. She'd originally planned to leave her in a good home, but ultimately could not bear the thought of starting over all alone. Caspar had come into her life at a time she was needed the most and she prayed that she would be able to keep her. Where was she?

The rain continued to pour. She glanced down the street to the road that led into town, but still nothing. At least the boardwalk provided some protection from the storm, but she was already soaked near through. The thought of riding all the way to Kansas City in a wet dress was dreadful. With one more glance at the empty road, Elizabeth strode down the boardwalk to the dressmaker's shop.

"Oh, my dear," Mrs. Weaver, the shop owner, said as she walked in, "you look like a drowned cat. Can I get you something warm to drink?"

"That's very kind of you, ma'am, but I was hoping you might allow me to use one of your rooms to change into something dry before the stage arrives." She reached into her satchel and pulled out a portion of her new dress.

"Of course, my dear. Are you leaving Stone Creek?"

"I am headed out with the others from the Matchmaker Agency. I am afraid Colorado is destined to be my new home."

The shopkeep tsked. "I heard about you girls leaving to be mail-order-brides. Frankly, I don't know how you do it. Leaving home for dreams of a better life out west with a man you've never met. I don't know whether to admire the bravery or berate the silliness."

"It sounds like you do a little of both," Elizabeth said with a smile.

The dressmaker smiled too. "It must be hard moving around so much," she said as she pushed open one of her room dividers. "Why, you just got to Stone Creek, Mrs. Jessup. We're still getting to know you. I hate to see you go so soon."

She was a little surprised at the woman's sentiments. She'd spent a mere eight weeks in this place, where she'd once believed she would make her home. The time here had not been nearly enough, but she just couldn't chance her father finding her. He'd make her return to England and that was the last place she wanted to be. She had to get away. To live her own life. Away from the horrible influence of her family.

She stepped behind the divider and quickly shed the wet garment and replaced it with the dress Grace had given her.

"After the fire," her voice bounced off the wall, amplifying her volume, so she quieted and tried again. "After the fire, I realized that I did not want to be somewhere where I would be all alone. I want to settle down, have a family, and a place of my own. This is an opportunity that I would be a fool to dismiss."

"It's a real shame about Ferg's place. It was a beautiful home." Something scratched against the floor on the other side of the divider like Mrs. Weaver was moving around some of her furniture. "There *are* a few eligible bachelors here that you could settle down with," the woman said with a laugh.

"The Redbournes?" Elizabeth asked, repeating the sentiments of most every woman with whom she had come into contact.

"You have to admit, they are very handsome, hardworking, and certainly aren't poor."

"With qualifications like that, no wonder women come from all the surrounding territories to garner their affections."

What was it with the women of this town? Elizabeth's thoughts returned to her encounter with Will Redbourne and she understood. He was handsome by all accounts and she'd once dreamed of him being a part of her life—the way a girl dreamed of having her own Mr. Darcy from Jane Austen's novel. But things were different now. She needed to focus on Pastor MacKenzie. She had to accept that her future was in Silver Falls with him, not here with the Redbournes.

"But, from what I hear, there are not nearly enough of them to go around."

They both laughed, though a pang of longing settled in Elizabeth's belly as she fastened the last button on the front of her dress and stepped out into the foyer.

"You're not wrong," Mrs. Weaver said, resting her folded hands in front of her. "There are plenty of unmarried women in Stone Creek, but not nearly enough men to go around." She stepped behind the counter and reached for a pencil. "I guess I understand why someone might be enticed to travel west for a man."

"Thank you," Elizabeth said as she smoothed the inevitable wrinkles from the front of her skirt. "I have a feeling this trip is exactly what I need." She turned to Mrs. Weaver and handed her a few coins from her purse. "I truly appreciate your help."

The shopkeep shook her head and closed Elizabeth's fingers over the money. "What on earth are you going to do with that sopping thing?" she asked as she pointed to the dress dripping a puddle on the middle of the floor.

Elizabeth gasped. "I am so sorry for the mess, Mrs. Weaver." She darted a glance around the room for something she could use to clean up the mess. "Have you got a towel or a wash cloth?"

"Oh, leave it be. I'll get to it in a minute. Why don't you go put it in the basket over there?" She pointed to a table near the back of the shop. "Once this storm passes, I'll hang it out on the line and it will be as good as new."

"I wish I could. It is my only change of clothes. Whether I like it or not, I will have to take it with me." She carefully folded up the damp dress and opened her bag, ready to shove it inside, but one glance at the leather-bound copy of her Lewis Carroll novel and she couldn't bring herself to chance ruining her books.

"Nonsense," the shop owner said, pulling the dress from her hands. She walked over to the far end of the shop and draped the wet dress over the basket on the table near the back

Elizabeth glanced up and her reflection in the mirror stopped her in her tracks. The rain had smothered her hair flat against her head. She looked a sight.

One pin, then two, she removed several from the back of her head and made quick work of unbraiding the bottom. She flipped her head upside down in hopes of regaining some of its fullness, then separated three sections to the side and re braided it. At this point, it seemed useless to try to pull it back up into the coiffeur she'd had earlier in the day.

After careful inspection in the looking glass, she tucked one loose tendril behind her ear, heaved her shoulders up, then down, and exhaled. The braid would have to do.

"I was saving this for a special occasion, and I think this qualifies." Mrs. Weaver took down a simple brown skirt with a coordinating pale pink blouse from a hook hanging on a line in the window. "I think this will fit just perfectly."

"Oh, it's beautiful, Mrs. Weaver," Elizabeth said with awe. She reached out to touch the top with its lacy lapels and strings, but her fingers stilled before they actually made the connection. "I'm afraid it's just not in my budget, but thank you," she said sincerely.

A little bark sounded before a black and tan coonhound puppy emerged from behind a curtain at the back. The shop owner laughed as the animal pranced out into the store across the floor. She scooped him up and allowed him to lick her face with a giggle.

"After my Harold passed, it got a might lonely around here. This little rascal has been the best thing that has happened to me in a long time."

Elizabeth scratched the pup behind the ears. "He is a cute one, isn't he?"

"You don't know what it meant to me, Eliza, to have his companionship. When you and Grace brought him to my door, you were truly an answer to my prayers. I want to return the favor in some small manner. So, how about you trade me that soaking wet dress of yours and I'll give you this one."

"That doesn't seem like a fair trade for you. It's too much." It wasn't like the fancy dresses her father had always purchased for her back home—it was better.

"On the contrary." She placed the dress over Elizabeth's arm. "And let me show you a little secret," Mrs. Weaver said, motioning with one finger.

Elizabeth strained to look down to where she had pointed.

The woman reached down and separated the material of the dress to reveal a split skirt. "It's perfect for riding and I'd imagine you'll be doing a lot of that in a place like Wyoming."

"Colorado," Elizabeth corrected with a smile. "You...are a brilliant dress maker, Mrs. Weaver. I cannot believe your generosity. Thank you!" She leaned down and hugged the unsuspecting woman and squeezed her close. "Oh, thank you!"

A scratching sound caught Elizabeth's attention. She pulled away to find her own little red coonhound, head tilted as she peered through the glass, pawing at the frame of the shop's door.

"Caspar, there you are, girl!" she said as she went to the shop's entrance.

Mrs. Weaver took the ensemble from her and walked behind the counter.

One look at the wet dog and Elizabeth realized she could not let her into the shop. She glanced over at the sweet shopkeep who came out from behind the counter with the skirt and blouse all packaged up in brown wrapping, and a large towel.

"Go on," she said as she handed the parcel to Elizabeth. "And good luck to you on your journey, Mrs. Jessup. God speed."

Guilt found its way back into her soul and her heart sunk a little at the deception she had woven in this town. She managed a grateful smile. "God speed, Mrs. Weaver."

Elizabeth carefully placed the package inside her satchel, then opened the door, knelt down next to Caspar, and set the towel on top of the dog, rubbing vigorously. "Let's stay out of the rain, girl, or they are not going to let you come with us."

"I certainly hope you are not thinking of bringing that mutt along," the woman who'd been with Opal said.

"I am sorry," she said with the warmest smile she could muster, "I do not believe I have had the pleasure of making your acquaintance."

"Gertrude Arnold. Charmed, I'm sure," she said with a rich southern accent and a hint of a curtsy.

Oh, my. How long is this trip again?

"You aren't going to bring that...that thing, are you?"

"Caspar," she scrunched down, addressing the dog, "this is Gertrude and Opal. We are going to be travelling companions for the next little while. Can you say hello?"

Caspar barked and sat down on the wooden planks of the boardwalk.

Gertrude groaned, her nose upturned and her face squished like she smelled something bad.

Elizabeth sniffed discreetly. Despite her best intentions at drying Caspar off, the distinct odor of wet dog lingered on her fur.

"It's here!" Opal exclaimed, her hands folded together as if to contain her obvious excitement. "It's here. It's here. It's here," she recited under her breath.

Elizabeth stood up and looked down the road to where the large reddish brown wagon appeared between the two tallest buildings in town—the bank and the hotel. She was anxious to get on the road, but if this driver was anything like the other stagecoach drivers she had encountered, he would want to get something to eat and rest for a bit before leaving again. She waited at the edge of the boardwalk, still protected from the rain by the wooden overhang.

The run from Redbourne Ranch must have worn Caspar out, because the dog lay in a heap at her feet, her eyes open and watching everything around her, but not caring much to get up and run.

The door to the telegraph office opened and Will stepped out alongside another man a good half-foot shorter than him with a receding hairline and prominent nose. Elizabeth whipped back around and stared forward at the approaching stage as if her life depended on it. The sooner she could get away from him, the better.

"Doesn't look like it is going to stop anytime soon." The sound of Will's deep voice sent tingles up her spine. Elizabeth cursed the havoc the man wreaked on her senses.

"Professor," Will called loudly as he stepped around her to greet the man she'd encountered on the street yesterday—the man who'd recognized her.

She turned her back to the men, but could still hear their conversation quite well at this distance.

"Will. I came to see you off. I am heading back to Boston in the morning, but I wanted to let you know that the administration has decided that they would like you to join us the first part of August instead of September. Your letter of requisition should be arriving soon."

A twinge of guilt poked at her gut, but she could not force herself to stop from listening in on their exchange.

"Thank you, Professor. I am looking forward to it."

"As for the, hmhmm, other matter we discussed. I hope you're right about him. I would hate to have us miss out on this opportunity. I understand why you feel you need to take this last job, but...be careful."

"I will. And I will see you before you know it."

"The University of London is lucky to have you, son. Just do me a favor. Don't get yourself killed in the meantime."

London? He's going back? Elizabeth could not believe her ears. How could he return after everything that had happened? With the danger he would be in?

"Yes, sir," Will said with a laugh.

"Oh, and Will? They don't have any objections if you were to bring a wife. The faculty actually prefers its professors to be married. Think on it."

Heat flooded Elizabeth's face again at the thought.

Will cleared his throat. "That won't be the case, but thank you all the same, Professor."

The stage finally pulled up to the telegraph office. It appeared as though several people had been crammed inside.

The door flew open and a woman with thick, blond curls wearing a dark red dress spilled out onto the walkway, followed by two portly gentlemen who bickered with intensity as they also stumbled from the coach. Will jumped up onto the boardwalk to offer his assistance to the young woman while the stagecoach driver climbed up on top of the wagon and started tossing suitcases and other boxes down to the muddy ground below.

Elizabeth was shocked at the man's blatant disregard for the passengers' belongings. The shorter gentleman who had been in the telegraph office with Will strode into the street and collected the bags from the ground, then heaved them up onto the covered footpath in a few short stacks.

"William Redbourne?" The woman in the red dress squealed his name. "Well, I'll be." She pushed back the tendrils of hair that had come loose during her fall and leaned in even closer to him. "Oooooo," she squealed again as she threw her arms around his neck. "I've missed you so much." She pulled away and tilted her head back as if expecting…a kiss.

Elizabeth's heart fluttered wildly inside of her chest and she stomped her foot on the wooden planks of the boardwalk in attempt to stilt the motion. Surprised by her actions, she took a sideways glance over at Will, who caught her staring, so she snapped her head around toward the last passengers leaving the confines of the stagecoach cabin, refusing to give him the satisfaction of knowing she'd been affected by the display.

Why, Elizabeth Archer, you are jealous!

She shook her head at the mere idea. She was leaving. Today. Right now, if she could help it. So, there was no point in continuing her once fanciful daydreams and wishful thinking. Who Will Redbourne courted was certainly no concern of hers.

Three children, with an appearance of ages ranging from six or seven to twelve or thirteen, stepped down off the stage. Each of them had a paper pinned to their clothing, but they were too far away for her to see what was written.

A man and a woman stepped out from beneath the awning.

The woman was shaking, her hands clutched in front of her chest as they approached the children from the stage. They seemed nervous somehow and Elizabeth wondered why.

Shameless sounds of a woman's laughter filled her ears, but she refused to glance back at Will and his 'friend.' The need to get away now superseded her curiosity about the anxious couple and the children with the tags.

"Excuse me," she said, placing a hand on the stagecoach drivers arm as he climbed down off the rack at the top of the wagon, "would you mind if I just waited inside for our departure?" She motioned to the curtain encased cabin.

The man looked at her as if she was a few pickles short of a jar—something she'd heard Grace say.

"I've been on the road for hours, lady. I'm going to get myself a nice meal at Millie's, then grab a quick nap. We'll start loading up in an hour or so."

"Before you go, I would like to discuss…" How could she say this delicately? "…my dog."

"I'm sure there's plenty to discuss, but we'll talk about whatever you'd like in an hour. After my supper and my nap." His tone indicated it was not up for debate.

One. More. Hour. She could wait that long. After all, it was only sixty minutes.

"Our train leaves Kansas City at half past six." Elizabeth couldn't resist one last reminder. She turned around only to be greeted with the sight of the woman who had come in on the stage fawning all over Will and she turned back toward the street. She didn't want to be anywhere near them, so she decided that she would head over to the mercantile and ask Mrs. Day if she could bide her time reading in the corner of the store until the driver had finished his little break.

"Come on, Caspar," she called.

The coonhound dragged herself to her feet and followed Elizabeth as she headed down the boardwalk. When she came to the break in the walkway, she paused, searching for a way to protect herself from the still pouring rain as she crossed the street. She had her satchel, but was hesitant for anything inside to get any wetter than they already were—especially her books. The rain continued to fall in a cascade of showers. Fat droplets pelted at the ground creating a host of puddles forming in the ruts of the dirt road.

A strong arm swooped around her, urging her down off the step and into the street. She glanced over at Will's smiling face as he covered her with his jacket until they arrived under the next covered boardwalk.

Caspar howled, still following close behind.

"I decided that maybe I was the one who wanted to snuggle a little longer," he whispered with a grin on his infuriatingly handsome face. "You cleaned up fast. I like the braid." He winked.

Elizabeth stood there. Stunned.

He flashed another smile that spread across his face, showing off whiter teeth than she had ever seen on a man—especially a boxer, then he turned back toward the stage and left without any further interaction.

Didn't he know what he was doing to her? Of course, he didn't. He had no idea who she was and that irked her even more. How dare he flirt with her after nearly kissing that other woman. Maybe it was for the best that she was moving a thousand miles away to marry some preacher from Colorado. Maybe it was for the best that she would never see Will Redbourne again. Maybe, in her heart, she was still a wishful thinker.

She headed into the mercantile, now, more intent than ever on losing herself in a good book. She would just forget about him and his voice that sent gooseflesh down her arms to her toes.

Will Redbourne who?

CHAPTER TEN

Will could not stop thinking about the woman's lips. How close they'd been. How full and inviting. He'd never seen her around Stone Creek before and was a little saddened he wouldn't have the opportunity to learn more about her or get to know her before he left.

"Hey, Paulie," he said when he got back to the telegraph office, "do you know her?" He grabbed the other outrider's arm and spun him to face the mercantile just before she slipped inside.

"Nope," Paulie dismissed and turned back around. "Never seen her before."

Someone had to know who she was.

"You met Otis's replacement yet?" Raine asked as he walked up behind Will.

"Just at a glance. Didn't get much of a feel for him yet."

"The bank is transferring a lot of money. I'd feel much better if I were coming with you."

"Why don't you?"

"The sheriff needs me here."

"You mean the town needs you here in the absence of the sheriff."

"Very funny. Sheriff Butts—"

Will sniggered under his breath.

"—has done a lot for this town."

"Recently?"

Raine didn't answer immediately.

"Either way, it's up to you, little brother, to make sure that this bankroll gets to Kansas City. I couldn't trust anyone more."

Will reveled for a moment under Raine's praise. He wanted nothing more than to make his brothers, and his father, proud.

"By the way," Will said with an amused snort, "you'll never guess who came in on the stage today."

"Oh, Deputy Redbourne." The sing-song sound of the woman's voice almost made Will feel sorry for his brother.

Almost.

Raine closed his eyes and shook his head.

Will laughed. "Yep."

"MaryBeth," Raine said as he spun around to face the lavish blond woman. "When did you get back to town?"

"Didn't Will tell you?" Her mouth extended into an exaggerated pout. "I've been visiting my mother in Colorado and just got back this afternoon."

"Does Cole know you're back?"

"Oh, no. I thought I would surprise him. Do you think I'd be able to stop by later this afternoon?"

As much as they'd all tried, Cole wouldn't listen to reason when it came to MaryBeth Hutchinson. All he saw was her bouncing curls and slender waistline. He couldn't see past the exterior to see that she was only looking for a man of status and wealth—all of which, every Redbourne son would have as part of their inheritance if they married before their twenty-sixth birthday. For her, it seemed, nothing else mattered and none of them wanted to see Cole get hurt.

"He's working with Tag out in the corral today. I'm sure he wouldn't mind if you stopped by," Raine said with a smirk.

Will elbowed him in the side.

"Are you both going to be home for supper?" she asked,

feigning innocence.

"'Fraid not," Raine said, pretending disappointment, "there's a lot of work to be done here in town. But, I am sure Cole will be pleased to see you."

Her toothy smile exposed a large portion of her gums and her eyes lit up with delight—though he imagined that the prospect of courting any man of status would have the same effect.

MaryBeth's heavily floral scent lingered long after her uncle had come to retrieve her.

"Dad's going to have your hide for sending her out to the ranch."

"Nah. Cole will learn sooner or later. And you have to admit, it's amusing to watch." Raine laughed to himself and Will joined in.

"Poor Charcoal."

While Mr. Phillips switched out horses for the stage, Will and Raine headed over to Millie's to grab a bite to eat before the short journey ahead. They were seated by a window with a perfect view into the mercantile where the woman he'd given a ride into town sat in the corner reading.

"Raine," he said after finishing his last bite of chicken fried steak, "who is that woman over there?"

His brother looked out the window. "Which woman?" he asked as several young ladies passed by the restaurant in small groups.

"The one reading in the mercantile. I've never seen her before, so she can't have lived here long." Surely, he hadn't been so preoccupied with his own life that he wouldn't have noticed a beauty like her.

Raine squinted. "I'm not sure. It looks like it could be Mrs. Jessup. Why do you want to know?"

Mrs.? Will fought the disappointment that rose up in his throat. Then the last name struck a chord in his mind.

"Jessup?" Will ignored his brother's question. "The woman

who bought Old Ferg's place before it burned down?"

"One in the same."

"What's her story? Why would somebody want to burn down her house? Has she been here long enough to have earned a grudge against her?"

"I don't think it was Mrs. Jessup they were after," Raine said with a shake of his head. "Ferg had gotten himself into some trouble with some seedy people. He left in a real hurry and I think Eliza Beth paid the price."

Will's conversation with Professor Cromwell ran through his mind and now his curiosity was piqued even more.

"Is she English?" he asked, suddenly distrustful of the beautiful woman. A man couldn't be too careful where Sterling Archer was concerned.

"I don't think so, but honestly, I've barely spoken with the woman. Grace and Ethan were pretty protective of her ever since that first night when they took her under their wings. They are who you should be asking—though, apparently, she moved here with her husband, but he's not around anymore."

"Why not? Where is he?" Will cursed himself for his interest. He didn't have time to ride back out to the ranch and talk to his brother and his wife.

"Honestly, I'm not sure the man even existed. There is something about that woman that just doesn't fit, but I don't get a bad feeling about her." Raine stared at him for a moment. "Why are you so interested?"

Will's gaze returned to the window. Mrs. Day had a large broomstick in her hand and was shooing a dog from her store.

"Huh? Oh, I'm not really. Just curious."

"Mmmhmmm," Raine replied unbelievingly. "I've seen that look before."

Will pushed away from the table and set some coins down in place of his plate. "I'll be back," he said, grabbing his hat from one of the empty chairs at their table and headed out the door.

What had she called the dog?

"Caspar," he said with a follow-up whistle. The pup happily made her way toward him and he led her over to the livery where she would be able to rest out of the rain. Most animals were accustomed to being outside in most types of weather, but for some reason, he liked the thought of having something that belonged to Mrs. Jessup—if that was indeed who she was. He gave the liveryman some money to hold onto the hound and to keep her from wandering off.

"She's not a horse," the man protested loudly as Will walked away.

He turned back over his shoulder. "You'll make do."

Mr. Phillips may act grumpy, but Will had a feeling that by the time he returned, the liveryman would be reluctant to relinquish the dog back into his custody.

By the time Will walked back into Millie's place, Raine had already finished his food and was in a deep, seemingly heated conversation with the sheriff, who looked like he'd just stepped out of the saloon.

The sun peeked out from behind the clouds, though drizzles of rain continued to fall, lighter now, but wet all the same. He leaned up against the doorframe of the café, waiting for Raine to finish his business.

"Let's go." Raine's jaw flexed, his eyes fixed on a point in the road as he pushed past Will and marched toward the jailhouse.

Water collected in the brim of his hat and fell in a stream in front of him. "What bee's gotten into your bonnet?" Will asked, trying to lighten the suddenly darkened mood.

"Control your thoughts, control the fight," Raine muttered under his breath.

Will smiled with a level of satisfaction he couldn't have imagined from such a small thing. Raine had just recited one of the mantras that Will had learned while training with Jem Mace in England. He'd tried many times over the last little while to share the wisdom in his mentor's words, but, until now, had believed they'd fallen on deaf ears. It was nice to hear.

"He let them go," Raine said, his jaw flexing and his hands clenching and unclenching. "Told them to get out of town."

"Who?"

Raine took off his hat and shoved his hands through his hair. "Those blasted Reynolds brothers. They are the ones who went to Ferg's house the other day and harassed Mrs. Jessup. It was their whiskey bottle that I found in the burned wreckage, and it was them who burned down that house."

"How can you know for sure. You just said you didn't have any proof."

"The sheriff had proof. He'd overheard them laughing about it over at the saloon. When he found out that I had arrested them, he sobered up long enough to make his way back to the jailhouse. He told them that if he ever saw their scrawny hides again he would keep them locked up."

"Why would he do something like that? This isn't the first time they've been in trouble." Will tipped his hat at Millie, who passed by with a wink, then closed the door behind them.

"He said that he didn't want to break their mama's heart," Raine strode purposefully toward the telegraph office. "I think he was just too drunk to think straight."

"Can we go after them?"

"I'll send a wire out and we can have Charcoal draw up a wanted poster to be circulated, but I am not sure what good it'll do. As long as they never show their faces in Stone Creek again, I guess I'll have to be good with that. For now. It's just not in my jurisdiction."

Will could see the conflict on his brother's face. He'd always said that wrong was wrong, no matter where you lived. He wondered if Raine ever felt envious of Rafe, being able to chase the bad guys down wherever they were, but refrained from asking.

"Besides," Raine said, turning back as he pulled open the door, "you're headed out in less than an hour and you've got plenty on your plate to do when you get back before you head to England. Things will all work out around here. It always does."

Will glanced up in time to see the stagecoach driver step out of Millie's and head toward the saloon. He hit Raine's arm with the back of his hand and jutted his chin in the man's direction.

Raine nodded and allowed the door to the telegraph office to close.

They hurried to catch up with him.

"Excuse me," Will said as they reached him. "I just wanted to introduce myself. Will Redbourne, one of your outriders for this run."

"Redbourne, huh?" the man asked as he pulled up short and narrowed his eyes at Will, then moved his appraisal to Raine. "I knew a Redbourne once. You any relation to a Rafe Redbourne?"

Both Will and Raine chuckled.

"He's our brother."

His face lit up and a reluctant smile broke onto his face. "Best damned bounty hunter I ever met." He pulled at his suspenders and let them snap back into place. "He's real good at spottin' a problem. You as good as him?"

Will wasn't sure what to say. He'd spent the better half of his life trying to make his older brothers proud, to live up to the expectation that they'd created, and to be worthy of being called a Redbourne. Before he could say anything, Raine interjected.

"You won't find a better rider, fighter, or guard. Ever. He's not only good with a gun, but he's excellent with his fists, and with his brain. You'll be glad you have him along and on your side."

Will looked at Raine, trying to keep the surprise from his expression.

"Well, glad to hear it. Name's Ellis Glenn." He stuck out a hand for Will to shake.

"It's nice to meet you, Mr. Glenn."

"Ah, just call me Ellis."

"The bank is ready with their shipment, Mr…Ellis, whenever you are," Raine told him.

The driver glanced longingly over to the saloon then back to Raine. "Just as well. Half hour isn't going to do me much good anyway. I'll catch some shuteye when we stop over in Kansas City tonight."

"I'll let them know." Raine tipped his hat, exchanged a knowing glance at Will, then strode off toward the bank.

"The storm doesn't look like it's going to clear anytime soon. Do you have any concerns with the safety of your passengers?"

"The man in the telegraph office told me there will be three women travelling with us all the way to Silver Falls, Colorado. It may take a while, but we want to keep on schedule as much as we can. If you're as good as your brother says you are, Mr. Redbourne, we'll all be just fine."

No pressure.

"I'll actually only be accompanying the stage as far as Kansas City and the delivery of the bank roll. You'll be fine with Paulie the rest of the way. How much trouble can three women be, right?"

Ellis snorted. "Son, I take it you don't know women."

"I have a sister. And a mother."

"Eh, you're still a pup. You'll learn." Ellis took a deep breath. "Well, what are we standing around here for? We have a stage to pack, passengers to load, and a run to make."

After a quarter of an hour, Opal Gailey and Gertrude Arnold were sitting happily in the back of the stage. The guards at the bank stepped out of the building, along with an armed Raine, toting a large safe with their shipment inside. All packages had been loaded in the racks on top and the outriders were both mounted and ready for the ride.

"Where's the last passenger?" Ellis asked as he finished securing the strong box with multiple chains and locks.

Will pulled back the curtains. "Ladies? I wonder if you know who the last mail-order-bride is who will be travelling with you."

"Why, Mr. Redbourne, so nice to see you again," Gertrude said as she pursed her lips and fluttered her eyelashes in his direction.

He flexed his jaw, willing patience. "Thank you kindly," he said, imitating the most polite Mountie he'd once encountered on a trek up through Canada. "The last passenger?" he tried again.

"That would be Eliza Beth," Opal stated confidently.

The news washed over him like the rain and he remembered the conversation they'd had over dinner last night—though he'd been distracted enough that it hadn't registered that Grace's friend was the same woman who had caught his interest, who may or may not be lying about her identity, and who was already promised to another man. And he was the one who was supposed to escort her. At least he would only be accompanying the stage to Kansas City. He wasn't sure whether to be apprehensive or delighted.

"Do you know where Mrs. Jessup is?" he asked, offering a smile for their cooperation.

They both shook their heads. He stood up straight and glanced around the town. Surely, she wouldn't still be reading in the mercantile. She had been very aware of what time the stage had been supposed to leave and he couldn't imagine that she would have forgotten.

"I'm afraid if she's not here in the next five minutes," Ellis said, "we're going to have to leave without her."

For a man who'd wanted to take a nap earlier, he sure was in a hurry.

"Just stay here until I return," Will instructed.

Ellis nodded.

He strode down the street to the mercantile and threw open the door. He marched to the back of the store to where he'd seen her curled up and reading. He stopped short when he came upon the vision of a woman, eyes closed, book tipped against her chest, sleeping. If angels walked the earth, certainly she would be one of them. Her bright red hair spilled across the big white cushion in which she lay. Her nose and cheeks were sprinkled with light freckles and he couldn't help but wonder if her shoulders were that way too.

He took a step closer, but as if he didn't quite trust himself to actually touch her, he reached for a long stick that had a feather attached to one end and reached out, the tip brushing lightly against her face.

Her hand batted at the motion, but she didn't wake, so he tried it again, though this time, he started with her ear and trailed the feathers down the side of her face to the delicate skin at her neck. Her nose twitched and her fingers brushed across the length of her face. Then, without warning, she smacked herself hard on the neck and opened her eyes wide, shooting bolt upright.

Will couldn't help himself. Laughter filled his throat and bubbled out into the air. "Are you ready to leave, ma'am," he said, nearly choking on his merriment.

"Ready?"

"The stage is leaving ma'am, and I have been instructed to tell you that if you are not on it in five minutes, it will leave without you."

Will liked seeing her a little flustered. She collapsed the book she had been reading, shoved it into the bag she had at her side, and attempted to stand with some difficulty.

He held out his hand to her. When she placed her fingers into his palm, his heart sped up enough that he jerked her out of the cushion and into him.

"Sorry about that."

"If you'd wanted to hold my hand a little longer, all you had to do was ask," she said with a smile as she pulled her satchel up into her arms and walked past him down the aisle of the general store.

Will stood still for a moment, a grin spreading across his face. He needed to get to know this woman.

"Thank you, Mrs. Day," she said as she left the mercantile in a rush.

Will finally got his feet to move. He tipped his hat at the store owner and chased after Elizabeth. She'd stopped again at the break in the walkway.

"Allow me," he said, swooping her up into his arms and crossing the street.

She squealed as the light rain sprinkled her hair and face. Once he placed her down and her feet touched solid ground, she shook her head with a laugh.

"Don't forget to ask next time you want to sweep me off my feet."

"Why, if I didn't know any better, I would think you were flirting with me."

You're playing with fire, Redbourne.

She bit her lip, smiled, then headed to the end of the boardwalk to where the stage awaited.

"Here is my ticket, sir," she said as she handed a soggy piece of paper up to Ellis.

"It's about time, Redbourne. If we're going to get these ladies to Kansas City before their six thirty train, we need to be on our way." He winked at Mrs. Jessup. It seemed there was something about the woman that could soften the grizzliest of bears.

Several people stood in front of the telegraph office to wave goodbye to the ladies. Raine had Indy by the reins and handed them over to Will.

"My dog!" Mrs. Jessup exclaimed as she poked her head out of the window.

"I almost forgot…" he said under his breath as he tossed the reins back to Raine and ran into the livery. When he emerged, a big red coonhound graced his arms. He opened the stagecoach door and set the pup on Eliza Beth's lap.

"Thank you," she said as she scrubbed the pup behind the ears. "I must say, you and I have had quite the adventure today. I am sad it has come to an end."

"The adventure, ma'am, has only just begun."

Her brows furrowed together and she searched his face.

"I'm the outrider, ma'am. And it will be my pleasure to escort you and these other lovely ladies as far as Kansas City." He tipped his hat and pushed away from the stage door.

"Achoo."

Will couldn't tell from which lady the sneeze came, but he smiled to himself as he walked away and up to where Raine stood, still waiting with Indy's reins in hand. His brother drew him into a tight embrace.

"You be safe, little brother. We'll see you real soon."

"Thanks for everything, Raine." Will clapped him on the back and pulled away. "I should be back sometime tomorrow morning," he said before mounting his horse.

Kansas City was only a couple of hours from Stone Creek and he fully expected to be back in time to meet up with Jem. Then, he'd have plenty of time to spend with his family and prepare for his trip to Boston. The thought of his ship brought a smile to his face. He pulled Indy around.

"Let's go, Ellis."

The stage driver nodded and snapped the straps. The wagon creaked as the wheels had their first go around, before settling into the rhythmic lull of motion.

This was going to prove to be a very interesting ride. He just hoped for his sake, and hers, that Eliza Beth Jessup was exactly who she said she was.

CHAPTER ELEVEN

Elizabeth smoothed her hand over Caspar's head and down the length of the dog's body. She was grateful that the hound wasn't jumping all over the cabin and the other passengers as she did not want to let her out to run in the rain next to the stagecoach just yet. She preferred to get on their way where there would hopefully be fewer distractions to take the dog's focus.

She couldn't stop thinking about Will Redbourne. The feel of his chest beneath her fingertips seared a place in her memory and she smiled as she remembered his shocked reaction to their playful interactions.

He'd been quite the gentleman today, offering to bring her into town, covering her with his jacket when she crossed the street—then, with heat filling her face, she recalled the moment when he scooped her up into his arms and carried her. Will Redbourne was a force to be reckoned with and despite her best intentions to forget him, he'd made quite an impression on her. Again.

She glanced out the window and there was a rider at the back and another at the front. She didn't remember having two guards for the stage when she'd come into Stone Creek and she wondered what they could possibly be carrying to warrant two of them. She looked over at Gertrude who now laid her head on Opal's shoulder, both women sleeping soundly, and she couldn't imagine it was for either of them. She determined that she would ask at their next stop.

Elizabeth opened her satchel and pulled out one of her favorite novels. She'd often dreamed of coming to America to see all the wonderful things that she had read about in her books. She loved fictional novels, but more often than not, enjoyed the factual books that contained some of the more interesting traditions and legends behind the people and civilizations that had lived in the ancient Americas. She loved learning about the Indians of various tribes, about miners who'd found gold in the mountains of California, and a plethora of other stories often recounted by explorers of all kinds, searching for the unknown.

She missed the library back home where information was always at her fingertips. She'd learned various tasks and skills by delving in, reading about, and then practicing some of the techniques illustrated inside the pages.

Bump.

Caspar's head shot up.

Bump. She'd forgotten just how rough the stage ride could be.

Without warning, Caspar jumped from the seat at her side onto Gertrude's lap.

She bolted upright and screamed.

The stage shuddered to a halt.

"I am so sorry. She doesn't usually jump up on people. Maybe she just needs to go out."

She was both grateful and surprised that Mr. Glenn had been willing to allow Caspar to join their journey, and she didn't want anything to jeopardize that.

"Is everything all right in here, ma'am?" the other mounted guard asked as he approached the window. He placed a hand on the opening to peer inside.

"No, it certainly is not," Gertrude said as she shoved Caspar off of her and brushed at the newly formed wrinkles in her dress. "I am a lady and frankly I am abhorred that I must share this stage with a...a...horse."

"She's hardly a horse, ma'am," the rider said, "but maybe we should let her stretch her legs a bit."

"Thank you," Elizabeth mouthed at the man.

He opened the door and Caspar happily jumped down and started running ahead toward the place where Will had pulled around on his horse and waited.

Gertrude lifted her nose into the air, avoiding Elizabeth's gaze. "My husband-to-be had better not have any animals."

"He's a sheep herder, Gertie," Opal said. "Of course, he's going to have animals."

"Well, sheep and dogs are very different beasts," she said, as her hands both dropped into her lap emphatically.

Elizabeth didn't have the heart to tell the woman that dogs were a widely used resource in sheep herding.

The stage started moving again with the familiar little creak of the wheels. She guessed they were a little more than half-way to Kansas City.

She envied Caspar a little and wished that she could get out and stretch her legs for a spell.

CRACK!

A ricochet bounced off of the steel box on top of the stage. "What was that?"

"Get down," Elizabeth commanded the other women. She was all too familiar with that sound. She'd heard it plenty. Her father had seen to it that she'd become an excellent markswoman and she had practiced for years on end, though she'd never had or ever wanted the need to use that skill.

CRACK!

Another shot rang clear, but this time it seemed to have missed the stage completely.

Elizabeth darted a glance out the window as it sped

forward. Will and the other rider were closer to the stage than they had been for the first leg of their journey this far.

CRACK!

They were under attack. She chanced another look out the window. Will and the other outrider had weapons drawn and had ridden up close to surround the stage. She couldn't tell how many bandits there were, but they were headed into a ravine and the outriders needed help.

CRACK!

The wood near her head splintered off, startling her. She pulled back long enough to see the damage that had been done, then, with gritted teeth and a firm determination, she climbed out the opposite window, grabbing onto the steel railings from the top of the coach. She felt around for her footing, inching herself along the side of the enclosed wagon, until she reached the driver's box. It was a good thing she had donned minimal underclothing when she'd changed into the dress or there was no way she would have been able to make the climb.

"Mr. Driver, sir," she tried to get his attention, but to no avail. He was busy trying to keep the stage upright as he drove despite the bullets flying around them. "Hmhmmm!" She cleared her throat loudly. Still nothing. "Gun?" she screamed.

The man dared a glance down at her, his eyes widening with surprise.

"Get back in the coach!" he yelled.

"Where is your gun?" she prodded.

He shook his head, but motioned to the grooved section behind his seat.

A large rifle perched against the back of his foot space. She'd never have imagined such intricate work engraved into a portion of a stagecoach that would hardly ever be seen. She wrapped her arm around the iron bar holding up the running lamp and reached into the partition, struggling to pull the gun from its roost. When it finally gave way, Elizabeth lost her footing, but refused to let go of the rifle. The driver reached down and, with little effort, heaved her up into the seat next to him.

"Forgive my saying so, ma'am, but you're mad. You should get back down into the coach with the other females."

Without gracing his comment with a response, Elizabeth turned around and climbed up next to the steel strong box. Luckily, the three women's belongings only took up half of the compartment, leaving plenty of space for her to climb in. She braced herself against the railing and leaned down over the steel contraption with the rifle in front of her.

CRACK!

The shot had come from a cliff on the edge of the hilly ravine. She took aim.

CRACK!

That time, the shot came from her rifle. A tree branch broke very close to her mark. She gritted her teeth in irritation. She'd missed. It didn't help that she was riding atop of a very fast moving stage. She cocked the gun, aimed, and fired again.

CRACK!

This time, a loud groan sounded from the distance, and a man fell out from behind the cluster of bushes and tall sycamore trees dotting the landscape, and tumbled down the hillside to the ravine floor.

Bile rose in her throat, but she shook her head clear of any thought, and forced herself to look for another threat. Splatters of mud were like clouds ushering in the approaching threat at the mouth of the ravine. Their only way out. They were headed straight for trouble. She worked her way back to the front of the stage, heaved the skirt of her dress over the bench, and sat down next to the driver.

CRACK!

That shot had come from her right.

One of the men ahead of them fell off his horse.

Will.

She caught the outrider's eye. His jaw clenched tightly and

even from this distance she could see the flare of his nostrils. He was not pleased. She couldn't worry about what he thought right now. They were under attack and she would do her best to help them keep the threat at bay.

CRACK!

The shot shattered the glass on the lamp, startling Elizabeth. She grunted. "I don't think so," she said as she raised the rifle and brought the man at the forefront into her sites.

CRACK!

He fell backward, but managed to remain seated on his mount. She'd only winged him. She cocked it again.

Bullets exchanged heavily on both sides.

"Hi-yah!" the driver yelled as he encouraged the horses to run faster.

Elizabeth took a deep breath, reloaded the gun, then, staying as low as she could, climbed back into in the railed storage section and lay flat against the wood. Another twenty feet and they would be on top of the hijackers.

At the driver's whistle, Elizabeth pulled herself up behind the strong box and took aim, following her target as the assailants spun their horses around to catch up to the stage that had passed them without a second thought. At this close range, she could see the men's faces and suddenly, killing one of them became all too real. She aimed, but could not make herself pull the trigger for a kill shot. She shifted slightly and pegged the closest man in the leg.

He screamed a few obscenities at her, but did not stop his forward pursuit.

The belt of extra bullets had slid just out of her reach and before she maneuvered close enough to collect it, one of the men had grabbed onto the side of the coach and began climbing up toward her. She wished she'd paid more attention to all the fighters that had come through her house. They had always been talking about the most effective methods to take down their larger opponents.

Improvise!

She turned the gun around and smacked the man in the face with the butt of the rifle. A thick gash oozed with blood as he jerked backward, but he did not lose his grip on the railing. He touched his face and upon seeing the blood, narrowed his eyes and curled his lip into a snarl before he spit a mouthful of blood at the ground.

"You're going to pay for that, Missy," he spat as he pulled himself up on top of the stage.

The driver glanced back over his shoulder. He pulled the reins slightly to one side and then the other. The man approaching her wavered with the stage, but kept his footing as he got closer.

Elizabeth placed her hands to her sides to brace herself, her fingers touching the edge of the ammunitions belt that had slid back within reach. With a little more effort, she scooted sideways until she could grip the buckle and pulled it toward her.

The man reached to his holster only to discover that his gun was not there. He growled in frustration, still inching his lumbering bulk toward her.

One bullet was all she needed. Just one. She managed to slide a pellet from the belt and scooched backward up against the driver's box as her fingers fumbled with the casing, trying to load it into the rifle.

Hurry, Beth! Hurry!

The man now stood hunched over her. His meaty hands reached down, touching the tender flesh just above her collar.

CRACK!

His large, bulky frame fell forward on top of her, squeezing the breath from her lungs. Half of his body dangled over the side of the railing.

But, how?

She hadn't fired.

"Help me," the man gasped, blood encasing his lips, a rotten stench rising up and filling her nostrils even as the life drained out of him. He pawed at the wood, grasping for anything he could, until he connected with her wrist as he fell, haphazardly pulling her over the side with him.

She screamed, closing her eyes and bracing herself for impact, but before she hit the ground, she was scooped up into her rescuer's arms and swung up in front of him. She breathed out a sigh of relief and collapsed against Will's chest. He felt good and she snuggled closer into his neck, smiling when a deep-seated groan escaped him. It was as if nothing could touch her when she was encircled in his embrace and she wanted to stay there for as long as she could.

He slowed the horse to a trot and the stage slowed down along with it.

"But, the bandits," she said, darting a look over his shoulder.

"The last two turned and high-tailed it for the hills. We're safe. For the moment." He looked down at her, his face mere inches from hers.

She glanced at his lips, then back to his eyes.

He cleared his throat and returned his gaze to the road before them.

"Then, you can put me down and I'll get back onto the stage."

"Not until we're out of the ravine." His face, now stoic, looked like one of the chiseled sculptures her father had in his office. Perfectly carved, but with a little scruff that accentuated his perfect jawline.

She all of a sudden felt the need to defend her actions.

"I had it under control," she said, knowing it was a bold-faced lie.

"We'll argue about that once I get you safe and onto solid ground," Will said falling back behind the stage. "What were you thinking?" he asked, exasperation lining his every word. "You could have been killed back there. How am I supposed to protect you when you pull a stunt like that?"

"I thought we were going to argue about that later."

He tilted his head, the cords of his jaw flexing. With a little nudge of his foot, he urged the horse to pull up alongside the stage driver. "Let's head on into Plain City and we'll send word to the territory Marshal that they will find those men in the ravine," he said to the man. "I can't be sure, but I think they were part of the Reynolds Gang."

A sinking feeling suddenly hit her and she sat up as tall as she could. "Where's Caspar?" she asked, straining against him, looking around for any sign of her dog.

"She's a good dog. I'm sure she'll catch up to us sooner or later."

"We can't just leave her out here." Elizabeth whistled. "Caspar!" she yelled. "Here girl."

"We can't wait out here where we are exposed. I'm sorry, ma'am, but we have to—"

"Caspar!" she yelled again, searching the darkening hillside.

"You want me to stop to let the lady back onto the stage?" Mr. Glenn asked.

"Yes!" Elizabeth jumped at the chance. "Let's stop, just for a moment. I'm sure she's around here somewhere."

"Let's just push through," Will said firmly. "The lady won't be able to get into any more trouble from here." He tightened his hold on her.

The driver chuckled. "Yes, sir," he said with a nod and snapped the reins once more.

"You don't need to look after me. I will be just fine in the coach with the other ladies."

"Maybe so, but this was the next best thing to holding your hand."

She pushed away from him enough to look into his face. As much as he tried to keep his facial expression at an even keel, his dimple betrayed him. She narrowed her eyes playfully and smiled through pursed lips. A grin broke out across his face.

After everything that had just happened, this was proving

to be a very interesting trip.

It took a while for Will's heart to return to a normal beat. As if it hadn't been enough to have an assembly of bad guys shooting at and chasing them, the woman had climbed out of the wagon and before he knew it, she was on top of the stage shooting back. He'd admired her courage, but had found it difficult to focus on the task at hand. At least three men had lost their lives today and Paulie had gotten shot—though the bullet had just grazed his arm.

Mrs. Jessup, or whoever she was, leaned against him, strands of her brilliant red mane tickling his chin. But he liked the feel of her in his arms. She was unlike any woman he had ever met. Most would have reacted just as Opal and Gertrude had by hugging each other and whimpering in the back of the stage, but this woman had demonstrated courage in the face of a very real danger and he couldn't help but be impressed. Even if it had scared the living daylights out of him.

He still felt guilty about leaving the dog behind, especially since there were still some intermittent showers, but he was responsible for the cargo on the stage. Not just the money, but the women too, and they needed to get somewhere safe before it got completely dark. He prayed the pup would find her way as Mrs. Jessup seemed quite attached.

The sunlight disappeared behind the hills to the west just as they reached the small town of Plain City. He hoped they would all be able to find accommodations for the night. With a bankroll as large as the one they had, he didn't want to take any chances by travelling through the night.

He looked down at the beauty now sleeping peacefully in his arms—which had very little feeling left in them. The ride into town had taken a little longer than he had anticipated, but he refused to acknowledge his discomfort.

He cleared his throat. Mrs. Jessup stirred, but then snuggled more deeply into him, her forehead nestling perfectly in the curve of his neck. He cleared his throat again—more loudly this time.

"Are we there?" she asked with a sleep-laced voice.

"Yes. I am going to drop you off in front of the hotel where Mr. Glenn has taken Opal and Gertrude. They should have a room for you for the night."

He was greeted with silence, so he looked down to see if she'd fallen back to sleep. Her eyes were open, but she didn't speak.

"I'll just be in the livery if you need anything," he told her huskily.

"You won't be staying at the hotel?" she asked quietly, still leaning against him.

"I'm on duty. I can't leave the stagecoach unattended, but I'll catch a few hours of shuteye in the room at the back of the livery while Paulie takes the first watch."

Silence.

"Don't worry," he said, sensing her reluctance to be alone, "it's just down the street."

"What exactly were those bandits after?" she asked, now fully awake and looking up at him.

He cursed himself for allowing the beauty to sleep in his lap. He was quickly becoming too familiar with the woman. If she kept looking up at him like that, he may not be able to stop himself from partaking of her plump and slightly parted lips. He shook his head, dragging his gaze from her luscious mouth.

"Three beautiful mail-order-brides," he told her with a wink.

"I'm serious," she said, raising her chin even higher.

He groaned. Did she have any idea what she was doing to him? He cleared his throat.

"We're carrying a bankroll into Kansas City." There was no sense keeping the truth from her.

To his disappointment, she dropped her head, nodding acknowledgement.

"I wish someone had told me what we were carrying. I would have been much better prepared," she said quietly, almost in a whisper.

"You…" He raised her chin until she raised her lashes to look at him and he leaned in a little closer. "…were amazing out there." He closed the distance between them, his lips so close to hers he could almost taste them.

It took every ounce of strength in him not to claim her lips in his kiss, but what kind of gentleman would he be if he succumbed?

"It's late, ma'am," he said as he pulled up in front of the hotel. "I should get you to bed." Heat flooded his neck and face. "I mean, I should allow you to retire for the night."

Smooth, Redbourne.

"Thank you for everything you did for me today," she said before sliding down off his lap.

"For saving your life?" he goaded her with a grin.

She smiled warmly. "Yes."

"The pleasure was mine, ma'am." He tipped his hat. "I'm sorry we didn't make Kansas City in time for you to catch the train," he added as an afterthought before turning Indy back toward the livery. "We'll leave just after first light," he called over his shoulder. "Around seven."

Will breathed in the night air, feeling lighter than he had in a good long while. Feeling had started to return in his arms, yet somehow, they felt empty. It had been a long time since a woman had affected him in such a way. Then, the nagging thought came into his head.

What if she really is Sterling Archer's daughter?

CHAPTER TWELVE

Elizabeth stepped inside the hotel and leaned against the front window until Will was out of sight. She couldn't stay there. Her satchel, which contained every cent she had left, was still in the stagecoach and if the station would not exchange the train she missed for a new one, she would have just enough to buy another ticket to Silver Falls. No, she couldn't spend money on something as frivolous as a hotel room when there was a perfectly good stagecoach sitting empty in the livery.

She'd fallen asleep, comfortable in Will's arms, for the better part of the last hour as they'd made their way into the small town of Plain City, Kansas. At least, it had stopped raining somewhere along the way and she'd been able to rest. At first, she hadn't appreciated Will's insistence that she ride with him on a single horse, but it had proven to be more pleasant than she would have expected. They hadn't spoken much, but she'd felt safe. Protected.

Elizabeth peeked out the window, watching Will until he was out of sight. As soon as he disappeared around a corner, she ducked out of the hotel, determined to get back into the stage. Unfamiliar with Plain City, Elizabeth wasn't sure exactly how she would be able to get into the building undetected, but had every confidence an idea would strike her by the time she reached the livery.

As she stood just outside the stock house, she saw that Will's horse had been tied up to the post in front of the telegraph office. A small light flickered in the window and Elizabeth guessed he'd woken the operator. If she slipped inside the livery right now, she may be able to do it unnoticed. She pulled open the unlocked door and with light, careful steps made her way over to the stage. A crunching noise drew her attention to the left of the coach and she turned over her shoulder to look behind her when she bumped into someone in front of her. She gasped and jumped backward behind the rear of the stage, her heart thumping wildly in her chest.

"Who's there?" a male voice called out, the light from a lantern filling the space behind her. After all of the drama they'd had in the last few hours, the last thing she needed was to get shot as an intruder.

"Eliza Beth," she said, cursing the quake in her voice as she peeked around the corner, then stepped out into the dim light.

"Mrs. Jessup?" He held up the light to illuminate her face.

She smiled and waved.

"I didn't mean to scare you, ma'am," he said. "Is there something I can do for you? I'd a thought you would be all settled in over at the hotel by now. It's been a long day."

"No. I'm fine, Mr...?"

"It's Paulie, ma'am. Just Paulie."

"Then, just call me Eliza Beth." The name seemed to fall off her lips as if it truly belonged to her. She paused for a moment, then motioned to the stage. "Paulie," she nodded, acknowledging that she'd used his given name. "I was just headed in to collect my things from inside the stage and I will be on my way."

"Ms. Arnold and Ms. Gailey both required a bag for the night as well." He held the lantern in one hand as he started to climb. "Which one is yours?" he asked.

"I just have my satchel, Mr...Paulie. It's just there." She pointed at the large brown bag with the straps dangling over the side.

Paulie moved a few bags, overlooking hers.

"Might I say, ma'am, you are quite handy with a rifle," he told her, wincing and sucking in a breath as he reached for her bag. "That was sure some good shootin' today. You were as good as any outrider I've seen. I'd say you probably saved my life." He raised the lantern to reveal a bloody shoulder.

"You were shot?" she asked, horrified that he was acting so nonchalant about the injury.

"Just grazed me, ma'am, but it coulda been a whole lot worse."

"There must be a doctor in this town. Don't you think you should have it looked at?"

"Nah. It stopped bleeding. It'll be fine."

"Mr..."

He cleared his throat.

"Paulie," she corrected, "the last thing you need is for infection to set in. Better come on down here and let me take a look at it."

"I haven't gotten to your bag yet."

"That's all right. It's not going anywhere."

Paulie climbed down from the stage and sat on a stool next to the work table.

On many an occasion, Elizabeth'd had need of stitching up a fighter or cleaning up his wounds after a fight. She imagined that a bullet wound that had just grazed the skin couldn't be any worse than that, but she'd also seen what could happen to the simplest wound if not cared for properly. Unless this small town had a doctor, she doubted they would be able to find many of the appropriate supplies. The General Store would be closed at this hour, so she'd have to think of something else that might help.

"Do you think you could go over to the saloon and pick up

a bottle of something strong?" Heat filled her cheeks as she realized what that must sound like coming from a lady. "We need to disinfect the wound," she clarified. "Unless you happen to have some iodine or other disinfectant on hand."

He thought for a moment. "Nothing like that, but I saw some medicine for horses right over here," he said as he made his way to a small shelf next to a cluster of open stalls.

Elizabeth picked up the bottle and looked at it. She did not recognize the name on the front, so she unscrewed the lid and took a whiff. Whew. Whiskey. "This will have to do. Now, let me see that wound."

Paulie gingerly worked at unfastening the buttons of his shirt and pulled it down off of his shoulder so she could get a better look at the injured area. While the bullet had certainly passed through, it was deeper than she had expected. It was more than a simple graze. Blood had caked all down his arm and absorbed into the sleeve of his shirt.

"Do they have a water pump around here?" she asked as she squinted into the darkness.

Without hesitation, Paulie stood up, grabbed a bucket from the floor next to a doorway, and stepped outside, holding up the lantern in front of him—though it was easy to tell that the weight pained him.

Elizabeth rubbed her arms against the night chill, grateful to be out of the evening's breeze. She caught a glimpse of a nice thick hunting knife sitting at the edge of a work table and reached for it. They would need some bandages and she doubted she would be able to find much out here.

A low rumbling sound emerged from a darkened hallway. Her curiosity compelled her to move toward the darkened doorway. A sliver of the moon's light spilled into a small room where she could make out two sets of bunkbeds and, by the shadows that filled the bottom bunk of the first, it appeared as if a man slept there. He was snoring.

Elizabeth laughed to herself. It was the stagecoach driver.

She backed away slowly, but tripped over a feed bucket, then knocked into a water pail that fell, tumbling to the ground with a loud clatter.

"What in tarnation?" the driver yelled, shooting out of his bed, weapon cocked and held up in front of him. He marched out of the little room, but stopped short when he nearly ran her over.

"I did not mean to wake you," she said as she bent down to pick up the offending cans. "I am so sorry."

"Mrs. Calamity Jane, is that you?"

Elizabeth felt the blush creep into her face. She'd heard tales of the frontierswoman who was good with a gun.

"I was just looking for some bandages for Paulie's arm," she offered.

The driver grumbled a little as he appeared from the darkened room and made his way over to the stagecoach. He climbed up into the driver's seat.

"Sure appreciate what you done today, young lady. I don't know if we would have made it this far with our full cargo with just the two outriders. I told 'em we'd need more than two, but do they listen to the likes of me?" He shook his head. "You've got some real skill with a rifle," he said as he turned around and fiddled with something behind him.

Elizabeth beamed at his praise.

A few loud knocks and clanks and he climbed back down off the wagon, handing her a smaller, rectangular, wooden box.

"In case of emergencies," he said. "Never know when you might need something like that in this line of work. Now, I am going back to sleep," he said as he stumbled back toward the bunk room. "Wake me when its morning. And try to keep it down out here." He waved and disappeared again into the darkness.

Elizabeth set the small box down on the work table and felt around for a latch to open it.

Nothing.

Paulie returned with a full bucket of cold water and the lantern. He set it down on the table and retook his seat, pulled his sleeve down off his shoulder to expose the wound, and waited.

"I hope that helps," he said.

With the added light from the lantern, Elizabeth found that the box Mr. Glenn had given her had a sliding mechanism built into it. When she pulled it open, she found a few rolls of gauze, liniment, a small bottle of spirits, a thin piece of wood, and a couple of washcloths.

Perfect.

She pulled out one of the rags and dunked it into the water, then turned to the wound in Paulie's arm and dabbed at the dried blood. She repeated the action, wringing out the dirty water into an empty bowl she'd discovered under the table, until the wound itself became visible and all of the dirt and dried blood had been cleaned away from it. Angry red skin surrounded the hole, but it did not yet look infected.

"This is going to hurt, Paulie. Are you ready?"

He had been a good patient thus far, but Elizabeth imagined that even cleaning the wound had been painful.

Paulie nodded, bracing himself against the work table.

She opened the small bottle of spirits from the box, but before she could pour some of it over the wound, Paulie snatched it out of her hand and took a quick sip. With a little shrug of his shoulders, he handed it back to her.

"Now, I'm ready."

She poured a little over his arm, then with the wash cloth scrubbed at the open sore until a light wave of fresh blood came out onto the rag, then she poured a little more.

Paulie's jaw clenched tightly together and he pounded several times on the table while exhaling loudly.

"Just a little while longer, and you'll be almost as good as new." Elizabeth poured a good portion of the remaining bottle on top of the wound for good measure, then retrieved one of the dry washrags from the box, dabbed around the injured area, and wrapped it tightly with several layers of gauze dressing, securing it with a pin she'd also found in the little medical kit.

"All done," she said as she stepped away from him.

"Thank you, ma'am."

"Thank *you*, Paulie, for helping to keep us safe."

He beamed at her appraisal.

"Goodnight, ma'am. You best be getting back to the hotel. I'm sure you'll want some rest after the day we've had. Morning'll be here before you know it. Speaking of which, it's time I had another look around."

Elizabeth nodded and turned toward the stage, walking slowly.

"Goodnight," she called after him.

Paulie stood tall, and held the lantern up as he stepped outside the livery to start his walk of the perimeter.

Elizabeth lifted her foot up onto the metal plank that served as a stair up into the stage and reached as tall as she could to retrieve her satchel. The handle dangled below the railing and it appeared to be clear of any other obstructions. She tugged on the leather strap until it tumbled over the edge, then she quietly slipped inside the stage and pulled the door closed behind her, keeping her head low. At least it would be dry, if a little cold.

She sat in the seat, leaned against the side with her satchel tucked up behind her head like a pillow, and closed her eyes. Paulie had been right. She longed for rest—even a few hours would be better than none at all.

After a moment, her back started to hurt and she twisted and turned until she achieved a position that felt comfortable. As she began to relax, visions of everything that had happened today passed through her mind and instead of slowing down, her breathing became more rapid and ragged.

She'd almost died today.

Had killed a man.

How could she live with that?

She rationalized that the lumbering oaf would have killed her had she not defended herself, but the realization that they'd only been after the money left her questioning her course of action.

Oh, Lord, forgive me.

All of the emotions that she'd held back to get her through the day came bubbling to the surface. She raised a hand to her face and wondered if Caspar was all right, wherever she was, and she longed for the attention the hound would have been sure to have given her.

Elizabeth wrapped her arms around herself.

She missed Stone Creek and wished that she could talk to Grace. And as much as she hated to admit it, she missed home. England. Her family, no matter what they'd done, she still loved them. If she'd ever needed someone in her life, it was now, but…she was alone. She forced herself to focus on the positive things that had happened, but only one came to mind.

He almost kissed me.

Just that one thought warmed her from the inside out. She could focus on that. Emotions swirled about her as her body finally gave in to rest.

CHAPTER THIRTEEN

The telegraph operator's eyes were red beneath his small, round spectacles, and his white night dress was still crumpled from sleep. Will had felt bad about waking the man, but he'd needed to get a message off to Stone Creek as quickly as possible. He hoped that Marshal Fenton was still in the area and that he would be able to get some men together to find the bodies of the bandits who had attacked them. Animals were not likely to leave the corpses alone for long.

"Thank you, sir," he said as he placed coins down on the table, double for the inconvenience. He moved his neck in a circular motion and stretched his shoulder blades backward, looking forward to a few hours of sleep. He collected his hat, nodded at the tired telegrapher, and headed outside toward the sheriff's office, lantern in hand.

By morning, he would be the least popular man in this little town.

Knock. Knock.

If the lawman in town was like most, his quarters would be in or around the jailhouse. He knocked again. Still no answer. He stepped sideways and peeked in through the window. A man in one of the cells, raised a hand, presumably to block the lantern's light from shining in.

"Can I help you, son?" A low, scratchy voice came from around the side of the building. A large, bearded man stepped into the light, his badge displayed prominently on his chest.

"My name is William Redbourne, Sheriff." He extended his free hand. "The stage came under attack on our way into your little town. Three of the culprits are dead, but two of them got away. Now, I don't know if they're headed this way or not, but I thought you'd appreciate the advanced notice."

"I do." He dipped his head affirmatively and then raised a brow at Will. "You said three are dead? You bring 'em with ya?"

"No, sir. There wasn't time. That's why I'm here. I also sent word to the territory marshal."

"Fenton? Been a while since he's been out in these parts." The sheriff cleared his throat and walked around him to the front of the jailhouse. "Where'd you say ya left those men?"

"Out in the ravine."

"You a lawman?" he asked as he moved to the chair stationed right outside the jail's door and pulled a cigar from his pocket.

"I'm not a marshal or a sheriff. I'm an outrider. Accompanied the stage. We're carrying some sensitive cargo."

"An outrider, huh?" The man eyed him through narrow slits.

Will nodded.

An outrider didn't carry the same authority as a regular lawman, but he was endowed with a responsibility to uphold the law—deputized in the line of his duty.

"What kind of cargo?" the sheriff asked, seeming satisfied with Will's response.

"The sensitive kind, sir. Along with three mail-order-brides."

"Mail-order-brides?" He struck a match and puffed on the cigar now protruding from his mouth. "Do folks really do that?"

"I'm travelling with proof, sir," Will told him, amazed himself that it was true.

Of course, it was natural for people to want to settle down and have a family. Wasn't it? And if there were no other opportunities…

The burly sheriff exhaled a thick stream of smoke and crossed his legs, leaning back into his chair. "Hmmmm." He seemed to ponder that thought for longer than was probably necessary before glancing back up at Will. "I'll get word over to the hotel, restaurant, and saloon to be on the lookout for any suspicious strangers in town."

"Thank you, sheriff."

"Where you headed?"

"Kansas City."

"Leaving tomorrow?"

"Yes, sir."

"Glad to hear it," he said with another puff of smoke.

Will tipped his hat. "Evenin'."

"Evenin'."

After collecting Indy's reins, he took his time walking back over to the livery. The wind from the storm had cleared the night sky of all clouds and the stars shined brightly in the heavens.

So much for an easy job, Sven!

Amidst all of the things that had gone wrong today, he could not help the smile that emerged on his face as thoughts of the red-headed woman invaded his mind. He'd never met anyone quite like her. The only women he knew who could shoot that well, were those in his family.

Most of the womenfolk in Stone Creek were all too willing to let the menfolk carry the guns—though he imagined some of those living outside of town would know their way around a shotgun or two.

Will tipped his hat at Paulie as he walked into the livery. He relit the lantern and carried it into the stables and hung it from the nail protruding from a beam above the gate.

"You must be tired, boy," he said as he walked

Independence into one of the stalls. He ran a hand over the horse's nose, then moved to his side, pulled the saddle down off his back, and hung it over the side of the stall.

He made quick work of brushing down and watering his mount. Loud snores greeted him from the bunk room where Ellis was sound asleep. He released a relenting sigh and fell onto the bottom bunk of the opposite set of beds.

Even though he was as tired as all get out, sleep eluded him. His mind raced through the events of the day and he called up a quick prayer of gratitude that they'd all made it through alive.

It had hardly seemed like any time had passed when Paulie came into the room and placed a hand on his shoulder.

"Will?" he said with a light shake.

"What's wrong?" he asked, sitting up quickly, and hitting his head on the boards of the upper bunk.

Blast it all.

"Everything's fine," Paulie said. "It's two o'clock and I am tuckered."

"Right." Will rubbed his head as he climbed out from the bed. He took the lantern from his riding partner and got out of the way, so Paulie could lie down.

The man pulled off his shirt and hung it over the footboard.

"Where did you get the bandages?" Will asked in a whisper, as to avoid waking Ellis.

"Eliza Beth found a box of supplies and she cleaned it up real good."

Will tilted his head, taken back a little by this information. "And just when did she do that?" he asked.

"Back about a half hour or so. She's a smart woman, that one. Good with a rifle too. And she is sure something to look at."

Will's jaw clenched and released.

That woman was trouble. She'd left the hotel after he'd dropped her off. He'd trusted she would do the smart thing and head on in to bed. A woman should not be out on the streets of an unfamiliar town alone in the middle of the night. He should have seen her inside. Made sure she'd gotten to her room safely before he'd left.

"Did she say anything?"

"Just that she needed to collect something before heading back over to the hotel."

Will shook his head.

Women.

Although, this woman was unlike any other he'd ever met. He liked her and that irked him. He walked out of the room without another word to start his rounds. It wasn't like he could go over to the hotel in the middle of the night and demand they check to see if she'd made it there.

There were still two of those bandits out there, and while Will still believed that they'd headed in the opposite direction of this town, he had no doubt that there were still people looking for this bankroll and he wasn't about to let anyone have it before he reached the train depot.

He checked both of his pistols and retrieved his rifle from the holster on his saddle bag. No one was going to get into this livery tonight. Not on his watch.

Once he stepped out into the street in front of the livery, he stretched again, peering out into the darkness. The sound of gravel crunching caught his attention and he strained to see ahead, his hand moving directly to his hip. Something in the distance, a blur in the shadows, was moving quickly toward him. He pulled his gun, resting it at his side, and held up the lantern high over his head to light the path.

Ruff. The lantern served as a beacon for the lost dog as she ran up to him like an old friend, pawing and dancing around his feet.

"Where'd you get off to, little one?" He holstered his weapon and scrunched down to scratch Caspar's head, behind the ears. "I'd thought we'd lost you, girl. Where'd you run off to?"

She jumped up and licked his face, but her tongue seemed awfully dry and it seemed her energy had been exhausted in finding them. He stood up and strode over to the water pump at the far edge of the livery yard and drew a few streams of water from the spigot.

Caspar lapped it up with enthusiasm.

"Are you hungry, girl?" he asked, pulling a couple of pieces of dried meat from his pocket.

Eliza Beth would be so relieved that her pup had found them. *He* was relieved that she'd found them. He didn't know what his family would do if they'd lost Seamus, their large white and gray sheepdog, and he couldn't imagine how difficult it had been for the woman not knowing if she would ever see Caspar again.

After she'd had her fill of the water, the red coonhound ran up to the door to the livery and scratched at the wood.

"What is it, girl?" Will asked. "Do you smell something?" He walked to the far side of the livery yard, scanning for any hint of trouble. After he took a quick round about the place, he would take Caspar inside for a bit and find her a place to sleep.

A noise caught his attention as they approached the backside of the building.

"Shhhh," he instructed quietly as he again pulled his sidearm. Will stood with his back up against the wall and carefully peeked around the corner. He couldn't see anything, but something rustled in the leaves a few yards ahead.

Without warning, Caspar shot out from behind him, barking loudly.

"Caspar!" he called in a loud whisper.

"Leave me alone," a young voice called out. "Let go."

Will peeked around the corner to see the coonhound biting the denim pockets of a small boy, who twisted and turned, trying to get away from the dog. He holstered his pistol again and strode up to them, the lantern high in the air.

"Hello," he said kindly. "It's all right, girl," he said, then clicked his tongue. "Caspar, let go." He blew a short, curt whistle and the hound released the boy's pants and sat down.

Without waiting for permission, the boy started to run, but Will caught him by the arm and swung him around, crouching down to meet him at eye level. He removed his hat, fingering the brim.

"It's late," he said, meeting the boy's eyes. "Your parents must be worried sick about you."

"I ain't got no parents," the youngster said loudly.

Will nodded his understanding. "That's got to be rough. Where are you staying?"

"I don't know."

"What are you doing out here all alone?" Will asked.

"I don't know."

"What's your name?"

"I don't know."

"Well, that's quite an unusual name, I Don't Know."

It looked as though the boy hadn't eaten in days. His face was smudged and his skin sallow.

"You hungry?"

The boy didn't say anything for a minute. "I don't know," he finally muttered with a single shrug.

"I've got some roast beef, potatoes, and corn bread inside."

The boy licked his lips, his eyes opening wide.

"Would you like some?"

He shrugged.

"Fruit jerky." Will stood up and walked back toward the front of the livery, Caspar at his heels. It probably wouldn't be the most enticing meal for a child, but he was grateful that his mother had been worried enough about him that she'd packed a knapsack full of foodstuffs that would last him days on the trail.

"Candied pecans," he continued, hoping to entice the boy further. Lottie's candied pecans would rival any of the large confectionaries out there. He moved slowly, smiling when he heard the tiny footsteps behind him.

Caspar reached the door first and immediately began scratching again at the wood.

Will opened the door and turned back to invite the boy in, but he wasn't there.

Damn.

He looked around for any sign of where the kid may have gone. He breathed out a laugh when he realized where he'd gone. The tip of his shoe was visible, peeking out at the bottom corner of the building.

"A slice of fresh-baked apple pie," Will called enticingly, continuing his list before going in and gently closing the door behind him.

He quickly walked back to his saddle bags and pulled out his knapsack, praying that he had caught the child's attention. He grabbed the chair that had been propped up against the livery office door and placed it in plain view of the window, setting his rifle at his side, then hung the lantern on a nail just above him. With very precise movements he peeled back each corner of the knapsack until the bounty of food was displayed prominently.

Movement in the window brought another smile to Will's face. He didn't want to look up directly at the child, but somehow, he knew the boy was there. Finally, after a few minutes had passed, Will finally looked up to see the look of longing on the boy's face, but as soon as he saw Will, he dropped back down out of view.

Will laughed as he stood up, walked to the door, and opened it.

The young orphan was crouched down, his arms around his knees as he looked up.

"Would you like to come in?"

After a moment's hesitation, he nodded.

The child stepped into the livery, glancing around as if he was researching all the exits. Will held up one finger as he strode over to the bunk room and reached inside the door to the left where he remembered seeing another chair. He pulled it out and set it next to his, inviting the youngster to sit.

"Roast beef?" Will asked.

His answer came in the form of a hearty nod.

Will pulled a fresh handkerchief from his pocket and set it on the boy's lap, then dished up a good helping of food. The kid stood stock still as if afraid or waiting for permission. Will didn't know which.

"Go ahead," Will prompted.

In seconds, the boy was trying to stuff everything into his face all at once.

"Whoa, slow down there, partner. You'll make yourself sick if you eat it like that."

"Okay," the muffled words came from between two very stuffed cheeks and the boy exaggerated his ability to chew.

"How long has it been since you've had a good meal?"

"I don't know," he said once he'd been able to swallow the food he had in his mouth.

Will raised a brow.

"Honest, I don't remember. A day or two, maybe. Name's Albert, by the way." He wiped his hand on his pants and held it out for Will to shake.

"Hello, Albert. I'm William."

"That's my brother's name," the boy said as he reached out for another piece of fruit jerky.

"Where is your brother?"

"Aw, he's with ma and pa. They're with God." He bowed his head, then slipped a small chunk of the jerky into his mouth.

Will had a lot of questions for Albert, but figured they could wait until after the youth had gotten some food into his belly.

A soft whimpering sound reached Will's ears, followed by a long bout of scratching against wood. He glanced over at the door, but Caspar was not there.

"I'll be right back," he told Albert, lighting a lantern to leave by the boy and taking the other on his venture to find the dog.

When he rounded the stage, he found Caspar scratching on the door into the coach.

"Silly dog," he said with a quick shake of his head. "Come on."

Caspar turned to look at him and sat down, whining softly.

"You don't need to sleep inside the cabin, girl. There are plenty of other places for you to lay your head. Come on." He hunched down and patted his legs, calling her to him.

Nothing.

"Oh, all right," he finally caved and walked toward the dog. He figured it wouldn't hurt anything to have the pup spend the night inside of the stage. She could probably still smell the lingering scent of her beautiful owner.

Will grabbed the latch of the door and pulled it open.

There, sleeping at an awkward angle, was the red-headed beauty who haunted his dreams.

"She looks funny."

Will whipped around to find Albert standing on the wheel axle and glancing through the open window at Eliza Beth.

"She drools." He seemed disinterested in her at that point and jumped down off the stage. "You got anywhere a man can sleep around here?" he asked with his seven-ish-year-old voice.

Will decided that he would have to come back and deal with Eliza Beth in a moment, but for now, he needed to settle the boy. At least until he could figure out what to do with him. Will guided him to the bunk room and bent down to meet his face.

"Now, there are other men sleeping in there, so you have to be real quiet. Do you understand?"

"Yes, sir."

"You can climb up onto the top bunk."

Albert nodded and Will patted him on the back.

"Do you love her?" he asked in a whisper before going all the way into the room.

"Who?"

"The drooly lady?"

"Go to bed," Will laughed, making a shooing motion at the boy.

Of course, he didn't love her, but he couldn't deny the attraction he felt to her. Besides, they'd only just met. People didn't fall in love that quickly. Did they?

Will walked back to the stagecoach and leaned against the open door. It would be a shame to wake her, but he wondered why she hadn't just stayed at the hotel where the beds would be much more comfortable than being strung out over two short, squat benches inside the very cramped enclosure of the wagon.

An idea struck and he quietly shut the door, walked out to where he'd enjoyed a short meal with Albert, quickly collected what remained of his food in the knapsack, and strode to the back of the livery where the horses slept.

After a few minutes of shoveling hay into one of the empty stalls, he grabbed his saddle blanket and the quilt his mother had made for him and spread them out over the bed of straw he'd created.

All the way back to the stage, he tried to figure out the best way to pull her from inside without waking her. The compartments were much smaller than he'd remembered. As he leaned in, he found it difficult to maneuver and realized the task was an impossible one. He couldn't just leave her there. She'd have a crick in her neck for days to come.

"Mrs. Jessup," he whispered, reaching out to touch her face, but she didn't rouse. "Mrs. Jessup," he called again, this time a little more loudly.

One eye opened half-way before closing again. She shifted in the seat and her satchel fell to the ground, spilling out all its contents. He finally just reached in, took a hold of one of her arms and pulled until she came willingly into his arms.

"Where are we going?" she asked sleepily.

"Go back to sleep," he whispered as he carried her into the back stall, the lantern dangling from his fingertips. He pulled back the quilt and gently laid her atop the makeshift bed.

She snuggled right down into the saddle blanket, twitching her nose a little before she settled back to sleep.

"Thank you," she muttered quietly.

Will tucked the quilt up around her neck and shoulders, then stood back and nodded in satisfaction. At least it would be more comfortable and warm than the benches in the stage's riding compartment.

When he returned to pick up the contents of the satchel he had arbitrarily dumped all over the floor of the compartment, he found that she was travelling very light. His sister Hannah would pack more than this for a trip into town and here this woman was moving across the country to start a new life. He figured she must have lost a lot when Ferg's place had burned to the ground.

Will reached into the compartment for the near empty bag and stuffed the brown paper-wrapped package back inside. A necklace with a large ruby pendant splayed across the floor and he picked it up, draping it over his hand. If it were real, it would have to be worth quite a bit. He dropped it back into the satchel, then reached down to collect several coins that had fallen to the floor.

Surely, the woman didn't just carry her money loosely in her satchel, so he looked around for some type of a coin purse. He decided it must still be inside the bag. She couldn't possibly be travelling cross country with only a few coins to her name.

Then, it dawned on him. The woman barely had two pennies to rub together. No wonder she had chosen not to sleep in the hotel last night. He shook his head, picking up a couple of books and photographs that had fallen.

He found a nice pocket at the side of the bag, but as he went to tuck the photographs inside, there, staring back at him were Sterling Archer, his wife, two sons, and Eliza Beth, wearing the same necklace he'd placed in the bag.

The red-headed woman who'd worked her way into his

waking thoughts was indeed Elizabeth Archer. He'd known it was a possibility, but somehow the truth of it felt like a punch to the gut. He held the photograph so tightly that he had to fight with himself in order to resist the urge to crumple it in his hands and throw it in her face.

What did she want with him? Had her father sent her? This was low, even for Sterling Archer and why have her pretend to be a mail-order-bride? How could she have possibly known he would take this job? There were so many questions that needed answers, but for now, he still had a job to do.

He picked up his rifle, placed his hat firmly on top of his head, and set out into the cool evening breeze. A brisk walk around the perimeter of the livery was just what he needed to clear his head.

Elizabeth Archer.
Damn.

CHAPTER FOURTEEN

Saturday

Elizabeth awoke to the wet, slobbery kisses of her coonhound.

"Caspar," she said, pushing the dog from her face.

It took a moment for her to remember where she was, then both eyes shot wide open and she sat up straight atop a large pile of hay. Her hand flew to her heart and she breathed a sigh of relief that the hound had made it into town unscathed.

The last thing she remembered was falling asleep in the stagecoach passenger compartment. Then, a hazy recollection of William Redbourne swarmed inside of her head. He'd done this. For her. She smiled.

The morning was quite chilly, so Elizabeth pulled the quilt up around her shoulders. She sniffed the material. It had to be Will's. It smelled like the soap he carried. She flopped back down onto the makeshift bedding. Why did the man have to be so attractive? It wasn't just his chiseled features and strong physique, but his protectiveness, his manners.

If she hadn't seen him fight in the ring, she would say he was a gentle man in every sense of the word, but she *had* seen him fight. Had seen the damage his fists could do to another person. He was beautiful. A man to be reckoned with. And somehow, that excited her and made her feel alive—safe, for the first time in a long time, but it also scared her a little. She needed to tell Will the truth. To clear the air between them.

She stayed put for a few more moments, then rolled off the bed—not considering what 'presents' may await her on the floor of a horse's stall. She pulled herself to her feet and, to her delight, she avoided any mishaps with manure.

In a matter of minutes, she'd folded both blankets and strung them over her arms as she walked up to the front of the livery.

"Hello," she called, but no one answered. She took a few more steps, surprised at how dark the room appeared for the morning hours. She'd seen the sun peeking through one of the slats in the livery's walls, so she knew she couldn't be mistaken about the time.

"Oh, hello," a balding man with a short, white apron said as he walked out of the livery office. "You must be the young woman Mr. Redbourne was speaking of. You're travelling west on the stage?"

She nodded. "Where is everyone?"

"It's just me and Nathanial around most of the time. Your Mr. Glenn has gone down to the restaurant for some breakfast and the outriders just stepped outside."

The clock on the side of the wall struck seven.

"If you'll excuse me, ma'am. It is time to open my doors," he said as he walked to the front of the building.

It took her a moment to remember that Mr. Glenn was the stagecoach driver. Breakfast sounded nice, but she figured that she would be all right to wait until supper was served on the train. For now, she couldn't wait to find Will and thank him for his consideration with the hay bed. And the quilt.

The liveryman grabbed ahold of one of the enormous barn-like doors and swung it wide, securing it to one of the posts at the opposite end of the livery, then moved to do the same with the other.

The morning rays poured into the stable like water from her mother's crystal vase. Elizabeth loved the sunshine. It reflected her cheery mood. She moved to the front of the building and leaned against the doorframe. Nothing could dampen a day like today.

She sucked in a breath as Will strode with purpose up the wooden planks that served as a boardwalk in this little town. As he moved toward her in his tan-colored shirt and black suspenders her whole chest seemed to fill with light.

"Good morning," she said as he passed her by without the slightest acknowledgement.

Maybe he didn't see me, she rationalized and hurried to catch up with him.

"I wanted to thank you," she started, moving her feet as fast as she could to keep up, "for the blankets last night. It was very kind o—"

"Mr. McFadden," Will said, ignoring her completely and speaking to the liveryman, "thank you for your hospitality. I know we came in late last night, but we appreciate the accommodations." He pulled something from his pocket and placed it in the stableman's hand—presumably money.

"I'm glad I could be of service. It's been a pleasure doing business with you." The man nodded and walked back into his office.

"Paulie," Will called out to the man pacing back and forth in front of the livery, "why don't you head down to the hotel and tell the ladies that it is time to go," he said, excusing the other guard from his sentry duty.

"As I was saying," Elizabeth tried again, but Will turned on his heel and headed toward the back of the building toward the stalls.

She stood there as he prepared his horse to ride, smiling to herself as he looked around for the saddle blanket.

"Are you looking for this?" she asked, holding it up.

He recognized her presence for the first time this morning, making eye contact.

"Thank you," he said gruffly as he walked toward her. He reached out for it, but she still held on until he met her eyes again.

"What's wrong with you?"

It took a moment before he responded, as if he were debating what he should say.

"I'm just trying to stay on your precious schedule." The overt anger in his voice confused her, but she let go of the saddle blanket all the same.

"I do not know what has happened to make you so angry with me, *Mr. Redbourne,*" she said, a little fire in her voice, "but I wanted to thank you for...for everything."

He looked at her, the hardness in his eyes startling her. "You are most welcome, *Miss Archer.*"

Elizabeth blinked.

He knew.

Heat filled her face and seeped down into her neck.

"Mr. Redbourne…" She didn't know what to say, so she fumbled with the quilt still in her arms. "Let me explain." She raised her chin into the air.

"Don't bother. There's nothing to explain," he bit back at her. "I'm supposed to be in Boston buying a beautiful ship that will give me the opportunity of a lifetime, but instead, I am here with you." He threw his saddle over his horse's back and worked at fastening the straps. "Look, I have a job to do and that is to get you and the others on the train in Kansas City, and that is exactly what I am going to do. Nothing more. Nothing less."

"I will not make excuses for my choices," she replied coolly. Her jaw clenched together and she wanted to say something snide back to him, but thought better of it. A lady was better than that. "Thank you again for all of your help…" *That was good.* "But I assure you, I require nothing further from you." She draped the quilt over the stall gate and walked away—a single tear threatening to fall down her face. She wiped it away briskly, straightened her gait, and headed for the stage.

This was looking to be the longest ride of her life. At least it would be over in a couple of hours.

"Damn!"

Will threw the grooming brush against the far wall.

"Mama said curse words show a person's lack of proper schooling."

Will turned to see the young orphan boy he'd encountered last night standing at the base of the stall staring up at him, Caspar protectively at his side.

"Good morning," he grumbled, bothered that he could not remove the irritation from his voice.

"Mama also said sometimes a man fights with the people he loves most."

"I don't love her, Albert."

"Why not? She's awfully pretty."

He did not want to answer the boy's questions any more. "How did you sleep? Are you hungry?"

"I think there was a bear in the room last night. He growled awful loud."

Will laughed, feeling better for the first time this morning. "Nah, I think that was just Old Ellis. He kind of sounds like a bear."

Will took Indy by the reins and led him out of the stall and into the main hall of the livery next to the stagecoach.

Paulie had returned with Opal and Gertrude, and Ellis was helping them load their bags back on top of the wagon. Elizabeth was already seated inside, reading one of her books as if she hadn't a care in the world. It was hard to imagine the daughter of Sterling Archer as a mail-order-bride and a pit formed in his stomach.

He turned to Albert. "What do you say we head over to the restaurant and get some breakfast?" They would be leaving soon and he needed to find somewhere for the boy to go. Somewhere where he'd be safe and well taken care of, and he needed time he didn't have to find that.

"I don't wanna put you out none," Albert said, craning his neck to look up at him, his bravado shining through admirably.

"I think I'll manage." Will laughed. "Come on." He stopped next to Ellis. "I'll be back shortly. You and Paulie have everything under control here."

"Looks like you found yourself another stray," Ellis snorted.

Will placed a hand on Albert's shoulder. "Don't listen to him. He's just jealous I make friends wherever I go."

"Eh, get outta here." Ellis waved his hand in the direction of the café. "But don't be too long," he called after them as they headed over to the restaurant, followed closely by Caspar.

When they arrived at the eatery, Will pulled the last piece of meat jerky from his pocket and placed it on the boardwalk in front of the pup before they walked inside.

"Well, aren't you two just the cutest things I ever seen," the waitress said as she walked up to their table. She raised an eye at Will and smiled coyly.

"We'll take the special with a large glass of milk for my friend, here," Will said with a wink at Albert.

"One hearty plate of flapjacks and bacon coming right up."

"Albert," Will started once they settled down into their seats, "where have you been sleeping at night?" The boy had to have run away from somewhere in town. He hoped the sheriff would know where to find them.

The boy shrugged. "I don't know. Here and there, I guess."

"How long have you been alone?"

"Willie died last year and I've been pretty much on my own ever since."

The woman brought a large glass of milk and set it down in

front of Albert. He looked up at Will as if waiting for permission.

Will nodded.

Albert picked up the glass and started to drink—and didn't stop until the very last drop was gone.

Will raised a hand to get the woman's attention. "We'll have another please."

Albert beamed as he used the back of his arm to wipe the milk-made moustache off his upper lip.

How was he supposed to find a place for Albert to go in the next half hour? Will didn't know the people in this little town. And, he had a job to do, which did not include finding homes for orphans, so, why did he feel responsible for this kid?

Once the food had been placed on the table and another glass of milk in front of Albert, Will watched as the young boy started shoveling flapjacks into his mouth. After a moment, Albert glanced up at him. He sat up straight, wiped the sides of his mouth with a napkin, and swallowed the food already in his mouth. With great care, the boy picked up his fork to cut off a small piece of the hotcake.

Smart.

"Can I get you kids anything else?"

It had been a long time since someone had called him a kid. Will shook his head. "Thank you." Then, just as the woman turned to leave he thought better of it. "On second thought, would you mind bagging up a couple of muffins and some pie?"

"Of course. I'll be right back."

It didn't take long before they had some boxes to take with them.

As they walked outside, Caspar jumped up and happily followed them back toward the livery. Will pretended not to notice, but Albert had shoved a handful of crisp bacon into his pocket and now the coonhound would reap the benefits.

"The ladies are all loaded and we are ready to go." Ellis looked down at the boy. "I see you've still got yourself a friend,

Redbourne."

"Albert," he said, "this is Mr. Glenn."

"Pleased to meet ya," Albert said extending his hand. "Officially."

Ellis looked from the boy to Will and back again before shaking his hand. There was a little rivet that formed on the man's forehead and his brows scrunched together as if not knowing what else to say.

The time had come. Will had to decide what to do.

"Albert," he said, dropping down onto his haunches, "I'm going to take you over to the sheriff's office. He's going to help us find you a place to live."

"Why can't I live with you?" he asked innocently.

"I don't live here, Albert. We're just passing through. The stage is headed for Colorado."

"Colorado sounds nice. Who's he?"

Will chuckled. "Colorado is a place a little west and north from here."

"Doesn't God live up north?"

How did he answer a question like that?

"God lives in Heaven, little man. I'm afraid we can't get there on the stage, or train, or even walking, but He is always in our hearts. Just like your ma and pa and Willie. They live in your heart too."

Will could see the wheels turning in the boy's head.

"I see," Albert said, dropping his head to look at his chest. He climbed up into the chair in front of the work table, his legs dangling, his elbows resting on his knees, his chin in his hands.

He sat there quiet for a few minutes, then he sat up tall and poked Will in the chest.

"How'd you get so big and strong?" he asked simply.

The question caught Will off guard, but he thought about it for a moment before answering.

"Work." And being a Redbourne didn't hurt.

"In case you haven't noticed, I'm kind of small. I'm going

to need to make some room or it's going to get really crowded in here." Albert pointed to his chest.

The sentiment pulled at Will's heartstrings. He wrapped an arm around the kid and pulled him in tight.

"I bet you already have more room than most, kid." He ruffled Albert's hair.

Caspar barked happily, then nudged into the boy, licking his face.

Albert giggled.

"Excuse me, Mr. Glenn, but how long before we leave?" Elizabeth stepped down off the stage, avoiding Will's eyes. "We are already three quarters of an hour behind schedule."

Will was sure that last part was for his benefit.

"We're just making one little stop and then we'll be on our way, Mrs. Jessup."

Will's jaw flexed.

Elizabeth nodded and turned back, climbing into the coach.

"She's still mad at you, you know," Albert said matter-of-factly.

"I know."

"Ma said the hardest part about fighting is saying you're sorry, but it's always worth it in the end."

"Your ma was a pretty smart lady, Albert." Will clapped him on the shoulder. "Can you stay put for a just a few minutes?" he asked the boy. "I have to stop in at the telegraph office and then we'll head over to see the sheriff."

Albert nodded, but Will had seen that look before. The kid was a runner.

"Paulie," he called to his partner, "can you watch Albert until I return?"

"Sure thing, Will."

The telegraph office was only a few doors down the boardwalk. Try as he might, the idea of leaving Albert in this little town all alone did not sit well with Will and he wondered if there was anyone looking after the boy since his parents and brother had passed. If so, were they abusive or cruel and that is why he'd run away from them, or were they good folks and Albert just hadn't given them a chance? Either way, he couldn't leave Plain City until he knew the youngster had a home and would be taken care of properly.

Mrs. Day, the mercantile owner in Stone Creek, had been working to unite orphaned children with couples from the valley who'd been unable to have children of their own. Will knew that there were plenty of families in his home town who would be able to provide a loving home for the boy. A quick telegram home explaining the situation would assure that his mother would be on the next stage to collect Albert and sort out the situation. She was good at that.

"Thank you, sir," he told the telegrapher with a nod as he passed the man a small piece of paper with his scribbled note for this mother.

Less than a quarter of an hour later, he returned to the livery. He walked over to Indy and untied him from the hitching post.

"Thanks, Paulie," he said to the man sitting in a staring competition with the young boy.

"Paulie can wiggle his ears without moving his face, Will. You should see," he said without blinking.

"Maybe later, Albert. We need to get going, and I need to talk to you. Come here."

The youngster quickly broke his stare and joined him. Will lifted the boy up into the saddle and then climbed up behind him.

"You know, you should be in school, Albert," he said as they rode to the edge of town and around the corner toward the jailhouse.

"I don't have much need for schoolin'. Besides, I already know how to add. Two plus two is four. And I can spell. Albert. A.L.B.E.R.T. See?"

"That's very good. Did your mama teach you that?"

"Uh-huh."

"Well, I know a place where there are lots of other boys your age and I think you'd really like it there?"

"Where?" he asked brightly.

"It's a place called Stone Creek and it's not too far from here."

"Will you be there?"

"Not for a while, but my family lives there."

"Why aren't you with your family?"

Albert was full of questions. Will loved seeing the boy's curiosity and wonder and hoped they would be able to find somewhere very special for him back home.

"I have a job to do. I made a commitment to the stagecoach company that I would make sure this stage makes it to its destination safely. Do you know what a commitment is, Albert?"

"Is that like a promise?"

"Sure is. And do you know why it's important to always keep your commitments?"

Albert raised his hand to his chin and pondered the question.

"So people will trust ya?" he asked, both eyebrows raised as he turned around, looking up at Will and anticipating his response.

"That's right. Now, I need a commitment from you, Albert."

The boy turned to look forward so Will could no longer see his face.

"I need you to promise me that you will be good and stay put. I can't be worried whether or not you're getting a square meal or that you might not have someplace to sleep while I'm on this job keeping the others safe. Can you do that for me, Albert?"

The young boy twisted his head to one side and then the other.

"Albert," Will coaxed.

"Okay. But where will I be staying and who's going to make sure my meal is square?"

Will laughed.

"You'll stay with the sheriff in this town until someone from my family can make it up here to collect you."

"Does that mean I'm going to be your...your brother?"

"How about we just say we are brothers in spirit for now?"

"Okay," Albert's shoulders rose and fell in a shrug.

When they reached the sheriff's office, Will climbed down off the horse, leaving Albert sitting in the saddle. "Wait right here for a minute, okay Albert?" he said as he hung Indy's reins over the hitching post there.

The boy nodded.

The sheriff sat leaned back in his chair, his feet crossed on his desk, and his hat resting peacefully over his face.

Will cleared his throat.

"Is someone dead?" the sheriff asked dryly.

"Yes, as a matter fact they are," Will responded with the same sarcasm. "Three outlaws. Out in the ravine."

The lawman took the hat from his face, returned the chair legs to the floor, and looked up at him. "What can I do for you, Mr. Redbourne?" he asked, folding his hands in front of him on the desk.

"I met a young boy last night who claims he has no folks looking after him. I can't very well take him with us on the stage, but I want to see to it that he is provided for and kept safe while I'm gone. I was hoping I could leave him here with you until someone from Stone Creek can come to collect him."

"This boy, is he about yay big," he held up his hand about Albert's height, "light straggly hair, and a real fast talker?"

Will laughed. "Sounds like him all right. You know him?"

"I think you're talking about Albert Henshaw?"

"You know Albert?" Will asked, his forehead crinkling into ruts.

"This would be the third time this month the boy has run away."

"He has a family?"

"Well, I don't know that I'd call them family exactly." The sheriff scratched his chin with the back knuckles of his hand. "The Bartlett's took him in last year and have him helping out on their farm."

Will sat down in the seat opposite the sheriff, irked with himself for not asking more questions and blindly trusting what Albert had told him.

"So, what was he doing out behind the livery in the middle of the night? Do the Bartlett's not know or care where he is?" Now, Will was beginning to get angry—though he reminded himself that it would be easy to not realize the boy had been missing until morning. Still, it was getting on in the day. How could these people not be worried sick that a seven-year-old boy was missing?

"I'm sure he just snuck out again and they haven't noticed he's gone yet."

"Haven't noti—" Will stood up, his hat in hand. "I need to meet these people, sheriff."

"I thought the stage was leaving this morning."

"We are." He needed to talk to Albert.

"It might take some time to get out to their farm." The sheriff pushed himself away from the desk and placed his hat on his head.

Will nodded. They were already a day behind thanks to those ruffians in the ravine, a couple more hours couldn't hurt. When they walked outside, Albert and Indy had disappeared. Will shook his head. How could he have been so...so...naïve? Something was obviously wrong to make the boy so wary of going back to the Bartlett's. Will glanced down the street and saw nothing. He made one loud whistle, followed by two short whistles, then waited.

It wasn't long before Indy moseyed around the corner at a

leisurely pace with Albert still in the saddle. Thank heaven his brother, Tag, had trained Indy well.

"No, boy," Albert was saying as he pulled on the reins, "this way." When the kid looked up and caught glimpse of Will, his eyes grew wide and his lip started to quiver.

What on earth had the Bartlett's done to this child that he would respond with actual fear?

Will took a deep breath.

In. He counted to four. *Out.* He counted again.

"Where you going, Albert?" he asked casually.

"I don't know."

Not back to this again.

"Come here," Will said. "I'd like to have a talk with you, man to man."

Once Indy was within range, Will took ahold of his reins, wrapped them around the hitching post, and reached up for the boy.

"I'm not going back there. I'm not!" Albert said stubbornly, folding his arms in front of his chest, his mouth scrunched into a pout and his brows firmly knit together. "And you can't make me. Nobody can," he said, his eyes narrowed as he looked up at the sheriff defiantly.

"Don't you think Mrs. Bartlett will be awfully worried that you didn't come home last night?"

"No. But, she'll be real mad that I didn't milk the stupid cow. She'll have to get Richie or one of the other boys to do it."

Will knelt down next to him.

"Now, I'm sure that's not true, Albert."

"Sheriff!" A woman marched up onto the planks in front of the jailhouse, her face red, her mouth curved into a snarl.

Albert jumped behind Will.

"I see you found that little brat of mine. Where was he this time?" She reached out toward the boy, but Caspar hopped up onto the boardwalk between her and Albert, teeth bared and a deep growl offering a warning. She barked, her stance ready for a fight.

Will raised up to his full height, keeping himself between the boy and the woman.

"It's all right, girl," Will said, reaching down and scratching the top of the pup's head. "You must be Mrs. Bartlett," he said with the most charming smile he could muster. He tipped his hat. "My name is Will Redbourne. I'm a friend of Albert's."

She snorted. "That boy doesn't have any friends."

Caspar growled.

"You'd better keep that mutt away from me," she spat, still recoiling from the animal.

She wasn't making it any easier to like her.

"And, don't you think you are going to waltz in here and take that child away from us. We done paid ten dollars for that brat, not to mention his room and board, and he ain't done his chores this mornin'."

Will swallowed, then looked down at Albert who shot him an, 'I told you' look.

In. Two, three, four.

Out. Two, three, four.

"A whole ten dollars?" Will whistled, trying to calm himself. "That's a lot of money."

"You're tellin' me. Now," she tried a smile that did not reach her eyes, "may I have the boy? Please?" she squeaked out with false politeness, her teeth grinding together, her nostrils flaring.

Will placed a hand protectively at his side, and rubbed the boy's shoulder.

"See, I just don't think I can do that."

"Wha...? Sheriff," the woman said in warning.

The coonhound leapt toward her with a bark. She quickly recoiled, a sour look contorting her face. Will could see the indignation stirring in her eyes.

"Caspar!" Will called with sternness. The dog whimpered lightly, hung her head, then backed up and sat down next to

Albert.

"Mr. Redbourne, the law is pretty clear in the matter," the sheriff said. "The boy belongs to her."

"The boy doesn't *belong* to anyone." Will's mind raced. He could not take Albert with him, but he was not about to leave him in the care of this woman. "How much do you want for him?" Just the words on his tongue left a bitter taste in his mouth.

If he knew anything, it was people, and he knew that this Mrs. Bartlett did not care two hoots for Albert. He narrowed his eyes at the woman and waited for her number.

CHAPTER FIFTEEN

Will had been gone for nearly half an hour. What could possibly be keeping him?

Elizabeth wanted nothing more right now than to get on the road and be on her way to her new life. While the idea of being a preacher's wife still terrified her, it had to be better than being on the trail or worse yet, living out her life a spinster in the west. At least this way, she would finally be able to settle down in a quiet little place with a home of her own where there wasn't drama at every turn. She hoped. She needed to be somewhere she would be safe. Protected. Somewhere she could live a good life with a good man, out from under the scrutiny of London society.

Safe, she repeated the word in her mind. Was that really what she wanted? To be safe?

How many times had she been in the throes of one of her novels and wished that she could have some of that adventure in her life?

Too many.

However, she knew exactly what it was like to be in the middle of excitement all right. Only it had been the kind that had landed professional boxers in her lap to be stitched up— something she had never been trained to do, but had done anyway—or nursed back to health after a beating. She was glad to leave that life behind her and to look forward to something new. Something…good.

She turned back the page in her book, unable to remember what she'd just read. After scanning a few paragraphs that suddenly looked like script from the Greek alphabet, she snapped it shut and pushed open the compartment door.

"Where are you going?" Opal asked.

"We're supposed to stay put," Gertrude added. "I thought you wanted to stay on schedule."

Sitting still in the overly small compartment of a stagecoach with two prissy mail-order-brides was not going to get them closer to their destination any faster.

"Don't get your knickers in a bunch," she said to a shocked Gertrude. "I'm just going to stretch my legs for a few minutes before we get on the road. We certainly will not be leaving without our escorts, now will we?"

She slipped outside before either of the women could respond.

"Mr. Glenn," she said, looking up at the driver's box to the man who looked as anxious as she felt to get on the road, "are we still waiting on Mr. Redbourne? Do you know where he has gone?"

"He found a stray and is trying to get the matter settled."

A stray? Odd.

"I am sorry, but could you tell me where?"

Mr. Glenn flicked his wrist down the road. Her gaze stopped at the telegraph office, but she did not see Will's mount there anymore.

"Thank you," Elizabeth said before trekking down the street, the hem of her dress gathered up in her hands, so it didn't drag on the street.

The sun shone brightly this morning—a far cry from the rain-filled cloudy day they'd had when they'd arrived in this little town. Puddles still accentuated the road, but that was the only sign a storm had blown through. She passed the telegraph office and continued down the street toward the blacksmith shop that capped the end of the road. There was still no sign of Will.

As she rounded the corner, Elizabeth froze. Will stood in heated conversation with a pinched-faced woman, tension pulsing through the air around them like stones grinding wheat. She quickly moved to the edge of the street, next to one of the buildings and watched.

Movement pulled her eyes to the dog sitting protectively next to the boy, ears alert.

Caspar!

She quietly made her way to stand behind them.

The woman bent backward slightly, shoving her arms together, folding them in front of her. She tilted her head back and closed one eye until it was a mere slit as she eyed Will, considering something he had said. Elizabeth quietly stepped forward, straining to hear their conversation.

"You think money would fill the hole it would make in our lives if we lost him? He already has a nice home with us," she said. "Siblings who care for him. A place to run and play. A father and a mother."

"You are not my mother!" the young boy yelled as he stepped out briefly from behind Will. "My mama wasn't mean like you. She baked fruit breads. She smelled like cinnamon. And she read to me every night. She didn't make me sleep in the barn. Or pull my hair when I did something wrong. She loved me!" He looked up at Will. "She loved me," he repeated.

Elizabeth's breath caught in her chest and she longed to pull the boy protectively into her arms and offer him comfort.

The woman laughed uneasily.

Will's jaw flexed, his hands balled into fists.

"How much?"

"Fifty dollars!" Mrs. Bartlett blurted, as if that were some astronomical amount.

Will wanted nothing more than to wipe that self-satisfied smirk off the woman's face, but that wouldn't accomplish anything.

Albert nudged in a little closer to him, then tugged at the bottom of his shirt.

"Sheriff, you heard her?" Will asked, turning to look at the lawman.

"Yes, sir. I did."

Will turned back and bent down to face Albert at eye level. He caught a glimpse of Elizabeth standing in the background next to Caspar. He shook his head and focused his attention on the boy.

"Do you want to go to Stone Creek, Albert?" He spoke in low tones.

The youngster nodded hesitantly. "But…," he looked down at his feet, "fifty dollars is a lot of money. I…I can't let you do that for me." He stepped around Will and took a step toward Mrs. Bartlett before pausing and looking back over his shoulder. "I appreciate all you done, Will," he said, "but I'll go with her. Maybe you could come visit me sometime." His eyes were big and his brows lifted with hope.

Will bit his lip to hide the amazed chuckle that threatened.

Mrs. Bartlett reached out toward the boy, a haughty expression distorting her already pinched face.

Caspar growled. The low, rumbling sound grew until it culminated in several barks.

Elizabeth reached down and patted the top of the pup's head.

Will nodded at the animal. "I wouldn't push it with that one," he warned the woman trying to take Albert. He strode over to where his black and white mount waited, reached into his saddle bags, and fiddled with the roll of bills he kept there.

"Will," Elizabeth whispered loudly, "do something. You

cannot just let him go. Not with the likes of her." She'd settled easily back into her British accent.

He didn't say anything, didn't even look at Elizabeth, but he held the money firmly in his hand and closed his eyes in a silent prayer for strength. As much as he hated giving money to the likes of a troll like Mrs. Bartlett, he wanted Albert to know he had value. And not just as a stable hand or indentured servant.

The woman had already turned back toward her wagon, Albert firmly gripped beneath her hand on his shoulder, but before Will could say anything, Elizabeth stepped forward.

"I'm afraid I cannot let you take him," she said as she reached into her pocket.

"Are you with him?" Mrs. Bartlett asked, nudging her nose toward Will.

Elizabeth locked eyes with him, then turned back to the woman.

"She's…my…" What did he say? His wife? His sister? His charge? The woman who hates him? He moved closer to her and wrapped his arm around her shoulder.

She looked up at him incredulously. "We're travelling together with the stage," Elizabeth filled in for him. "He's the outrider accompanying us to Kansas City."

Will leaned down slightly and whispered into her ear through the corner of his mouth. "What are you doing?"

"Saving a boy from the likes of that woman," she responded under her breath. "And I don't need to be…*anyone* to you to do it."

"I've got it under control."

Elizabeth ignored him and stepped out from under his arm toward Mrs. Bartlett and Albert. "I'm afraid I do not have fifty dollars, but I am sure we could come to some other arrangement." She pulled out a few bills and held them out for the woman to see.

Will stood there, astounded at Elizabeth's gesture.

"That's barely what I paid for him," Mrs. Bartlett sneered. "Wouldn't be near enough to cover expenses for another one. Not to mention the days' worth of work that won't get done in the meantime. No, Albert is coming with me."

The boy's eyes lit up at Elizabeth's offer, then he smiled in resignation and waved as they turned back for the wagon again.

"My father," she called loudly, then her voice softened a little, "has money. I'll even give you something extra for your time."

Of course, she would turn to her father.

Mrs. Bartlett stopped and turned around. "Why do you want him anyway? He's just a scrawny little brat. Not much good for working the fields yet."

Will could not believe the audacity of the woman. How dare she speak about Albert that way? He suddenly felt sorry for her husband and children and had a new appreciation for his own mother. Heaven knew she'd put up with a lot from her eight children.

"How much extra?" Mrs. Bartlett mulled over the offer.

"Elizabeth," Will called to her, hoping to make her understand that he was prepared to take care of the situation right now.

"Shhhh," Mrs. Bartlett snapped. "Don't interrupt the girl, Mr. Redbourne. I want to hear what she has to say."

Will held up a fifty-dollar bill and the woman swallowed hard.

Elizabeth's jaw dropped.

"I believe we were in agreement first. Here is your money, Mrs. Bartlett." He pulled it tight between his hands, then turned to the lawman. "The only stipulation I have, Sheriff, is that the Bartlett's do not get to 'buy' any more children to be like an unpaid hired hand on their farm." He turned back to the woman. "It is one thing to have your own children doing chores, but to use any child the way you have used Albert is just wrong."

"We've never used Albert like a hired hand," Mrs. Bartlett

protested indignantly. "He works to earn his keep. We feed him, clothe him, and provide a bed for him to sleep in just as if he was one of our own."

"It's all right, Will. I can be strong like you—even if Richie gives me another black eye or I get another lickin' for running away." Albert stood between him and the woman.

Will's jaw clenched together and a fresh wave of determination washed over him. "Those are my terms." He held out the money. "Do you agree?"

Mrs. Bartlett eyed the bill, the temptation apparent on her features. After a few moments, she rushed forward, snatched the money from Will's hands, and shoved Albert toward him. "You can have the lazy little thing," she said, admiring the money and licking her lips before turning to march away.

"Sheriff?" Will said, placing a protective hand on Albert's shoulder.

"I'll see to it," the sheriff responded with a nod, unsmiling.

Albert ran toward Will who scrunched down, scooped him up, and hugged him, Caspar dancing on her hind legs at his feet.

"I can't believe you did that. Just for me."

"Just between you and me, kiddo, I would have paid a lot more for your freedom," he whispered.

Albert beamed.

Will set him back on the ground and handed the sheriff a few bills.

"I don't want your money, Redbourne. It was enough just to see the look on that woman's face. Don't you worry none. I'll keep him with me until your kin comes for him."

Will extended a hand and the sheriff took it in a firm shake. "You ought to be catchin' up to that little lady of yours, Redbourne. She's quite a beauty. Didn't look none too pleased with you, though."

Will turned to see Elizabeth disappear around the corner, headed back toward the livery.

"Mr. Redbourne, sir?" someone called from behind him.

Will twisted around.

The telegraph operator stopped right in front of the boardwalk and bent over, his hands on his knees to catch his breath. "I'm so glad I caught you before you left." He stood up long enough to hand Will a telegram.

"Thank you," he said with a grateful nod of his head. "Are you all right?" he asked, when the man hunched back down and exhaled loudly.

"I don't get out…" he swallowed, "from behind that desk," he inhaled sharply, "nearly enough," he said, nodding. "I'll be fine." He made a shooing motion with his hands as he staggered back toward the telegraph office.

After scanning its contents, Will turned back to the sheriff. "My father will be in Jacksonville on Thursday to pick up a load of lumber. He'll be by to collect Albert sometime that afternoon." He handed the man some money. "This should be enough to look after the boy until then."

The bright light he'd seen in Albert's eyes just a moment ago quickly extinguished. "You're still leaving me behind?"

"How about we talk to 'the drooly lady'…" Will started.

Albert perked up at the use of his term for Elizabeth.

"…and see if she'll allow Caspar to stay here with you and keep you company?"

Albert nodded heartily.

Caspar barked.

Will laughed.

"It's settled then."

CHAPTER SIXTEEN

As Elizabeth stepped up onto the metal stair into the stage compartment, the welcoming sound of Caspar's bark filled her ears. She looked back and saw the coonhound running toward her in front of Will astride the black mount that looked like it had a shooting star on his forehead.

She swallowed, unable to deny the attraction she felt for the man. He was so handsome. Heat seeped into her cheeks as she noticed the way his denims clung to the muscles in his legs.

You are angry with him, Elizabeth Archer. Don't forget that!

Her focus returned to the dog and she stepped back down off the metal rung and dropped to her haunches in greeting. However, when Caspar reached her, the hound was still moving too quickly and knocked Elizabeth backward and onto her hind end. Now, the heat rushed into her face as Caspar licked her cheeks and chin. A resigned giggle escaped her lips as she brushed the dog's head with her fingertips.

Will slid off his horse in one smooth movement and was at her side in a moment, offering her his hand.

She blew a stray hair from the front of her face and, reluctantly, slipped her hand into his. He pulled her into a standing position—a little too close to be comfortable—and looked down at her, his eyes unreadable.

"Thank you," she said, unsmiling.

"I'd like to talk about what happened back there."

"I wouldn't," she responded coolly.

"Look, I know you are still angry with me, but...I have a proposition for you," Will said as she turned back to the stage.

She whipped around, eyes narrowed, and ready to attack.

"Bad choice of words," he laughed uneasily. "Not that kind of proposition."

Elizabeth turned to face him head on, her hands together resting in front of her. "I'm listening."

"I'd like to buy your dog."

That was not at all what she had been expecting. She glanced over at Caspar, who was busily lapping up water from the bucket the liveryman had placed at the door.

"You want to *buy*...my dog," she repeated incredulously. For the moment, they were together, why would he need to buy the dog from her?

"Yes."

Caspar had been by her side when she'd had no one. She'd already thought she'd lost her. Twice. And she didn't know if she could stand the thought of willingly giving her up. She'd had a hard enough time placing her puppies.

"Why do you want to buy my dog?"

"Does it matter?"

"Yes."

Will looked down at his shoes and then back at her, the dark brown varnish of his eyes warming her from the inside out.

"Caspar is not for sale." Though she was down to her last few dollars and couldn't deny having money in her pockets again would make her feel better about moving across the country. Still, it was Caspar.

"Come with me." He held out a hand.

She eyed him warily. "Why?"

"Trust me."

"Trust you?" Elizabeth shook her head and started to turn

away.

"Will," Mr. Glenn called down from the driver's box.

"Can you give me just ten more minutes, Ellis?"

When the driver nodded, Will turned back to look at her, his face a little closer than she had remembered.

"Can we call a truce?" he asked. "Just for the moment?"

He was the one who started all this nonsense to begin with. *Argggg!* She wanted to yell her frustration.

"Fine," she relented.

He swept a hand in front of him, indicating his intention to get her back on his horse.

She didn't budge.

"Please?" he asked.

Elizabeth imagined that he got most anything he wanted when he used that smile as a weapon. She shook her head in annoyance, exhaled loudly, and stepped past him toward the horse. Without waiting for his assistance, she lifted her skirt, put her foot in the stirrup, and using the saddle horn as leverage, pulled herself up into the seat. At least she'd worn the new split skirt Mrs. Weaver had traded to her.

"I do learn things from my books, you know," she said at the surprised expression glancing off Will's handsome face.

He chuckled and pulled himself up behind her.

They rode a single block down the road to the sheriff's office. She wanted to make some quip about him wanting to snuggle with her, but she didn't feel like lightening the mood.

"We couldn't have walked one block?" she asked instead.

"Maybe, but I didn't want you to have any place to run."

When he lifted her down off the horse, he set her on the ground, but did not let go of her waist until she looked up at him and met his eyes.

"We have a lot to discuss, but try to remember that it is me you are upset with."

"You're taking me to jail?"

"Albert!" he called.

The sheriff stepped outside and a small boy came rushing forward.

"What did she say?" he asked, his eyes wide with anticipation.

"Miss Archer, this is Albert."

"Hi, drooly lady." He took a step forward with his hand extended.

She looked at Will. "Drooly lady?"

"It's a long story," Will replied, nodding his encouragement.

Elizabeth placed her hand in the small boy's and he bent down to kiss her fingers. "It's a pleasure to make your acquaintance, ma'am," he said with a slight bow. He turned to Will. "Did I do it right?" he whispered loudly.

"What a little gentleman," she said, losing the American accent. "Surely, he didn't learn that from you," she teased, despite her best intentions.

"You did just fine, Albert," Will told him, ruffling his long, straight, and straggly hair. "Elizabeth…"

She squirmed a little. Nobody had called her Elizabeth in months, yet Will had used the name several times this morning.

"You talk funny," the boy said matter-of-factly.

"That is because I am from a place called England. Have you ever heard of it?"

"Uh, huh. My mama said it was across the whole ocean. How did you get here? To this consonant?"

"I think you mean, continent."

"Right."

"Well, I travelled in a carriage, then I got onto a giant boat…"

"You mean a ship?" He looked at Will with a grin.

Will nodded his approval and winked at the boy.

Elizabeth laughed.

"Yes, Albert, you are right, it was a ship. A really big one. Then after taking a train, riding in a covered wagon, and walking a lot, I arrived in Stone Creek where I met up with Mr. Redbourne and he brought me here on the stage."

"I think you had him at 'ship,'" Will teased.

"I'm going to ride on a train someday. And sail in a ship," Albert said proudly, puffing out his chest. He exhaled and took a step toward her, tilting his head to look up at her. He slipped his hand into hers. "Thank you for everything you done. It was real nice of ya. Especially, since you didn't know nothing about me."

"Anything," she corrected. "I didn't know anything about you."

"Right." He turned to Will. "I see why you like her," he whispered loud enough for Elizabeth to hear. "She reminds me of my mama."

She glanced over at Will, who smiled at her uneasily.

"Is Caspar your dog?" Albert asked in the sweetest little voice she had ever heard.

"Yes."

"She's real special. I can tell."

"What makes you say that, Albert?" she asked, curious at his assessment.

"'Cause I don't feel all alone when she's with me. Does she do that for you too?"

She looked at Will and then back at the boy.

"You know, Albert," she said as she moved to sit on the top step leading up to the sheriff's office, "I think she is special for just that reason. It wasn't very long ago that I was all alone, travelling to a new place to live, and she found me."

"She found *you*?" he asked disbelievingly.

"She did. And she has stayed by my side ever since. She even scared off some bad guys when they threatened me."

"Whoa!" he exclaimed as he sat down next to her, his eyes wide. She had his full attention.

"Caspar is playful and fun, but she is very courageous too. Did you know that she even pulled me out of a burning house?"

"She did?" Will asked. "I think I missed that part of the story."

"It doesn't matter. It's over now and I am headed someplace else to start over."

"You must be real special," Albert said. "Caspar wouldn't have come to you otherwise." As if on cue, Caspar loped up to the side of the boy and sat down, her head resting on his lap.

"You seem pretty special too, Albert."

"Albert lost his parents a while back," Will chimed in, "and then his brother last year. I found him late last night out behind the livery. I guess he's been living with a family who…um…"

"I saw. Or did you forget?"

"It's okay," Albert said. "The Bartlett's took me in when nobody else would. But, they just weren't very nice folks. Not like you and Will. So, I ran away." He scratched the pup's ears.

Elizabeth didn't know what to say. Maybe it was time to let Caspar help somebody else. She stood up. "Well played, Mr. Redbourne."

Will raised his hands, shrugged his shoulders, and shook his head as if he hadn't known what would happen.

"You know, I was thinking, Albert…" Elizabeth took a deep breath to muster the courage to do what she was about to do. "Colorado is pretty far away and a really long walk for a dog like Caspar. Would you want to watch over her for me and keep her safe with you?"

"Oh, boy, would I ever!" he said, jumping up and throwing his arms around her.

Caspar barked happily and Elizabeth giggled through the tears that had collected in her eyes. One slipped down her face, then two. The choice to leave her family behind and start over all alone had been hers. Albert hadn't had that choice and she reasoned that he needed the young coonhound more than she did. She hugged him to her a little tighter as if gaining strength from his excitement.

"Okay, enough of this," Will said, tugging on Elizabeth's

arm. "I'm afraid we have to be going, Albert."

"Don't worry, Miss Archer. I'll take good care of your dog. When you and Will get to Colorado, I can write you a letter and tell you all about our adventures."

"I would like that a lot, Albert. Thank you." She bent down and placed a light kiss on his forehead.

"She kissed me!" he said, eyes wide, a hand rubbing the spot her lips had touched his head, then he turned to look at Will. "Do you like her kisses?" he asked innocently.

Will laughed out loud. "Well, I don't know, Albert. She hasn't kissed me yet," he said with a wink.

"Don't worry, I'm much too young for her and I think she's a little sweet on you anyhow."

Elizabeth gasped, unable to believe what had just happened. Her cheeks burned. Her mouth went dry. How was she supposed to respond to that?

"Is that true, Miss Archer?" Will asked with a raised brow.

"If you'll excuse me," she said, gathering her skirt and skittering down the steps. As she reached the last one, her foot caught on a protruding nail in the board and she fell forward.

Will acted quickly, stepping in front of the staircase, catching her before she could fall.

"Seems you're making a habit of falling into my arms."

She hit against his chest, feeling the deep rumble of his amusement.

"I have never been so clumsy in my life." *Seriously, Elizabeth. Pull yourself together.* "You must be cursed and I've been around you too long." She made a mental note to be much more careful with her surroundings in the future. She did not need Will Redbourne to save her. She was a smart, capable woman. Now, she just needed to prove it.

"Quite the opposite, I assure you, ma'am. I am feeling quite blessed today." He winked at Albert, who giggled happily.

Why did this man seem to blow so hot and cold? Wasn't it just this morning he was giving her the cold shoulder?

"I can assure you, Mr. Redbourne, I can make it back to the livery all by myself. You can let me go now."

He did as he was told, but he'd been so quick to respond that she wavered backward and he reached out a hand to steady her.

"I'm fine," she said, holding up a hand, then brushing at the imaginary wrinkles in her skirt. She turned around and crouched down. "Come here, girl," she said, patting the tops of her legs.

Caspar jumped down off the platform.

Elizabeth braced herself this time, determined that the dog would not knock her off balance. As she held Caspar's face between her hands, her fingers rubbing the sections behind her ears, she didn't know what to say. The dog licked her face.

"Thank you, Caspar," she said, wrapping her arms around the dog's neck. She held on for a few moments, kissed the side of her head, and stood. "Go on," she said, motioning toward Albert. "Goodbye, Albert," she said with a light wave.

He waved back. "Thank you!" he called after her as she made her way down the road on foot toward the livery. Tears welled up in her eyes again and she chastised herself for being so...so weak. She knew that leaving Caspar with the boy had been the right thing to do, so why was she crying?

"Can I give you a ride, ma'am?"

Elizabeth refused to look at Will. She didn't want him to see that she'd been crying and she didn't want to give him the satisfaction. She could walk one block back to the livery for heaven's sake. And she didn't need Will to help her make it there safely.

"Come on," he said playfully. "Elizabeth?"

That was it.

"What makes you so special that you get to call me by that name?" she said, spinning on her heel to face him.

"It is your name, isn't it?"

"Yes. Well, it was." She loved her name and if the truth be told, she liked hearing it again.

"Was?" He was goading her and she knew it.

"You know what?" she said, tossing her hands in the air. She took a few more steps forward, then stopped to say something, but thought better of it and started walking again. "You don't know me, Will Redbourne. You...you..." She didn't know why she was so irked at him.

"I want to," he said as he dismounted and walked alongside her.

Elizabeth stopped and stared ahead. Enough of this. Didn't he know she was on a stagecoach headed west to marry a preacher from Silver Falls, Colorado? When would they possibly have time to get to know each other? His job was to guard the stage to Kansas City, while she rode inside of it, and then they would part ways. Likely, for good.

When she'd left England, she'd never imagined that she would come face to face with the man who'd inspired her to leave her family behind and brave an adventure across an ocean. She hadn't realized the danger she'd been in everyday with the kind of men her father and brother associated with. She hadn't known the kind of man her father was.

"I thought women were the ones who were supposed to be hard to understand," she said aloud.

"You are."

"Well, so are you." She felt foolish standing on the street having this conversation with him.

Thoughts about the night she and her family had received word that her brother was in the hospital, near death, flooded into her mind. She'd been angry at Will for putting him there and had been devastated and confused that he would do something so out of character from what she'd seen, until she'd learned the truth. Will was a good man with a good and honorable heart, and he'd had every right to defend himself against a plotted attack.

Elizabeth took a deep breath. The past needed to stay in the past. Though, she wished she'd had the opportunity to meet him then. It would have made this whole situation so much easier.

When they arrived at the livery, Opal and Gertrude were pacing outside of the stage and Paulie was in handcuffs sitting on a chair by the front door. A large ominous looking man with a stubbly face and black trench coat stood close by in a heated conversation with Mr. Glenn.

Will handed her the reins to his horse and strode quickly toward the hard-looking man, reaching him in mere moments.

"What are you doing? Paulie had nothing to do with it, Fenton," Will said loudly. "You know it."

Elizabeth pulled her shawl tighter around her arms and hurried to catch up. As she passed the wagon on the opposite side of the stage, she caught a glimpse of what was inside. The bodies of three men wrapped in cloth planted a pit of dread deep in her belly. The man talking to Mr. Glenn must be the territory marshal Will had sent for.

"I'm telling you, Redbourne, it was an inside job."

The two men stood almost nose to nose, although Will had an edge being slightly taller than the other.

"If he were involved, why did they shoot him?"

"Maybe he was a liability."

"We have a job to do," Will said, defending his friend. "Just because you have some age-old grudge against me doesn't mean you need to delay these ladies their passage, nor the client their bankroll."

"I do my job, Redbourne, just like you. And my gut is telling me this was an inside job."

Will scratched his chin vigorously with the backs of his fingers. "Why don't you escort us to Kansas City? We can get the ladies on their train and settle this mess once we get there."

The marshal didn't respond.

"I tell you what, if Paulie is guilty, you can have his share of our pay. If he's not, you can have mine. You'll get paid either way." He turned to the other outrider. "Is that fair, Paulie."

"Will, I can't let you—"

"It's settled then."

The marshal opened his mouth, as if to protest, but raised an eyebrow instead. "You are willing to give up your paycheck to prove the man innocent?"

"I am."

"Will, you can't—"

Will stuck out his hand for an agreement. He and the marshal shook on it.

"Now, can we please get on the road? We've had too many delays as it is."

"After you?" the marshal said with a tip of his hat.

"What about these?" Paulie asked, raising his hands into the air.

After the marshal unlocked Paulie's handcuffs, he turned around and caught Elizabeth's stare. His face lit with a smile that touched his eyes.

"This better not be a mistake, Redbourne," he called back to Will as he made his way to her. "Hello," he said, removing his hat and running a hand through his hair. "My name is Marshal Darius Fenton and I would very much like the pleasure of making your acquaintance."

"She's off limits, Fenton," Will said. "One of the brides."

The man's stubbled jaw was square, his eyes the brightest blue Elizabeth had ever seen. She bowed her head in acknowledgement.

What name did she use? She looked at Will. His eyes narrowed at her and the muscle in his cheek pulsed.

"Elizabeth...Archer," she allowed the name to spill from her lips as she extended a hand toward him. Her past would catch up with her sooner or later. It was time for her to stop pretending. Will already knew the truth. That was all that mattered.

"Why, Miss Archer, you are simply the most beautiful sight I have seen in ages." He took her hand and brought it up to his lips.

She could feel the heat of Will's stare, but she avoided looking over at him.

"It sounds like you will be joining us as far as Kansas City."

"With you along, ma'am, I may just have to join you for the remainder of your journey."

Elizabeth enjoyed his praise. It had been a long time since a man had showed respectful interest in her and she liked it.

CHAPTER SEVENTEEN

A tight knot gripped Will's chest and would not relent as he watched Elizabeth's interaction with the marshal. Every breath was becoming increasingly difficult. When he'd discovered that Elizabeth was an Archer, he'd wanted to be angry with her, had wanted to make her pay for her father's and brother's mistakes, but when she'd looked up at him with that trust in her eyes, he'd realized there was more to the woman than he'd expected. He wanted to get to know her better. To understand her reasons for being here. For changing her name.

He supposed a lot of women would find a man like Fenton appealing, but he did not feel like punching a tree when other women smiled at him, so why did he feel that way watching Elizabeth with the man? It took a moment before he realized that he wanted to be the one she smiled at, laughed with…

Elizabeth reached out and playfully tapped the marshal's arm.

…touched.

Will took the few steps that separated them and reached out for the reins.

"Ms. Jessup, I mean, Archer," he knew it was childish to say, but hadn't been able to stop himself. If he was honest with himself, he was jealous that Elizabeth was being so open and honest with the marshal. And now, the marshal would be accompanying them to Kansas City. At Will's request. How could he have been such a dolt?

She narrowed her eyes at him, raising a brow. She was calling him out, but Will pretended everything was as it should be.

"Thank you for holding onto him, ma'am," he said as he reached down and slipped Indy's reins from her hands. When his fingers brushed against her skin, his gut tightened and his jaw flexed. How did she have such an effect on him?

"We need to be getting on the road, ma'am." He tipped his hat and led his mount back toward the livery entrance where Paulie waited.

"Thank you, Will," Paulie said as he rubbed his wrists. "Why would the marshal accuse me of any wrong doing?"

"He wouldn't. Unless he knows something that we don't."

Paulie's eyes opened wide and he shook his head slowly.

"Will, I would never—"

"You don't have to tell me, my friend. I've known you near my whole life. But, Fenton is a lot like my brothers. Rafe's instincts are unparalleled when it comes to sniffing out trouble and Raine has a way of uncovering the truth in any situation. I think those natural abilities are what drew them to the law. I'm guessing the marshal's not any different."

"What do you know about him?"

"Just that he's a straight arrow—even if it's sometimes blinded by revenge," he added given his previous encounter with the man.

"You do something to make him mad?"

"Let's just say we both took a liking to the same pretty girl and it cost the man an ounce of his pride." He couldn't help but see the irony in the situation and he refused to be on the other side of the coin.

Elizabeth giggled.

Will swung up onto his horse.

"We've got a bankroll to deliver, Paulie, and I've delayed us long enough this morning. Let's get on the road."

His childhood friend and partner walked over to where Opal and Gertrude stood watching the exchange between Elizabeth and the marshal. Neither of the ladies seemed too pleased. Paulie caught their attention and motioned toward the stagecoach.

Will would be glad to finally get back on the road. He could use the time alone on his horse to think. It wasn't like he could win Elizabeth over, nor should he. His job was clear. Escort the stage to Kansas City. After all, she was headed west to meet the man who'd sent for a bride in good faith. It was none of his business. He was leaving. Going to England. It was best that he put all thoughts of Elizabeth Archer out of his head and focus on the job at hand.

For months he had dreamed of the ship that would be under his command as he travelled across the seas. Being a professor was a means to an end. He would teach at the University and then lead expeditions of discovery. He couldn't think of a better adventure. Except one.

Stop it!

He glanced back over at Elizabeth. When Fenton placed a kiss on the back of her hand, it was enough. Will couldn't watch any longer. He nudged Indy forward.

"Excuse me, ma'am, but like I said, we really need to be getting on the road."

For someone who had been so keen on getting to Kansas City as soon as possible, she was certainly taking her time. He stared at her until she finally met his eyes. She glanced back at the marshal with a smile Will wished had been intended for him.

"If you will please excuse me, Marshal." She dipped in a slight curtsy.

"I look forward to speaking with you more, Miss Archer," the marshal said.

Will locked eyes with her again. His jaw set firm, unsmiling.

"I need to drop this wagon with the undertaker." Fenton directed his comments to Will, but Will's eyes did not defer from Elizabeth's. "I'll meet you at the edge of town," he said with a bob of his head as if trying to get Will's attention.

"I'm boarding," Elizabeth said, pulling her shawl around her a little tighter as she headed toward the stage.

"Redbourne! I'll meet you at the—"

"I heard you the first time, Fenton." He didn't mean to snap.

"Don't think I've forgotten what happened in Hesterville." The marshal raised a challenging brow.

"Edge of town. We'll wait," Will said, leading his horse away from the man and up alongside the stage.

It would be nice to get back to some sense of normalcy.

Will raised his arm above his head and made a circling motion with his hand.

"Heading out!" Ellis called from the driver's box.

Will rode on ahead, toward the edge of town, to wait for Marshal Fenton. He brought the horse to a stop, leaned forward, and rested his arms across the saddle horn.

By the time Fenton arrived, the stage had only been idle for a minute or two. With Paulie bringing up the rear, they slowly embarked on the new leg of their journey.

Fenton pulled up next to Will a few hundred yards ahead of the stage.

"What's her story?" he asked as if they'd always been on friendly terms.

"I think that is something you will have to ask the lady." Will did not want to talk about Elizabeth Archer to this man.

"But you seem to know her pretty well."

"We only just met yesterday." It was true, but somehow it felt as if he'd known her a lot longer.

"Yesterday?" Fenton asked with surprise. "I'd have never guessed by the way you two were acting towards each other," he said knowingly.

Tension suddenly swarmed the air around them like the marshal had something more to say, but never voiced it. Will cursed the man who was more like his brothers than he cared to admit.

"You take the east," he said, turning the focus back to the job. "I'll take west, and when we reach Kansas City, we'll reconvene.

At least if the marshal was outriding, he wouldn't be near Elizabeth. Will didn't know why he cared, but he'd have a couple of hours to figure it out.

"Shhh."

Elizabeth whipped her head around at the sound and strained to listen. An odd shushing noise was coming from the back of the stage coach. She shook her head, chalking it up to her imagination.

A simpering whine came from the same spot, followed by a scratching noise. If she hadn't known any better, she would have said it sounded an awful lot like Caspar, but, she rationalized, she was just missing the pup. It was the first time since crossing into Missouri that she hadn't had Caspar there with her, other than the few hours she'd gone missing yesterday.

"Shhh," the sound came again, followed by a distinct giggle.

"Did you hear that?" she asked the other two women who'd been staring out the windows at the trail for the better part of half an hour.

"I didn't hear anything," Opal said. "Did you, Gertie?"

"Just the relentless creek of the wheel beneath me," Gertrude said, her voice laced with a whine.

Knock.

"What was that?" Opal asked, sitting up and grabbing onto Gertrude.

Something, or someone, lurked in the baggage boot.

Elizabeth grabbed a hold of the handle just to the side of the window and pulled herself upward, sticking her head out into the fresh air.

"Mr. Glenn," she called, realizing it might be hard for the driver to hear her from down here. She bit her lip, contemplating her next move.

"Is there something I can help you with, ma'am?" She glanced out the window to find Marshal Fenton riding alongside the stagecoach.

It took a moment to recover her surprise, but she threw on her best smile. "Can we please stop the stage?"

"We're just another hour or so outside of Kansas City. Can it wait?" he asked.

"Well, I think we might have a stowaway in the boot," she responded.

Marshal Fenton looked from her to the rear of the stage, then quickly pulled forward enough that he could engage Mr. Glenn in conversation.

"Whoa," the driver yelled and within a few moments, the stage came to a halt.

Elizabeth pushed through the door, nearly tripping over her own feet as she hustled off the step and toward the back of the wagon. She reached for the leather lifting strap at the same time the newly dismounted marshal did and their hands brushed across one another's.

"Excuse me," she said, turning to look at him.

"I didn't mind," he replied with a smile that could have melted the heart of an ice queen.

Elizabeth found the marshal charming and handsome, but his touch didn't incite any thrill or anticipation from her. There was no spark, no butterflies.

"Why did we stop?" Will asked as he rode up.

Elizabeth shifted her gaze to Will, whose jaw now flexed tightly, his eyes like steel. Flutters filled her stomach and her breath caught in her chest. He was seriously the most handsome man she had ever seen and, while she tried to be contrite for her current positioning with the marshal, her heart lifted a little at the thought that Will might just be jealous.

"Miss Archer heard something in the baggage boot."

"Who is Miss Archer?" Gertrude asked, glancing from Elizabeth to Opal.

Elizabeth smiled at the woman as she relinquished her hold on the leather strap and raised a reluctant hand just high enough to be acknowledged.

The marshal lifted the cowhide flap covering the storage space at the back of the stage and Elizabeth gasped as Caspar barked and jumped out of the boot at a very surprised territory marshal. His hand shot to his hip, but he recovered quick enough that he didn't draw.

Elizabeth's heart jolted and she placed a hand up against her bosom as if stopping it from leaping right from her chest.

"I guess she couldn't wait," a small voice came from the baggage boot.

Albert looked up at her, eyes wide, shoulders shrugged, and a triumphant grin spread across his face.

Will was off his horse in an instant and pulled the boy out from the back and set him on his feet.

"Albert," he said, "we had an agreement." Will dropped down onto his knee. "Do you remember when we talked about commitment?"

"Yes, sir," the boy said, dropping his head, then he looked up brightly. "But it doesn't matter on a count of I crossed my fingers." He held up both hands, fingers crossed.

"Albert." Will tilted his head.

"I know." Albert dropped his hands to his sides. "But, what if you didn't come back?"

"Of course, I'd come back. I made a commitment to you, didn't I?"

"That's what Willie said too and he never came back."

Will stood up and ruffled the kid's hair.

Elizabeth watched the exchange with admiration. Will was good with the boy.

"Who's Willie?" Opal asked, her hands at her chest.

"Will someone please tell us what is going on around here." Gertrude stomped her foot and folded her arms, her lips pursing together to show her displeasure.

"Willie was Albert's brother," Will told her, then glanced around at the others in the group. "Well, we've got him now." He looked at Mr. Glenn. "I'll take care of his passage, Ellis." He nodded at the driver. "Then, I'll wire my father *and* the sheriff," he said turning to look at Albert with a raised brow, "once we get into Kansas City."

Caspar dashed from one side of the stage to the other, running circles around the people all standing around.

"I think she's happy to be out of that trunk," Elizabeth said, dropping down onto her haunches and allowing the dog to lick her face. "It's good to see you, girl." She hugged Caspar tightly.

"What are we supposed to do with a dog?" Marshal Fenton asked.

"Don't worry, Darius," Will said, "she'll just run alongside the stage or with us. When she gets tired, she'll have to ride on Albert's lap in the cabin."

Albert nodded heartily, but the look on Gertrude's face distorted her otherwise pretty ordinary features and she threw her hands up in the air and climbed back into the travelling compartment.

"Come on, Opal. You heard the marshal," Gertrude turned and smiled at Marshal Fenton, "it's only for another hour or so."

The rest of the ride from Plain City into Kansas City was unexpectedly uneventful. The delightful aroma of freshly baked bread greeted them as they rode into town. Several passersby came in and out of the Walnut Street bakery. A man leaned against the pillar in front of the barbershop, raising his head in acknowledgement as they passed. Horse drawn streetcars trod the dirt road down both sides of the street, and buildings two and three stories high towered over them. It reminded Elizabeth of home.

Bittersweet feelings bubbled up inside of her. She missed her mother more than anyone and wished she could come to America also, but Margaret Archer had refused to believe what kind of a man her husband had turned out to be. She was blindly devoted to the man and would never leave the comforts of London society and their home.

Elizabeth breathed in deeply, her mouth watering at the delicious smells filling the air, and she sat up straighter in her seat. If her new life was supposed to happen in the middle of God's country, she'd take it.

CHAPTER EIGHTEEN

Sometimes, Will missed life in the city. He loved the clarity that working on the ranch had often provided as he worked through one problem or another, but there was something to be said for the hustle and bustle of a town like Kansas City.

They passed the building where they were supposed to deliver their cargo on their way into town. It looked empty. After Ellis had sent word from Plain City to the benefactors of the bankroll that they had been delayed, he had received a telegram with new instructions to meet at the land office at noon.

Will slipped his watch from his vest pocket and flipped it open. Eleven o'clock. They were early. Luckily, there was a livery next to the building where he hoped they would be able to secure the stagecoach in the interim. He motioned for Paulie and the marshal to join him.

"We have another hour before we can deliver the bankroll," he explained. "In the meantime, I will head over to the telegraph office and wire back to Plain City, and to my father, to let them know about Albert." He glanced over at the stage.

Elizabeth's head pushed against the window, her eyes closed, her mouth slightly open. He couldn't decide if she was actually tired or if she'd slept to avoid listening to Gertrude

Arnold chatting incessantly. He smiled.

"The train station is supposed to be at this end of town," he told Paulie and Fenton, "so I'll see if I can pick up a train schedule for the ladies. They'll need to exchange their tickets. Then, I'll stand guard while you both take Ellis and the ladies to get something to eat." He knew the marshal would never agree to leaving Paulie alone with the bankroll.

"Then we'll settle our business," the marshal said with a nod.

"Sounds good, Will," Paulie joined his agreement.

The stage pulled up behind them into the livery yard and Will dismounted. He paid the groomer who met them out front to take care of Indy until he returned. He spun around to find that Marshal Fenton had beat him to the stage. He opened the door and held out his hand for the ladies.

Will removed his hat and thrust a hand through his hair. Thoughts tumbled like weeds through his mind. He hadn't felt this conflicted in a long time. He started for the boardwalk and caught Elizabeth's gaze as she stepped down off the stage. It was hard to believe that a woman who looked like that was any relation to Sterling Archer, let alone his daughter. She was beautiful. Breathtaking. His eyes lingered longer than was probably appropriate, but when she smiled at him, his heart turned to butter in the sun.

The marshal held onto her hand longer than was necessary, and leaned down again to kiss the back of her hand.

Will rolled his eyes.

Marshal Fenton must have said something amusing because Elizabeth smiled up at him and did a little curtsy before joining the other women.

"Arggg." He wished he had more time. It wasn't really Fenton that he needed to worry about as much as the preacher she was headed to marry in Silver Falls—though he still cursed the streak of jealousy that rose to the surface whenever she smiled at the marshal. What could he do now? He barely knew the woman. Maybe it was for the best.

When he arrived at the telegraph office, he was surprised to see that there was a line. He pulled his pocket watch again from his vest. His stomach grumbled. He'd been so upset this morning that he hadn't had anything to eat, and now, his belly protested a little too loudly for comfort. He smiled uneasily at the woman in front of him who turned around and shot him a disapproving look.

In a small wooden display on the wall, the train schedule had been written out for the day. The next train to Denver would be leaving at one thirty. If things kept moving along, he would have plenty of time to run by the station and possibly even pick up a little something to eat on his way back. The idea of riding all the way back to Stone Creek tonight—especially, if he had a young boy and a dog in tow—did not appeal to him. Maybe he would stay the night in Kansas City before returning home. He just hoped he wouldn't miss Jem.

"Next," the kindly old man behind the counter called.

Will stepped forward and placed his scribbled note down in front of him. An odd, empty feeling started in Will's chest and spread throughout his gut. Something was wrong. He glanced around over his shoulder at the others in the room, but nothing seemed off or suspicious.

The bankroll.

He needed to go.

Now!

As soon as the telegrapher confirmed the telegrams had been sent, Will hurried outside and looked around. He caught a hazy glimpse of a familiar tall, blond man slipping around the corner toward the livery before he could get a good look at him.

It can't be.

Will strode to the edge of the building and peeked around, but the alleyway was empty. Unable to shake the uneasy feeling, he rounded the corner and took the first few steps back toward the livery at a normal pace, but something inside of him urged his feet to move faster and he quickened his pace until he was at a full run. He stopped short as he approached the wooden building, drawing his gun as he pushed open the door. The place was unnaturally quiet.

"Hello?" he called, his voice like an echo coming back on him.

He glanced around, gingerly making his way across the floor, peeking into each stall as he moved toward the back where they'd planned for the stage to be kept while they waited. There was no sign of Paulie, the marshal, or any of the passengers the stage had carried. They must have still been out, getting something to eat.

He took in a deep breath and strained to listen. The sound of low, but urgent grunts were barely audible above the silence. He pulled back the hammer on his pistol. Something wasn't right.

"Paulie? Fenton?" he called as he passed through the dark stable.

Tension rested on the air as thick as his sister's black-rye bread. Some of the horses pranced about in their stalls and others swished their heads back and forth accompanied by a few snorts. Something was definitely off.

"Mr. Liveryman?" he said, feeling foolish for not knowing the man's name.

A knocking sort of noise caught his attention from the direction he was headed. The hairs on the back of his neck stood on end and gooseflesh ran down his arms. He took another step.

Light poured in through an open door at the far edge of the stable. Will aligned himself with the wooden wall and followed it until he came to the opening. He darted a quick look around the corner, only to discover that there was an entirely different space behind what he'd believed to be the hay and grains storage area.

Double doors had been swung wide open at the back and the stage was parked just a few feet away from him. The horses were still hitched to the stage and they pranced about in place, blowing and twisting their heads anxiously.

The muffled sound of voices pulled him to the left. There, on the floor behind the stage, lay Paulie and the marshal, both bound and gagged. Will looked around, but didn't see anyone else. He slipped over and knelt down next to Paulie, noticing bright red stains growing on the material of his shirt. He was bleeding again.

Will holstered his gun and worked quickly to untie the man.

"Where are the ladies?" he asked quietly as he moved to help the marshal.

"They've already gone down to the café with Ellis," Paulie said after taking the handkerchief from his mouth and spitting rapidly.

Will removed Fenton's gag, but as he was working to untie the man's wrists, he noticed that the strong box, that should have contained the bankroll locked inside, lay all catawampus on the floor next to the wagon's wheel, pried open and empty.

"We were going to join them once you got here, but—"

"Will, look out!" The marshal yelled.

He turned and ducked out of the way just in time to see a shovel head swinging toward him. The unmistakable sound of a cocking gun filled his ears and he glanced up to see a sweating and pallid Sven, holding him at gunpoint.

Sven swallowed hard and wiped the sweat from his upper lip with the back of his sleeved arm.

"Where is it?" he asked calmly, with the hint of a smile.

"Sven?" Will asked, shocked to see him here in Kansas City, let alone out of bed. "What are you doing?"

"Where is it, Will?" Sven screamed, his voice scratchy and weak, as he pounded the tip of his gun against the air. "Don't mess with me."

Will had his hands raised to his shoulders and took a step forward.

"I don't want to hurt you," Sven said shakily, "but I will if

I have to."

"What do you want, my friend?"

The Norwegian's eyes darted to the right and he shot the ground by the marshal's feet. Will guessed the gun tucked in Sven's belt belonged to the lawman. He took a step backward, stepping protectively in front of Fenton, hoping the man would see the holstered gun at his hip.

"You're sick, Sven." Will could see the man growing weaker by the moment.

"You don't understand," the tall brute said quietly, a whimper escaping his lips. "I have to get it. Where is it?" he sobbed.

"Where is what?"

"The bankroll!" he screamed.

Will didn't understand. The strong box had been opened. There was nothing inside. Sven had to have the bankroll, nothing else made sense.

"Sven, why don't you just put the gun down and we'll talk about this."

"Like you talked to my friends? To my brother?"

Will's brows scrunched together. The man was talking nonsense—presumably from the fever.

"You killed them," he said, his voice sounding more irrational as the moments passed.

The puzzle pieces started to fit together. The only men who had been killed were those who'd attempted to rob the stage in the ravine outside of Plain City.

"Sven, tell me you didn't do this. Tell me you are not the one who arranged to steal the bankroll. Tell me you were not involved with those men who shot Paulie and tried to kill Elizabeth."

"I need that money, Will. Where is it?" Sven dropped to his knees, the gun wilting in his hands.

It wouldn't be long before the large Norwegian would pass out. Will just needed to stall a little longer. He took a step toward him. The man had been his friend and he couldn't just let him die on the floor of a livery like an animal.

"Hold it right there." Another man, with a wide girth and meaty hands, stepped inside of the livery through the large open doors, his gun pointed at Will.

Will put his hands up again.

"Please, we need to get a doctor. Can't you see that this man is very sick?"

"What's it to you?" the man asked, pushing up the brim of his hat with the tip of his gun.

"He's my friend," Will stated, non-apologetically.

A light came on in the man's eyes. "You must be Redbourne."

Will nodded.

"Sven said you were a good man. Couldn't stop whining about how he wanted to be more like you, didn't you, son?" He grabbed Sven by the shirt collar and hauled him to his feet. "Wanted to be more like you than his old man." The old brute scoffed. "I believe the man asked you a question, Redbourne," he said the name with disdain, directing the comment at Will as he pointed his gun at Will's chest and pulled back the hammer until it cocked.

Will backed up until he ran into the seated marshal's knee.

"Where is *my* money?" the older man demanded.

A light tug on his hip told Will that the marshal had picked up on his hints.

CRACK!

The old man fell backward and Sven dropped back down to his knees, falling over to the ground. Another man darted in from around the corner, gun raised, and with another precise shot, the marshal took him down.

Will rushed forward.

"Sven?" he called, trying to rouse the man. He put the Norwegian's arm over his shoulder and lifted him into a standing position. Will groaned. The weight was too much. He wouldn't last long trying to carry him like this.

The marshal removed the gun from Sven's hand and retrieved his own from the sick man's belt, returning it to his empty holster.

"I'm going to need your help," Will told the lawman.

"Where are you taking him?" The marshal placed his arms beneath Will's to help support the man. "He's officially in my custody."

"That may be so, Fenton, but he needs a doctor."

Together they carried Sven over to the cart that sat at the edge of the stable.

"It might be faster if you put him on a horse."

The marshal had a point. He ran back to the stable where Indy had been stalled and opened the gate.

"Come on, boy," he coaxed, grabbing the bridle from a nail on the side of the stall.

Within a few moments, they had Sven in a saddle with Will right behind him to keep him upright. There were several doctors in Kansas City. He just needed to find the closest one. He eased his heels into Indy's side and urged him out of the livery and into the street.

It had been a while since Will had visited, but he seemed to remember one of the medical offices being on Fourth Street. He headed that direction, followed by the marshal, and was relieved when he came upon a little white house with a sign out front that read, *Office of Dr. Vernon Hicks, Physician.*

He dismounted awkwardly, trying to keep Sven from falling off, then gently pulled his friend from the horse. The man was getting heavier and Will struggled under his bulky frame until Fenton was able to reach them. With a joint effort, they carried the Norwegian up the front steps and to the door.

Before Will could call out that they were there, the door swung wide open and an older man in a white shirt, black vest, and spectacles ushered them inside and directed the men through a long, white curtain to a room with a large table. They laid Sven down as gently as they could and took two steps back, allowing the doctor access, each sucking in a lightened breath.

"What's wrong with him?" the doc asked.

Will proceeded to tell him about everything that had happened yesterday morning back at Redbourne Ranch, but he excluded the details about him working with a band of outlaws.

"He a friend of yours?"

"No," the marshal said.

"Yes," Will said at the same time, pulling the hat from his head and running a quick hand through his hair.

The doctor looked up at the marshal.

"He's in my charge," Fenton replied as he pulled back his coat to show his shiny marshal's badge.

"He do something wrong?" The doc asked, while he proceeded to examine him.

"Seems so, Doc," Will said, now fidgeting with his hat.

He glanced up at the clock on the wall. A quarter of twelve. They only had fifteen minutes before they were supposed to be at the land office. He reached into his pocket, pulled out a few bills, and handed them to the doc.

"I hope this will cover it, but if not, the marshal here knows how to find me." He turned to Fenton. "I've got to go," he said apologetically. "Will you look after him?"

The marshal nodded. "You know he's going to jail, right?" he whispered.

"I know, but at least he won't be dead." He handed the marshal money the equivalent of what his share of the job would be, but the lawman shook his head.

"Keep it," he said, jutting his chin out toward Sven. "I got what I came for."

Will stared at the bills a moment before returning them to his pocket. He looked up, nodded curtly, then hustled from the office.

On his way back to the livery, he rode past Ellis, the three women, Albert, and little Caspar. He exhaled heavily. *This was just supposed to be an easy day trip. What a mess.*

When he got back to the stables, Will rode around to the back of the livery and dismounted. The doors were still wide open and Paulie stood on top of the stage, the closed strong box already secured back in place. He looked up at Will.

"Sven?"

"He's with the doc now." Will dismounted and lashed his reins around the top rung of a stall gate just inside the doors. "We only have a few minutes. I hope Ellis is on his way back with the ladies."

"Oh, no," Paulie said as he climbed down from the top of the coach. He ran toward a door at the far end of the big open space.

"What is it?" Will asked, surprised by Paulie's sudden exclamation.

"I forgot about the liveryman," he said as he threw open the door to the tack room.

The poor livery owner jumped, squinting as the light hit the dark room. He sat with his hands and feet tied to the legs of a chair, his mouth also bound with a cloth gag. Paulie rushed inside and worked quickly to free the man.

Once unrestricted, the stable owner, rubbed his wrists.

"What took you boys so long?" he asked, annoyance permeating his voice. "I heard gunshots, then everything went quiet. If you weren't dead, then why did it take you this long to come get me?"

"Yes, we are alive, thank you. And we caught the bad guys. And we saved your life. You'd think a little gratitude might be in order."

"Yes, well...thank you," he said. His face dropped, his eyes grew wide, and he backed up toward the office. "Are they...," he swallowed, pointing to the two men lying on the floor, "dead?"

"Yes." There was no use sugarcoating it.

"Oh, my. I'll just go get the sheriff." He ran from the room, breathing heavily.

"Paulie, we're going to be in a lot of trouble here. Do you have any idea what happened to the money that was supposed to be in that strong box?"

"I was just as surprised as you when he opened it and nothing was there." He moved to the stall where his horse was housed.

Will wasn't sure what they were going to do, short of asking for an investigation.

"Think, Paulie," he said quietly, "was there ever a time when you stepped away from the stage while you were guarding it?"

"No, Will. I swear. I walked the perimeter a few times, just like you, but I never abandoned post. I wouldn't."

"Then, we have to ask ourselves the same question Sven did. Where is the money?"

"I can answer that," Ellis said, as he stepped into the light.

They both turned to look at him.

"Follow me."

Will's eyes locked with Elizabeth's as she stepped out from behind the driver, her arm around Albert's shoulders. She smiled—a light, a beacon, in an ever darkening situation.

Ellis climbed up onto the driver's box. "Well, come on, we've got a bankroll to deliver."

Will stepped over to the travelling compartment and opened the door. "Ladies," he said, removing his hat and bowing his head lightly. "And, gentleman," he said to Albert, who boarded just in front of Elizabeth. He closed the door and reached through the window, ruffling the boy's longer, blond hair "Albert, how was your meal?"

"I had a stack of flapjacks this tall," he said with one hand around his belly and the other up to his chin.

"That's a lot of flapjacks," Will said with a smile. "I'll bet you're ready for a nice long nap, then."

"I ain't no baby, Will," Albert said, folding his arms and

scrunching his brows.

"Albert," Elizabeth said as a gentle reminder.

"I," the boy looked up at her, "*am not* a baby, Will."

Elizabeth nodded her approval.

Will laughed and winked at her and her smile turned into a light giggle.

"I know, kiddo. You're practically a man, but even the strongest of men deserve a nap once in a while, don't you think, Miss Archer?" He turned to look at Elizabeth.

She shrugged. "Somehow, I cannot imagine that you, Mr. Redbourne, are a nap taker."

She had him there. He couldn't remember the last time he'd indulged.

With the passengers all loaded, Will had a matter to discuss with Ellis. He'd been hired as an outrider to guard the stage as it carried a bankroll deposit to Kansas City along with three mail-order-brides, but now, the money was gone and there was no reasonable explanation that Will could see. The driver seemed to have some answers.

"Ellis," Will said as he climbed up into the box next to the driver, "there's been a little mishap."

"Paulie told me all about your Norwegian friend. That is exactly why my benefactors decided to take some extra precautions," he said with a sly smile.

"What *kind* of precautions?" Will raised a brow, but narrowed his eyes.

"The kind that allows us to deliver our cargo on time," he said, raising an arm. "Head out!" he called out with a loud, booming voice, then turned back to Will in quieter tones. "Everything will be all right, son. Don't you worry."

Will narrowed his eyes at the man. He climbed down off the stage and mounted his horse. He'd been left out of the loop on a job he was responsible for and he didn't like it one bit. How was he supposed to protect the payload if he had no idea where it was being kept? When he glanced inside the coach as he rode by, he met Elizabeth's eyes. She smiled briefly, then returned her attention to the boy and his dog. Caspar climbed up and stuck her head out the window, her tongue out as she panted her excitement.

Will laughed as he rode to the front. "You heard the man," he called out to Paulie who awaited his cue. "Head out!"

He led the stagecoach across town to the land office just east of the train depot.

When they pulled up in front, a man with a long, silvery coat stepped out onto the porch to greet them, accompanied by two rather large armed guards. He waved at Ellis, then tipped his hat to the outriders.

Will pulled up next to the window of the stage and leaned down to address the passengers.

"Please stay inside until our dealings here are complete."

Each of them responded with a nod.

"Thank you, kindly." He tapped the window sill, then rode up to the porch. Paulie stayed at the back to guard the coach. Ellis pulled on the long, wooden brake and wrapped the reins for the team around it before climbing down.

"Mr. Danvers," he said, hopping up the wooden steps and greeting the man in the silver coat. "It's nice to see you again."

They shook hands.

"Likewise, Mr. Glenn. I trust you have my package," he said, nodding toward the stagecoach.

"Yes, sir."

"Any trouble find you along the way?"

"Nothing these outriders couldn't handle, sir."

The gentleman turned to Will. "You Jameson Redbourne's kid?" he asked, taking a step toward him.

The question surprised Will.

"Yes, sir."

"Jameson's a good man."

"Thank you, sir."

"Thank *you*. For all you've done here. I know it wasn't an

easy task to get the stage here without incident. Although, I must say, I was astounded to hear that a Redbourne was stepping in as an outrider." He crouched down on the platform, so he was eye-level with him on his horse. "You're the one who studied in England. William, right?"

"Yes, sir," Will said slowly, narrowing his eyes slightly, surprised by the man's familiarity with his family. "May I ask how you know so much about us, sir?"

The man laughed. "Jameson and I go way back. We knew each other as children and we have done business together many times throughout the years. You could say I owe him my life. And my wealth." He leaned in closer to Will and spoke more quietly than before. "He's very proud of you, you know?"

Will didn't know what to say. Sometimes, in a family as big as his, he'd felt alone, invisible almost. "What makes you say that?"

"Last time he came to Denver, he couldn't stop bragging about his son studying at Oxford. He said the two of you are more alike than you'd probably care to admit." He laughed. "Said you'd taken up pugilism while you were there. You still fight?"

Will was still trying to process everything he'd just learned. He looked up at the man, realizing he'd been asked a question. "Fight? Right. Not professionally. Not anymore."

"That's a shame. We're getting ready for a big match in Denver and we could really use a man like you."

"In another lifetime maybe," Will said with a tip of his hat. There was no use recounting his whole story to this man. Besides, he would be setting sail soon and heading for England. He didn't have time for another diversion in Denver.

"Well, you're lucky to be a part of such a wonderful family. And to think I've come across two in one day."

"Two, sir?" Now, Will was really confused.

"I ran into your brother, Levi, over at the train depot not an hour ago. He just got in with that pretty little lady of his.

Looks like there will be another Redbourne in the world soon enough," he said with a chuckle.

Levi's in town?

Will hadn't seen his brother since Christmas.

"Wait, did you say Cadence is expecting?"

"Not in so many words, but I do believe she is. You didn't know?"

"No."

An uncle. A smile spread wide across Will's face. He was going to be an uncle!

"Well, I wish you luck with your future, young man." He handed Will an envelope, which he guessed contained payment for the run.

"Thank you, Mr. Danvers."

The man stood up and joined the rest of them at the stage, followed by his guards.

Will pulled his horse around to see what had made Ellis so confident that the bankroll had not been lost.

The man climbed up into the driver's box. When he pulled a metal lever, carefully absconded beneath the seat, the entire bench swung open on large metal coil hinges. Will watched as the front panel at the back of the box gave way, revealing a secret compartment at the back of the driver's box, ornately decorated and keenly disguised.

Ellis pulled out several large cream-colored sacks and handed them down to the guards. When the last of the bags had been retrieved, the stagecoach driver shut the compartment with a satisfied grin. He worked his way down from the stage, shook Mr. Danvers' hand, and turned with a wink.

Clever.

The job was done.

Now, he just needed to see the ladies off to the train station, make sure they could exchange their tickets, and then, if he could find his brother, he would forgo the night in Kansas City and head back to Stone Creek today with Levi, assuming that was where they were headed.

He dismounted, walked over to the stage, and opened the door. Caspar came bounding out with a gleeful bark as she ran circles around him in the gravelly dirt.

"Ladies," Will said, tapping the brim of his hat.

Albert looked up at him, his brows squished together and his face scrunched into a scowl.

"And gentleman," he added, nodding at Albert.

The boy's face brightened immediately and he hopped down out of the travelling compartment to chase after his dog.

Will raised a hand to help Gertrude down, then Opal. When Elizabeth came to the door, she hesitated before slipping her hand into his. He swallowed hard at her touch. He hadn't expected the warmth that radiated from his belly into his chest by merely holding her hand.

"Miss Elizabeth," he said a little more huskily than he'd intended.

"Mr. Redbourne," she responded as she stepped down onto the ground. She looked up at him for a while before he realized he had neglected to release her hand.

"My apologies, ma'am. Are you ready to head over to the train station?"

"I suppose I am as ready as I will ever be," she said quietly.

"I thought you'd like to know that the next train leaves at one-thirty, which should give us plenty of time to get your tickets exchanged."

"Thank you."

Ellis was on top of the stage tossing down the ladies' luggage. When he picked up Elizabeth's satchel, he pitched it down to Will with a satisfied *humphhh*.

"Can I walk with you, ma'am?" he asked.

"Suit yourself," she said, reaching for her bag.

"I've got it." He turned away from her enough that her satchel was out of reach.

"Why, Mr. Redbourne, if I didn't know any better, I would

say that you think me incapable of carrying my own luggage."

"Well, I'd hardly call this luggage, Miss Archer, but I think you are very capable of doing whatever you put your mind to."

He smiled at the color that crept into her cheeks.

Crash!

He looked over at Paulie who was trying to balance several large luggage cases in his arms.

"Excuse me a moment." He ran over to help the man get organized.

"Here, gentlemen, maybe this will be of assistance." Mr. Danvers pulled up in a small, four-seated horse-drawn cart, stepped out, and proceeded to help load the women's baggage into the back."

Will smiled at the man's timing. He could see how Mr. Danvers and his father would be friends. "Thank you again, sir."

"Of course. And, Mr. Redbourne, if you ever change your mind about getting back into the ring, you look me up." He tucked a card into Will's front pocket.

Elizabeth looked up at him, her eyes and mouth wide. Then, as quickly as the horrified expression had come, anger flashed through her eyes and she marched down the road that led to the train. Alone.

What just happened?

CHAPTER NINETEEN

All of the reasons Elizabeth had left London came flooding back into her mind.

"Elizabeth, wait," Will called from behind her.

She plodded forward, unable to stop her feet from moving one after the other. She wanted to run, to get away, but something inside of her would not allow that. She stopped cold and spun on her heel to face him.

Will nearly plowed into her, but stopped just short, his horse nearly running them both down. He stood mere inches from her, his chest rising and falling with quick, labored breaths.

"Where are you going in such a hurry?" he asked, readjusting the reins in his hands.

"I..."

Why was she so angry? It wasn't Will's fault that he was a talented boxer.

"I..." she started again. She looked up into his face, his eyes searching hers as if to understand, and the anger seemed to melt away to acceptance. "I have a train to catch," she said quietly, turning back around and taking another step toward the station.

"What happened back there? We were being civil and then Mr. Danvers...Ah," he said as if he'd just received the answers to his questions. "Does this have anything to do with...your father?"

She paused, turned to look at him, then started walking again.

"It has everything to do with my father." She breathed out a heavy sigh. "I left home to get away from that life. Away from the man who nearly had you killed." She choked on the last word, then pondered for a moment what more she should say. "Can I ask *you* a question?"

"I'm an open book," Will said with a smile.

"What happened between last night and this morning that made you so angry with me? Then, what happened to make you not angry with me anymore? See," she said, placing her hands on her hips, "hard to understand."

Will slowed his pace, stretched his neck backward for a moment, and shoved his free hand into his pocket.

"Not so hard, really. I found the photograph of you and your family."

"And you saw Thom and my father. That's how you knew who I was." She nodded, understanding finally dawning on her.

"I thought that after the way I left things, maybe he'd sent you to do some of his dirty work, or that maybe you were here for some type of revenge."

She didn't know whether or not she should take offense to the comment. She kept her eyes focused on the road ahead of them. "My brother's predicament was one of his own making. I still can't believe they tried to force you to throw a fight." She shook her head. "I'm sorry about what they did."

He shrugged. "I'm sorry too. The last thing I wanted to do was hurt Thom, but…"

"It was him or you."

"Exactly. I'm glad you understand."

"And, what changed your mind about me?"

He thought for a moment. "You gave Albert that dog."

Elizabeth glanced behind them at the little boy and Caspar running around together behind them.

"I knew at that moment you wouldn't be capable of doing half of the things I'd imagined."

They walked in silence for a few minutes. Elizabeth couldn't blame him for the things he'd thought. Her father was the head of an organization fraternizing in illegal gambling and alcohol distribution, along with many other shady dealings. She'd been so naïve for so long.

"You did me a favor, Mr. Redbourne." She turned to look up at him. "Back in England." She returned her gaze to the road. "I was blind to what my father and brother were doing. I think that Jeremy, my brother just younger than Thom, tried to protect me when he left. He must have known what was going on and didn't want any part of that life. He tried to take me with him, but I didn't understand at the time. I just thought he wanted to try something new and I didn't want to leave my fancy clothes or the luxuries that were at my command," she admitted.

"And yet, here you are on your way to marry some preacher in Silver Falls. Colorado. In the middle of nowhere. With few luxuries and fewer fancy clothes."

She opened her mouth feigning shock. "How did you know he is a preacher?"

Will smiled, but did not respond.

"I learned the truth about my father and what he was doing the night you put Thom in hospital. The curtain was pulled back and I was forced to recognize what I unwittingly had been a part of, but I am most ashamed that I'd let myself be so ignorant at the expense of others. It took me a long time to accept, but I finally realized that everything I had, the fancy life I knew, had come from the literal blood and sweat of an endless number of fighters and innocent men and women whose loved ones had gotten caught up in my family's schemes."

"Did you know that there is a reward for your safe return to England?"

"I wish I could say I was surprised. I was 'daddy's little girl' and I did what he asked of me. Wait," she said, pulling back to look at him, "you're not thinking of turning me in, are you?" She was half playing, half serious.

He looked at her, a cross between hurt and disbelief playing over his features.

She couldn't deny the attraction she felt for the man, but now it was somehow more than the girlish infatuation she'd had for him before.

"Your father will never find you because of me."

"Do you think me a terrible person?"

He stopped.

She stopped, biting the inside of her lip as she waited for his response.

"I think you were very brave, coming to America all alone because you wanted a better life. And I don't mean with 'fancy clothes and luxuries,' but a good, honest life."

Elizabeth smiled. In the beginning she'd thought it would be impossible, but now...

Hissing steam released into the air and the chugging sound of an arriving train sounded with methodic rhythm. She'd hardly noticed the time as they covered the distance to the station.

"Thank you, Will. I have wanted to tell you that for a long time and I never thought I would have the chance. I did not want to leave without taking advantage of the opportunity." She held out her hand for her satchel. "Who would have guessed that I would have tried to find my place in the same little town where you grew up?"

Will strapped Indy to the hitching post just outside of the depot and pulled the watch from his vest pocket. "We still have another half hour before you need to be on the train. Can I buy you some lunch?" he asked, pointing to a small café at the edge of the station.

"I don't think so, Mr. Redbourne." She held out her hand to him, this time to shake his. "I'd rather not press my luck. Seems it has not been with us since we left Stone Creek."

"I thought we'd gotten past all that *Mr. Redbourne*

nonsense."

"Goodbye…Will."

"When are you coming back, Miss Archer?" Albert ran up to stand beside Will.

"Albert," Elizabeth said as she bent down to him, "remember your promise to keep Caspar safe?"

"Yes, ma'am."

"Good. You listen to Mr. Redbourne and do exactly as he tells you, all right?"

"Yes, ma'am, but…I think you should stay."

"And why is that, Albert?" she asked, unable to keep the smile of being wanted off her face.

"Because Will loves you."

Will choked and pounded on his chest to stop from coughing.

Butterflies filled her belly and she stood up straight, daring a glance over at Will.

"Mr. Redbourne and I are friends, and friends, Albert…care about each other. But sometimes, we have to say goodbye to the people we care about. At least for a little while. Do you understand?"

"Not really. Grownups are hard to understand sometimes." He wriggled his nose and rubbed the tip with the back of his hand.

Will and Elizabeth looked at each other and laughed.

Caspar barked.

Elizabeth dropped down on her haunches again and scratched the dog behind her ears before leaning forward and kissing the pup on the head. "Goodbye, girl," she whispered.

"We're gonna miss you a whole lot, ma'am," Albert said, moving to stand next to her. He leaned down and whispered in her ear. "Don't worry, I'll take care of him until you get back."

Elizabeth was about to correct the boy and remind him that Caspar was a girl, until she realized that he was referring to Will.

"I'm sure you will, Albert." She stood up, meeting Will's

eyes again. She could get lost in those eyes.

Snap out of it, Elizabeth!

She dipped her head and took a step toward the ticket office, then spoke one last thought to the man who'd unknowingly given her everything. "You're a good and decent man, Will Redbourne. I hope you get what you're looking for out of your life. I wish you the very best of everything."

He waved with a half-hearted jerk of his raised hand.

She smiled.

She regretted that she hadn't had more walks like this with him where there were no misunderstandings or secrets between them. That she hadn't gotten to know the things he wanted out of life, but it was for the best. She needed to focus on her future and that was with Pastor Adam MacKenzie. With the handle of her satchel in both hands, she stepped up onto the platform.

Denver, Colorado, departs at one-thirty, the sign read. She nodded her head and stepped up to the ticket office to exchange her train voucher for the next departure.

Once she had the new ticket in hand, Elizabeth sat down on a bench on the main platform and waited. She glanced up at the ornate black clock at the center of the boardwalk and exhaled. She still had fifteen minutes before they would start boarding.

One-thirty.

"Will?" a familiar voice called out and he spun around to see his older brother, one of the twins, all dressed up in fancy duds striding purposefully toward him.

"Levi!" He closed the distance, meeting him half way and embracing the man heartily. "Mr. Danvers from the land office told me he'd run into you and Cadence down here this morning. I didn't know you were coming home."

"I'm afraid it's only for a short time, little brother. The

railroad has me busier than ever with new lines shooting off from the main route. We may even get one that will take us all to Montana."

"Hmhmmm," a woman cleared her throat from behind him.

"Will, you remember Cade." Levi stepped aside to reveal the most beautiful pregnant woman Will had ever laid eyes on. Her dark, wavy hair framed her face perfectly and her high cheeks were light and rosy.

"And when were you planning on telling me that I'm going to be an uncle?" Will asked, his eyes inadvertently resting on Cadence's belly. He stepped forward and leaned down to place a kiss on his sister-in-law's cheek. "It's good to see you, Cade."

She laughed. "I'm still not sure he believes it's real."

Albert tugged on Levi's pant leg.

"And who might this be?" Levi asked as he dropped down to see the kid.

"Hello," the boy said. "I'm Albert. Are you going to be my brother too?" he asked innocently.

Levi stood up, his forehead crinkling, and a brow raised.

"It's a long story. I'll tell you on the ride home," Will assured him. "But, Albert here is coming to Redbourne Ranch until an appropriate family can be found." Will placed a hand on the kid's shoulder and squeezed him close.

"I've purchased a wagon from the smithy," Levi said. "While Cade insists she can ride, I thought it more appropriate considering her condition. It should be delivered any time now."

"Condition?" Cade smacked him on the arm. "You talk as if I have some disease. Women have babies every day, my love."

"Not mine," Levi said with a laugh as he placed a light kiss on his wife's lips. He turned to Will. "Have you had lunch?"

"As a matter of fact, we haven't."

"Would you care to join us?"

Will looked down at Albert, who nodded with exaggeration.

"Sounds perfect."

There was a small café at the edge of the station that boasted, *'Cities finest fried chicken.'* They walked inside and were seated immediately at a small table in the corner. Will sat down in the chair next to the window, admiring the vantage point of being able to see the train's platform from his seat. The savory scent from the man's supper at the next table wafted beneath Will's nose and his mouth started to water, followed by another low grumbling in his stomach.

Food. He hadn't realized just how hungry he was.

Will was grateful when their meals arrived a few minutes later. Albert had just finished telling Levi and Cade about finding 'the drooly lady' in the stagecoach sleeping. The kid had no problem telling it like he saw it, but he wasn't sure he wanted his brother to know that Albert saw that there was something unexplainable between him and Elizabeth.

The train whistle blew and Will looked up to see a small throng of passengers gather together, waiting in line to board. He scanned the dock for Elizabeth. It didn't take long to find her brilliant fiery curls amongst the growing crowd. He'd become fairly acquainted with the light tugging on his heart, but this time, he found it difficult to subdue.

Then, an uneasy feeling settled over him and a familiar nagging in his gut told him to be alert.

It can't be regret, he reasoned with himself. *I've known her all of thirty-six hours.*

They'd seen more than their fair share of adventure today, and he couldn't imagine there was more to be had. The bad guys had been caught, the bankroll delivered, train tickets exchanged. He turned back to the conversation and food at the table, pushing the nagging in his gut away.

"So, then, the marshal kissed the back of Miss Elizabeth's hand and you should have seen the look on Will's face." Albert's eyes narrowed into slits, his eyebrows scrunched together and his lips pursed into a pucker. He raised his hands and balled them into fists, then shot them open again, repeating the gesture.

Levi and Cadence laughed. Albert joined them.

"Why didn't you tell us about Elizabeth before, Will?" Cadence asked with a growing smile on her face.

Will narrowed his eyes at the little traitor. "Because there is nothing to tell. Despite what Albert says."

"Miss Gailey said that Elizabeth even knows how to shoot. Just the other day, they were under attack from a group of outlaws trying to get the treasure they had on board and she had to kill one of them before he killed her."

"Will, is that true?" Levi asked, his amusement turning to concern.

"Albert, how…?"

Will closed his eyes briefly and shook his head. "We ran into a little trouble on the way into Kansas City and Elizabeth was…quite brave. Almost got herself killed in the process, but yes, she shot one of them."

"That sounds like admiration in your voice," Cadence said.

"He's a Redbourne," Levi said. "We like strong women."

"I didn't say I like her."

"You didn't have to, little brother. It's evident."

"Well, it's no use. She's headed to Silver Falls to marry a preacher as a mail-order-bride. Who does that?" He glanced out the window again, just in time to see Elizabeth step up onto the train. He bit into the warm and savory breast of fried chicken, grateful for the hot meal, then took a sip of his lemonade while Levi regaled him with tales of life on the rails. Albert's eyes were glued to Will's brother, who reveled in his little audience.

It wouldn't be long before Levi and Cadence would have to find a place to settle. Will imagined it would be difficult to travel with children in their lines of work. His sister-in-law was a Pinkerton—of the spy sort—but wondered how that would work with a baby on the way. It wasn't like they needed the paycheck. Between Levi's job and his inheritance, Cadence could do whatever she chose to do and their little family would be more than comfortable.

The man dressed in a perfectly tailored, pin-striped suit, sitting at the table near the door, stood up, tossed a few coins on the table, and placed a dark fedora on top of his head. Will ignored the nagging feeling that tugged again at his gut. Although, there was something familiar about the bloke. Will moved to one side, hoping to catch a glimpse at the man's face to no avail.

Stop being so suspicious, he rationalized, chastising himself for his idiocy and took another sip of his drink.

He watched as the man from the café strode out onto the train's platform and without any luggage, stood in the line to board the same train as Elizabeth. Will set down his drink, not taking his eyes off the man, a pit forming around his still nagging gut. Then, the man turned just enough that Will could see him clearly.

Asa Henchley, one of Sterling Archer's men.

He stood suddenly and pulled some money from his pocket, handing it to his brother. "I can't explain right now, but I have to go," he said as he pushed himself away from the table. He took a large gulp of his lemonade. "Will you take Albert with you to Redbourne Ranch? Mama is expecting him. Also, Indy is tied up at the hitching post just outside." He spoke so fast he wasn't sure they'd understood a word he was saying.

"Where are you going?" Levi asked as he stood up from the table.

"He's going after Elizabeth," Albert said knowingly, excitement written on his little features. "Her train is supposed to leave at one-thirty o'clock."

Will looked at Cadence, pleading.

"Albert, Independence, Redbourne Ranch. Got it," Cadence said. "Go!"

Will nodded, then turned to the boy.

"Listen, kiddo…"

"Go, Will! You'll miss it."

"Levi and Cadence are going to take you to Stone Creek."

"I'll be okay."

"Do not run away, Albert. Do you understand me?"

"Go! Argggg."

"Albert," he said again, a warning in his voice.

"All right."

"Let me see your hands."

Albert raised his hands in the air. "I promise."

Will nodded, brushed his hand across the boy's head, and turned to Levi.

The man had disappeared onto the train car.

He had to go.

Now.

He still needed to purchase a ticket and make the train before it departed.

"I'm sorry," he said, pulling his now standing brother into his embrace. "And, thank you." He bent down and kissed Cadence on the cheek. "I'll see you all very soon."

"Good luck," she said. "She's quite beautiful."

How did they always know? He didn't have time to get the details, he just smiled and headed for the door before he remembered one last important detail. He skipped back to their table.

"Oh, and…uh, Caspar, Albert's dog is waiting just outside the door." He patted Levi on the shoulder and headed out before his brother could protest.

Will only stopped long enough to pull a small travelling sack from his saddle bags and then darted to the train station's ticket office as quickly as his feet would carry him.

"I'm afraid the train is full," the pinched-faced man with the balding head told him from behind the counter.

"It can't be that full," he said sardonically. "People are still being loaded.

"I'm sorry, the only place left would be in the luxury sleeping car?"

"I'll take that one."

"You don't understand, sir. It is quite expensive and—"

Will put up a finger to stop the man from speaking, pulled the cash from his bag, and laid it on the counter in a heap. "Do you think this might cover it?" he asked, still breathing heavier than normal.

The man pulled back, surprise lighting his face beneath his white and red visor.

"What?" Will said, realizing he was acting like an arrogant blowhard. "Haven't you ever seen a rich man in denim before?"

"No, sir. I mean, yes, sir. I mean—"

"Just get me the ticket. Please," he added in his most kind voice, mostly to remind himself he wasn't a total heathen.

He needed to watch his spending. He'd just spent his wages on one sleeping car. If he wasn't careful, he wouldn't be able to make his share of the ship. He couldn't think about that now. He'd find a way to make it work. For now, Elizabeth's safety was all that mattered.

The train whistle blew two long horns.

The ticket clerk passed Will the thickly printed paper. "You'd better hurry. It's already moving."

Will looked out the window, and sure enough, the train had started to move.

"Thank you," he called back to the man as he ran out the door onto the platform. There were still several train cars before it would leave the station completely. He draped his bag over his shoulder, his ticket between his teeth, and he prayed— harder than he had in a while—as he sprinted, nearly tripping over a sleeping man whose legs protruded from one of the benches.

He recovered just as the last car reached the edge of the platform.

Jump.

Holding his breath, Will caught onto one of the ladder rungs on the back of the caboose. He pulled himself over the railing and tumbled onto the metal surface at the ground level of the train. With a loud exhale and a hand over his heart, he lay back against the flooring and laughed. He'd made it. His satisfaction lasted only a moment, when he remembered why he'd made the jump in the first place.

He needed to get to Elizabeth.

CHAPTER TWENTY

Elizabeth felt like she was nearly sitting on the woman's lap next to her. Thank heaven it wasn't a man sitting there.

It might have been nice if it had been Will.

She bit her lip.

Elizabeth Archer, watch your thoughts.

She'd been one of the lucky ones and had gotten a seat next to the window. She stared outside the glass, hoping to catch one last glimpse of the man who'd instigated her new venture. While several men and women hustled about on the platform and around the station, there was no Redbourne to be seen. Even as the train left the station completely, she still scanned.

Her heart dropped. She yanked the curtain closed and stared straight ahead. He was gone. And any hope of getting to know the real him, and not just the idea of the boxer she'd admired, vanished with the station. She lifted a hand and awkwardly swiped at the lone tear she didn't care to admit had fallen down her cheek.

It had been a long day and the trip to Denver promised to be a long one. Elizabeth pulled a book from her satchel. She'd already read it several times, but it was one of her favorites. The heroine was strong and smart and the hero demonstrated his undying love for her over and over throughout the pages, not to mention the adventures they took together. She seemed to get caught up in the story every time she read it. It would be nice to lose herself again in that world where dreams came true and happily-ever-afters were real.

A baby started to cry. The man in the seat across from her sneezed. The child the row behind her kept popping his chewing gum. What she wouldn't give to have a room of her own in the sleeping car right now, but those days were long since passed. She slammed the book shut. The hero was about to save the heroine from a fate worse than death, but she found that she could not concentrate enough to enjoy the passage.

Opal and Gertrude had been seated together a few rows behind her, but their voices carried enough that Elizabeth could hear them busy in conversation about the letters they had received from their soon-to-be husbands. She thought now might be a good idea to learn a little about the preacher she was travelling west to marry. She patted her satchel, where the pastor's letter had been tucked away, then stood up from her seat and made her way to the back of the car. Maybe out on the back platform, she would be able to hear herself think.

"Excuse me," she said to a gentleman who had his legs sprawled across the aisle, his black fedora resting over his face.

He pulled his feet in enough for her to pass, but made no other gesture to accommodate. He certainly was no gentleman.

Elizabeth squeezed between his knees and the bench across from him. When she finally reached the compartment door, she swung it open and was greeted by a wash of fresh air swirling around her hair and face, and found it a refreshing change from the otherwise stuffed accommodations.

She stepped out onto the miniature platform, resting her back against the newly closed door. After a few deep breaths, she retrieved the pastor's letter from her pocket. It had been intended for Winnie and was supposed to contain details about the town and about the man.

Elizabeth felt silly, like she was intruding on someone else's private conversation, but she had to know something about him. She was the one he was going to marry after all.

The sky shone with its brilliant blue hues, scattered with several shades of feather-like clouds. Elizabeth moved to the balcony where she could get a better view of the countryside and thought how grateful she was that she didn't have to make the entire trip by stagecoach.

She leaned against the railing and unfolded the letter.

Dear Winifred,

I thought you might want to learn a little bit about your new home. Silver Falls is a beautiful place with a sense of community that would rival any other. I purchased a parcel of land right outside of town with access to the stream, a beautiful view of our mountainside, and green as far as the eye can see. I have already begun construction on our home. All that is missing is a woman's touch. Your touch.

I am a man of average height and build, but I am a loyal friend and love God. I enjoy reading, and…

A short burst of wind came unexpectedly and blew the letter from Elizabeth's hands.

"No!" she screamed against the breeze as it floated just out of reach. "No," her voice descended to a pleading whisper. "Please, God."

A large hand reached out from the platform on the car opposite her and snatched her letter from the air.

Elizabeth closed her eyes in gratitude.

"Thank you," she started, opening her eyes to see who had saved the only connection she had with her new life.

Will?

She blinked a few more times. It was him.

"Mr. Redbourne?" she said aloud. "What…? What are *you* doing here?" She hated that she had to yell to be heard.

He stepped down onto the small staircase of his train car, reached over to the railing on hers.

Elizabeth's heart raced.

Will made the jump between the two with ease.

Once he was safe on the platform with her and no longer in danger of falling, she hit him on the chest.

"Worried?" he asked.

She caught her breath. "Of course, not."

He raised a brow as if calling her bluff.

"What are you doing here? I thought you were headed back with Albert to Stone Creek. Wait," she asked, looking around him into the other car. "Where's Albert? And Caspar?"

"They are just fine and on their way to Stone Creek."

She opened her mouth to say something, but he raised a finger and placed it on her lips. Her heart beat faster and a wave of gooseflesh travelled down her arms at his touch.

"I ran into my brother and his wife at the station," he said, dropping his hand to his side. "They will make sure that Albert and your pup are safe."

She unwittingly brought her fingers to her mouth at the loss of his touch. "I...um..."

Spit it out, Elizabeth.

"You...uh, still haven't answered my question, Mr. Redbourne."

"Why I am here."

"Yes."

"Well, I thought you might want this." He held up the letter from the preacher.

"Oh," she clasped the button just below the neck on her dress, "thank you," she said, reaching for it.

He pulled it just out of her grasp.

"A love letter?"

"Just a..." What was she supposed to say? In a way, it was a love letter of sorts, but it didn't belong to her.

The truth.

"It's a letter. But it does not profess love. The preacher is expecting Winnie and he's going to get me instead."

"He's getting the better end of the deal, if you ask me," Will said playfully. He handed her the paper, his fingertips grazing her hand.

Why did his touch have such an effect on her?

"Thank you, but I'm not so sure." The thought occurred to her that she probably should have sent a telegram letting the good preacher know that things had changed and she would be taking Winnie's place, but it was too late now. Maybe she could wire him from Denver. At least he would have a little bit of time to prepare himself.

Elizabeth refolded the note and placed it into the pocket of her skirt. She would have plenty of time to read it later.

"Mr. Redbourne, what are you really doing here?"

"I'm taking you to Silver Falls," he said as if that ended the matter. "And the name is Will."

"I thought you had a precious boat to buy. Won't you miss out on the *opportunity of a lifetime*? I think that's how you put it."

"There will be other *boats*," he emphasized the word, copying her, "but I would not be able to forgive myself if something happened to you…or Opal or Gertrude, of course."

"Of course." She eyed him warily. Then, she remembered the conversation that she'd overheard between him and Mr. Danvers at the land office.

There was a big fight coming up in Denver and Mr. Danvers had been trying to recruit him. He must have changed his mind and was headed to Denver to fight. That was the only thing that made sense.

The air suddenly deflated from her sails.

This is not one of your fanciful romance novels, Elizabeth.

"Well, maybe we should go back to our seats," she said, reaching for the door.

Will held it open as she traipsed inside.

"I don't need an escort," she quipped at him.

"My seat is also this direction," he informed her, unaffected by her newly cool demeanor.

This time, the man with the long legs was not taking up half the aisle, in fact, he wasn't in his seat at all. When she arrived at her bench, she groaned inwardly at the woman, two rambunctious children, and an infant who must have exchanged places with the woman who had sat there previously. She turned back to look at Will with a smile.

"Well, this is my seat." She moved to sit down.

"Are you sure you would not rather join me at the front of the train?"

"The front?" she asked longingly. The luxury cars were in the front. She cleared her throat. "I think I will be just fine back here, but thank you for your kind offer, Mr. Redbourne."

"It's your choice ma'am, but it is my understanding that they are serving roast and sautéed potatoes for supper. With a French crème brûlée," he added to really taunt her.

Her mouth watered at the thought. But she couldn't. She couldn't risk losing any more of her heart to someone who wanted to fight for money. She'd seen all too often the pain and suffering that kind of life had on a person and she did not want to be one of those women who lived in constant fear that her husband wouldn't make it back home, or if he did, that he would be a broken man.

Husband. The thought was outrageous. She was no more going to marry Will Redbourne than the man with the long legs who'd slept with a fedora on his face. Her future was laid out for her now and those plans included one preacher from Silver Falls.

Elizabeth looked at the little brown-haired girl with the braided hair. The pretty youngster climbed up onto the bench and stuck her tongue out at Elizabeth.

"Ahhh," Elizabeth gasped. *How rude!*

Then, the girl pulled an icky face as she started to jump up and down on the padded cushions of Elizabeth's seat.

"Sara Marie, that is not nice. Stop jumping on the seat. Sit down right now and read to your brother," the frazzled woman said, bouncing a crying infant in her arms.

Elizabeth turned back to Will. His nearness startled her and she steadied herself by placing a hand on his chest. "Maybe," she cleared her throat, "just for a minute," she said, glancing up into his face.

His head bent down toward her—his mouth so close to hers.

"After you," he whispered with a hand over hers. He took a step back and swept the air in front of him, indicating the way.

She had a feeling that Will would be difficult to avoid on this trip—especially, if he provided some peace and quiet.

"I don't think I can," Elizabeth said, clinging to the railing at the front of the passenger car.

Will stepped around her, climbed down onto the train steps and held out his hand.

"I'll help you."

Elizabeth shook her head.

"I guess you can just go back to your seat and read your letter," he said, taunting her into getting over her fear.

It worked.

She moved her satchel around to her back and with one look at him, turned around and took her first step backward down the metal steps, her knuckles turning white as she gripped the iron rail.

"Look at me," he said, waiting for her to meet his eyes. "Give me your hand."

She slipped her fingers into his and he gripped them as tightly as he dared. "Now, place one foot on this step." He stomped on the bottom rung.

She squealed as one foot dangled in the air, not quite able to reach the step.

"One more time," he encouraged, wrapping his arm around

the railing, then reaffirming his grip on her hand.

She glanced over at him, the fear apparent in her eyes.

"Do you trust me?" he asked.

"I don't know," she retorted. "Should I?" She giggled uneasily.

He firmly planted his foot at the edge of his own step and nodded. "Jump!"

As soon as her foot left the metal stair, he slipped his free arm around her waist, pulling her into him as he released her hand, and planted her firmly on the top step of his platform.

"I did it!" she breathed. "With a little help," she added sheepishly.

He liked the color that seemed to stain her cheeks when he was around. He only dared hope he might be some of the reason for that.

"You're a natural adventurer," he praised.

As they worked from car to car, they practiced the same technique, until they got to the last. The steps were just too far apart to attempt the jump. Elizabeth looked up at him, her eyebrows scrunched together. Will chuckled as he pulled a lever on the front of the car they were on and released a bridge made of corrugated metal that swung around onto the other car and locked into place.

Elizabeth put her hands on her hips. "Do they all do that?" she asked, wide-eyed, a smile dancing on her lips.

"Yep," he said unapologetically.

"Why, Will Redbourne, if I didn't know any better, I would say that you wanted to be close to me."

"Is it that obvious?" he asked.

He stepped onto the bridge and reached back for her. She slipped her hand into his and they crossed with ease. Will pushed on the connecting slab until it clicked back into place.

"The dining car, I presume," he said as he opened the door. He'd been on several trains across country since the railroad had been completed last year, and with Levi Redbourne as his brother, he'd been privy to a lot of the luxuries offered to those who could afford it.

They stepped inside of the cart and Will smiled at Elizabeth's awed intake of breath.

"It's been a while since you've been on a train."

"It's been a while since I've seen anything so fancy, let alone been inside of it."

She turned to look at him and he swore he could see stars twinkling in her eyes.

"I hadn't realized just how hard it would be living out west without all the luxuries that London offered. That my father provided."

"May I see your ticket, sir?" A man, dressed in a white shirt, black vest and pants, and a black flat-topped hat extended his hand, a ticket punch in the other.

Will pulled his ticket from his bag and handed it to the man.

"Your compartment is just this way, Mr...?"

"Redbourne," he provided.

The conductor nodded and led them down the short hallway, through a thick red-velvet curtain and stood aside, his arm sweeping in front of a door with ornate gold foil patterns embossed around the edges.

"Will you be needing anything else at the moment, Mr. Redbourne? Mrs. Redbourne?"

It was probably for the best that the man believed the notion. The last thing he wanted was for talk to start among the passengers and crew.

Elizabeth opened her mouth to protest.

Will glanced at the man's nametag, then stepped slightly in front of her. "I think Mrs. Redbourne and I are fine for now, Lionel. Can you just tell us when dinner will be served?"

Although his family had money, they rarely used it for this type of expense. Guilt tugged a little at his gut when he thought about how many more jobs he would need to take to make up for this expenditure, but he wanted to enjoy it while it lasted. He would get the money he needed for the ship. One way or another.

"Dinner will be served at four-thirty, sir," Lionel said with a bow before disappearing back through the curtain.

The first-class compartment consisted of a large, stuffed bench-like couch with several throw pillows that extended almost the entire length of the cabin, a small table and chair in the corner, and a folding accordion door that separated the main compartment from the sleeping quarters.

An awkward silence ensued as Will realized they were alone together. In his room.

"Why did you do that?" Elizabeth asked quietly.

"Do what?"

"Let him believe we are married?"

Will nodded, understanding her reservations. "You're going to be spending time in my compartment and the last thing I want to do is give others the wrong impression. You are a lady who deserves their respect. People are just too quick to judge these days and I wouldn't want to be the cause of an ill-fitted reputation." Especially since Levi was constantly on the rails. A Redbourne with a loose woman in his compartment wouldn't be an easy rumor to shake.

The train jerked a little, throwing Elizabeth against him with a little squeal of surprise.

"I seem to keep doing that," she said as she pushed away from him. "Sorry."

"I'm not complaining," he said with a smile.

She shook her head with a laugh.

"Maybe we should go back out to the dining car."

"Yes." She was quick to respond, not meeting his eyes as he pulled back the curtain and she hurried past him, that beautiful stain returning to her cheeks. There was a little skip in her step as she walked back into the large, open car with a few guests lounging in chairs or in conversation at one of several tables dispersed throughout the cabin.

"Shall we sit and have a drink?" Will suggested.

"That sounds lovely," Elizabeth said, opting for a seat near the front of the car by the window.

"Good choice." He was surprised to see flowers adorning each of the tables in the dining car and thought how lovely one of the pale blue flowers that matched her eyes would look tucked up against Elizabeth's beautiful red curls.

Movement caught his eye and he looked up to see Mr. Henchley lurching out of sight behind the door in the next car. Did the man really think he could follow them and not be seen?

Will had no idea what the brute was up to, but he felt better knowing that Elizabeth was not sitting back there alone in a passenger car full of people where no one would have noticed had she gone missing.

He smiled.

"I still can't believe you came to America all on your own. You've done quite an impressive job of taking care of yourself," he commended. "If we don't count the last few times I've saved your life." He chuckled at the look of indignation she shot his way.

"Okay," she relented. "Twice."

More, if you count now, he thought, but didn't say it aloud. He did not want to alarm her. And as long as Henchley kept to himself, there wouldn't be any trouble. He'd see to that.

CHAPTER TWENTY-ONE

Elizabeth turned around to see what Will kept looking at. There was nothing there, but a couple of gentlemen playing cards and the door.

"Is everything all right? Am I boring you?"

"What? No. I mean, yes. Everything is fine."

She turned around again. "Did you want to play a game of cards?"

He jerked back a little and leaned against the back of his seat. "Now, aren't you full of surprises?"

"Why are you really here, Will?" she asked. "The truth this time."

He shook his head, shoulders shrugging, and chuckled uneasily. "I'm sure I don't know what you mean."

"I like to play games, but the physical kind, not the emotional kind. I learned a few things working for my father and one of them was to spot a tell when someone is lying. And you, Mr. Redbourne, are lying."

"Tell? What tell?"

"That doesn't matter. I know about the fight in Denver."

Now, he seemed genuinely confused.

"The fight Mr. Danvers was talking to you about. He wanted you to participate."

"You heard that?"

"It was hard to miss. I was sitting in the stage. The windows…were open."

"Then you must have heard me turn him down. I enjoy the sport of fighting, the challenge of it, but I learned all too well, at the hands of your father, the dangers of that world." He glanced behind her again.

She turned to see what he was looking at. Still nothing.

"Do you remember a man by the name of Asa Henchley?"

"Of course. He works for my father. Why?"

"Because I saw him board this train right after you got on."

Elizabeth whipped around and looked toward the back of the train and through the last window.

"Is that why you keep watching that door?"

Will nodded, then leaned forward. "You want to know why I really boarded this train? I was…"

"Worried about me?"

He shifted in his seat. "Yes," he said, placing his hand over hers. "I don't know what it is about you that makes me think…" he swallowed, "makes me feel…"

"Yes?" She sat up taller in her seat and waited for him to formulate the words.

"That makes me…"

Elizabeth held her breath.

"…care what happens to you."

It was a nice sentiment and she was glad that he cared, but a woman wanted to hear all of the reasons she was cared about, not that there was some mysterious reason that couldn't be pinpointed.

"Well, thank you," she said, followed by pursed lips. "I *care* about you too."

"I didn't mean it like that, Elizabeth."

"I'm sure."

"Will, I can't go back."

"I know."

Their four course dinner arrived and it was better than anything Elizabeth had tasted in months—maybe with the exception of the meal she'd eaten at Redbourne Ranch. They ate making small talk between bites. Elizabeth tried to enjoy the conversation, but she couldn't stop thinking about the lurking man. How had he found her? If Mr. Henchley followed her all the way to Silver Falls, she could be putting the people there, including the preacher, in danger and that didn't sit well with her. She had to think of something. She finished up the last bites of her meal and wiped her mouth with the corner of her napkin.

"Well," she said as she scooted to the edge of her bench and stood up, "Thank you for the meal. I should probably be getting back to my seat."

"If you think I'm letting you go back alone with him out there, you'll need to think again."

Elizabeth weighed her choices. On one hand, crying babies, bratty little girls who didn't mind their manners, and a determined henchman set on returning her to England to a life she didn't want to live. On the other hand, a ride full of peace and quiet, a place to stretch her legs, and a very handsome man to keep her company. There really wasn't much of a choice. She sank back into her chair.

"What do you think Mr. Henchley wants with me? Do you think he is here to return me to my father?" She thought about the type of work she imagined the man had done for her father and gasped, a quick intake of air filling her lungs. "Certainly, you don't think he would...hurt me?"

"Of course, not. I know how much Sterling loves you. The man has many faults, but his love for his family is not one of them."

"It sounds like you admire him."

"I admire..." he paused as if thinking of the best way to phrase it, "his determination and drive to get what he wants out of life, but I cannot forgive the way he chooses to go about getting it."

Elizabeth understood that sentiment all too well.

"It's getting late," Will said. "I think I'll stay out here for a while if you'd like to head back to the compartment and get some sleep.

She thought about arguing, but she knew it wouldn't do any good. Sleep sounded nice after a day like today, and now, with Will there, she could rest easier. She picked up her satchel, scooted to the end of her seat, and stood.

"Thank you," she said, placing a hand on his shoulder.

Will slipped off the bench. "Ma'am," he said as he made the motion of tipping his hat, although the Stetson remained on the seat. He plucked one of the flowers from the vase on the table and handed it to her. "Sleep well."

The deep, rich sound of his voice shook her insides and she smiled, in spite of herself, biting her lip. She reached out for the stem, but he shook his head.

"Allow me," he reached up to her face and pushed her hair back behind her ear, then tucked the small, blue flower there. "Goodnight."

Elizabeth didn't trust herself to speak. She smiled and turned away from him.

Once she reached the cloth separator, she pivoted so that half of her body was hidden by the thick velvet curtain. She watched Will for a moment as he slid onto his bench, his back to her, and she smiled lightly as he ran his hands through his already unkempt hair.

"Goodnight," she whispered, then slipped into his first-class compartment.

As soon as the door was shut, she leaned up against it, her heart pounding heavier than usual in her chest. She bit her lip, a smile forming on her face.

"I fancy Will Redbourne," she stated with disbelief to the empty room.

Then, as quickly as the smile had lightened her face, a feeling of apprehension and sadness overtook her. How could she entertain thoughts of Will when she was on her way to marry another man? A man who would already be getting a big surprise upon her arrival.

She reached up and removed the flower from behind her ear. Life had such a funny way. A week ago, she was all alone in a home she'd purchased under an assumed name, ready to start a life as someone else in a small little town in Kansas. She hadn't realized just how much she missed being Elizabeth Archer in these last few months, but every time Will said her name, she felt...free.

She laid the bloom on the table in the corner of the compartment and slipped out of her dress so it wouldn't become too crumpled in her sleep. She hung it over a bar in the sleeping chamber. With a last look at the empty cabin, she closed the accordion doors and lay back, staring at the ceiling.

What a predicament.

She closed her eyes and, despite the looming dilemma, she smiled.

Will could not get the woman's face out of his head. He'd rather enjoyed their supper, liked the way she laughed. She was unlike any woman he'd ever met before. He was used to having strong women in his life. His mother was the most resilient woman he knew, but Elizabeth was different. She didn't fawn all over him like so many of the women back home often did. She was her own person and he admired that about her.

"Lionel," he said to the conductor, "I wonder if I might have a slice of apple pie."

"I think we can manage that, sir."

He had a craving for something sweet and the pie would have to do for now. He smiled devilishly to himself, then, his mother's face floated to his mind.

Respect.

Leah Redbourne had engrained the concept into her children from an early age. She'd taught them well, but Will was the first to admit that he'd often chosen to experience life's lessons the hard way.

"Here is your pie, sir." Lionel leaned over as if telling a secret. "And I added a scoop of ice cream."

Will liked ice cream, though he'd never tasted any as good as Lottie's. The family cook, who'd been like a second mother to the Redbourne children, was as talented as they came. Her delicacies could rival any New York establishment.

He took a bite of the pie with a smidgeon of ice cream, but just as he brought it up to his mouth, Mr. Henchley peeked through the window into the dining car. He took one look at Will, and ducked back into the previous compartment. Will set his fork down on the plate, wiped his mouth with the napkin, and decided now was as good a time as any to confront the man.

Elizabeth had made it clear that she did not want to return to England, a thought that had disturbed him from the moment they'd met, but it was her choice and he would make sure that her father would respect that choice.

He moved easily into the next car as Mr. Henchley hadn't taken the time to return the bridge to its position. He glanced around, scanning the sleeping passengers, but did not see him. Then, the thought hit him. Distraction—a most effective technique. It was possible that Mr. Henchley had not come alone. In fact, Will remembered quite clearly the band of brutes he generally kept around. Maybe he wasn't working alone. Maybe he'd doubled-back.

Elizabeth.

He needed to get back to the first-class dining car. If he was going to confront Sterling's thug, he would make the man come to him.

People draped over the seats, trying to get some sleep. The small windows allowed for very little light to come into each car, making it difficult to navigate through the darkened cars. Will tripped over several sets of legs and travelling cases before he made his way back to the front of the train.

When he arrived at the dining car, the lights still burned brightly to accommodate several other passengers who'd taken a late meal. By the time he reached his table, his ice cream had already begun to melt. He slipped a bite into his mouth on the way to his quarters.

The accordion door to the sleeping quarters was cracked lightly, but not enough for him to verify that she was still inside. Either Elizabeth hadn't thought to lock it, or something was amiss and he decided that he'd rather err on the side of caution, so he stepped toward the open door, feeling his hip for his gun.

With a deep breath, Will wove his fingers beneath the handle, his gun now drawn and raised to his shoulder.

A loud snort came from the room, startling him and bringing a smile to his face. He slipped his gun back into its holster and stood there a moment longer...just to make sure. Sure enough, another little snort, accompanied by several mumbled sentences, alerted Will that she was indeed inside the sleeping compartment and all was well.

"Will..."

His name crossing her sleeping lips caught his attention, though it was followed by several mumblings he couldn't quite make out. Intrigued, he wanted to stay a little longer, to listen a little longer, but his conscience bid him leave. He chuckled inwardly as he backed away, bumping into the couch attached to the wall. He sank into the cushions, biting his hand to stop the curse from leaving his mouth as his knee now throbbed severely from where it had knocked against the wooden corner of the furniture.

Will lay back against the cushions for a moment to allow the ache to subside, reasoning it wouldn't hurt if he were to stay for a little while. He was there to protect Elizabeth and there would be no better place to do that than right there in the cabin.

"Goodnight, beautiful," he whispered, knowing full well

she could not hear him. He'd enjoyed their time together today. It was the first time in a long time that his ship and new position at the University of London had not consumed the majority of his thoughts. Now, they were haunted by the beautiful woman in the next room with the fire-red hair and a small, blue flower tucked behind her ear.

Get some sleep, Will.

He forced himself to stand long enough to secure the door, then he lay back down on the couch, closed his eyes, and smiled.

They still had a few more days together on this train and as long as he could keep Mr. Henchley away from her, he vowed not to waste a moment.

Sunday

Elizabeth awoke to the lulling of train wheels spinning over the tracks. She opened the curtains covering the book-sized window just above the suspended spring-board bed. The sun played peek-a-boo with the clouds, but it looked to be a promising day as the sky no longer appeared menacing.

She threw off the covers and reached for her dress. A crack in the accordion doors reminded her just how tired she'd been when she'd lain down last night. She'd been too exhausted to sit up and had simply latched it closed. When she slid the door backward, her eyes grew wide as Will's sleeping form draped over the couch.

She slammed the doors closed harder than she'd expected. Her hand shot to her mouth as she was afraid the loud banging sound may have woken him. She reached for her satchel and dug inside for her change of clothes—a nice sage green skirt and a beautiful cream blouse. She made quick work of getting dressed for the day, though it was awkward in such a cramped space and was unable to put her feet on the ground due to the height of the mattress.

It would be nice to get something new once they arrived in Silver Falls. While the dress Mrs. Weaver had given her was lovely, Elizabeth didn't know how appealing it would be to wear day in and day out over the course of the next week or so. She pinched her cheeks and tried to run her fingers through her hair. With little success, she pulled out her hairbrush and spent the next several minutes trying to untangle her curls. At last, she was able to pull her unruly locks together and braid them at the side of her head. It would have to do for now.

Once she was satisfied that she didn't look like a poodle in a lightning storm, she pulled back the doors to find that Will had slipped out of the room while she'd dressed. She bit back the disappointment that sank into her chest, climbed down from the bed, and walked out into the dining car where the mouth-watering scent of cooking meat and hot bread knotted her stomach.

Several gentlemen dipped their heads in acknowledgement as she made her way to the table where Will was already seated.

He looked up at her and scrambled to stand. Though he was unshaven, his hair had been brushed and he'd changed into a fresh shirt. Elizabeth's belly tumbled at the sight of him.

"I thought you might be hungry," he said with a wave of his hand at the seat across from him. "I ordered you some scrambled eggs and bacon. I hope that's all right."

"You read my mind," she said, trying to keep the conversation light. "I'm famished, but…"

"Everything has already been paid for, Elizabeth. There is no need to worry about that."

How did he know?

Was it that obvious that she was out of money—or nearly out of money?

Heat filled her face, but she couldn't bring herself to object.

"Thank you," she said with as much grace as she could muster. She was truly grateful for everything he had done for her.

They sat in companionable silence for a few minutes as Will glanced over the newspaper in front of him.

"How long before we reach Denver?" she asked, wishing for as much time as possible because she knew that once they arrived in Colorado, it would only be a matter of time before they would have to part ways.

"I expect we'll arrive sometime Wednesday evening." He looked up from the paper. "Are you getting nervous?" he asked as he folded it up and set it on the table top.

"Nervous? Why would I be nervous?" She chastised herself for the crack in her voice.

Will laughed.

"I would have never thought a girl like me, the daughter of an English…businessman, okay, criminal mastermind, common thug…would be on her way to marry an American preacher in the middle of nowhere."

"What did you think would happen…for a girl like you?" His tone was sincere and not at all attacking.

"Up until last year, I thought I would marry some wealthy aristocrat my father had introduced me to." She giggled uneasily. "I thought the path for my life had already been determined. I thought I…I thought my father was a good man."

"Is that what you want?"

"For my father to be a good man?" She looked at him as though he were daft. "Of course, I do."

"No, I mean, do you want to marry an aristocrat? Do you want that life?"

"Not now. I spent my whole childhood believing my father could do anything. He was a hero in my eyes. If I could have been deceived by someone I saw every single day of my life, someone I loved, how could I ever trust anyone in that world, especially one that I've only known a short while?"

"You've trusted me," he said simply.

"That's not the same. I watched you. I saw you fight. I saw

the integrity with which you comported yourself. I..." she stopped speaking, realizing what she'd just let slip. Not knowing how to recover, she just looked at him and shrugged.

"Unlike you," he said quietly, "I had good examples in my life and was taught from an early age that a man without integrity is like a bucket full of holes." He picked up his napkin and placed it on his lap. "Doesn't carry much water."

A woman who Elizabeth hadn't seen before placed plates in front of them full of delectable food items.

"And now, here you are," Will continued as he picked up a piece of bacon and placed it on his plate. "You left everything in your life that was familiar to come to a foreign land all to seek out a good, honest life. If that is not integrity," he said, plunging his fork into a large pile of eggs, "then I don't know what is. You are an extraordinary woman, Elizabeth Archer." He met her eyes and held them captive to do with as he desired. He smiled, winked, and lifted the food to his mouth.

Elizabeth lowered her lashes and looked at her hands, now folded in her lap. She had never really thought about it like that before. She'd felt like she would carry the stain of her father's actions, his world, with her wherever she went. Maybe marrying a preacher wouldn't be such a bad thing—as long as he was not the kind preaching hellfire and damnation all the time. She didn't know if she could stomach a man like that.

She looked back up at Will as she reached for a slice of bacon sitting at the edge of her plate. The temptation was simply too great to ignore. Elizabeth was quickly discovering that the meat wasn't the only temptation in front of her. With an audible sigh, she bit off the corner of a crispy piece of pork, and smiled.

She may only have two days, but it was enough, for now.

CHAPTER TWENTY-TWO

The next couple of days were fairly uneventful. Mr. Henchley had not shown his face since that first night and Will sat on edge, waiting for the man to make his move. Why would he have boarded the train if not to accost Elizabeth?

They'd discussed everything in their lives from the kinds of foods they liked to the dreams they most wanted out of life. He hadn't wanted to make Elizabeth uncomfortable by continuously reminding her that one of her father's men loomed somewhere on this train, but a nagging feeling wouldn't let him alone as they approached the Denver station.

He needed a plan. Something that would deter the man from whatever his objective may be. If Mr. Henchley didn't get what he'd come for on the train, Will had no doubts that the man would just follow her to Silver Falls and he didn't know who would be there to protect her. A measly and frail little preacher would be no match for a trained thug. No, it just would not do. He had to take care of the situation before they arrived at the depot.

Maybe he could just pay Henchley off, although, he imagined it would do little good for a man who obviously held a grudge. Will had broken the goon's nose and three of his fingers while fending off a targeted attack. That night had haunted Will's thoughts since he'd returned home months ago. He'd politely declined Archer's 'invitation' to throw a big fight and ended up beating the regional champion in just four rounds. A record.

Elizabeth's father lost a lot of money on that fight and had wanted to teach Will a lesson, so he'd sent Thom, his eldest son, and three of his brutes to show Will what happened when someone crossed Sterling Archer. It didn't end well for Archer's men and Will was on the next boat back to America.

A payoff wasn't an option. Even if the man accepted, he would just be back when Archer offered him more. They needed a more permanent solution.

Elizabeth had not come into the dining car yet this morning. He'd spent the last few nights sleeping on the couch in the cabin, if one could call it sleeping. He'd tossed and turned, thinking of the woman who slept mere feet from him.

What is taking her so long?

He looked over his shoulder as if that would hurry her along, but he still could not shake the uneasy feeling that now seemed to have taken permanent residence in his gut. He stood, picked up his hat, and headed back toward the compartment.

Elizabeth screamed.

Will broke into a run. He shoved the curtain to one side and slammed the compartment door open, but she wasn't there. He looked down the hallway just as the hem of her green skirt disappeared through the outside door on the front platform.

How did Henchley get into the first-class car?

Will strode down the hallway at a run, reaching to his side and placing a hand over the butt of his firearm. As he approached the cab, he slowed his pace enough that he could prepare himself for whatever lay in wait. He pushed on the doors to each of the sleeping compartments they'd passed, but all were shut tight, locked. He glanced through the windows on either side of the tittering door. They were gone.

The air held a chill as Will stepped out onto the transition deck.

"Will!" Elizabeth screamed his name.

It came from above.

He looked right for a ladder, then left. Metal rungs jutted out from the side of the car. He took off his hat and shoved it into the cab in the space behind the fireman in the tender car, then reached for one of the handles.

"I'll be back for that," he told the striped-capped man, whose dirty face was nearly as dark as the coal itself.

"You can't go up there!" the fireman called after him.

He couldn't hear the rest of what the man yelled as he'd already crested the car. At the top of the ladder, Will glanced over the edge. Several men on horseback rode alongside the train. It appeared that he'd been right. Mr. Henchley had not come alone.

How did the man think he was going to get off the train?

Please, God, don't let him toss Elizabeth down.

Will placed a foot on the roof and started to pull himself up.

"Stay where you are, Redbourne!" Henchley screamed over the deafening wind from the moving train. He held a fighting Elizabeth over his shoulder as he inched his way to the opposite end of the train car.

Will held his breath. The slightest wind could knock them both to their deaths. How had he been so stupid to have let this happen? He was supposed to have protected her.

"You're going to get yourself killed, Asa," he called out. "Just put her down."

His keen forethought had served him well in the past, but he'd let her down. The only way Henchley could have gotten to Elizabeth without him knowing was if he'd climbed over the roof of the first-class car and snuck in from the front. How had he not thought of that?

Why hadn't he made sure the door had been locked behind him?

"Come on, Henchley, I'm sure we can come to some type of agreement." His words were drowned out in the sheer volume of the current of rushing air.

While the man's back was turned, Will climbed up, over the last rung, until both feet were planted on the top of the train. There was nothing to hold onto and it took a moment before he gained his balance.

It would be a miracle if any of them survived this debacle.

Will crouched down low and, with practiced steps, danced his way toward Elizabeth and the man holding her captive.

CRACK!

A bullet pinged off the steel casing next to Will's foot—too close for comfort.

CRACK!

This time, the projectile entered the cabin below and Will held up his hands to show he was backing off. There were people on this train and if the man kept shooting, it was likely that an innocent passenger would get hurt.

Elizabeth's arms raised into the air and with a powerful grunt, she landed a punch to Henchley's backside with enough force that it brought him to his knees and he flipped her forward, flat onto her back, against the hard metal air vent riser at their feet.

Her hands shot to her chest as she gasped for air.

The brute recovered quickly. Once upright, he pulled back the hammer on his gun and aimed it at a winded Elizabeth.

Will bent forward, closing the short distance between them in moments, and lunged at the man, ramming his head into Henchley's gut, knocking the gun from his hand. It slid from view as the two men tumbled rapidly toward the edge.

Will grappled for his footing while his opponent dug into his shoulder with a vice-like grip. It took all the strength Will could muster, but he was able to maneuver far enough away that he could land a punch across the man's jaw and separate himself from Henchley's clutches.

It didn't take long for him to locate Elizabeth. She had dragged herself into a kneeling position and was attempting to make her way toward him, her chest still heaving from labored breaths.

"Stay!" Will cautioned as he crept along the rooftop in her direction. They needed to get off the top of the train before someone got killed.

"Are you all right?" he yelled the question as he reached her position. He forced himself to his feet and extended his hand.

She nodded, the wind twisting her hair and twirling it wildly about her face. She shoved it out of her eyes and slipped her hand into his without hesitation.

He glanced backward. Henchley was gaining on them and Will urged Elizabeth in front of him. He had to create a barrier between her and the man who'd come to take her back to England and back to her father.

Once they reached the end of the car, Elizabeth turned around to lower herself over the edge and down onto the ladder at the front of the train. She looked up, above Will's head, and gasped.

"Will, look out!"

He whipped around and rolled sideways just as Henchley took a swing at him. It threw the man off balance and he toppled over the side of the luxury car as he slid downward, his body quickly disappearing from sight.

Will gripped the railing with one hand to stop himself from following the brute overboard and reached out with the other, scrambling to grab ahold of the man's arm as it slid through his fingertips. He forced his hand to tighten and finally it caught successfully around Henchley's wrist, stopping him from falling to his death.

"I don't need your help, Redbourne," he spat, his feet dangling just above the mechanical rods churning the wheels.

Two men on horseback had their mounts at a gallop beneath them.

CRACK!

A shot pinged off the railing next to Will's arm.

"Just let me help you, Asa."

"You've. Done. Enough."

Will could feel the man's hand slipping through his fingers.

"Let go!"

CRACK!

Will ducked his head down to the roof.

"Take the win, Redbourne," Henchley urged. "It is not over yet." He yanked his arm free of Will's grasp.

Will collapsed against the roof on his belly, his breath coming in ragged heaves. Reluctantly, he moved away from the ledge and turned back to where Elizabeth still peeked over the top of the train.

"Are you all right?" he repeated his earlier question.

"Mmhmm," she affirmed. "You?"

He nodded, then dropped his head back down until his forehead rested against the cool metal roof. After a moment, he pushed himself up and made his way to the ladder. He hadn't recognized any of the men on horseback, but if they were with Henchley, he could bet that they would hunt Elizabeth until their mission was complete.

She'd already climbed to the bottom of the transition platform and Will followed as closely as he could. When his feet hit the ground, Elizabeth flung her arms around his neck and he pulled her in tightly to him, holding her close for longer than he should have.

"Let's get you inside," he said, pulling her away from him and rubbing her shoulders. He reached into the little cubby behind the fireman and retrieved his hat. "Thank you, kindly," he said with a smile he didn't feel, and then opened the door into the first-class compartment car.

As soon as they got back into their cabin, Will grabbed his bag and Elizabeth's satchel. They were not that far outside of Denver. Once the train pulled into the station, they would need to hurry. There was no time to waste.

"I'm thinking that rather than wait for the stage, it might be better if we just borrow or purchase a wagon or horses and make the drive ourselves," he told her as he set their things down next to the door.

The horses the men had been riding would need rest and would not be able to make it to the Denver station today. That would give them a good day's head start. He didn't like the idea of trying to outrun them, but he was out of options.

Elizabeth sank down onto the couch. "Does that mean you're coming with me to Silver Falls?" She looked up at him, her eyes searching, scared, hopeful. She rubbed her arms.

"You're shivering."

She was beautiful, there was no doubt about that. He pulled one of the blankets from the rumpled bed in the sleeping quarters and wrapped it around her shoulders.

"You didn't think I would just leave you to your own devices with someone like Mr. Henchley and his brutes out there, did you? My mama taught me better than that."

She smiled faintly. "I don't want to be any more trouble than I've already been. I can make the trip on my own. Truly. You've done so much for me already."

"The matter is settled," he said, leaving no room for argument—not that she wouldn't try.

"But, Will…"

He looked at her, one brow raised.

"Your ship," she said quietly—the one thing that struck a chord.

He sat down next to her and slouched against the back of the couch. He couldn't believe that she'd remembered.

"She's a real beauty," he said dreamily. "I'll have her one day."

"Her?"

"The ship."

"What is it about this…*ship* that draws you to…*her*?"

Will laughed. "I want the freedom it provides, I guess."

"Freedom? That is the last thing I expected to hear from a Redbourne."

Will sat up and turned to face her. "Don't get me wrong. I love working the ranch and being with my family, but something about exploring new lands and learning about different cultures and civilizations calls to me."

"So, you want to be a sailor."

"Me? No." He sucked in a deep breath, shaking his head, and grinned. "I will be the captain and commander of my own vessel." He sounded like a school boy with dreams of adventure. "And someday, not only will I have explored all corners of the earth, but I will be a renowned shipping tycoon." He laughed again.

She nodded slowly.

"You think me foolish?" That was exactly why he'd waited so long to tell his family about England.

"On the contrary, I find your choice brave and awe-inspiring."

Will didn't know exactly what he'd expected her to say, but that was not it. He wasn't sure how to respond.

"What about you? Surely, you have a dream."

She opened her mouth, then closed it again.

"What? It can't be that bad."

"It's not bad, it's just…Well, my dreams used to be similar to yours."

"Used to be?"

"Things changed when I left England. I'd read so many books as a child that were full of adventure and romance," she looked at him, the familiar red stain returning to her cheeks, "and people *doing* something with their lives. As I grew older, I realized it was no longer enough to read about those things. I wanted to experience some of them for myself."

"What changed?"

"Everything changed. Look at me," she said, pushing

herself into a standing position and holding the blanket open for him to see her dress. "I am hardly the woman I once was. I have exactly two dresses to wear. No home to speak of as it burned to the ground—almost with me inside. I'm down to my last few dollars, and I'm in desperate need of a bath. Not exactly the future I had envisioned." She leaned up against the wall, next to the window, and pulled back the curtain to stare outside.

"Why Silver Falls?"

She shrugged. "Adam MacKenzie."

"Who?" he asked, joining her at the window.

"The preacher. He's my future now."

He leaned forward and whispered in her ear. "How do you know?"

She pulled the blanket tighter around her shoulders and flicked her head enough that her hair spilled back behind her shoulder. "I…" She stopped, not finishing her sentence.

"From the way things are going, it seems like your father doesn't agree with your choice to get married to the man."

She whipped around and faced him, fire alight in her eyes. "My father does not control me anymore. He does not decide who I will marry or where I will live." She cleared her throat, took a step backward, and breathed deeply. "Besides, I only made the decision last week. There is no way he could have known of my plan to marry the preacher."

"Why *are* you marrying him? This preacher whom you've never met before?" Will regretted the question the moment it left his lips. He had no right to ask. Unless…

NO!

He was not even going to entertain the idea.

Marriage was not something to be taken lightly. He'd heard that his inheritance was a lofty sum, none of his brothers would confess the amount, but even a palace of gold was not enough to justify marrying for anything other than love. He didn't want the answer.

He still had plenty of time before his twenty-sixth

birthday—years even. So what if he lay awake at night thinking of her? So what if he had feelings for the woman that he'd never had for any other? Besides, Elizabeth had promised herself to another man. A man who was expecting someone else.

Will shook his head of the nonsense running through it. He looked down at her, placed a crooked finger beneath her chin, and lifted it so he could see her eyes. How a criminal like Sterling Archer had raised such an amazing daughter was a mystery. Elizabeth was smart and sassy, courageous, and thoughtful.

His gaze fell to her mouth and slowly, he lowered his head toward hers, wanting nothing more than to claim her lips with his own.

Two long blows of the train's whistle, followed by a short and another long, signaled their arrival in Denver. Will closed his eyes and clenched his jaw.

What are you doing, Redbourne?

"We need to go," he said quietly. He stepped away from her, picked up their bags, and draped them across his body, then held out his hand for her. "Now."

Denver reminded Elizabeth of home. The train station bustled with people. She'd seen plenty of tall buildings and crowds in New York and Boston, but never imagined that such a large city existed this far beyond the Mississippi.

Will held a hand out to help her down from the train car. She didn't have any luggage boxes or travelling cases to worry about, just the lone satchel that contained everything she owned, so she placed her hand in his, a gesture becoming all too familiar, and climbed down the metal steps.

"If we get moving and purchase a good pair of horses, we may just make it into Silver Falls before nightfall." Will did not let go of her hand, but ushered her through the bustling crowd toward the doors.

Once out in front, there was a large sign with the word, stagecoach, written across the top with an engraved image of the passenger wagon.

"Will, I already have a voucher for the stage." She slipped her hand from his and reached into her satchel to retrieve the ticket. "We don't need to spend more money getting horses or a wagon."

"It's too dangerous. Besides," he pointed at the sign with the next appointed departure, "it looks like the stage north only comes through here once a week. And that was yesterday. So, we can either find another way of getting to Silver Falls or we can wait until next Tuesday and give Henchley and his men time to catch up and find us. Is that what you want?"

"Of course, not." Her hands were tied. She had run out of options. How did she explain to him that she didn't want to take any more of his money? "But, who are you to decide what is too dangerous for me? I have to learn how to make my own way and if you are always there with an upgraded fancy sleeping car or hot meals that I didn't have to cook myself, it will just be that much harder when I have to face the reality of living without those conveniences."

His jaw pulsed. He removed his hat and ran his fingers through his hair before returning the Stetson to his head.

Elizabeth had taken every precaution to make sure that everything had been planned out down to the last detail for her trip, but the unexpected delay in Plain City had changed everything. She barely had enough funds remaining to buy herself a decent meal, let alone pay for a week's worth of room and board in Denver. She stepped toward him and placed a hand on his arm.

"Will, I appreciate everything you have already done for me more than you know. But your job was finished in Kansas City. I can't let you sacrifice any more than you already have for me."

"Just like you, I can decide for myself if something is too big a sacrifice." He paused a moment, then his voice quieted. "If it's the money you're worried about—"

"It's not just the money, Will. It's…you."

He stared at her, his eyes unreadable, searching.

"I've grown quite fond of you over these last couple of days. Grown to depend on you, but what happens when you're not there anymore? I think it's best that we part ways now, before…"

"Before what?" He closed the short distance between them and took her hands into his. "What if I don't leave?"

"What are you saying? That you are going to give up your dreams to what? Escort me into the arms of another man?"

"Not *another* man."

Her heart skipped a beat.

"Will," she shook her head, "I care about you too much to let you do that. I can't be the one who stands in the way of what you want out of life."

"What if what I want has changed?"

"Has it?"

His eyes moved back and forth between hers, his brows scrunched together as if he were searching for the right answer, conflicted. When he didn't respond immediately, she pulled her hands from his with a squeeze and smiled.

"It's all right, Will. I can make my own way."

"I don't doubt that for one minute." He raised a hand to her face and caressed her cheek with his thumb. "But, I'm still accompanying you to Silver Falls." He turned and strode down the street.

"Where are you going?" she asked, following after him. "Maybe you should leave my satchel here with me."

He didn't stop.

She nearly had to run to catch up to him. "You are a stubborn man, Mr. Redbourne."

"Then, I'm in good company." He looked down at her and winked.

Elizabeth shook her head, but laughed.

When they reached the livery, two men stood out front in casual conversation. The man in black leather cuffs and a filthy, once-white apron leaned with one elbow on a fence post, while the other man in a ridge-top hat had his foot propped up on the edge of a trough.

"Good morning, gentlemen," Will said, walking toward them and extending his hand. "I'm looking to get a couple of good riding horses and gear."

"Where ya headed?" The man with the hat stood up straight and met Will's hand with a shake.

"South. Figure we have about a day's ride ahead of us."

South?

They were headed north toward Boulder. What was he up to?

Elizabeth's eye caught on the shop across the street. She'd never seen dresses like those displayed in the window and wanted a closer look. She didn't hear the rest of their conversation as her focus was now diverted elsewhere.

The clothing was of fine quality, but she was intrigued by the brown one with buttons in two rows down the front. The skirt was split in the center like men's trousers, but it looked like an appropriate dress for a woman, similar to the one Mrs. Weaver had given her.

She stepped inside the shop.

"Hello," the woman greeted her. "Are you new in town or just passing through?" she asked, her chin lifted slightly into the air.

"I'm afraid we are just passing through, but I saw the dresses in your window and was intrigued. I've never seen anything quite like them."

"Ah, yes, the split skirts. Many of the women folk from the surrounding towns asked for something that would allow them to ride a horse and maintain their sense of propriety. Francine, my assistant, came up with the design and well," she clapped her hands together, "might we say they have been a very popular item." She led Elizabeth to a section of the store where there were several of these skirts already made up in a few different sizes.

"The dressmaker in Stone Creek, Kansas gave me something similar before I left," Elizabeth said, wishing she'd worn that skirt today instead of the rosy blouse and skirt Grace had given her. "I would love to have a few more. The work on these is exquisite," she said with awe as she ran her fingers over the stitching in the fabric.

"Thank you," the woman replied, her hands crossed in front of her belly.

Elizabeth looked up and caught a glimpse of Will through the window, looking frantically from one side of the street to the other.

"If you'll excuse me," she said as she gathered her skirt into her hands and headed for the door. "We are leaving shortly and I do not want to keep him waiting. You understand?" She opened the door to the shop. "You do beautiful work," she called over her shoulder as she skittered down off the boardwalk and headed back across the street.

Will had been so concerned for her safety and she didn't want him to worry that she'd disappeared.

CHAPTER TWENTY-THREE

It had only been a moment.

Will scanned the street for any sign of Elizabeth. She'd been right behind him. His gut had never failed him before, as much as he'd grumbled about not knowing how to trust it, and he did not like it one bit. Why had he not sensed trouble earlier? He chastised himself for taking so much time perusing the horses the liveryman had for sale that he'd let her absence go unnoticed for too long.

He started back toward the train station, his heart beating fiercely inside his chest, his breaths now coming more rapidly as the thought of losing her washed over him.

"Will!"

He stopped so quickly he slid on the gravely road, but thankfully he managed to stay upright as he spun around to the sound of her voice. Relief washed over him when he saw her cute little form step down from the boardwalk on the opposite side of the street from the livery and wave at him. He placed a hand over his heart, willing it to calm.

In—two, three, four. Out—two, three, four.

"I'm sorry," she said innocently, "were you looking for me?"

It took all of his will-power to stop himself from chastising her for disappearing, but she was not a child to be rebuked. He'd do best to remember that.

"Are you all right?" He didn't trust himself at the moment to say anything else.

"I'm fine. I hope I didn't worry you."

Will shook his head. "You can take care of yourself, right?"

"Right!" she said with a firm nod of her head.

The sunlight added a backlit glow to her hair, accentuating her vibrant red curls. There was a fire in her eyes that added a brilliant sheen to the vivid blue color.

He looked down at her lips, surprised by a desperate desire to claim them.

He cleared his throat and took a step back.

"We should be going," he said more briskly than he'd intended. "I found what we needed." He managed a smile as he led her back to the livery.

"Here you are, Mr. Redbourne," the liveryman said as he handed Will the reins to two strong Quarter horses.

The man hadn't had any horses that even rivaled Indy, but these two were strong and Will hoped the mare would be gentle enough for Elizabeth. The liveryman had directed him down the road to a saddle maker. He wouldn't have the luxury of a custom rig, but at this point, a nice, sturdy saddle for each of them would suffice.

"*Two* horses?" Elizabeth said, her hands on her hips and a smile touching the corners of her mouth.

"I thought you might change your mind." Will shrugged. "Come on," he said as he led their new mounts down the street behind them.

Once they had all the supplies and tack they would need for the day-long journey, Will stood next to the buckskin mare he'd selected for Elizabeth. He held out a hand to help her up, but she just stared at the horse like riding was a foreign concept.

"We're not going to get very far if you don't actually get on the horse. Don't tell me you don't know how to ride." Will thought about the short trip they'd taken into Kansas City with her riding in front of him on his lap. Not that he didn't like the thought of being that close to her, but if his arms were numb after just an hour or so, then he couldn't imagine what two or three hours would do.

"Of course, I know how to ride," Elizabeth said, her hands on her hips. "Well, I know how to ride the horses back home. I cannot say I have ever ridden on one of those contraptions." She pointed to the western style saddle. "I am certainly not afraid to try it, but…" she looked down at her skirt, scrunched up her face, her eyes narrowed, and tried to pull her dress up enough to stick her foot in the stirrups. By the time she finally managed to get her boot into the straps, she couldn't lean forward enough to reach the saddle horn.

Will stepped forward and lifted her up, but her bunched dress made it nearly impossible for her to swing her leg around the other side and the cloth inched up her leg until her knees were exposed.

Once seated, she looked forward, a stoic expression hardening her features, but a bright shade of pink flooded her face and neck.

Propriety. She was worried about showing her knees.

He dropped his head. He could see her point. He'd never had to worry about that before. His mother and sister both had appropriate riding attire, but now that he thought about it, most of the other women he knew did not ride much, if at all. They usually rode in wagons or carriages or walked wherever they went. Now it made sense why.

"I have an extra pair of denims, but I doubt you could even get rope to hold them up."

"I don't know that I've ever ridden…like you before. Like a man, I mean."

It took him a moment before he realized what she meant.

"You mean straddling the horse?"

She nodded.

Riding side-saddle on a western style rig would be dangerous, let alone uncomfortable, for such a long ride. He could see that would be a problem.

"Mrs. Weaver gave me a split skirt that I could change into, but…" Elizabeth shrugged.

She'd have to learn how to ride sooner or later, but he wasn't sure it was wise to have her first experience be on a day-long journey.

"Maybe we should just rent a wagon. It might take us a little longer, but you'll probably be more comfortable. It's not a short drive."

"Will, I know you've gone to a lot of effort and expense on my behalf, but I can't let you spend any more money or time. Give me a minute and I'll just find a place where I can change."

"And here I thought you were ready for the kind of adventures you've read about in your books." He raised his hands up in the air to pull her down from the horse. "Trust me, a sore backside will take the fun out of any undertaking."

Elizabeth placed her hands on Will's shoulders. He took a step backward and pulled her toward him, off the horse. Her hands slid down his chest as he set her on the ground, but he grabbed them before she could snatch them away and held them close to him. She looked up at him, searching his eyes.

This was becoming more complicated than he'd anticipated.

"Thank you," she said, her eyes a warm, dusky blue.

"If you'll allow me, ma'am," he said with a playful smile, "I'll be your outrider for this adventure."

She giggled.

Will released her hands to allow her room to adjust her skirt.

"Come on," he said, collecting the horses' reins in his hands. "We need to get a move on if we're going to make it to Silver Falls before nightfall."

"I would like to make one stop first, if that would be all right." Elizabeth asked.

He raised a brow, but did not object, though he was surprised when she paused in front of a jeweler's shop.

The ruby.

He'd remembered the necklace he'd found in her bag. It was the only explanation. She'd said herself that she was low on funds and he couldn't help but wonder if she was trying to sell the piece. She'd held onto it for this long, it must mean something to her.

"May I have my bag, please?" she asked, pointing at the satchel that Will had secured to the saddle of her horse.

"The wainwright's shop is just around the corner," he told her as he worked on the straps holding her bag in place. "I'll head over there and pick up a wagon."

She nodded.

He'd debated leaving her alone, even for a few minutes, but figured they had quite a lead on those that were after her. He handed her the satchel, tipped his hat, and made a mental note to stop by the jeweler's shop before they left town.

"Do you need help with anything?" he asked, pointing at the shop with his chin.

"I'll be fine. Thank you," she said with a smile.

Will watched as she disappeared inside the shop. He didn't know whether he should be grateful or apprehensive about sharing a seat with the beautiful woman for the next several hours. She made him feel invincible, and, in this line of work, that was dangerous.

"Come on," he said aloud as he climbed up onto his mount.

There was certainly nothing dull about Miss Archer.

"The horses need a break." Will stopped the wagon near a small copse of trees.

The sound of rushing water drew Elizabeth's attention to the falls cascading down the hillside just a few yards upstream and she climbed down off the wagon's seat to explore. Her legs wobbled from unuse, but it didn't take long before she'd regained her footing.

They had been travelling for the better part of the day and the sun waned in the sky. Elizabeth figured they still had another couple of hours before reaching Silver Falls and was grateful for the opportunity to stretch out.

Will unhitched the horses and led them to a small, grassy meadow near the river to graze. Elizabeth watched with amazement as he led them down to the water's edge and then brushed them down with skilled hands.

She'd watched him fight in several tournaments back in England and had admired the finesse and style of his movements as he worked his way up to becoming a heavyweight champion, but now, after everything he'd sacrificed for her, she had a new appreciation for his abilities outside of the ring. He was a natural protector and she felt safe when she was with him.

What am I doing?

She sat down on a large rock and removed her shoes and stockings to stick her bare feet in the cool ripples of the stream. She closed her eyes and leaned backward, allowing her hair to flow behind her in the afternoon breeze.

The deliciously sweet and spicy aroma of cinnamon and apples filled her nostrils and she breathed deeply.

"Hungry?"

Her eyes shot open.

Will waved a muffin from a Denver café beneath her nose and her stomach grumbled softly. She licked her lips. Slowly, he drew it upward just out of her seated reach and then raised it to his mouth. The next moment he sunk his teeth into the delicacy and smiled with satisfaction as he chewed.

He held it out again for her, only to repeat the motion, taking another bite.

"Oooo, you are a cruel man, Will Redbourne," Elizabeth squealed as she pushed herself up onto her feet in an attempt to grab it away from him, but he lifted it a little higher, but just as her fingers brushed across the wrist of his loaded hand, she slipped on one of the rocks and tumbled sideways, unable to catch her balance.

Will's arm shot out and he scooped her up before her dress hit the water. When she glanced up at him, his face was dangerously close to hers. She could feel his warm breath on her face and she drank in the musky scent of him, reveling in his nearness.

"You really must be more careful, Miss Archer," he said with a grin. "Any other man might not be such a gentleman and take your actions as a flirtation to be rewarded with a kiss."

Heat crept up her neck, through her face, and extended to the tips of her ears, but her gaze did not falter.

The humor disappeared from Will's features and his eyes fell to her mouth. Elizabeth's heart quickened and she bit her lip. Why did he have to be so attractive?

The horses neighed and the spell was broken.

"You can put me down now," Elizabeth said with a smile.

"I don't think so." Will scrunched down, balancing her in his arms, and retrieved her shoes. Then, he carried her over to the buckboard and placed her on the back fold.

"I am perfectly capable of walking across a meadow, Mr. Redbourne."

"And, I am perfectly capable of carrying you." He reached behind her and pulled a bag full of foodstuffs. "I thought you might want a little something to eat before we get back on the road." He pulled a small box from the bag and opened it to a delightful savory scent.

"What is in there?" She pulled back one of the box sides to peer inside.

She was greeted with pork medallions, fried potatoes, and corn bread. Elizabeth's mouth started to water. "I am starving."

"I thought you might be." He chuckled and handed her a napkin with one of the medallions on it.

"I still want some of that muffin," Elizabeth said, as she lifted the pork for a bite.

Will reached into the bag and pulled out a basket with several more of the cinnamon apple treats.

She pushed on his arm.

He laughed, but did not look at her as he turned around and hopped up on the back of the wagon beside her and scooped a bite of potatoes into his mouth.

"Thank you," Elizabeth said, swallowing her last bite of cornbread. "I was going to wait until we arrived in Silver Falls, but…" she twisted around, reached for the straps of her satchel, and dragged it across the back of the buckboard until it was in her lap. "…here." She handed him a few of her newly folded bills.

It had taken all of her strength to sell her ruby necklace, but when the appraiser had told her how much she would get for the piece, she'd reasoned it would be an investment in her new life. She wanted to start out by paying Will back for at least some of the extra expenses he'd incurred escorting her across country.

"What's this?" Will looked down at the money in her hand and raised his brow, then picked up a napkin and wiped at the corners of his mouth. "Well," he said as he hopped down off the back of the wagon, "we'd better get on the road. I'd like to make it to Silver Falls before dark. Come on." He held out a hand to help her down.

"Willlllll?"

He ignored her outstretched offering and scooped her up into his arms again, carried her to the wagon seat, and set her down.

"Stay put," he said before heading to the back and packing up what was left of their food.

Elizabeth didn't know where he thought she would go without her shoes.

Stubborn man.

A leather corner of Will's traveling bag protruded from

under his side of the seat. She glanced back to see him closing up the back of the wagon. With the money still in her hand, she leaned down, opened the flap of the side pocket, and quickly slipped the bills inside.

When he finally joined her on the wagon's seat, he handed over her shoes and stockings, then grabbed a hold of the reins. "I don't know what kind of impression you want to make, but showing up barefoot to meet that preacher groom of yours would be a right bold move."

Elizabeth opened her mouth in protest, but when she saw the smile that played with his handsome features, she closed it again and turned to face forward.

"Some men like bold," she quipped, not offering him the satisfaction of another glance.

Will chuckled.

"That we do. That we do." He snapped the reins and they started the last leg of her mail-order journey.

Silver Falls, Colorado

As they pulled into the dusty streets of the small town, Elizabeth's heart began to beat faster and her lungs filled with something seemingly lighter than air. Flutters twirled about in her belly as she sat up straighter, watching as many of the townsfolk stopped to watch them as they pulled up to the livery.

"Whoa," Will called.

He pulled back on the brake and wrapped the reins around it before jumping down and running over to her side.

"We made good time," he said with a satisfied grin. He wrapped his hands around the sides of her waist and helped her to the ground.

"Thank you," she told him, allowing her hands to linger a little too long on his strong forearms.

He winked. "Stay here," he said before disappearing into the stables.

Elizabeth glanced around at the curious faces looking at her as the onlookers talked amongst themselves. She brushed down her skirt at the creases their travels had placed in her dress.

The town was quaint, reminding her somewhat of Stone Creek. It was just missing the huge clock in the center of town. School would have long been over by this time in the day, and yet she saw several children playing stickball in a small field just off the main street.

She took a few steps toward the restaurant across the street until she saw a man dressed in dark colored trousers and a charcoal grey shirt with a white clerical collar, his sleeves rolled up to his elbows, skipping down the steps of the eatery, whistling cheerfully. Certainly a man of the cloth would not be dressed so casually, nor would he be so handsome.

Would he?

Intrigued, she watched as he greeted several passersby before heading into the mercantile.

Curiosity pecked at Elizabeth's mind until she gave in to its lure. Unable to stop herself, she pulled her shawl up around her shoulders, crossing her arms in front of her, and strode over to the store. She peeked inside the window where she could see the preacher speaking to the woman behind the counter, his face all but obscured. She looked back at the livery. Will glanced up and their eyes met.

At least, this time, he would know where she'd gone.

After a moment of trying to collect her nerve, she pulled open the mercantile door and strolled casually inside, attempting to get a better look at the man while browsing their humble selection of food stuffs, home improvement materials, and sewing notions.

"I hear the stage has been delayed," the woman behind the counter said. "We're all anxious to meet this mysterious bride of yours, Mac."

Mac?

"You and me both," he said with a wink.

Elizabeth sucked in a breath. She quickly picked up a large box of four candles and raised it in front of her face. She'd met several preachers in her lifetime and none of them looked like that.

"It's such a shame she won't be here to join us for the celebrations on Saturday."

Movement outside the window caught Elizabeth's attention and she glanced over to see Will striding up the boardwalk toward the mercantile. He stopped in front of the shop next door, then disappeared. Elizabeth leaned forward, attempting to see where he'd gone.

"Hello."

Elizabeth spun around to find the woman from behind the counter walking toward her.

"Hello," she replied with a smile, daring a glance at the handsome reverend. He was a little older than she'd expected, but that did not detract from his appeal.

The woman and the preacher both stared at her expectantly.

"Forgive me. My name is Elizabeth Archer," she started, gulping with her next breath. "I was supposed to be coming in on the stage."

This caught the preacher's attention and he turned to face her, leaning on the counter.

"We ran into a bit of trouble on the way into Denver, so when the stage was delayed, we decided to come by wagon."

"We?" the storekeeper asked.

How did she explain Will?

"The outrider who escorted me here," she said matter-of-factly. "And me."

"And the rest of the passengers on the stage?" the preacher asked with interest, pushing himself away from the counter and taking a step closer.

"I knew two of the other women who are on their way, but

we got separated and I am not sure when they will be arriving."

"I'm Matilda Patterson, by the way. This is my place," the woman said, glancing around the store. "Tell us, dear. What brings you to our little town?"

Elizabeth looked at the preacher and gulped. She looked down at her feet, then back up again. "Well, you see...I'm—"

The bell just above the door rang and Will walked into the room.

She exhaled loudly.

"Elizabeth," Will called. "The horses are settled for the night, but we'd better head on over to the church if we want to find that pastor of yours before it gets too dark." He turned to the shop owner. "I don't suppose you could direct us to the Lord's house, could you, ma'am?"

Elizabeth laughed nervously. "Will," she said, grabbing his arm and pulling him up in front of the man she'd come all the way to Silver Falls to marry.

The pastor stepped forward, his hand extended. "I'm Mac, the preacher here in town. Are you looking for me?"

"*You're* the preacher?" Will asked incredulously. It appeared it was his turn to be surprised. He glanced over at Elizabeth with a raised brow.

Heat rushed into her cheeks.

"Yes, sir," he said with a nod. "Were you expecting someone else?"

"You could say that," Will said, accepting the man's shake. "That's quite a grip you've got there, pastor."

"Sorry," Mac said, releasing Will's hand and raising them slightly in front of him. "Comes with the job."

"Well, now isn't that fitting? I guess my work is done here. Ma'am," he said with a tip of his hat as he stepped back toward the door. Then, he turned around and faced the preacher. "If you don't mind my asking, Mac, why would a man of your...standing," he forced out, "have the need for a mail-order-bride?"

Elizabeth could feel the blush in her cheeks deepen.

The preacher narrowed his eyes curiously to look at Will.

"Well, now, how would a stranger in town know something like that?"

Will looked over at her again, his dark brown eyes unreadable, and Elizabeth's mouth went dry. She managed a sheepish smile and took a step between them, facing the preacher.

"Because, I…*am* the mail-order-bride."

CHAPTER TWENTY-FOUR

Will didn't know what he'd been expecting of a small town preacher, but Pastor Mac was not it. He'd counted on the man to be...unappealing at the least, and had never imagined that Elizabeth might actually be attracted to her unseen groom. But, by the way she was gazing up at him...

A huge knot formed in his gut.

"You're not Winnie," the preacher said skeptically to Elizabeth.

"No." She shook her head. "I'm not."

She looked at Will as if to garner courage, but he had no intention of sticking around long enough to watch the woman he'd grown to care so much about over the last few days offer herself up as a bride to a man she'd never met before.

He needed air.

"If you'll excuse me," he said with a nod toward Mac. "I've got some business to attend to." He turned back to the door.

Elizabeth leaned toward him. "What business?" she whispered, her eyes leaving the pastor briefly to search Will's.

"You found him, Elizabeth. I'll find a place to stay tonight while you two get acquainted."

"But, Will..."

"Ma'am," he said with a tip of his hat, then he turned to the man to whom Elizabeth would be wed. "Pastor." He nodded his goodbye. "Elizabeth."

Without waiting for her response, he marched from the mercantile and down the road back toward the livery, his breathing staggered, his heart racing, and his fists on fire.

He needed a fight.

Elizabeth and the preacher walked the length of the boardwalk and out beyond town to a small pathway that led down to a large, rushing stream, as they discussed their unique situation.

"I must admit, in this job, there's not much that surprises me, Miss Archer, but you surprise me."

"How so?"

"Well," he rubbed his lightly bearded chin, "you're in love, yet here you are, fixing on getting married to a man you've known for all of an hour."

"I am not in love. Why would you say such a thing?"

Love? Will was the most annoying, controlling, arrogant, beautiful man she'd ever met, but did she love him?

"Don't be telling me that you haven't noticed how that young man looks at you. How you look at him."

She shook her head.

"Don't bother denying it. Sometimes, the Lord works in mysterious ways and sometimes he just lays it out plain as day, and darlin', today it's as plain as day."

"If that's what you believe, then why are you here walking with me? Listening to my life story?"

He shrugged. "I'm the preacher here. That's what I do."

"You are not angry?"

"Why should I be? Getting a mail-order-bride wasn't my idea in the first place. I come from a place called Thistleberry, Montana, where there are ten or more times the men to women.

The folks there believed that a man of God should have a good woman by his side. I don't disagree, but instead of allowing me to find someone on my own, they placed an ad for me with a matchmaker service. I'd actually hoped that it would happen for me naturally."

"And why hasn't it?" she asked.

"I guess I just haven't found the right woman. It is challenging when the odds are ten to one."

"Maybe for a lot of men, but look at you. I'm not convinced."

Did I just say that out loud? Heat rose in her cheeks.

"I, I mean, I cannot imagine you having trouble gaining favors with any woman you wanted."

That wasn't any better. Change the subject!

"What kind of woman is right for you?"

He laughed. "I imagine she'll be a lot like you—brave, strong, smart," he leaned into her and whispered, "beautiful."

"Why Pastor MacKenzie, I do believe you are flirting with me."

"It's Mac. And, if I thought for one minute that I'd have a chance at having you look at me the same way you look at Will, I'd whisk you away and marry you right now."

It still hadn't sunk in. She was attracted to Will, there was no doubt, and he had been her hero, saving her from disaster more than once, but love?

"That *is* why you paid my way to Silver Falls. To get a bride out of the bargain."

"Is it?" He turned to look at her, one eye mostly closed.

"Now you are just teasing me."

"Guilty as charged," he said with a slight bow.

The pastor was very easy to talk to and she already felt comfortable with him. This solution was supposed to have been the simple one. Move to Colorado, marry a preacher, lead a peaceful life and live happily ever after. It was turning out to be much more complicated.

"You may give Mr. Redbourne a run for his money yet," she said, smiling up at him as she wrapped her hand around his crooked arm as they walked.

"Redbourne? Not Leah's boy?"

He surprised her at every turn.

"Yes. How did you know?"

"I met Leah years ago when she brought her children out to visit their granddad in Thistleberry. I am just a year older than her oldest son, Raine. I knew they were from Kansas and since that is where Winnie lived, I figured the chances were pretty good."

"Sounds like you know them better than I do." Elizabeth shrugged. She realized just how little she knew about Will's family—other than what she'd learned in the few days she'd spent with them.

"I doubt that. I was working for Mr. Deardon at the time. Leah's father, well, his sons now, God rest his soul, own the largest ranch in the territory, and the work kept me too busy to do much fraternizing."

Elizabeth looked up at him and stopped, her eyes wide. "You worked on a ranch?" she asked, surprised by the revelation.

Mac laughed. "I wasn't always a preacher." He bent down and picked up a small pebble and tossed it into the river. "Liam, Mr. Deardon, got me back on my feet after I lost my parents. His grandsons—Deardon grandsons," he clarified, "have become like my brothers. I'm afraid the only one of Leah's children I had much interaction with was Raine."

"That makes a lot more sense. If the Deardons are anything like the Redbournes, you'd fit right in." She was being forward and she knew it, but somehow, it didn't feel wrong. "What is their secret? They seem to be the perfect family."

"Well, I don't know if I would call them perfect, they've had their trials, but I've never seen a family more devoted to each other."

"It sounds wonderful. Why would you ever leave Montana?"

"I was offered a position here. A parsonage of my own. And it just...felt right."

"So, what made you want to become a preacher?" She knew she was asking a lot of questions, but she couldn't help herself. Mac was a very interesting man—and, if she were honest with herself, she liked the connection he had to Will and his family. "I can't imagine it was for the money."

Mac laughed again.

She liked the deep, rich sound of it.

"Have you ever just felt like you were meant to do something with your life?" He picked up another rock.

"Will and I just had this conversation. Yes."

"Well, let's just say I didn't have the same type of childhood as the Deardons, or the Redbournes. After my parents passed, I was lost. Liam took me under his wing and I finally found a place where I was...I don't know...loved, encouraged, challenged to be a good man." He tossed the rock into the river. "Listen to me running off at the mouth. Maybe *you* should be the preacher." He smiled.

"I was prepared to be the preacher's wife," she said with a little laugh, "but that doesn't appear to be my calling either."

Mac was a very handsome, attentive man, so why did Elizabeth's thoughts keep returning to Will? She wondered if he'd found a place to stay for the night.

"Speaking of my calling," the pastor said, "we are having a community bazaar on Saturday to raise enough funds to build us a new church and school. We've already got most of the lumber and will be having a competition between some of the men to get the framework built as part of the festivities. We could sure use another pair of hands."

"I don't know that I would be much help, but I'll try."

The pastor shook his head. "I meant your Will."

"Well, he's not *my* Will, but he is a good man and I am sure he would be happy to help, if you ask him."

"Somehow, I think it would be better coming from you."

She turned to look at him, his eyes sparkled with mischief. "I'll ask." She giggled.

"Well, we'd best be getting back. You would not believe the talk that goes on in this town." The preacher held out his crooked arm and she took it. "Mrs. Patterson will have all of the ladies abuzz by now. They'll probably have us already married and have names picked out for at least three of our children."

They both laughed as they headed back to town.

"Will?"

Will turned to see Alaric Johannson, Cole's young friend, astride a lofty wagon seat as he pulled into town.

"What are you doing here?" the kid asked, leaning down to rest his elbow on his knee.

"I could ask you the same thing." Will had forgotten until now that Alaric had kin who lived in Silver Falls. It hadn't been that long ago that the youth had been sitting next to Cole during his little fight with Sven in their barn.

"I come here to visit my granddad every summer. Just heading over to the mercantile to pick up a few supplies for the upcoming week." He motioned for Will to follow him across the street to the mercantile. "I must admit, I would have never expected to see you around these parts. Denver maybe." He pulled to a stop in front of the store and jumped down off the seat. "I hear there's a big fight going on down there."

Will wished Denver were a little closer right now.

"It's a long story, kid, but I'm heading out at first light."

"Redbourne business?"

"Not exactly." He thought for a moment. "Outrider business."

"Ahhh…How exciting. You'll have to tell me all about it. It

is too bad though, that you won't be sticking around for the church bazaar on Saturday. They're going to have fireworks." Alaric's eyes grew wide and his speech became faster and louder. "Hey, they're going to have a boxing match with some of the locals to raise money. They said I'm not old enough to fight— not like granddad would allow it anyway, but, you should enter. You'd win for sure."

"Now, I don't know about that. But you said they are trying to raise money?"

"The preacher wants to build a new church and schoolhouse. I guess the roof on the old one caved in last month while school was in and a few of the students got hurt."

Will raised a brow. "This preacher, tell me about him."

"Mac? He's great! Beats that old reverend that used to stop by every couple of months or so, usually sloshed. He taught me and some of the other boys how to fish. He even knows how to throw a curveball."

He certainly does, Will thought with disdain. He didn't even know the man, but didn't like him just the same. He needed to get out of town and fast. He couldn't just stand by and watch Elizabeth marry him. It was time to stop chasing whatever fairy tale this was and get on with his own life. In England.

Will unclenched his fists.

"What kind of fight?"

"Huh?" Alaric's brows scrunched together.

"At the bazaar. Is it an organized match?"

Alaric shrugged. "Not sure. They just said they were looking for men who would step into the ring for a good cause."

Fighting was not always the answer, but sometimes it helped to relieve a little tension and right now, Will needed to release some of his pent up frustrations and if it was for a good cause even his mother couldn't object to that, now could she?

"Where do I sign up?"

"Really?" Alaric said, popping up straight, his eyes alight. "I think you just have to tell the mayor."

"Where do I find him?" Will asked.

Alaric pointed down the road. "He was out at the McCallister place earlier today, but I think he's back. He's usually in the restaurant having his supper about now. I'm sure you can find him there. If not, I can take you to out to the McCallisters once I'm done at the mercantile. It'll give me a chance to see Abby."

"Who's Abby?"

"Just a girl. McCallister's daughter."

"You sweet on her?"

Alaric shrugged. "She's like no other girl I've ever met. And I find that interesting. I like being around her."

Will nodded. He understood more than the kid would ever know. "Good luck," he said with a wave as he headed back in the direction of the restaurant.

Maybe he would be staying in Silver Falls longer than he'd anticipated. At least a day or two. As he approached the center of town, he glanced sideways, his heart dropping into his gut. Elizabeth and the preacher walked arm in arm up the side road laughing and talking comfortably.

At his size, it was unlikely Will could hide behind the mercantile pillar. Instead, he stopped and flicked his hand in a curt wave.

Elizabeth slipped her arm out from the preachers and made her way over to him.

"Will," she said, "I'd wondered where you'd gone." She brushed at her dress like he'd seen her do many times over the last couple of days.

His hands balled into fists and opened again.

Why did she have to be so beautiful? He forced a smile onto his face.

"I figured the two of you needed some time to get to know each other. Marriage is a pretty big commitment."

"Yes, it is," the preacher said with an odd smile. "Elizabeth, it's been a pleasure. Remember what we talked about." He met her eyes meaningfully.

Will turned away from the sight, not wanting to witness how well they got along.

"I have a pulpit that isn't going to finish itself," the preacher said with a laugh.

He's a carpenter too? What woman in her right mind wouldn't marry the man?

"Elizabeth, Miss Verla has a room all made up for you over at her restaurant next to the old church." Mac pointed to the quaint little house-like structure with two large white pillars in front, obscured slightly by a dilapidated old building. "I'll meet you at the restaurant in an hour and we can get some supper. I know the womenfolk around here are anxious to meet you, but I think we can put them off until tomorrow." He winked. "You two must be exhausted, travelling all the way in from Denver today."

"Thank you, Mac." Elizabeth beamed at the pastor. "I'll see you in an hour."

"Will," Mac looked up at him, "it's good to see you again." He tapped the brim of his hat.

Will returned the preacher's nod, then watched as the man strode up the street. He and Elizabeth seemed awfully cozy. Too cozy. What had he expected? She was supposed to marry the man after all. He knew he should be grateful that her intended was so…so perfect for her, yet somehow, that just irked him all the more.

"So, you're already on a first name basis with Pastor MacKenzie?" he asked with a raised brow.

"Why, Will Redbourne," her eyes narrowed at him and her lips curved into a smile, "are you jealous?"

Hell yes.

"Of course not. Jealous? Me? Why would I have reason to be jealous?"

Her eyes searched his for a moment. "Oh," she said with a quick shake of her head, "before I forget to tell you, there is a big town bazaar tomorrow and they are going to be building the framework for a new church and school."

"So, I've heard." Try as he might, he could not keep the dryness from his voice.

"I know you probably want to get on the road as soon as it's light, but…" Elizabeth took a deep breath. "…do you think you might be willing to stay and help the others? They could use an extra set of hands. And, I thought it would be ni—"

"I'll be here," he interrupted her. "I've been invited to participate in a boxing match. All in the name of charity."

Her jaw dropped. "Wait. You're staying because…because you're going to fight?"

"It's all for a good cause."

"But, I thought…never mind. So, you're staying?" She nodded to confirm.

"It looks like it."

"And you'll help with the school?"

"Yep."

"Great."

He tried to ignore the moisture that touched the brims of her eyes.

"Great," he replied flatly.

She picked up her dress with a nod of acknowledgement and stepped past him before turning back.

The wet streak that extended from eye to chin did not go unnoticed and Will's gut ached with regret. He wanted to pull her into his arms. To say he was sorry for being such a dolt. To kiss away her tears and let her know that everything would be all right. He started forward.

"Thank you, Will. For…everything," she said as she adjusted the satchel around her shoulders, then whipped around, away from him, and hopped up onto the boardwalk, heading the same direction as the pastor.

Now, he really felt like a heel. Would it have been so hard for him to show a little courtesy, a little respect? His mother would not be proud and guilt nudged at his gut. Again. He stood still and watched her until she disappeared into the restaurant at the edge of the town's center.

"Great," he muttered aloud.

Alaric stepped out of the mercantile with a large box in his arms. He loaded it into his wagon and started back up the stairs. "Did you find the mayor?" he asked hopefully.

Will shook his head. "Haven't made it that far yet," he said, taking a step up. "Here, let me help you with that," he said, picking up one of several crates that awaited the boy at the top of the porch.

"Thanks."

"Mr. Johansson," a rotund man with a big green vest and yellow bowtie called from a few lengths down the boardwalk. "I have been looking for you." His red, bulbous nose twitched as he pulled a handkerchief from his pocket. "ACHOO! Excuse me. I need to get some more of Miss Verla's honey. It seems to help. I think there is something in the air today and it's put me into fits." He wiped his face and tucked the cloth back into his pocket. "Mrs. Patterson tells me that you are friends with a real boxing champion from England and that he is here right now in our very little town."

Alaric's ears turned a deep shade of red.

"Well, is it true?"

The kid hesitantly turned and looked at Will.

"Yes, sir," he said aloud. "Sorry," he mouthed in Will's direction.

Will chuckled as he stepped forward and held out his hand to greet the man he guessed was the town mayor. "My name is Will Redbourne, sir."

"Redbourne, huh?" He mulled over the information for a moment before continuing. "Any relation to Leah Redbourne, son?"

He shouldn't have been surprised, since his Granddad Deardon owned property here.

"Yes, sir. She's my mother."

"How delightful," he said, clapping his hands together. "I've known Leah since we were children. She and your uncles used to spend countless…" he looked up and cleared his throat. "Yes, well, I'm sure you aren't interested in such things." He cleared his throat. "Are you the boxing champion to which this young man was referring?"

Will cast a tired look at his younger friend. "I don't know about that, but I've won a few bouts in the ring."

"Splendid. Splendid." The man clasped his hands tightly in front of him. "Oh, forgive me. I am Mayor Tuttle. Has Mr. Johansson informed you about our little charity bazaar tomorrow?"

"Yes, sir. He has."

"Oh, good. Then, can we count you in as one of the participants?"

"Yes, sir."

"Oh, this will bring folks from miles away." He spread his hands in the air as if rolling out a banner. "Leah Redbourne's son, a real honest-to-goodness fighter, here in Silver Falls. I'll send Mitchell Patterson over to Middleton at first light. We've got to spread the word." He clapped his hands again. "Leah Deardon's son," he said under his breath, nodding unceasingly. "Good to have you here, my boy," he said, slapping Will on the shoulder. He turned to Alaric. "You take good care of him, Mr. Johansson. And tell Miss Verla that she can put all of his meals on my tab."

"Yes, sir!" Alaric said with enthusiasm.

After the mayor left, Alaric turned to him, his tongue licking his lips. "Granddad's not a bad cook by any means, but Miss Verla's cookin' is almost as good as Lottie's."

The mention of his family cook, made Will's stomach grumble. He hadn't realized just how hungry he was. It had been hours since they'd eaten the pork medallions and cornbread from the café in Denver.

Will smiled, despite himself, as he thought of their interactions near the river and he patted his pocket, the ruby necklace inside of there a constant reminder of her.

Once the wagon was loaded, Alaric climbed up onto the bench. "You're not staying at the old Deardon place, are ya?" he asked.

Truth was, Will hadn't thought much about his accommodations for the night. He knew his Granddad Deardon had purchased several homesteads and parcels of land here, but until now, the stories about the man's adventures had been just that. Stories. "Is it even still standing?"

"Barely," Alaric said with a laugh. "Hey, why don't you come home with me. I know granddad would want you to. As soon as I drop off these supplies, we'll come back and eat at Miss Verla's. Granddad would like that too."

Will had never met Alaric's grandfather, but he knew that Friedrich Johansson and his own granddad had been friends many years ago. "All right," he said as he climbed up on the wagon next to the kid. "Let's go."

CHAPTER TWENTY-FIVE

Elizabeth folded her hands in her lap and waited at the table near the window for Mac to arrive. Several townspeople had stopped by to introduce themselves and to welcome her to town. The bell above the door rang and she glanced up to see Will. He met her eyes with a smile, tipped his hat in her direction, then followed a young boy and an older man, with white hair and a cane, to a table on the opposite end of the restaurant.

As if he didn't already occupy the majority of her thoughts...

She stood up and moved to the seat across the table that faced the window. She didn't want to stare at his back all through supper—or worse, his handsomely chiseled face.

"May I join you?"

Mac pulled out his chair and sat down. He'd changed his clothes into a nice pair of dark brown trousers and a blue shirt that matched the color of his eyes. His clean-shaven face and combed hair reminded Elizabeth that he was not only a preacher, but a man. Honest-to-goodness fine-looking man.

"Nothing like a man taking his beautiful, would-be mail-order-bride to dinner to cause him to reflect on his destiny."

"Reflection looks good on you." The words were out

before she could stop them. Heat rose in her face and she folded her lips together.

Mac laughed out loud, evoking in her an uneasy giggle.

Miss Verla walked up to the table and set a plate of chicken fried steak and mashed potatoes in front of each of them. "I've got some warm pie and custard in the kitchen," she said with a wink.

"Thank you." Mac nodded at the woman. "Harold is a lucky man to have won your hand, Verla."

The woman lit up under his praise. "I'll be back with that pie," she said with a wink.

The meal was delicious and Mac charming. In another time, another place, Mac would be the perfect suitor, the perfect husband, but right now, she couldn't get Will out of her mind.

Stars twinkled in the vast open sky and the scent of burning pine from someone's fire left a light trail in the air. Elizabeth stepped out onto the boardwalk while Mac waited for Verla to box up one of her pies.

Lights from the hotel flickered across the street and reminded her of the estate back home. She yearned for a warm bath and bed to rest her weary form. She leaned against one of the large wooden pillars adorning Miss Verla's porch.

The door opened and Will stepped out of the restaurant onto the boardwalk followed by his supper mates. He strolled down the steps and stopped to help the old man climb up onto the seat in the wagon.

"You have to tell him before it's too late."

She hadn't seen Mac leave the restaurant and jumped with surprise at the sound of his voice behind her. She breathed a laugh and shook her head.

"He's leaving." Her head rested against the pillar. "There's a boat, a ship," she corrected, "waiting in Boston to take him back to England."

"And you don't want to go. Because of your father?"

She nodded. "I do not want any part of that life." She

turned to look at the handsome preacher. "How is it that I have known you only a few hours and you know more about me than almost anyone in the world?"

He chuckled. "It comes with the collar," he said, his smile revealing a small dimple at the corner of his mouth. "I tend to have that effect on people."

She turned back to her post and rested her head against the wood as the small wagon disappeared around the smithy and out of sight.

"Did you find your room upstairs acceptable?" he asked.

"Yes, quite. Thank you." She reached into her pocket and pulled out the money she'd intended to use to cover her expenses. "Miss Verla said that you have already paid for the room, but I cannot let you do that." She handed him the money. "Not now. You have done so much for me already."

"Nonsense. You, Miss Elizabeth Archer, are worth every penny. And, since the other two brides have not yet arrived, I imagine you'll have the place to yourself—except for Verla, of course. She lives in the section in the back." Mac took a step down onto the street and looked back at her. He reached up and brushed a stray lock of hair from her face and rested it behind her ear. "I'll just be down the street at the parsonage on the other side of the mercantile if you need anything."

"Thank you, Mac." She leaned down and kissed him lightly on the cheek.

He nodded. "Goodnight, Elizabeth."

There was a lot to think about. Mac was a good man with a good heart. He would be a good husband, of that she had no doubt, but he was right. Elizabeth had fallen in love with the outrider, despite her best intentions. But even if he felt the same, she didn't know if she could return to England after everything that had happened and she would not be the one to stop him from living his dream.

The night air had grown chilly and she briskly rubbed at her arms before resigning to the evening. A good night's sleep would help her to think more clearly in the morning.

She hoped.

Saturday

It had been a while since Will had awoken to the cock's crow. He stared at the ceiling for a few minutes, watching the morning's rays bouncing across the room, before shoving the covers aside. He sat up, rubbed his face with both hands, and took a deep breath.

He appreciated the Johanssons' hospitality. It had been a while since he'd had a good night's sleep in a real bed. And it had been a long time since he'd stepped into an actual ring. Even though today's match was for a good cause, the old pressures still weighed on his gut like MaryBeth Hutchinson's fruitcake. Just the thought made him groan.

After today, he'd be making all the necessary preparations and then in a few weeks' time, headed for England.

England.

He reached for his clothes. When he pulled his trousers off the back of the large armchair next to the bed, Elizabeth's ruby necklace tumbled out onto the floor. The sun's rays glinted off the deep red gem. He picked it up, the cool metal chain draping across his hand, the ruby pendant dangling, glittering in the light.

Elizabeth deserved a happy life. And if that life did not include him, he would bow out graciously. He closed his fist over the jewelry and closed his eyes.

Time to go.

He slipped the necklace back into his pocket and proceeded to dress. In another half hour, his horse was saddled and he was ready to leave. Alaric and his grandfather were already loaded on the wagon. Will was impressed at how young Mr. Johansson still seemed. The old man had hurt his leg working with one of his horses last month, but another week or so and he would be as spry as any of them.

The Johansson stead was only a couple of miles from town. The days were getting warmer and Will was grateful that they had opted to start work on the church and school house early instead of waiting until the sun sat high in the sky.

When they pulled up to the building site, the place was already booming with men, women, and children hustling about in anxious preparation.

"We appreciate your coming, Mr. Redbourne," the pastor said as soon as Will walked up to the meadow just beyond the mercantile. "We can use all the hands we can get. And I understand you are quite handy with a hammer and nails."

He supposed that anyone who'd grown up on a horse ranch would know his way around the tools and shrugged. "I've built my fair share of fences."

Mac smiled and clapped him on the back.

Elizabeth stood behind a table, adorned with a long white cloth, pouring several large glasses of lemonade. When she looked up, Will couldn't help the grin that spread across his face. Her hair had been pulled back on the sides, but the length of it was curled, cascading down her shoulders, and she wore a cornflower blue dress that matched the color of her eyes.

She waved, then picked up another glass, biting her lip with a smile.

Will groaned.

Why did the preacher have to be a good guy?

With the majority of the menfolk in the town helping, the frame for the schoolhouse was erected before lunch. He imagined that it would probably take a few weeks for them to finish the building to any respectable level.

He wiped the sweat from his forehead with a handkerchief as he leaned up against the hitching post, waiting for a spot to open near the water pump. It seemed unusually warm for a day this early in the year. Men surrounded the table where the ladies were dosing out lemonade, the preacher at the front of the line.

Elizabeth handed the man a tall glass full of the frosty drink and laughed at something he said. Will kicked at the dirt, willing the men in front of the pump to go faster. He wanted to dunk his entire head below the cold water.

Enough of this. Either get the girl or let her go.

"Thought you might could use a drink."

Will looked up to see Mac holding out one of the frosty glasses of lemonade for him. How had he gotten over to him so quickly?

"Don't mind if I do." He took the glass and took a small swig.

"Elizabeth's quite a lady," Mac said, leaning over the top of the post.

"I'm aware." He wiped the excess from his lip with the back of his forefinger.

A few moments of silence passed between them.

"Alaric wasn't wrong. You really are good with a hammer. I don't know that we could have got this frame up so quickly without your help. Thank you."

"I didn't do much."

"Don't be so modest."

Funny—his mama would say he needed to develop a better sense of modesty.

"So, the mayor tells me you'll be fighting this evening in the ring."

"Yep."

"You really a regional champion?"

Alaric!

"It's just a title." One that had come at a great cost.

"Well, all the same. I wish you luck."

"I haven't ever known a preacher that condoned fighting."

"Well, now, it's for charity. Besides, it's not fighting. It's boxing. I would have thought you, of all people, would know the difference." He nudged Will, a grin set on his face.

It was hard not to like the man.

"So, Preacher, what brought you to Silver Falls?"

He needed to know that he would be leaving Elizabeth in good hands.

"It was time for a change of scenery. When this parsonage opened, an old friend of mine recommended me for the position, and well, here I am."

Could he have been any more ambiguous?

"How long have you been here?"

"Since March."

Will turned to look at him, surprised by the information. By the way the people here embraced and admired the reverend, he would have thought that the man had been here for years. That still didn't mean anything. Swindlers made a living doing the same thing.

"Where were you before this?"

"A little town up north called Thistleberry."

"Montana?"

"Yep. And, yes. I knew your grandfather." He turned around, arms folded, and leaned on the post next to Will. "You come from good stock, Redbourne. Liam was a good man."

"How…?"

Will narrowed his eyes at the pastor. How could he possibly know that Liam Deardon was his granddad?

"I know your family very well. Liam took me in when I was young, gave me a home. Seth, Daniel, and I used to get into all sorts of trouble together."

At the mention of his cousins, Will was a little nostalgic. It had been way too long since he'd been out to Whisper Ridge for a visit. They hadn't been able to make it when Granddad died. No wonder he liked the preacher—despite his best intentions. He'd already been given the stamp of approval by family.

"You're making it difficult not to like you, Pastor."

The man laughed.

"Were you looking for a reason not to like me?"

An older woman with white hair pulled up into a bun on top of her head, and an apron to match, held out a small wicker basket with cloth napkins protruding from the sides. "I thought you two gentlemen might like some hot fried chicken and hearty potato salad." The aroma of chicken mixed with cornbread made Will salivate.

"Mrs. Jensen, you are an angel sent down from heaven. You read my mind." The preacher stood up straight and relieved the woman of the basket. "Are there some of your berry tartlets inside?" He lifted the cloth on top to peer inside and then looked up at her with an appreciative grin.

"I know you like them." The woman's pleased expression took years off her otherwise wrinkled face.

"Thank you, ma'am," Mac said with a wink. He moved over to the mercantile steps and sat down, placing the hamper at his feet. "Will?" He held up a chicken leg.

He didn't have to be asked twice.

"That's mighty kind of you, ma'am." He tipped his hat at Mrs. Jensen, then joined Mac on the stairs.

By the looks of things, everyone in town was pitching in to do their part. Some of the materials for the church had been donated by local merchants. Others contributed their time, food, and baking talents to provide meals for those who had been willing to help with the building.

He caught sight of young Alaric sitting on the edge of the boardwalk, laughing at something a young girl with reddish blond pigtails had said, and a sprig of jealousy pricked at his gut. *Smart kid.*

Normally, with a big fight pending, Will would forgo the meal right before the bout. His stomach would knot up, his palms would sweat, and he undoubtedly acted more aggressively toward the people around him. However, for some inexplicable reason, he wasn't experiencing any of those symptoms. He felt calm, hungry even.

He reached in and pulled a nice big breast from the basket

and leaned down onto one elbow before indulging with a bite into batter covered meat. He closed his eyes, reveling in the juicy food.

"Mrs. Jensen is a good cook, is she not?" The woman's question surprised him and he opened his eyes to find Elizabeth standing at the base of the mercantile steps, her head blocking a good portion of the sun. The light shone brightly through the unruly red tendrils that framed her face.

He sat up straight.

"Almost as good—"

"As Lottie's," she finished for him. "I know. We had her fried chicken the first night I met your family." She handed Will a plate with several small confections on it. Then, she handed one to Mac. "We thought you both might enjoy something sweet to finish up your meals."

"I just took the first bite," Will said, holding up his chicken as proof.

"Mrs. Jensen's tartlets will do just fine for me," the pastor said, raising one into the air.

The three-point clang of a triangle sounded and a man's voice, amplified by a conical ship-hailer, shouted a call-to-action for the resting crowd. "Just one more wall to go, folks. Let's get this frame finished up before we head on over for the rest of today's festivities."

Will looked over at the preacher. "Do they want us to inhale our food?"

"You've got brothers. You should be used to that."

"Not with my mama around. No, sir. If we acted like wolves, we ate like them too. Out in the coop. On the ground."

Mac laughed. "Poor chickens."

Elizabeth's brows knit together. "Did you decide not to fight?" she asked.

"No. I'm still planning on it." He looked at Mac. "It's for a good cause, remember?"

"Of course," she said, replacing her confused expression

with a reluctant smile. "It's just that I thought you didn't like to eat before a big fight."

Will narrowed his eyes at her. "How could you possibly know that?" he asked.

"Sterling Archer's daughter, *remember?*" she said, pointing at herself.

"How could I forget?" he mumbled under his breath before thinking better of it.

By the stricken look that crossed Elizabeth's face, she'd heard.

Damn.

"Elizabeth," Will called after her, but she had no intention of talking to him right now. The reality of his words stung. She was Sterling Archer's daughter and no matter how far away she ran or what name she used, the fact remained and there was nothing she could do to change what had happened. Will had every right to resent her father. The man had tried to have him killed for winning the heavyweight championship instead of throwing the match like he'd been instructed to do.

Elizabeth set the plate of pastries down on the refreshment table and briskly excused herself. She needed to be alone for a moment to reevaluate what it was that she wanted. Who she wanted. It was time to make a decision and stick with it. She slipped behind the mercantile and started down the same small path she'd travelled with Mac when she'd first arrived in town.

"I don't know what happened back there…"

The sound of Mac's voice brought her some semblance of comfort.

"…but, I do know that it won't be resolved by running away."

That is exactly what she'd done. She'd run away from home. She'd lacked the courage to stand up to her father, and now, she felt like a fraud.

"You heard him, Mac. I was a fool to think there could be anything lasting between us with so much history." She wasn't angry or hurt as much as she was sad. "I thought…"

"Shhh." Mac reached out and placed a comforting hand on her shoulder, but she spun to face him, delving her face into his shoulder and he welcomed her into his arms, holding her.

She fought back the tears that threatened.

"Seems to me that Will Redbourne is a good man who loves you." He pulled away from her enough that he could look into her face.

She met his eyes, blinking to rid hers of their wetness.

"He loves you." He squeezed her shoulders, then dropped his hands into his pockets.

"Maybe love isn't enough to bridge the gap between us."

"Have a little faith, Elizabeth. He has a plan for you." Mac glanced upward. "He has one for me. He has one for all of us. Trust in Him and He will guide your path."

"Pastor, come quick." The young man who'd been with Will at the restaurant last night darted up the path. "Eddie fell and he's hurt real bad."

"Excuse me, Elizabeth," he said apologetically as he turned back with the boy.

"Go," she urged. "I'll catch up." She picked up the hem of her skirt and hurried back to the building site.

A burley man with a thick beard and moustache lay on the ground, his head in Miss Verla's lap, his arm twisted at an odd angle. Several men and women had gathered around him and a man in a black frock coat and a string tie knelt over him, a brown leather doctor's bag at his side.

"I'm sorry, Eddie," the doc said, "but you'll have to withdraw from the match."

The man dropped his head, then looked back up at the doctor. "Can't you just move it back into place like last time? I can still fight."

"No, Eddie, you can't."

"Withdraw?" A rotund man in a brown canvas vest and cotton notch collar pulled a pipe from his mouth and fixed his gaze on the injured man. "Mr. Sanders, who did you name as your second?"

Silence.

"Every boxer was required to—"

"Me." Mac stepped forward and a hushed awe fell over the crowd.

No! Elizabeth's hand shot to her mouth.

"Pastor?" Mr. Sanders looked up at Mac, his brows furrowed, shaking his head. "I'm so sorry."

"It's all right, Eddie," Mac said, rolling up the sleeves on his shirt. "It's for a good cause."

Elizabeth had heard that phrase one too many times over the last couple of days.

Mac looked over at her and winked.

Men.

Will glanced across the ring at his final opponent. He should have known the moment he'd rolled out of bed that morning that it would come down to him or the preacher. He would have never believed he could hit a man of God, but after seeing Elizabeth in his arms that morning out by the river, all bets were off.

CHAPTER TWENTY-SIX

Elizabeth glanced down at the ticket in her hand, refusing to regret what she'd done. The realization that there was no future for her and Will Redbourne had come at a hefty price, but she was determined to stand by her decision, no matter the cost.

Ding.

Her gaze shot up to the ring and she watched with baited breath as the two men approached each other, neither taking his eyes off the other. How had she gotten herself into this mess?

Jab.

"Ohhhhh," the crowd hummed all around her.

The preacher was the first to make a move, striking Will directly in the nose.

Bold.

Images from the championship fight in England flashed through Elizabeth's mind, and although Mac had held his own and had made it successfully to the final round, she couldn't help but worry. Will was a talented pugilist and had learned the art of patience in the ring. He would allow his opponent to get comfortable, lead him into a false sense of security, then pounce.

She wasn't sure she could watch.

Jab.

The preacher struck again.

"Come on, Redbourne," someone called out from the crowd. "Show us the champion."

Elizabeth shook her head. She should have been thrilled to have two men fighting over her, but it meant little when she realized that either of them would be content to live without her. She scrunched the ticket in her hand and held it against her chest.

Faith. That is what Mac had suggested.

She'd wagered her future on the outcome of this fight. All of the money remaining from the sale of her ruby necklace had been placed on Will. He was the safe bet. If he won, she'd have enough money to get her back to Stone Creek. Somewhere familiar, with people who cared about her. After today, Will would be heading back to England, to teach at the University of London and, except for the rare occasion of a holiday visit, she would not have cause to see him again.

If Mac won, Elizabeth was prepared to stay in Silver Falls and convince him to marry her. He was a good man and it didn't require much imagination to believe that she could feel for him what she now felt for Will. Besides, she reasoned stubbornly, it was all for a good cause. Any money lost would be used to help rebuild the church and schoolhouse.

It was in God's hands now.

The winner of the final match would decide her fate.

Will's eyes watered. His nose throbbed.

Visions of Mac holding Elizabeth, laughing with her, marrying her, fueled his jealousy and he struggled to remember his training, to keep his emotions in check. He breathed in slowly, narrowing his eyes at his target, but all he could see was the collar that was no longer there.

They'd both lost their shirts after the first round with other opponents and it irked Will that the preacher was as fit as any man he'd battled in the ring, but what upset him the most was the way Elizabeth had openly admired the man's physique.

"You're not afraid to hit a preacher, are you, Redbourne?" Mac taunted him good-humoredly. "It's just the two of us here, Will. You and me."

They danced in circles, eyes trained on one another.

"I thought you were a champion, Will. A fighter. Show me." He tested with a feint to the right.

Will jerked his head backward.

"I've won a bout or two," he said, feeling collected, more in control of his emotions.

"She came here to marry me, you know."

"I know."

"That has to make you angry."

"Why would it? I got paid to do a job."

Mac threw another punch, but Will ducked out of the way and countered with a jab to the preacher's face.

He wiped a trickle of blood from the corner of his mouth and raised his hands again. "You love her."

Lead Right.

This time, the blow caught Will off guard and he stumbled backward a few steps.

Mac was no amateur.

"You...don't know what you're talking about." He was keenly aware of the red-headed woman seated in the second seat over, ringside.

Focus, Redbourne.

"I know that your job as an outrider was finished in Kansas City when you delivered the bankroll, but you chose to accompany her the rest of the way to Silver Falls on your own dime. I know that you paid for horses, saddles, and a wagon to get her here safely."

Will's jaw clenched. They'd known Mac for all of two days. How dare she share so much with him.

"Stop trying to get into my head, preacher."

"I'm just calling it like I see it. You love her. Admit it."

"No."

"Well, then, I guess you wouldn't mind if we named our first son after you?" Mac led with a jab, but Will countered with a shoulder roll and a hard counter cross to the preacher's jaw. He continued his combination attack.

Jab.

Jab.

Hook.

Cross.

Mac grabbed ahold of him and held him in a Clinch.

"She loves you too," he whispered in Will's face.

Stunned, Will stopped fighting the hold, his eyes nothing more than scrutinizing slits as he searched Mac's face for some hint of humor.

Mac's face remained stoic.

"What did you say?" He had to have heard the man incorrectly.

"I *can't* marry her, Will. Because she loves *you*." Mac released him with a shove backward.

Will's breathing now came in ragged heaves. He didn't dare believe. Didn't dare hope it was true.

Elizabeth loves me?

Distraction. He wouldn't have thought the preacher capable of such tactics, but...

"Why would you say that? How would you even know? You only just met a couple of days ago." Will circled his fists.

"Because she bet her last dime on you." Mac raised both of his brows and nodded as he countered the circle, matching Will's movements. "Mrs. Patterson couldn't wait to tell me that my bride bet on another man."

Suddenly, the imaginary cleric's collar returned to Mac's throat and Will no longer wished to fight the man. His pent up frustrations and resentment seemed to melt away.

"It's really hard not to like you," he repeated his earlier observation.

"Maybe this will help." Mac jabbed at his face, but Will raised his hands in a cover-up, blocking the hit.

"It'll take a lot more than that to get to me, Preacher. I am a heavyweight champion, you know."

"Thou shalt fear the Lord, thy God. He giveth and he taketh away."

"You talk too much."

"Will!" Elizabeth called out his name in a terrified plea.

He took his eyes from Mac's face to search for Elizabeth ringside, but her seat was empty. He scanned the crowd. There, at the edge of the building, Mr. Henchley had his large hand clenched tightly around Elizabeth's arm, dragging her toward the door.

Before he could tell Mac what was happening, the pastor surprised him with a haymaker punch to his face. The wild swing sent Will crashing to the floor of the ring. Pain sliced through his head like a hot knife through butter. He struggled to get up, but the relentless ringing in his ears and the throbbing in his jaw and face made it difficult to gain control over his ability to balance.

He shook his head slowly and collapsed again to the ground.

"I'm glad to see that the good Lord has finally knocked some sense into you," Mac said with a laugh.

"Henchley." The name was all he could force out of his mouth and he pointed toward the exit. "He's taking Elizabeth."

"Unhand me right now, Asa Henchley." Elizabeth had had enough, though she sounded braver than she felt. "You tell my father that I will come home when I am good and ready and not a moment beforehand." She yanked on her arm, but his grip was too tight. "You're hurting me."

The crowded building rang in a rousing chorus of excitement and disappointment as the man dragged her down the aisles of chairs toward the back of the livery. He stopped, just short of the door, and pulled her around to face him.

"The reward was for your return, Miss Archer. It did not specify what condition you had to be in when you got there." The warning in his voice made her shudder. Cold. Calculating. "Your little adventure is over."

Elizabeth still held the ticket in her hand with Will Redbourne written amongst several dark scribbles.

"Will!" she called out again, her voice dissipating in the cheers and jeers of the opposing spectators.

Ding.

The match was over.

Mac had won. It took a moment for the significance of his victory to sink in.

A preacher's wife.

Henchley shoved open the large barn doors and wrenched her alongside him out into the cool afternoon air. He looked down the street in both directions, sputtering under his breath, waiting.

"Where the hell did they go?" The irritation in his voice was evident with the menacing growl that rumbled in his chest.

Several women and young girls lined the large bowery, arranging their confections of pies, cakes, and other desserts on covered tables for display. All of them unaware of the danger that loomed in their midst.

The smell of freshly popped corn wafted beneath her nose and she turned to see several metal tubs filled with water and topped with bobbing apples. She scanned the area for anything she might be able to use as a weapon, and spotted a large knife sitting next to the beautifully golden rhubarb pie.

"Why, Miss Archer," Mrs. Patterson called to her as she approached, her arms full of sticks, material, and two fishing poles. "I thought you would be inside. I hear you have quite a vested interest in this particular fight."

"You are right. I did place a rather large bet. It's over. My betrothed won." She let the revelation sit for a moment.

"Mac won?" Excitement filled Mrs. Patterson's face. Her shoulders scrunched and her smile spread wide.

"You look like you could use a little help." Elizabeth stepped forward, her arms extended, but Mr. Henchley stopped her cold with a firm hand on her shoulder. The unmistakable sound of a cocking gun was followed by a painful jab into her side.

"I'm sorry, my dear, we are in quite a hurry. The lady looks like she can manage without your assistance." His smile looked like that of a snake about to consume an egg. "Isn't that right, madam?"

Mrs. Patterson's eyes opened almost as wide as her mouth and Elizabeth imagined this was the first time in a long time the woman didn't have something to say. She pursed her lips, readjusted her grip on her load, and scurried away from them, mumbling something under her breath.

Elizabeth had heard stories about Mr. Henchley and his devices. She hoped they'd been grossly exaggerated, but was unsure how far she was willing to go to test the man.

He pushed the barrel of his gun even deeper into her side, willing her toward the saloon where three horses had been tied to the hitching post outside. He glanced over his shoulder, back at the livery.

"He will come after me." She lifted her chin in defiance.

"Who? Redbourne? Let him come. We'll settle things once and for all if he does."

"Get out of here!" the barkeep yelled as he threw a man into the street. "And don't come back." He dusted off his hands and folded them across his chest.

Two other men burst through the saloon doors laughing loudly, but the moment they fixed their eyes on Mr. Henchley, they immediately sobered. Elizabeth did not recognize any of them.

"Sorry, Boss," one of them said as he hopped down off the last section of boardwalk and strode with purpose toward them. "We didn't think you'd get her so quickly."

They were Americans. Henchley must have hired them after he'd arrived here.

The man on the ground scrambled to his feet and dusted himself off. "We didn't see no harm in getting' a little drink while we waited for the wagon."

Henchley removed his gun from her side, pulled her in close to him, and placed the barrel beneath the man's chin.

He trembled, eyes wide.

Elizabeth held her breath.

"Where is that brother of yours?" Henchley asked, closing one eye and leaning close to the man's face. "That wagon was supposed to be here half an hour ago."

He shrugged.

"We've got a train to catch in Denver, boys. Saddle up. We'll have to start without them." He reset the hammer on his gun and removed it from beneath the man's jaw, to his visible relief.

"Yes, sir!" He picked up his dusty hat and shoved it atop his head.

A wagon with two men on the bench seat jostled up the dirt road toward them. The reward her father had offered must have been quite a sum to warrant the attention of her father's crony and five miscreant thugs.

"You're late," Henchley spat at them as he ushered her toward the front of the buckboard.

"Tim's horse went lame," the driver pointed to the man climbing over the seat into the back of the wagon, "and we couldn't find a replacement."

"I don't think you've thought this through," Elizabeth said quietly. "My father always said you were the methodical one.

The logical one. Disciplined to a fault. Aren't you sick of always having to clean up my brother's messes? Having to do my father's bidding?"

"Gag her," Henchley instructed the man they'd referred to as Tim. "I'm tired of listening to her yap. Throw her in the back."

As Tim pulled the grime covered handkerchief from around his neck and jumped down from the back of the wagon, Elizabeth gagged at the thought of the cloth coming anywhere near her mouth. She leapt toward the saloon, but Henchley grabbed her by the hair and roughly yanked her back. Tears welled in her eyes from the pain.

"Whoa now," one of the brothers from the saloon said, his hands raised waist high in front of him, "I didn't sign up to be hurting no lady. I thought we was just returning her to her pa."

Henchley rolled his eyes, then without warning, shot the man to the ground.

Blood immediately oozed out onto the dirt and the man clutched at his chest.

Elizabeth gasped. She started forward, but the brute still had a hold of her hair.

Women screamed and scrambled for cover behind the nearby confections tables and beneath the mayor's platform.

"You shot Wayne," exclaimed one of the men as he rushed to the fallen man's side.

"Would you like to join him?" Henchley took aim, but the man raised his hands, still in a crouched position.

Elizabeth couldn't allow someone else to get hurt. She jutted toward Henchley, crouched down below his arm, and jumped up, pushing against his wrist, using all of her strength to raise his aim and the shot fired into the air.

"Elizabeth?"

"Elizabeth!"

Both men's voices were a welcome sound to her ears. She turned to see both Will and Mac emerge from the back of the livery.

"Will!" she called back to them. "Mac! I'm over here!"

Henchley grabbed her around the middle and handed her off to Tim. "Get her into the wagon," he spat.

The hireling picked her up and tossed her over his shoulder, then threw her into the back of the buckboard and climbed up behind her. She glanced upward, the leader of the group still in her view.

"You two," Henchley motioned to the others, "keep them busy. Do what you have to do." He shoved the driver aside and grabbed the reins.

The buckboard lunged forward, the uneven road jerking the wagon about, pitching her violently against the wooden contraption as they made their retreat.

"I'll take care of these goons," Mac said as they emerged from the livery—which housed the make-shift boxing ring—out into the street, shoving their arms into their shirts. "Go get the girl."

"And just how am I supposed to do that?"

Elizabeth had been thrown into the back of a wagon with Henchley at the reins. Will's attention was drawn to the three horses that had been tethered to the hitching post in front of the saloon. Three brutes stood in his way, another lay on the ground, blood seeping from a hole in his chest.

Henchley. The hired gun never failed to live up to his reputation.

"That man needs a doctor," Will called out to Henchley's men.

"Doctor won't do him no good no more!" one of them shouted back.

"But, Homer, maybe he's right," the man kneeling next to the injured said just loud enough Will could hear. "I can't stop the bleeding." His hands were covered in blood and he'd wiped some of it onto his shirt and forehead.

"Shut up, Wendell." Homer spat into the dirt, his eyes fixed on Will. "Wayne's as good as dead."

"I'm just going to need one of those horses, fellas," Will told them as he stepped forward. He blinked a few times, his vision still a little off. "We're not looking for any trouble."

"I've got this," Mac said as he buttoned up his shirt and returned his cleric's collar to his neck. "Elizabeth needs you."

Will nodded. Henchley was a loose cannon and the longer Elizabeth remained with him, the more danger she was in. He casually felt his hip. He'd taken off his holster before the match had begun.

Within seconds, the stern and haughty expressions that had contorted two of the men's faces had now softened and they held up their hands, palms out.

Odd.

A stir behind him, pulled Will's gaze backward and he was greeted with one of the most beautiful sights he had ever seen. Men had filtered out of the livery and now stood as a single wall behind Mac and him.

"Go!" the preacher yelled.

Will didn't waste another moment. He ran toward the men, who parted for him to get through to the horses.

"I'm a doctor," he heard someone call behind him. "Let me through."

Will jumped up into the saddle of the brown and white Appaloosa closest to him and pulled the reins around in the direction the wagon had headed.

They can't have gotten far.

It wasn't long before he had them in his sites—though they were moving much too fast for what a normal wagon could handle.

One wrong move and...

Will couldn't finish the thought. His gut tightened and he

leaned down close to the gelding's body, urging him faster.

Each time the wagon hit a bump in the uneven road, it would rise into the air and quickly crash back down onto the ground with an awful crunching sound, causing Will's breath to catch in his throat until Elizabeth's head peeked up above the buckboard's back walls.

He exhaled.

As he gained on them, a man in the back of the wagon with Elizabeth drew his gun and attempted to aim at Will. With no way to steady the weapon, the likelihood of being hit was slim, but possible. He didn't care. Elizabeth's safety was all that mattered now.

Without warning, the man crashed through the back of the fast-moving wagon and he tumbled out onto the ground below, leaving a gaping hole of splintered wood in the background, framing Elizabeth's outstretched form. She'd kicked him right through the tailpiece and Will had to swerve to miss hitting him.

"That's my girl," he whispered aloud, not breaking his speed.

As he pulled alongside the wagon, he reached out, but Elizabeth was still too far away to pull safely into his arms. Henchley snapped his head around and locked eyes with Will. He handed the reins of the wagon to his cohort and clambered over the seat into the back with Elizabeth.

There was no choice. He had to protect her and the only way to do that was to make the jump onto the wagon. There would only be one chance. He kept pace with the wagon as he maneuvered into a position that would allow him to make the leap without getting caught in the wheel.

Have a little faith, Will. He could hear Mac's voice in his head.

Jump.

He sailed through the air and landed on a waiting Mr. Henchley. They slammed into the back of the driver's bench. The broken wood sliced Will's shoulder and he could feel blood oozing down his arm. Henchley landed a hard punch against the side of Will's face with a cruel laugh and pulled back to unleash another blow when the wagon shook brutally and the driver screamed. Will pushed against Henchley's face as he was pressed up against the splintered seat, then twisted enough to see that the driver and team of horses were gone. The bolt must have come loose from the wagon's hitch. Without a way to steer they were headed downhill, straight for a ravine.

Henchley growled as he reached for Will's throat, but missed as they hit another bump, and by some grace of God, the wagon remained upright. Will took the disruption as an opportunity to escape from beneath the man's weight, slamming his fist into the Englishman's gut. Henchley fell, kneeling on the wagon's bed.

Elizabeth screamed as she slid dangerously close to the gaping hole at the back of the wagon, desperately reaching for anything that would stop her from plummeting from the back. Will dived forward, catching her wrist as her feet scrambled to find footing at the metal corners of the tailpiece.

She nodded, then screamed as Henchley swung a piece of broken wood at Will's prone form. Will took the hit with a grunt and kicked out at the man, pushing him away against the back of the driver's seat. He pulled Elizabeth up as he stood, and his eyes widened in fear as he looked past the enraged thug.

Time was running out.

"Redbourne, I will not let you take this from me." Henchley shouted, his hands gripping either side of the wagon's corner, his eyes wild, crazy.

Will reached down and scooped Elizabeth up into his arms, stepped up onto the edge of the buckboard and jumped. He placed a hand beneath her head and shifted so his body would hit the ground first. They rolled several times, but finally came to a stop.

"Nooooo!" Henchley screamed as the wagon disappeared over the edge of the ravine.

Will exhaled and lay back down against the grassy terrain

and closed his eyes, his arms still wrapped protectively around Elizabeth's body, hugging her close to him.

"Elizabeth? Are you all right?"

She didn't move.

Panic gripped his heart.

What have I done?

He rolled over, so his body covered hers and he pushed himself up enough to look down into her face.

"I'm alive, does that count?" she said quietly, a soft smile dawning on her sumptuous mouth.

Her eyes opened, their blue shade complimented perfectly by her flushed cheeks. She was the most beautiful woman Will had ever seen. And he loved her.

"You had me scared there for a minute."

She didn't say anything at first, but then she looked up into his eyes, searching them. "You came after me."

"Of course, I did. I'm the outrider, remember? It's my job."

"Thank you."

Will laughed and placed his forehead against hers.

"When I thought I'd lost you, I…"

Elizabeth bit her lip and it was his undoing. He brushed a few stray strands of hair from her face and lowered his head to claim her lips with his own.

She raised her hand to cradle his tender, swollen jaw, her fingers grazing over the bruised flesh, then playing with the too-long tufts of hair right behind his ear.

He groaned, pleasure mixing with pain.

He lifted his hand to cover hers, then his fingers trailed the length of her arm. Warmth spread through his body like sunshine. His heart beat faster, his chest swelled, and he drank it all in, tasting, devouring the sweetness of her kiss.

He needed to pull away.

Now.

"Elizabeth," he said, waiting for her to open her eyes.

She looked up at him, then bit her lip again.

He groaned again, evoking a giggle from the woman he was determined to marry.

"I love you," he whispered with another soft kiss against her lips. "I love you."

She smiled, not taking her eyes from him. "If you wanted to cuddle a little longer, Mr. Redbourne," she said, her mouth widening into a grin, "all you had to do was ask."

He breathed a laugh and pushed himself off of her to stand up. He reached out a hand to help her to her feet. She slipped her hand into his and lifted her head to meet his eyes.

"I love you, too."

CHAPTER TWENTY-SEVEN

Three Weeks Later

Elizabeth had never been so nervous and excited all at once. Today she would become Mrs. William Trey Redbourne. The thought left butterflies fluttering about in her stomach and she smiled, realizing that her life would rival any of the romance novels in her collection.

"Will is not going to be able to take his eyes off of you," Grace said as she adjusted the flowers in Elizabeth's hair.

"I still can't believe you're here," Elizabeth said as she glanced up in the mirror at Grace's reflection. "You have no idea how much it means to me."

"I still can't believe that you are heading back to England. A whole ocean away."

"Five years isn't that long."

"You're right. And just think of all the adventures we will have to write each other about in the meantime." Grace bent down and rested her chin on Elizabeth's shoulder and they both looked into the mirror.

"Sisters."

"Sisters."

Knock. Knock.

Elizabeth glanced up at the photograph of her family she'd stuck in the edge of the vanity and lamented briefly the fact that none of them would be here with her on her wedding day.

The door opened and Mac's face appeared in the doorway. "It's time, ladies. But first, Elizabeth, there is someone here who would like to see you."

She turned around and stood up. Mac moved aside and a man stepped into the room with a large bouquet of flowers blocking his face.

"You didn't think I would miss my baby sister getting married, now, did you?"

Elizabeth's heart skipped a beat.

"Jeremy!" she squealed as she ran into his open arms. "But, how did you—?"

"Will's brother, Levi, found me in Detroit. When I heard what happened and that you are marrying Will Redbourne, of all people, I immediately made arrangements with work and well, here I am." He handed her the flowers.

"Thank you, Jer. They are just lovely."

Grace took them from her and set them down on the vanity.

"There is so much to say," Jeremy told her.

"There will be plenty of time to talk *after* the ceremony," Mac said with a playfully raised brow.

"Of course." Jeremy reached down and collected her hands in his. He squeezed and leaned forward to place a kiss on her cheek. "Congratulations, Lizzy."

Elizabeth's heart swelled and she looked upward.

Thank you.

"Ready?"

"Why am I so nervous?" She shook her hands in front of her and took a deep breath.

"I think all brides are nervous on their wedding day. But are you happy?" her brother asked.

"More than I would have ever imagined." Elizabeth smiled

and turned to Mac. "Ready!" she confirmed with a confident nod.

As she descended the restaurant steps, tears came to her eyes as she gazed upon so many of those whom she'd grown to love over the last couple of months. This was the family she wanted. Good, honest, hard-working people who cared about each other, who protected each other.

Albert sat in the front row on a chair next to Leah, who tapped him on the shoulder and pointed up at the staircase. He spun around and his face lit up, a huge grin spreading across his face, and he waved enthusiastically with both hands. Elizabeth giggled and winked at the boy as she raised her skirt off her ankles and took another step down.

When her eyes met Will's, he took her breath away, standing there in a dark grey three-piece suit with a blue brocade vest and black cravat. He was beautiful. And he was hers.

Mac nodded at Will.

"I know how much you would have liked to have your mother here," he whispered, reaching into his pocket, "so, I thought you might appreciate having something that would bring her close to your heart today." He held up the ruby necklace that she'd sold in Denver.

She sucked in a breath and scooped up the pendant in her hand. She looked up at him.

"How did you get this?"

He motioned for her to turn around, then fastened it around her neck. "I knew it was special to you, so I bought it the same day you sold it."

She hadn't thought it was possible, but…

"I love you, Will Redbourne," she whispered.

"Prove it," he said with a grin and a raised brow.

"If you wanted to marry me," she said with a smile of her own, "all you had to do was ask."

"Will you marry me, Elizabeth Archer?"

"Yep."

They turned to face Mac and he performed a beautiful ceremony.

"Well," the preacher said, looking at Will after their vows had been made, "what are you waiting for? Kiss your bride."

Will's smile extended across his face, his dimple more pronounced than she had ever seen it. He slipped his hands across her cheeks and rested them along her jawline, a thumb caressing her lips for only a moment, before pulling her into his much-anticipated kiss.

"I love you, Mrs. Elizabeth Redbourne. Forever."

And she felt it. The tingle of truth. All the way down to her toes.

"I know."

THE END

If you enjoyed Will's story, please consider leaving a review.

To sign up to receive Kelli Ann Morgan's new release alerts and newsletter, visit www.kelliannmorgan.com.

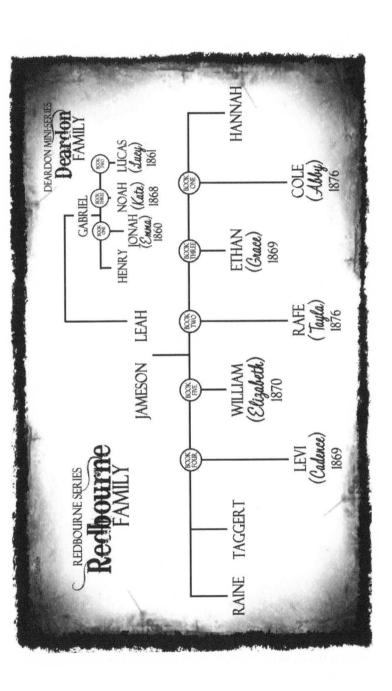

REDBOURNE SERIES
Redbourne FAMILY

DEARDON MINI-SERIES
Deardon FAMILY

RAINE   TAGGERT   JAMESON   LEAH

GABRIEL
HENRY   JONAH *(Emma)* 1860   NOAH *(Kate)* 1868   LUCAS *(Lucy)* 1861

BOOK ONE   BOOK THREE   BOOK TWO

LEVI *(Cadence)* 1869 — BOOK FOUR

WILLIAM *(Elizabeth)* 1870 — BOOK FIVE

RAFE *(Tayla)* 1876 — BOOK TWO

ETHAN *(Grace)* 1869 — BOOK THREE

COLE *(Abby)* 1876 — BOOK ONE

HANNAH

ABOUT THE AUTHOR

KELLI ANN MORGAN is a bestselling author whose western historical romance books have been downloaded over a quarter of a million times and maintain a better than four-star rating.

Kelli Ann lives in beautiful Northern Utah with her wonderfully creative and witty husband, her fun and imaginative teenage son, and two very playful cats. Before she started writing historical western romance, she worked as a photographer, jewelry designer, motivational speaker, corporate trainer and many other things, but has found fulfillment in living her dream of writing romance and designing book covers for herself and other authors.

She's passionate about creating stories with handsome, chivalrous men, intelligent, strong women, and in a world where there is always a happily-ever-after. Her novels are highly romantic and on the sensual side of PG—without all the graphic love scenes.

If you would like to receive new release alerts from Kelli Ann, please visit her website at http://www.kelliannmorgan.com where you can sign up for her newsletter.

FACEBOOK:
https://www.facebook.com/KelliAnnMorganAuthor

E-MAIL:
kelliann@kelliannmorgan.com

NEWSLETTER SIGN UP:
http://bit.ly/1iFvvwy